What You Pay For

What You Pay For

MARIETTA PUBLISHING
MARIETTA, GEORGIA USA

Other books by C.J. Henderson available from Marietta Publishing

The Occult Detectives of C.J. Henderson

The Things That Are Not There

PUBLISHED BY
Marietta Publishing
Bruce R. Gehweiler, Publisher
PO Box 3485
Marietta, GA 30061-3485
http://www.mariettapublishing.com

ISBN 1-892669-18-8

Printed and bound in the United States of America by Lightning Source, Inc.
10 9 8 7 6 5 4 3 2 1

Design: Robert Sommers
Cover Art: James Warhola
Copy Editing: Leverett Butts

There are many people who, over the years, pushed and prodded and encouraged me into becoming a professional writer when I would have probably preferred, deep down inside, to remain an anonymous voice.

Of all of them, however, there was only one whose respect I actually desired enough to summon the courage to throw off my cowardice. He was there when I needed him to not only push me in the right direction, but to give me the confidence to keep moving forward.

If not for him, I would in all likelihood, never have started writing these stories. And, if I hadn't started writing Hagee stories, there is a good chance no one would ever have heard of me at all. Thus, I dedicate this book to:

Marc A. Cerasini

He believed in me more than I believed in myself, for which I shall always be grateful.

Contents

Introduction

THE WAY I understand it, a good part of the job of the introduction is to get the casual browser interested enough to want to read (and therefore, by necessity, purchase) the book in question. There are, I'm assured, various methods of doing this.

But, it seems to me that, should I wish to convince you that this book is something you'll enjoy reading, I could do no better than to urge you to take a few moments, turn to the first page of the first story and read. If, within two minutes tops, you don't know for yourself whether this book is your cup of tea or not, how in the hell am I supposed to help you?

So whether I wanted to adopt the huckstering spiel of a used-car salesman or the effete tones of the learned academic, the truth is no amount of pestering, prodding or poking with a sharp stick is going to do any better job of selling you this book than a simple reading of the first few pages of actual content.

And nowadays with so many bookstores having big comfy chairs, there's really no excuse not to take a few minutes and allow yourself the pleasure of encountering C.J. Henderson and his tales of Jack Hagee, Private Eye. That said, it seems to me all I can reasonably hope to do, to honor the conventions of that peculiar literary institution known as the introduction, is tell you what it was about these stories that made me like them so much. Why does this collection of private eye yarns rate your attention instead of one of the many others available? And the answer to that can be both simple and complex.

The simple version is one word — BALLS! This is fiction with BALLS! and that is a very rare thing indeed. If you're tired of slogging through a lot of "sensitive" apologetic Pop-Psych 101 garbage masquerading as the essence of current private-eye fiction, then by all means skip the rest of this intro shit and start reading the stories. However, if you'd like a more detailed map of the road ahead, complete with the complex answer, stick around and hear me out.

What you've got here is a collection of 13 stories about a guy named Jack Hagee. Tough guy doing a tough job. Hard-boiled private eye eking out a borderline existence in the biggest and baddest city of all…and, at the same time, modern-day warrior-gladiator-samurai locked in a battle against the virus of decay that infests our crumbling civilization. So to speak.

This is the tale of the hero — an epic poem whose verses are short stories and novelettes — larger than life in a tradition older than we can ever know. It is surely no accident that author Henderson has Hagee attempting to finish reading Homer's Illiad in his office-bound downtime.

When the tale of the hero is done well, it has the power to not only captivate and excite, but inspire and instruct. And to live on, long past the time of its own creation. It is both an urgent plea in favor of observing a strict morality and a cautionary vision of the perils to be faced when you fail to do just that. And as such, its message is timeless.

Within these pages, it is done very well indeed.

It may appear that Jack Hagee operates in New York City, but really, Jack's universe is a hell that would do Dante proud. Jack is set against the usual sort of human antagonists one expects to find in crime fiction — murderers, thieves, cutthroats and politicians (pardon any redundancy) — but beneath these conflicts we sense the larger battle being waged here — man versus a world gone mad, a hostile prison of our own creation that threatens to overwhelm us and drag us down into untold depths of depravity.

Pretty heavy, huh?

But for any with eyes to see, this is our world — maybe not the view you get from your breakfast nook as you calmly ingest your morning paper and your bran muffin, but ask anybody who's been there when a body's been pulled from the river, or a near-frozen infant is rescued from a dumpster or the clean-up begins on the carnage caused by a babbling madman who's permitted to walk out of rigorous containment unchallenged whenever he feels the urge to go push someone's grandmother in front of a speeding subway train.

And make no mistake about it, these are not tales for the faint of heart, not because of a gory content (Henderson never flinches from the bloody reality of Hagee's continual combat; neither does he wallow in it) but because Jack's world-view is as uncompromising as the hellish void in which he struggles to survive. The right way is the hard way and Jack does things the right way. He suffers for it and so do those who stand with him. It is a hard life and it takes its toll.

When we first meet him, Jack Hagee is on the ragged edge. He's coming to the end of his years on the Pittsburgh Police Department and his marriage has just collapsed. But more importantly, Jack Hagee is still walking wounded from his part in Uncle Sam's dirty little war of attrition in Southeast Asia. He's teetering on the edge of the abyss and his gin-soaked, dope-fueled, red-eyed ricochet ride through Pittsburgh's underworld drags us along by the short and curlies as Jack makes one last desperate lunge to get clear of the black hole that's opening up inside his own heart. This yarn, "What You Pay For", gives us both the title of the collection and a distillation of the journey ahead. Soul-weary, but too fuckin' mean to give up, Jack slam-dances his way through the damned, the corrupted and the bodies of hapless victims only to emerge at a truth that confirms his own worst fears about the moral quicksand that surrounds and threatens to engulf him.

This is what is most properly referred to as a rockin' start.

The next story, "Nothing Comes Cheap", is Henderson's take on that traditional PI shuffle — working for the rich folks. A family whose massive personal fortune cannot buy off the skeletons in their closet, the Morgans give Jack his introduction to the Big Apple as he hangs out his PI shingle in Manhattan and goes toe to toe with the all pervasive evil that quickly comes to characterize Henderson's City That Never Sleeps. Jack shows an uncharacteristic pragmatism born of hunger and despair here and proves that, despite warrior skills of near superhuman caliber, he can prove fallible and his disillusioned romanticism can reassert itself at the worst possible moments.

This tale gives us the first tantalizing taste of the shadowy backroom machinery that runs the Big Town, a system that will alternatingly adore and revile Hagee, coax and threaten him, protect and attack him, use and accuse and abuse him but will never control him. This background of civic corruption, deception and rampant self-interest was a revelation in the original hard-boiled fiction of the twenties and thirties, yet, with a few notable exceptions, it is little used today. Henderson works this vein masterfully as the stale, rotten odor of "smoke filled rooms" lingers in the background of any number of Hagee adventures.

Nowhere is this element more in evidence than in "All's Well That Ends Well", as Jack climbs right into the middle of a Manhattan political firestorm and meets the first of Henderson's truly mythic villains — the killer, Stone. The scene of physical combat that provides the climax of this tale is action writing of the first order — vivid, breathless and gut-wrenching. Henderson has a penchant for setting his action in unique locations, where the geography becomes an integral part of the conflict. It is more than just fitting that Hagee battles the baddest bad guy he's ever encountered beneath the biggest bridge in the city. The bridge towers above them, symbolizing the titanic nature of the contest yet mocking its participants and their feeble attempts to assert themselves in an indifferent universe. What is truly remarkable about this scene is the all too real feeling that Hagee might not, in fact, triumph.

This story also provides our first encounter with Hubert, the information specialist with "a voice like a cartoon duck." He is described as a rather unremarkable looking fellow yet, despite the lack of any descriptive passage to validate my vision, I see Hubert resembling a dyspeptic Arnold Stang auditioning for the part of Ratso Rizzo. You know the type — you can dress him up, but he'll still leave a trail of slime across the carpet. All the more amazing then that Henderson will, over the course of the collection, make Hubert an endearing character.

Next up, we have a short mood piece that is one of my favorites. "Bread Ahead" is another showcase for Henderson's unique touch with action scenes. In addition, we get an amplified soliloquy on the cesspool known as New York City; a terrific setting for the conflict (where once again geography is very much a character in the play); and a slice'n'dice twostep through the shifting thought processes that pull pride and righteous indignation away from the battlefront to make way for sheer will and desperation. This one can be read in less than five minutes, but its imagery will have you waking up with night sweats for a long time to come.

Those who follow Hagee in his novel-length adventures will recognize "Bread Ahead" from its other later incarnation — the marvelous tone-setting Chapter One of the first Hagee novel — "No Free Lunch".

"Dance" finds Hagee working up a case that looks local, when, in a heartbeat, he's dropped hip-deep in international intrigue and ideological skullduggery. This tale has a lot to recommend it — crisp writing, taut suspense and the smell of true fear wafting off the page — but the central moment is one of absolute bravura hard-boiled storytelling: pedal to the metal, balls to the wall as Hagee plays a psycho version of chicken with the bad guys, inviting them to look into his eyes to determine his intentions. I can feel his white-hot stare as he stands there with his finger on the button and a lifetime of anger, hatred and despair egging him on to take the ultimate "Aw, fuck it..." way out and I don't doubt his intentions for a moment. The bad guys are faced with a lid-off look at the game of chance they've bought into and the price of a wrong move will never be higher.

As the skills Jack honed in the service of his country are called out of retirement, we also get to meet a new member of the Hagee extended family — Jack's former Military Intelligence partner, Grampy, who's leading a rather bohemian existence as a street busker. Their teamwork, despite the lengthy lay-off, is so smooth and natural that one hopes Henderson will, sometime, delve back into their past careers and present us with a tale of the old days.

The sequel to "Dance" is up next. "A Game To Be Played" sends Hagee south along the Tourist Trail to Florida with a secret message to deliver and a carload of enemy agents in pursuit. Hoping to keep himself out of trouble with the government, Hagee leaps out of the fryer into the fire, burning rubber down Interstate 95. Car chases, a cinematic convention, rarely work well in prose, but this story provides a kinetic exception to that rule.

It also provides some classic Hagee physical combat, some nifty deductive reasoning and a double-cross finale that paints an eerily convincing portrait of those who are supposed to guard our nation's security. In this swirling maelstrom of shifting loyalties, where allegiance to the highest bidder is the order of the day, Hagee stands tall as the classic American hero — straight-forward, resourceful and just.

We arrive, now, at what might be considered the odd duck in the bunch — "The Piper's Tune." Henderson has stated that one of the original goals of the Hagee stories was to lay to rest, once and for all, the absurd notion that hard-boiled meant urban crime stories exclusively. "Hard-boiled isn't a genre," he maintains. "It's a state of mind."

With this guiding principle, he set out to place Hagee into one of every different kind of story known — including old-fashioned adventure, fantasy, science-fiction and horror. Later, he began to worry that the Hagee fans (not as large a bunch as deserved, but oh so zealous) might be put off by having Jack encounter the supernatural and other-worldly. Personally, I would enjoy reading about Jack emptying his .45 into a werewolf or three, but I admit I would draw the line at seeing him outfitted in one of those cold steel and loincloth ensembles that passes for fashion in the sword and sorcery world.

At any rate, before the experiment was, well, not so much abandoned as deflected (dig C.J.'s series of Teddy London supernatural mysteries originally published under the pseudonym Robert Morgan to catch my drift), Henderson managed to pen this marvelous paean to the grand old adventure pulps like All-Story, Argosy and Golden Fleece Magazine. Hagee runs into trouble in the deserts of the Middle East and we're knee deep in Lost Patrol territory. Of course, Henderson couldn't resist bringing the tale into today with the sort of denouement that would never have gotten past the censors of old. It is, however, this aspect that saves the story from being a mere pastiche and moves it up alongside the rest of the Hagee canon as a stunning indictment of the arrogant irresponsibility that so often undercuts civilized man's noblest attempts to rise above his bestial origins.

Worth mentioning as well is the guest shot of "Bomber Brannigan" — author Wayne Dundee's pro wrestler support character from the Joe Hannibal series — appearing as Hagee's sturdy second in this adventure. I mention this only for those readers who are, like me, total suckers for this kind of insider stuff, but being familiar with the Hannibal series is not necessary to enjoy the story. It is, however, another recommended pleasure.

Now we come to a very unusual tale that, nonetheless, strikes me as the quintessential Hagee story. "Change From Your Dollar" is an anecdote related during a break in a marathon poker game. Hagee's cronies settle back as Jack relates an incident that occurred shortly after his return from the service. The incident follows the format of some earlier stories in the collection. Hagee's in a bad mood; he finds himself confronted with a situation that dictates caution and he proceeds to bulldoze his way through it. The situation turns out to be more complex and dangerous than expected and Hagee needs all his strength and cunning to survive. But unlike his encounters with cops, crooks, spies and politicians, this time Hagee manages to antagonize a substantially more formidable foe — a grizzly bear. Brutal, desperate, and as real as a broken bone, this story is a powerhouse.

At this point, I'd like to offer an observation: Possibly the single greatest compliment a writer can offer another writer is to say "I wish I'd written that." Now, Lord knows, that doesn't necessarily mean the other writer will take it as a compliment; that tends to hinge on who the first writer is — someone for whom you have a level of respect or an asshole. But everyone who creates can name some creations for which they wish they had been responsible. Off the top of my head, I can think of several: the novels "The Maltese Falcon" and "The Black Dahlia," the movies "Rio Bravo" and "Miracle on 34th Street," the songs "Heartbreak Hotel" and "The Return of the Grievous Angel," the pilot episode of "Crime Story," the collected rants of Dennis Miller and any number of short stories by Hammett, Chandler, Burnett, James Lee Burke and Harlan Ellison. There's more, of course, but you get the idea.

Add to that list the next story in the collection, "Nine Dragons." This yarn is (to use a favored term of my pal Pete the Schemer) *fucking ultimate*. It's got all the good things that make any of the Hagee tales enjoyable — sharp prose, nerve-jangling tension, humor, sentiment, action scenes that can give you whiplash and a healthy dose of that world-weary philosophy of life, war and New York City that Hagee does so well — but this story has one extra thing, something that lifts it to the pinnacle: resonance.

There are layers to this tale that I'm still finding each time I reread it. Small delights like the passage that explains how the mayor's insensitivity results in a rearranged schedule for an important N.Y. ethnic holiday, despite the traditions of the celebrants. Bigger joys like the location chosen for this story's climactic fight scene, a battleground that symbolizes the larger war Hagee has been waging since page one.

But to explain what I mean about resonance, pay close attention, if you will, to the instances in the story where a younger man and an older man square off. The wisdom of age is a most powerful weapon, especially when it is pitted against the arrogant pride of the young. It employs the single most profound element of the martial arts — using the enemy's own energies against him. The response of the loser in each of these contests shows clearly how accepting responsibility for one's own actions is the fundamental characteristic distinguishing the man who has honor from the man who has none. This is the truth that guides and propels the Hagee stories. It is a lesson worth learning and I will be forever envious that it wasn't me that wrote this incredible story.

Next up, we get our noses rubbed in the sick, sad remains of a marriage destroyed in "All the Money in the World." Hubert is the voice of unreason as he and Hagee deliver the bad news to a woman whose worst fear doesn't come close to the devastating reality of her husband's extramarital shenanigans. Hagee's diatribe is perhaps his most ferocious condemnation of our constant refusal to take responsibility for anything we do and it is aimed, oddly enough in a genre often condemned for its misogynistic excesses, at men who insist on letting their little head do the thinking. A very nice touch.

A tale that is new to this edition of the collection, "Woolworth's...For All Your Defensive Needs" is a splendid action tale of hunter vs. hunted, set loose in the forest primeval. A simple case of insurance fraud becomes a life and death struggle and Jack's fieldcraft is matched against man and nature in another of Henderson's marvelous action sequences. Despite the tension and violence, this tale finds Hagee mellowing a little as sentiment and humor are permitted a larger share of the proceedings than previously seen.

The last of the original group in the collection, "Toothpick" is a raw nerve of a story throbbing in gutshot agony. A serial killer is on the loose and New York trembles in fear — he tortures, kills and devours women. The carnage here is particularly repellent, but Henderson never crosses the line into splatterpunk. Hagee, unable to resist the entreaties of the latest victim's father, finds himself staked out as a sacrificial goat. Needless to say, he's just the man for the job.

And to close out this edition, another new tale makes an appearance — "The Things We Do." Henderson toys with the conventions of the private-eye tale and the "civilizing" elements that recent writers have imposed upon it to make his point as Hagee takes on a job of Honest-to-God babysitting and gets sideswiped in the situation. This tale shows Hagee cautiously opening his heart to a new love interest and coping with the way this relationship has caused him to lower his defenses. It also contains my single favorite line in any Henderson tale. No, I'm not going to tell you what it is — if you're a like-minded individual, you'll spot it; if not, what's the difference? But the crime, when it stands revealed, is about as petty and superficial as one can imagine and Henderson provides it as yet another brilliant condemnation of the arrogant, insipid, self-involved nonsense that passes for matters of import in today's sorry excuse for a culture.

Henderson has never tried to hide the fact that he uses these stories to rail about the insanity that runs rampant through our society. Relentlessly courageous, pragmatic, unyielding and unapologetic yet compassionate and, in the final analysis, not without some degree of hope, the Jack Hagee stories are epic tales of the hero residing in our hearts and they urge us to let him loose upon the land, so that we might get back on course, steering away from the flames of hell that beckon us each day.

It is unfortunate that these stories arrive at a time when their message of the individual taking responsibility is so out of fashion in both the real world and its distorted funhouse mirror, the world of publishing.

Jack Hagee appeared in three novels — "No Free Lunch," "Something For Nothing" and the perhaps prophetically titled "Nothing Lasts Forever." Then the publisher cut him loose. Regardless of what they might or might not have told old C.J., it's easy to see that it all came down to political correctness and marketing — both plagues upon the land. Henderson is by no means the only hard-boiled writer to lose his series. One disgruntled gent even went so far as to state plainly that he'd been promised an immediate contract for a new series as soon as he came up with a more caring, nurturing protagonist, preferably a woman.

Well, fuck that.

It's not that I have a problem with women characters or women writers although they don't often interest me very much, but I am goddamn sick and tired of this notion that the public can only handle one type of book at any given time.

You have an author here approaching the peak of his powers, and instead of trying to fit his work into some marketing asshole's cockeyed demographic by changing the titles and asking for a softer approach, somebody should have tried to find a way to let this guy do what he's here to do. Instead, he has to seek out paying gigs (fortunately fairly plentiful for a man of his talent but a waste of that talent nonetheless), because no one wants to publish his hard-edged books. There's a novel in progress and I've read the first two hundred pages of it and I am here to tell you it is a monumental motherfucker of a book. But nobody has the BALLS! to put it out.

So far.

But things are looking up. After all, these stories and the original series of novels are being reprinted by a publisher who sees a place in this world for fiction with BALLS! Can a contract for new material be in the offing? We can but hope.

And that brings us back full circle. Fiction with BALLS! If that sounds good to you, then you've picked the right book. Read it, then go get the novels, then grab up the Teddy London stuff and maybe, by then, a publisher with some BALLS! will let C.J. Henderson get back to doing what he does best — being that unappreciated guy holding a mirror up to our ugly world, urging us not to give up or give in.

In the meantime, meet Jack Hagee.

Jack Dolphin
Franklin Square, New York
June 30. 2003
(revised from my earlier introduction for the online edition)

What You Pay For

What You Pay For

THERE WAS SOMETHING familiar in the way the sun hit the railings along the turnpike; it was a reflecting red — the kind they use on the walls of family restaurants, the shade a cabbie's neck turns when he spots his customers really enjoying their ride. It reminded me of the way my eyes looked in the last three or four gas station mirrors, on the occasions I'd bothered to look. I'd left Pittsburgh with the stupid notion of drinking a shot every half hour until I drowned the stupider notion there was some way I could make things work with my wife.

Our final words kept haunting me. Three hours of final words that, when all the last-minute snipes and condemnations were peeled away, boiled down to the fact that Michelle and I had finally had enough of the seven-month farce I'd once convinced her would last a lifetime.

I listened to my car's motor, hoping it knew where we were going. I'd forgotten. I'd also forgotten the notion of death by gin poisoning. Attractive as it sounds, running away from one's problems never works for long. No matter if you do it when you're five with a pocketful of nickels and your favorite comic books and a couple of sandwiches rolled up in an extra jacket, or at thirty with two bottles of gin and an army blanket and an uncashed paycheck, eventually you have to get back to the "real world."

To me, the real world is a grey desk in a plasterboard corner of the Tenth Precinct. My name is Jack Hagee. I'm a detective.

I'd left on Friday night. My weekend had been spent wheeling around in circles, feeling sorry for myself, trying to replace bad memories with gin and self-respect with anger. By Monday afternoon, the gin and self-respect were gone, and I was too tired to deal with the others. All I wanted was a little sleep and a chance to put my life into an order I could recognize.

Hoping to hide behind my desk until my head only hurt as much as the rest of me, I left my Chevy between two patrol barges in the precinct lot and headed inside. Finding Capt. Wheelock waiting for me was not a good sign.

"Good afternoon, Jack-o." I nodded back to him. "Little late today, are we?"

"Oh, were you late today, too, Cap?" I hate that "we" crap of his.

"Can it, mister. I'm getting tired of you — of the lateness, and the lip, and the shit attitude you put on with your pants every morning. You didn't report in this weekend — no one knew where you were. Now you're late again today — dirty, no shave—"

"No sleep, either, but that's just because I'm hung over so bad."

Wheelock pulled back from my desk with a snarl. Lowering his tone, he continued, "You're a real funny guy, Jack-o. With such a good sense of humor, I'm sure you won't have any trouble laughing this off. As of now, you are officially notified — one more procedural break, your ass is on probation. You start following the rules, or hit the bricks. You understand?"

I nodded again, doing it lightly to keep my brains from spilling out of my forehead. I was grateful to see that was all he wanted. My skull was unraveling at the seams, and I needed some quiet time to put it back together. In less than three days, I'd allowed my wife, my home, and maybe my job to slip through my fingers. As much as what was left of me wanted to crawl into the nearest dark corner to get the dying over with, I knew it wouldn't be wise. I'd most likely only fall asleep, and then open my eyes to my walking papers. I hated to admit it, but it was probably smarter for me to stay awake during my shift. And the easiest way to do that was to see if Spenser was on desk duty.

He was. So was the pharmacy he kept in his day kit. As I approached his station, he greeted me sourly.

"What's up, plainclothes?"

"Wheelock thinks it would be a good idea if I stayed awake until checkout time," I told him. "Maybe he's right. You have anything to help that situation?"

"Gee, Jack...I thought you weren't the type to dirty up your body with such things."

Nothing stings worse than your own words from the other end of the barrel. Realizing the difference between need and pride, however, I answered:

"I'm not the type for a lot of things I've started getting used to." Spenser wasn't being a bad guy. I'd deserved a little hassling for all the comments I'd thrown his way over his "medicinal" habits. In truth, he could've been a lot nastier. Luckily for my hangover, he wasn't.

He looked me over while rummaging through his kit, asking, "When'd you sleep last? Friday…Thursday?"

"Somewhere in there."

"Christ, plainclothes. I suppose there's more than an ounce or two of gin in on top of that?" I nodded. It didn't hurt too much. "Yeah — that figures. Listen, I have something here that should get you around," he said, handing me two small white capsules. "I make these up for guys like you who don't spend too much of their recreational time at the drug store. Even though this isn't the most effective way to take this stuff, I'm not about to give you snorting lessons — not here, anyway. Besides, for what you want, oral is good enough. They're filled with crystal meth."

As I continued to stare at him vaguely, he explained.

"Take one now, the second one later *if* you need it. This stuff will kick in like lightning, especially for someone like you who doesn't use shit. It'll wake you up and keep you going. Once you get off shift, though, get home and get to bed, 'cause this stuff will trash your ass — good. But, it'll also get you through the day."

I asked him if he had anything milder? He told me.

"Sure, lots. Nothing that'll do you any good, though. If you want to stay awake and have the energy to get through the day, you have to give up something. After all, you get what you pay for."

Accepting Spenser's logic, I thanked him, slipped him his asking price, put the capsules in my pocket, and headed back toward the locker room. Twenty minutes later, after one of the powdered pick-me-ups, a shower, and a change into cleaner clothes, I suddenly found myself feeling much better, as if I'd snuck in a nice ten-hour nap and somehow not noticed. I could feel the extra weight in my arms dripping away through my fingers and, although my eyes were just as red as before, I couldn't find the crackles of pain that had been chipping away at my vision since Sunday night.

Deciding it wasn't worth thinking about the pain until it came back, I headed for my desk. There I found a number of messages from Linda Tibbs, the wife of one of my informers. It didn't figure to be very important, but it gave me an excuse to get out of the office. Since Spenser was the desk-badge on duty, I told him where I was going and headed out to see her.

Dodging my way through the jerking afternoon traffic did not improve my spirits. The Pennsylvania Chamber of Commerce is big on telling people how relaxing life is in their state. Pittsburgh is not one of the cities that help prove their point. Rusting traffic signs with multiple sets of green metal traffic instructions do not take the place of trees, and shoeless drunks picking at the scabs on their constantly bleeding feet, wedged between the buildings I passed did not make it as calming sights. Over the years I'd live in Pittsburgh, I'd allowed familiarity to blind me to the decay that gripped it. Maybe I was just in the wrong part of town; maybe I was in the wrong town altogether. The storefronts and restaurants and scattered office buildings all blended beyond one's vision, helping disguise the city's ills behind a mask of even calm. The place couldn't look any duller if the mayor ordered it completely repainted in battleship grey.

Shaking my head, I stopped viewing the terrain around me, trying to concentrate on my destination. Maybe it was the meth, or maybe the weekend had just opened my eyes to everything I'd been ignoring. Either way, it didn't matter at the moment. Behind the wheel of a car is not the place to get lost in thought.

I brought myself back to the mundane, wondering why Linda had called me instead of Tibbs himself. I didn't really care; I'd wanted an excuse to dust the station, and whatever the Tibbs' wanted was as good an excuse as any. Not that I ever especially wanted to see Tibbs.

Think of something fairly gross, like two quarts of vomit gurglingly stuffed into a quart-and-a-half bag. If you can imagine the bag with legs, arms, and two little piggy eyes, you'll have a fair idea of what Tibbs looks like, but only fair. I've known him since high school. He hadn't been much of a tryer then — graduation was his only goal. Linda had promised to marry him if he graduated. Marrying Linda put him in line for her father's body shop. Somehow, he managed to hold himself together long enough to graduate, get married, and inherit the station. If old man Ralston could have fought off the black cells eating his liver and brain for another year, the strain would've probably killed Tibbs first.

But, he'd made it. Now the two of them lived on scraps and pennies. She pumped gas and kept the station running. Tibbs played a lot, earning change by running errands for anyone who tipped high without expecting too much in return.

As I rolled up to the pumps, I wondered again what was important enough for Linda to call so many times. She waddled out from the office in response to the bell my car set off as I pulled in. She'd gotten heavier since the last time I'd seen her. I hadn't thought it possible.

"What's the problem, Linda?"

"Jimmy ain't here."

"That why you called me?"

"I mean he still ain't here." She scratched at her thigh, trying to nonchalantly tuck one of the rolls of fat that was showing back under her shorts. I wasn't sure why she was wearing them on a cold fall afternoon; didn't care much either.

"He went out to do a job on Saturday night," she explained, "and he ain't come in yet." With a few questions, I got the story.

Tibbs had left on his bike Saturday night to run an errand for someone, claiming he'd be back by midnight. That had been almost 48 hours earlier. She didn't know what the job was, or who it was for, but she did remember that he'd mentioned having to make a stop at The Big Valley, the local fast-food steakhouse.

I told her I'd check into things and get back to her. She smiled, telling me to drop in anytime, scrunching her fat left cheek into a fair approximation of a wink. She told me how lonely it was with Tibbs going off on his odd jobs all the time, letting what was supposed to be a girlish laugh struggle upward through her bloated frame to further sour the afternoon air. I thanked her noncommittally and headed back out into the traffic. I wasn't in the mood to hurt anyone's feelings.

I thought about Tibbs as I headed for The Big Valley. It wasn't like him to just disappear — not anymore. Sure, he'd pulled his share of stunts, daredeviling around town. Work never interested him — just goofing on his bike, really. Everyone always said his bike would buy him a one-way ticket someday. They'd been wrong, though. He'd grown up enough over the years to survive to thirty. At least I was hoping so.

I arrived at the steakhouse about twenty minutes later. The manager spotted me as I came in with the rest of the early dinner crowd. He came over to greet me, salad bowl in hand. Spooning some greens into his mouth, he sputtered:

"Hey, Hagee. What's up, Kojak?"

"Not much, Lou. I'm just checking around."

"What're you lookin' for?"

"Tibbs."

I watched his face. Nothing registered outside of the fact that he knew who I was talking about. Pieces of shredded lettuce dribbled down his front.

"Haven't seen him since, uummaa, Saturday. Why? Somethin' wrong?"

"I don't know, Lou. I doubt it. Linda's worried; he hasn't shown for a few days."

"Jeez. That pig. Think she'd be grateful, you know?" He spooned another mouthful of salad to his lips, chewing open-mouthed as he talked. "Ah, but, hell — can I treat you to a steak or somethin'?"

I honestly thought about it for a moment, but even though I hadn't eaten much more than potato chips and beef jerky for three days, I still turned him down. Linda's proposition and the meth and the smell of burning animal fat and blood filling the steakhouse had stolen my appetite. After three days I'd simply forgotten how to be hungry.

"Not today. Maybe later. I got to keep going right now. You have any idea where Tibbs was headed after he left here Saturday night?"

"Oh, sure. He was going over to Humphrey's to check on my order."

I thanked him for the info and headed back outside. I didn't bother to tell him about the crumbled eggs and bacon bits clinging to his sweater. They always fall off soon enough.

Walking out the door, I headed for my car, ignoring the early season chill. Maybe that was the meth, too — for some reason I wasn't as cold as I'd been over the weekend. I was glad for that; November nights in Pittsburgh are lonely enough without being cold as well. Unlocking my door, I got in and keyed the ignition, aiming myself toward Humphrey's.

Everett Humphrey was the local meat wholesaler. His packing plant had sat on the outskirts of town as long as people could remember. There were rumors about him selling other things, but then I'd heard the same rumors about Lou and Tibbs and half the people I knew. Cities can be as bad as any small town when it comes to allowing boredom to breed gossip. Stopping at the first pay phone I spotted, I rang Spenser to let him know what I was up to. He gave me a bit of news after I told him where I was heading and why.

"Don't bother going to Humphrey's."

"Why not?"

"Tibbs just called here. He wanted to talk to you; told him you'd probably call in in a while. He said he'd head over to the Top Dollar and stay put 'til you could get there. Where are you now?" When I told him, he answered, "Good. Tibbs was all the way over the other side of town. From where you are, you'll probably beat him."

I thanked Spenser for the message, then hung up. Getting back in my Chevy, I shot over the half dozen blocks to the Top Dollar.

The Dollar was the only decent bar at that end of town. It was also one of Tibbs' favorites. I suspect most of the appeal was tied to the distance between the bar and his home. Pulling across the railroad tracks separating it from the rest of the town, I left my car in the alley slashing the bar away from the next building and went inside. As I opened the door, Pete, the bartender, reached for the Gilbey's. I waved him off, taking a seat at the bar. I wasn't thirsty.

"Nothing for you, Jack?"

"No, thanks, Pete. I'm just looking for Tibbs. He been here today?"

"No, not today. He was scoutin' for ya the other day, though."

"Do you have any idea what he wanted?"

Pete leaned over the bar, closing the distance between us. In a tone trying to imply something sinister, he whispered, "Jack, I think Tibbs was gettin' himself mixed up in somethin'."

When I questioned as to what kind of something a tired, fat coward like Tibbs could get himself mixed into, I received a lot of stalling sounds until Pete finally came across with something I could understand.

"Okay, lissen. I think he was gettin' involved with fencin'. From what he said the other day, I think he was on to a lot of easy turnover property — watches, typewriters, computer boards, radios — quick-pay stuff. I think he was lookin' to test the waters — see if you'd play ball with him on movin' it around."

I wanted to ask Pete more, but someone thirsty screamed him over to their side of the bar. While I waited for him to come back, I mulled over what he'd said. I would've thought Tibbs knew me better; fronting stolen property, even turning a blind eye, was not my game. I'm not a very complicated guy — I'm only good for playing by one set of rules at a time. Besides, Pittsburgh had enough cops with their hand in the bag; they didn't need me in there, too.

Maybe Pete had gotten it wrong. Maybe Tibbs had floundered in over his head with someone who had the merchandise, and now needed me to bail him out of trouble. It wouldn't be the first time. Just as I called Pete back to test out my theory, the world tore itself apart.

Everyone turned toward the sound. Something outside was crashing — splattering itself over the scenery with a crunching, slippery, gurgling sound that grew in volume through every torturously long second. I was in the street before the first screams started to diminish. I forced something warm and gagging to stay in my throat as I saw what was screaming: Tibbs, his motorcycle, and the local freight express had all decided to play tag together for a moment. Tibbs lost.

I ran sickly to the spot where the majority of Tibbs had been thrown. I cradled what was left of him in my arms, trying to keep the loose, bloody bundle from slipping through my fingers. The remains of his bike, now dragged a half mile distant, exploded beneath the train, sending spurts of flame leaping out between the dark wheels of the passing boxcars.

Tibbs opened his mouth to say something, but nothing worked. Blood and other dark liquids spilled out instead of words. I yelled toward the growing crowd of bored and curious busybodies for someone to call for a wagon. Somebody yelled okay. I don't know who. It didn't matter; I hadn't asked anyone in particular.

I held Tibbs until the ambulance came. He'd died before whoever called for it had gotten the change out of his pocket. Even Tibbs had deserved better. Something had gone wrong. Maybe if I hadn't been wrapped up in myself for so long, a 20-block stretch of 8 1/2" gauge track wouldn't have been covered with blood and scorched body parts. I watched them load Tibbs into the ambulance, carrying him in a rubber bag instead of on a stretcher. I considered punching the side of the ambulance, but didn't bother. Turning away, I went back inside.

Suddenly, I was thirsty.

The boys in the morgue couldn't make up their minds who they were less happy to see — me or Tibbs. Both of us kept dripping on the floor.

"Fer Christ's sake, Hagee, if you have to mess the place up, toe the rubber, okay?"

I didn't needle the attendant. Being the one who got to try and put Tibbs back together had him in a foul enough mood. I stepped up on the mat, letting the occasional splatter of Tibbs' blood fall to its vinyl surface.

"What did he have on him?" I asked. My answer was a half-filled plastic box covered with dried brown fingerprints and a grunted:

"Why?"

"I don't know, really," I answered. "There's just something in this I don't like. Sure, I know Tibbs was reckless…"

"Who?"

"Tibbs," I spat, "the guy you've got your arms in up to their elbows."

I didn't have the right to be angry, but I didn't care. Spenser's goodie was oozing out of my system. I was getting tired; bits and pieces of my life were falling away like snow from a spring roof. I was sick of not being in control of anything around me, and of not being able to do anything about it. Deciding to do something about Tibbs, I pulled his effects toward me and started going through them.

He hadn't had much in his pockets. Just his wallet, some candy bars, his keys, some rolling papers, a pack of gum, and a handful of change. Certainly nothing worth dying for. At least not on the surface.

Things still felt wrong, though. Continuing to fight the retreating meth, I pushed my eyes open and went over everything again, looking for something to go on. I unwrapped the smashed and bloodied candy bars, going through the twisted caramel and broken clusters of peanuts and chocolate, but there wasn't anything there not listed on the wrappers. The pack of gum wasn't hiding anything, either. The papers were another story, however. I pulled the package apart to find a small plastic sample bag inside. It was slippery to the touch. Dragging a chair over to the mat, I fell into it and tried to puzzle things out.

I was feeling lousier the later it got. Before I could give up and head back to the precinct house, though, it hit me. What had been staring me in the face the whole time finally organized itself in my head. I stood up, shook away the tremors that were creeping into my legs, and headed for the door. I didn't mention the sampler to the morgue boys.

Outside, I opened it, taking the slightest of tastes. Unlike television cops, I can't stick a smear of heroin on my tongue and not only identify it, but stay straight as well; I'm not that good. I didn't have to be, though. All I wanted to prove was that what I'd found wasn't talcum powder or powdered sugar or any other legal substance. It wasn't. Not by a long shot.

Sealing the bag, I tasted the grease on the outside. The taste of animal fat made my teeth bite. I knew where I was going.

Back in my car, I returned to the outskirts of town. I thought about going home to take a shower and maybe even get the sleep I kept wishing for. Spenser's spell was wearing off, and I was turning back into a very tired and miserable pumpkin. I also thought about Tibbs' ruined face, the bleeding mouth and the words that wouldn't come out of it. That kept me going. So did the fact that I didn't have a home to go to. I was at Humphrey's before I knew it.

Stopping in his private lot, I cut my motor, parking near the only building still showing any lights. The front door was locked. I found myself wishing for some of those TV-cop skills again as I worked at the lock, trying to jimmy it. It isn't as easy as they make it look. Somehow, though, I finally got it open without being spotted. I went down the white-tiled hallways of the meat packing plant, trying not to touch the walls as I went. Tibbs had been spread over enough of the city for one night.

Suddenly, I heard voices coming from the meat locker area ahead of me. Looking through the small glass window in the door, I saw Humphrey with one of his workers. They stood talking in the middle of a few hundred steer carcasses hanging from the ceiling. My ear to the door, I tried to hear what they were saying. It didn't work. Giving up, I pulled out my service revolver, hoping the shakes in my hands wouldn't cause me to drop it. Standing up, I walked into the refrigeration chamber. Legally, I didn't have a leg to stand on, but I was too worn out to remember how the rules worked. Frost curled from my mouth along with my words.

"Okay, meat man — party's over."

"And just who the hell are you?" snarled Humphrey.

"My name's Hagee. I'm a cop. You want your rights here or at the station?"

Humphrey was a short, older man. He snapped back, "Save your breath, junior. I know my rights. One of them involves the concept of private property. Now why don't you explain what you're doing on mine while I kick your ass out of here."

"Sit down, Humphrey. You too, pal." I used my .38 as a pointer, waving them over to a brace of wooden chairs near the wall. As they sat, I told them, "Yeah, I'll explain what I'm doing here, meat man. You run drugs out of this place. It comes in those peeled cows you have strung up over there. I think once I run you two in and double-back with a search warrant, I'll find the additional evidence I need."

Without batting an eye, Humphrey questioned, "And just what put this notion in your bonnet, junior?"

"A package of street powder, all ready for sale — one covered with beef fat. It was found on a dead man last known to be headed out to see you before he disappeared. His name was Tibbs. You know, the guy you had killed tonight."

He tried to lie about it, but his eyes gave me all the proof I needed. A flicker of something less confident darted through them — a glance upward at the cows.

"Tibbs?" he stammered. "You mean that fat errand boy, the one with the motorcycle? He's dead? What happened to him?"

"What happened? I'll tell you what happened. My guess is he wanted a bigger payoff for ferrying this stuff around town for you. I've always wondered how he kept his place going, the way he neglected it. Now I know, don't I? His main pad came from messengering your appetizers around town. He got an idea of wanting more, though — so you had him iced."

Sweat was rolling down my forehead despite the temperature in the meat locker. Spenser had been right; his powder deserted with a vengeance. Forcing myself to stay standing, I said:

"I figure he made his demands Saturday night. You said no, of course — help like Tibbs must be a dime a dozen. Then I figure he made noises about turning you in, so you grabbed him and held him until you could set me up as your alibi. Your boys took him and his motorcycle, and threw them in front of the express at the crossing. Trying to beat a train at a crossing — just the kind of stunt everyone in town has been waiting for to cash Tibbs' chips in for him. It was sure to look like an accident, especially with a cop walking around saying stupid things like 'Yeah, I was there. It was an accident.' You'd be rid of him, all right."

Humphrey looked at me squarely. "And what has you so sure it wasn't an accident?"

"Because," I told him, "when your guys did their dirty work, they forgot one little thing. Motorcycles don't go anywhere when the driver still has the keys in his pocket." I pulled the crimson-crusted ring out, waving it back and forth. "Like Tibbs did. That's why I don't think it was an accident, meat man."

"That's too bad, plainclothes. That's honestly too bad." A new voice had come up behind me, one I recognized. "We tried to make this easy on you, Jack. We really did. Tibbs had to die; he was pushing too hard, in front of too many people. We had to make an example of him."

Even through the leaden haze settling throughout my system, I knew it was Spenser behind me. Remembering his now-obvious lies on the phone earlier, I kicked myself mentally for not having figured out his place in everything a long time earlier.

"Now, you give me your gun, Jack, and let's talk about this."

I turned slowly, knowing it would be foolish to try anything else. Spenser was too fast not to anticipate anything I could come up with. He and Humphrey, and who knew how many others, had obviously set me up with a lot of care.

"Really planned this out well, didn't you?"

"Obviously not as well as we thought. If we had, you'd be out trying to bring in a bunch of shop-rippers, not us. But we goofed and you didn't, so now it's time to talk."

Spenser didn't want to kill a cop. That made sense. But Humphrey didn't want to deal with me. Maybe I'd called him too many names.

"No," he ordered. "Kill him. Kill him right now and get it over with."

Spenser looked back at him from the corner of his eye. "I think this can be handled in a less clumsy fashion."

"No. Don't trust him. He's not our kind — kill him. Do it!"

They continued to argue, Humphrey growing more and more animated, Spenser trying to reason with him, but never quite taking his eyes off of me. Not that that mattered much. The meth had been the only thing holding me up, and it had disappeared from my system like rain from a summer road. I watched the scene at a distance; Spenser giving my gun to Humphrey's assistant. Spenser telling him to watch me. Spenser assuring him I was in no shape to give him any trouble. Spenser taking Humphrey out of the room to talk. Spenser telling him not to worry, and then the suddenly closing freezer door cutting off their conversation.

I was glad for that; it helped me ignore them. I worked at it, trying to get past them, and the guns, past the cold and the sweat and the dry, aching strain in my throat to something I couldn't quite remember. It was something that could help me — it was in my shirt pocket. Reaching in, I pulled out the other meth capsule Spenser had given me that morning. Humphrey's stooge looked at me with a grin. As he began to wonder if he should stop me, I flashed him the best I'm-harmless-and-silly smile I could muster and broke it open.

Hoping I wouldn't miss my nose, I steadied my hands and raised the two halves, drawing the powder deep into each nostril. My eyes pulled back painfully into my head with my next breath. After a minute, my arms and legs felt stronger than they ever had in my entire life. I was willing to bet up to a dollar they'd support me for at least a minute if I tried to stand.

Since more of Humphrey's screams were coming from the hall than Spenser's, I figured that minute'd better come soon.

Looking up at the stooge, I smiled again, but then faked a groan and doubled over sharply. While he tried to decide what to do, I groped about at the floor, angling toward him. He asked:

"Hey, somethin' wrong?"

As he bent over to check, I came straight up, slamming him across the chin — hard. I grabbed my gun from him at the same time; pulling back, I swung its grip around in an arc, bringing it back down across his forehead. He collapsed against me, toppling me into the chair I'd just emptied, bits of bone and grey frothing the air before me.

Pushing the limp body off me, I staggered to my knees, gasping for air. The meth was in me — snaking through my blood — pumping air into my brain — dancing my senses at an unfamiliar and uncomfortable rate. Putting my hands to my head, I steadied myself, listening for sounds from the hallway. I heard Spenser quieting Humphrey, making whispered plans. Humphrey's footsteps disappeared down the hall, taking him to either more men or another gun. Which it was didn't matter. Either forced me to make the next move.

I was certain there was no other way out of the meat room; Spenser would have come in after me if there was. Figuring I had only a few minutes at best, I braced myself, trying to blink the stars away from between myself and the door. The meth had jolted me awake enough to handle Humphrey's man, but some parts of my body were not happy with the arrangement. I doubled slightly as my stomach cramped; my shoulders kept reaching down, wanting to touch the floor, just for fun. Part of my brain thought that was a good idea; another part kept screaming something about getting past Spenser and out of the plant.

I shut my eyes, trying to drive the patterns back far enough so I could find the door. I ran to it, disgusted with myself for moving so slowly. Peering out its window, I could see Spenser, calmly positioned behind a desk in the hallway. I stepped back, looking for something to shield myself with. I told my brain I'd let it go to sleep just as soon as it helped me get out of the meat room alive, in the hopes it would throw in with me for a little while. It worked. I let my arms and legs move, doing what my brain told them. I was too confused to take charge. They moved one of the wooden chairs in front of the door, and then piled two of the hanging beef carcasses on it.

Taking a second, I wiped imaginery sweat from my brow and then shoved hard, driving the load before me through the swinging doors. Two shots barreled at me from the desk, driving deep into the meat. I shoved harder, pushing the mass at a run until I crashed into the desk. The top beef flipped up and over, slamming into Spenser, sending him tripping backwards, unable to bring his gun back around.

I stood up sharply, feeling the quickness of the move painfully in my forehead — down my back — in my knees. My gun fired in Spenser's general direction. I watched the bullet tear into the wall to his side, gouging out a line of tile-and-plaster splinters. His gun tried to aim itself again, slowed by the explosion of porcelain shards my shot had dislodged. My arm jerked sideways at the same time, firing a second shot. I watched this slug drive through Spenser's chest, covering the wall behind him with a dark splatter. I heard his teeth jam together as his head struck the wall.

This dazed him, but didn't stop him completely. Aiming vaguely, he managed to squeeze off one last shot. I watched the bullet erupt from the barrel of his gun, following its progress down the hallway toward me. Luckily, I remembered what it could do if it hit and stepped aside, letting it drive into my arm instead of my chest. The force spun me around, but didn't knock me down.

Spenser fell back against the wall at the same time, his eyes closing as he slid down it, smearing himself across the tiling, blood splotching its whiteness. I picked up his gun from where it had clattered, brushing away the bits of colored fuzz floating in the air in front of me. I still wanted to leave, but my legs buckled beneath me, sending me to the floor. My brain nagged at me, reminding me that Humphrey was still free. I told my brain I could handle Humphrey with my eyes closed. Then I passed out so I could prove it.

I woke in a hospital room. I was willing to believe the nurse when she told me it was Friday. It felt like a Friday. I had to wonder why my arm was so sore until she told me I was lucky the bullet hadn't struck the bone. I had forgotten about being shot.

I nodded gratefully for the information, my eyes promising I'd try to never get shot again. That seemed to please her.

Wheelock came in shortly after she left. He didn't seem as upset as I expected. He explained what happened to me between the time I'd passed out and then opened my eyes again in the hospital. Apparently Humphrey had panicked and run out on Spenser, trying to escape. A patrol car spotted him doing 70 mph, and went after him simply because he was speeding. Thinking they were in pursuit for other reasons, he'd gone faster, trying to make the freeway. The patrol called for backup; they bottled him up in the middle of a block, taking him without a shot. Not knowing they didn't know anything about me, he blurted a confession, trying to put the blame on Spenser. That meant an investigatory team and an ambulance to the meat plant, which got my car to the station parking lot, me to the hospital, and the bodies to the morgue.

As I mulled over the misunderstanding that had save my life, Wheelock said, "So, since Tuesday morning, the news media has been shoving the story of the drug-selling cop down Pittsburgh's throat with a vengeance."

A pause went on long enough for me to realize I had the next line. "Yeah?" I figured I didn't have to be clever until I healed.

"Yeah. Which means that once the reporters who have been kept down in the lobby, who are still coming here in shifts, waiting to hear what you have to say — once they're turned loose in here to pry what happened out there out of you, then..."

I finished it for him. "Then the in-quotes 'honor' of the department will be in my hands — right?"

Wheelock went stiff. "Yeah, right."

He stood over me, waiting for some kind of reply. Not knowing what else to say, I told him, "Let me think about it. Don't let the newsboys in — tell them I lapsed into a coma or something. Give me an hour — go get a sandwich — go get laid. Let me think about it."

Wheelock nodded and left the room. I spent the first few minutes testing out the idea of being alive. Somehow it still seemed natural. Deciding I was stuck in the "real world" for a while longer, I thought about what Wheelock was asking. It wasn't that much.

He didn't want me to lie; all he was asking me was that I implicate Spenser, all the way to the hilt, and let the department off free. He didn't want old wounds opened — or new graves dug. Sure, if I wanted to, I could draw lines to those cops who had to have been working with Spenser. Drawing them far enough, they might even lead back to Wheelock...but I didn't care.

I'd give the captain what he wanted, and as soon as I was able, I'd go to the station, get whatever they owed me and head out of Pittsburgh in the first direction I came to before I decided to try and keep playing cop, or call Michelle. Monday had convinced me those were games I didn't play very well.

Besides, I was tired of other people's rules. Trite as it sounds, whenever you let someone else tell you what to do, then you're not doing whatever you really want to be doing. At the age of thirty, with my wife headed in one direction and my career in another, both of them away from the hospital bed I was glued to by a bullet hole and my own stupidity, I figured maybe it was time I started making my own rules.

Like Milton told us — better to reign in hell. Spenser was right — you get what you pay for.

Nothing Comes Cheap

OVER THE YEARS, I've noticed the less work I have, and the fewer my chances are of getting any, the more time I spend in the office. Maybe it's desperation, or maybe without any work, I just don't have anything better to do; I don't know. It's always been that way, though.

The worst period was after I'd first moved to New York. Setting up as a private detective in Manhattan is not the easiest thing in the world. Once I'd greased enough palms to get my license transfer and a pistol permit, I found myself with just enough cash to afford lunches; all I had to do was skip breakfasts and pretend dinners were things that could be put off in the same fashion one delays the buying of a second car.

Having paid the deposit on the pair of rooms near Union Square I still call my office with promises dripping in all the sentimentality I could wring from a rural upbringing, I found myself spending a lot of time staying indoors, thumbing through the stack of magazines I'd found in the scratched metal desk that came with my "suite." I tried to keep reading because the only other thing to look at was the wall in front of me, and reading the magazines was driving me crazy quickly enough.

My one other diversion was arguing with the building manager, trying to get the painters sent up to put my name on the door. It was bad enough knowing my name wasn't in the phone book yet, I at least wanted people to able to find me if they by chance stumbled into the lobby, and maybe saw my name in the wall directory, and just happened to need a detective that day. You never know.

Of course I'd tried drumming up business in all the usual ways. Some of the local blues had promised to send anything my way they thought might help bring in the rent money. I'd spread my cards around throughout the neighborhood and far beyond. The first week I spent a lot of time on the phone calling lawyers' offices, department stores, small shops — anyone who might have needed a detective at the moment. No one did.

I spent the second week reading and staring at the phone and taking single shots of gin once or twice an hour. I'd take the bottle out of the drawer, open it, pour, close it, and then put it back in the drawer. It was a way of convincing myself that no matter how many shots I took, I wasn't drinking too much.

By the third week, the magazines were back in the drawer and the bottle was open on the desk. I was pouring myself a tumbler after my daily argument with the manager when my first customer knocked on the outer door, asking if she could come in.

I told her, "Sure." By the time she had showed up, even lunches had begun to become more a part of memory than routine. All of my cash, and most of my excuses, had dried up earlier that week. I was ready to track down missing bicycles for ten dollars a head. The woman coming through the door looked like she might have a better offer.

She was dressed in white, the kind of white they paint $2.50-a-scoop ice cream parlors. It was the color of prize-winning cats, the shade ski resort owners make pacts with the devil over to see it on their slopes just once. It started at the floor in the form of spike-heeled shoes that just peeked out from under crisply pure slacks. A tunic top flowed down from her shoulders, strapped in by a tight white leather thong belt. The thong dangled down her left side, its shining, milky beads clacking gently as she moved toward me. It was a nice sound. Carved ivory held her auburn hair out of her eyes; it also doubled out to keep one of her wrists and several of her fingers warm. I got up to greet her, hoping she wasn't collecting money to save the seals.

She took my hand, asking, "This is the detective's office, isn't it?"

"Yeah." To save time, I told her, "I'm the detective."

"Mr. Hagee?" I nodded. "Lorraine. Lorraine Morgan." I nodded again. I liked the sound of "Morgan." It had a hum of money to it that matched her outfit and the way she held herself. Mentally crossing my fingers, I asked what I could do for her. She took a seat and told me.

"My father was murdered, Mr. Hagee. Purposely. I want you to prove it."

As she talked, I began to put the pieces together. Morgan — Ralph Morgan. He'd been killed the week before; I remembered a few of the papers I'd been able to afford screaming about it — MILLIONAIRE MUGGING, they'd called it. Morgan'd been beaten and robbed several blocks from the skyscraper that housed the modest penthouse labyrinth he'd called home. The police'd found all the typical signs of a mugging, and had therefore labeled it a typical mugging. Ms. Morgan wasn't as sure as they were.

"I don't think Daddy was killed by some little brown P.R. junkie who happened to be in the right place."

"Why not?"

She looked at me as if I had started in on a salad with the wrong fork.

"Excuse me...," she asked. "What do you mean?"

"I mean...why don't you think your father was mugged? I assume you're trying to tell me you think he was killed with forethought — that he was made to look as if he was mugged. Okay, I'll buy that. Now I want to know what makes you think so, what you want me to do about it. You know, little things like that."

She swallowed softly. She'd made up her mind to tell me her suspicions before she'd entered the building. This was the period where she got her facts to the edge so she could push them out into the open. Confronting things out loud is difficult for a lot of people. Her fingers dipped into her bag, liberating a cigarette case. She pulled a hand-rolled affair from it, one fairly guaranteed not to be stuffed with anything the boys at American Tobacco sell. She asked:

"Do you mind?"

I shrugged. What'd I care? I was impressed she'd even asked first. New Yorkers aren't famous for considering other people's sensitivities before dispensing drugs in public. I guess finishing schools have their purposes after all. She lit her doobie, the end burning back by only the slightest red circle. She inhaled deep and long, but the joint only fired back about a quarter of an inch. That and the heady, thick odor coming from it told me the grass I could also smell had been heavily laced with cocaine. Once she'd held down two solid drags, she continued.

"Understand, Mr. Hagee, Daddy and I weren't what you would call 'close.' Rich families, at least the ones I know, aren't much like that. We liked and respected each other — Daddy said I have wonderful business sense." She fumbled for a second, then continued.

"What I'm trying to get at is that he trusted me." She puffed again, then started once more, holding the acrid smoke down without effort. "Last month, he confided to me that he was thinking of changing his will. He had had... second thoughts on some things — some people."

She exhaled then, letting the smoke curl up past the ivory. I stared at the cloud, trying to rationalize the fact that her escaping grey breath cost more than a decent meal or a bottle of Gilbey's. Then I just stared at her and waited for the rest. After all, I thought, maybe she had something. I was hoping she did. I needed a case, and hers was the only one in sight.

"Can you prove any of this?" I asked.

"I don't know," she said honestly. "I think Daddy made some notes on the changes and put them into one of his safe deposit boxes. I didn't want to go after them until I had a reason to. I could get the notes and a copy of his present will. If we compare them, it might give you something to look for, narrow the field."

"Why not just go to the cops?" I asked. "They *are* the ones who are supposed to solve these kinds of things."

She looked at me frankly this time. Taking another drag, she half-whispered, "I don't know that I can trust them, Mr. Hagee. My father was rich — I'm sure you can make some guesses as to how rich, and as to how far the reach of that kind of money can extend. The police have been known to be corruptible in the past. A lot of people in this town are owned. I want to know the truth, Mr. Hagee, but I don't want to get killed for it."

That made sense. After all, she had the money to hire me, and let me get killed for it. Whether or not owning me for a while would help her, I wasn't sure; I thought I knew what I could get out of it, though, so I asked her the only question I had left.

"Okay, I'm intrigued. I would like to know one thing, though."

"What's that?"

"Why me? What brought you here?"

"You wrote to one of Daddy's companies, looking for work. I came across your letter the other day. It said you'd been with Army Intelligence, that you'd been both a police and a private detective in other cities, and that now you were here in New York looking to be hired. Chances are if you've only been in town a few weeks, you're not in anyone's pocket yet." She stared at me with sharp, piercing eyes, "I don't think you are."

"No one but yours," I answered. She smiled. It was a warm one, edged with enough of a trace of relief to let me trust her. As she snuffed out her roach in my ashtray, she told me, "You know, you don't look like a detective."

"Is that good or bad?" I asked.

"I don't know," she replied. Looking at me with what could best be described as little-girl slyness, she asked, "Would you care to discuss it over lunch?"

"Do I need a tie?"

"Not really."

"The client picks up the check, you know."

"Only if the client picks the restaurant."

I agreed. The client could pick up the detective, too, if she wanted. I figured I wouldn't push that one, though. I'd wait until I got paid before I got arrogant. Thinking of that, I reminded her that she didn't know my rates. She assured me she could cover the bill. Testing, I warned her:

"I might be new in town, but I can be as greedy as the next guy." She answered over her shoulder:

"Nothing comes cheap, Mr. Hagee."

I had to agree with that. Assuring her I would eat anywhere she wanted to, I followed her out of the office. Making a mental note to use the right forks, I locked my unlettered door behind me and let my client take me where she wanted.

Lunch'd been found in Chinatown, the part most people can't afford. Maybe she felt better discussing her father's death in a place where the waiters didn't appear to understand the table conversation. It didn't matter to me.

We batted her few suppositions and fewer facts back and forth, found a little out about each other, and ate our lunches. I tried not to be too obviously starving; she tried not to too obviously notice. When the meal was over, the waiter brought us a small platter of honeydew, cantaloupe, and watermelon slices. I asked where the fortune cookies were. Lorraine explained that in some Chinese restaurants — "some" being her word where "expensive" would have been mine — the custom was to bring seasonal fruits instead. Maybe it meant fortune cookies were low class; maybe the rich don't need cookies to tell them what's coming next. I just ate the melons and made up my own future. It's what we all do anyway.

From lunch we headed for Daddy's old — her new — business offices. What I needed were copies of Daddy's wills, the old one and what Lorraine claimed was the new one, or at least the outline for it. Apparently "the office" was the place to find the first and get directions to the second.

I wasn't sure what to expect as we stepped off the elevator. Guys like me don't see much of midtown, not from a sixtieth-floor view anyway. I half expected every employee to stare me up and down, their faces reflecting the questions a detective raised by being with the dead boss' daughter. None of them did. A few people looked up from their work to say their good afternoons and the like to Lorraine, but no one seemed much interested in me. Maybe she was right; maybe I didn't look that much like a detective after all.

As we passed through the door to the executive suite, I began to wonder why I wanted to be one, either.

The room was "richly" decorated — the same way the Grand Canyon is "fairly" memorable. Plowing our way through a field of sea-blue carpeting, the kind that sells for a week's salary per square yard, we made our way to a desk piled high with papers. A receiving box sat deep with memos and opened letters. Other stacks of less important forms grew around the edges of a central blotter. Outside the newborn mountain range of business lay a few packages, and other odd-shaped deliveries that couldn't be broken down by size.

I told her, "Looks like you don't come in very often."

"No, not really," she answered. "I come in once or twice a week, pick up whatever needs my attention, and distribute the rest to whoever it really should have gone to in the first place. Let me go through some of this, and then I'll find Daddy's notes." While she dug through the outer foothills, I shoved the packages aside so I could sit on the corner of the desk.

She asked, "Who are the packages from?"

I read off the return addresses while she continued to hunt. Anything to get us back on the track, I figured. There were only a few. The largest one, though, had no markings on it except for the address of the building we were in, the postage that had gotten it delivered, and the word PERSONAL next to Lorraine's name block lettered on the front.

"The big one doesn't want to identify itself."

"That's odd," she said. "Pass it over, will you?"

I handed her the package, absently staring around the room, wishing we could get down to business. My fingernail caught on what felt like a string under the paper, irritating me further.

As Lorraine tore at the wrapping, I saw that it hadn't been string, but wire instead. That gave me a bad twinge, but I couldn't place why. As she went to cut it, though, it suddenly made an ugly sense. Knowing I couldn't stop her in time with words, I threw myself over the desk, grabbing her as her hand closed on the snippers. We tumbled over backwards, a fierce retort echoing through the office a hundred times before we hit the floor. I came back up on my feet, even as the door of the office opened, admitting the rank and file. I started giving orders before anyone else could.

"You. Call the police — tell them a bomb's been set off." I pointed toward another secretary. "Does this dump have a doctor?" When she nodded, I snapped, "Find him and get him up here."

As more of the curious started to jam their way in, I put a couple of the older matrons, the ones who looked like third-grade teachers, to the task of clearing the room and keeping it that way. Lorraine and I were alone again in less than a minute.

She asked me, "What was that? What happened?"

"Mail bomb." I pointed to a trio of nasty holes in the ceiling and the wave of plaster on the floor all around us. "More specifically, a mail gun."

I knelt down on the floor next to her, putting my arm around her shoulders. She shuddered against me, starting to cry.

"I think you're right about your father," I told her. "We're going to have to talk some more."

She agreed quickly, continuing to cry. While I held her, I reached down and picked up a piece of the bomb's wrapping — one that had a part of the block-lettered address. I scanned it quickly, and then shoved it into my pocket as a knock came at the door, followed by a cheery "Well, well, and what happened here?" The doc had arrived, and from the sounds out in the hall, the police weren't far behind. I whispered to Lorraine that we would talk later, and then started explaining mail-order redecorating to the company's pill huckster.

Court was set to reconvene at Lorraine's apartment that night. The doc had treated her for mild shock, but hadn't been needed beyond that. The police, led by a Captain Phillips, tied things together so neatly that they were gone in under an hour. One of the bomb squad team'd seen the same kind of wiring detailing before, so therefore the bomb obviously had to be the handiwork of the previous wirers.

Thus the police set out after a half-baked, home-grown terrorist organization no one had heard a peep out of in two years, giving the press a nice angle, my client a pat answer, and me the problem of figuring out who really had tried to restyle Lorraine's hair with three .22 shells.

I kept going over the facts available on my way to Lorraine's. The package had been compact and lightweight, for what it had accomplished. Someone who knew what they were doing'd built a triple-shot bomb, one that fired three bullets at the same time through the top of the box. Cutting the wire trigger released the bullets. My car radio told me three New York-based groups and two foreign ones were already taking credit for the blast. News travels fast in big cities, too, I guess. That meant no one would probably ever get actual credit for it; the police were usually too busy to bother investigating explosions where no one got hurt. Generally, not much was ever found out about the ones where people did get hurt, so I wasn't expecting much from them on this one. What I had been expecting was more of a hassle than I'd received, though.

Once they'd turned up I was a detective working for Ms. Morgan, and not the window washer or some other type of hired help the Morgan Corporation kept around to save its top execs from bombs, they'd left me alone. That'd struck me as curious. The one thing the TV shows and the old movies've pegged correctly is the fact that cops don't have much use for the private sector. Hell, when I was a cop, I didn't have much use for private dicks.

Maybe they did have some sort of interest in things the way Lorraine'd intimated earlier, I thought. Then again, maybe they just didn't catch a lot of TV or old movies. New York was a big place; maybe they only go to stage plays, I thought, leaving the late-night tubing to us out-of-towners. After all, they'd looked like an esoteric bunch — especially the sensitive one who'd finished his pizza while taking Lorraine's statement, leaving a smear of cold grease on her desk to mix with the exploded-plaster residue already there.

Be that as it may, I'd let it bother me to the point where I didn't get anything done. I'd spent the afternoon thinking about the unusual speed and friendliness of the NYPD and banking the check Lorraine'd given me at lunch. Looking at the half an address I'd scooped up in her office hadn't gotten me anywhere, nor had looking at Daddy's original will. It left too many people too well off to point any fingers on its own. The notes on the new will would have to tell the story, but those weren't to be pulled out until dinner was over and the butler was gone for the night. Lorraine had figured out in which bank they were tucked away — apparently Daddy'd kept all of his legal papers in one box — and had picked them up that afternoon.

Dinner at Lorraine's apartment was interesting. I didn't often eat in rooms twice the size of my apartment. It made me feel good to see that she liked things cozy. While the butler made me feel like a big man by pouring me a second cup of coffee before I had to ask for it, Lorraine left the room for a moment, returning with a package. She handed it to me. When I asked her what was inside, she told me to open it and find out.

"Go ahead," she said. "This one doesn't explode."

I pulled the paper away and opened the box, finding a hat inside. She told me, "It was one of Daddy's." Figuring what the hell, I slipped it on. It fit. She seemed pleased.

"Now you look like a detective," she said. "Just like Bogart."

Oh goody, I thought. Just what I always wanted. But it did seem to make her happy, and since happy clients tend to pay their bills faster, I figured I could grow to like wearing a hat, at least for a little while. After all, I've done sillier things to please women in my life.

As Jeeves cleared away the coffee cups, I asked her, "What say we retire to the den for a little business?" She nodded, the playful spell broken, and led me back through the apartment.

We wound up in the study; she indicated the seat behind the desk for me. I took it. She gave me Daddy's notes, which I read over while she went back out to tell the butler to go home early. Once I'd finished, I pulled out a list of figures I'd drawn up that afternoon that capsulized the original will. Comparisons between the two seemed to narrow things down fairly easily. I pointed out the differences to her.

"Take a look. Some people have been shuffled around a little, but these three I've checked off — they could be a little miffed."

Looking over the names and the figures, she agreed. The first one cut was Daddy's club. They'd been in for a nice chunk of change, but they'd been dropped completely. His executor, one Carl Larkin, given a lot of decision-making control in the first will, had to take a back seat to Lorraine, according to the notes for the now never-to-be new one. Most noticeable of all, however, was the provision that also cut my client's baby brother Richie out of the picture entirely.

"Interesting, isn't it?" I asked. "So who do you suspect?"

"I, I don't know. I mean, I—"

"Yeah, don't worry about it. This doesn't tell us anything conclusive. Sure, your brother might have done it. Maybe he wanted you bombed, too, just on general principles. Then again, Carl here would be the one who might want both of you out of the picture. Dad, so the will wouldn't be changed, and you, so you wouldn't do what you're doing right now."

"What about the club?"

"Who knows?" I answered. "Anything's possible. We'll need more than what we have to do anything against anyone, though." I shoved Dad's hat back from my forehead asking her, "So why did Dad cut Richie out?"

She lowered her eyes, embarrassed.

"They weren't seeing eye to eye on how Richie should be living his life. He, he has some 'habits' Daddy doesn — ah, didn't approve of."

She'd said "habits" in the same voice most parents use to discuss bed-wetting. Before I could follow up, though, she asked, "Why can't we do anything now?"

I explained little things to her, like evidence, or the lack of it in this case, and slander, et cetera. Her little-girl confidence in the hired gladiator seemed to slip a little, brand-new helmet or not.

"Then there's nothing to stop them from trying again. Now that I've hired you, they might — they might try to get rid of both of us."

Her voice cracked slightly, panic rooting itself toward the base. As she came near me, I held her again, telling her it wasn't very likely, that she'd be all right, that I'd take care of her — all the standard lies one tells a child when one doesn't know the truth.

We talked softly in the half darkness, her asking me to stay with her, me agreeing. Somehow the light faded, and I found myself with her in a different darkness. Neither one of us said much; we merely groped and sweated and tried to kiss and groan away the fact that someone might be sitting up somewhere trying to figure out a new way to get rid of us. I know men and women often have unspoken questions between them, but I can think of better ones.

As the night wore on, we finally seemed to get rid of our immediate anxiety. Lorraine stayed cradled in my arms, sleeping comfortably while I tried to decide what to do in the morning. None of the handwriting samples she had shown me before dinner'd matched up very conclusively. Small wonder; most people don't do any block lettering when they sign their names, and official papers were all Lorraine'd been able to find.

I was feeling ready to give up on the whole thing when I heard a noise in the hall. It had been a soft scuffing sound, like someone trying to move about without waking the rest of the household. But since my client and I were supposed to *be* the entire household that night, I found myself a bit suspicious.

Easing out of bed, I crossed the room to the doorway, listening for further noises, looking around for something I might use as a weapon. Before I could spot anything, the doorknob started to turn. I hung back in the shadows, watching a man the size of a small jeep enter the room, gun in hand. He glanced toward the bed and then, as if surprised to see only Lorraine, started looking around for someone or something else, probably me.

I didn't know why and I didn't care. Figuring what little surprise I might have was quickly running out, I waited as he turned completely away from me and then jumped him, our combined weights sending us crashing against the floor. I heard the gun go bouncing across the floor, but had no idea where it'd gone. I tried holding him down, but he was too big — like trying to hold back a bucking refrigerator. He threw me off and was back on his feet instantly. I was only halfway up when his knee crashed into my side. I hit the wall, first with my back, then with my head. As he closed in on me again I managed to pull to one side, avoiding a kick that broke the plaster next to my head.

By now Lorraine was awake, screaming and turning on lights, both actions surprising my pal. Taking the advantage, I pushed myself up from the floor into him, sending him over. As he came up, I grabbed a lamp from a nearby dresser and swung it, crashing the heavy base against his skull. He snarled, knocking the lamp from my hands, and suddenly we were on the floor again in a tangle.

He had one of my arms and one of my legs, and was pulling them over my back toward each other, wrestling style. All I could do was drag or push myself across the floor with my free limbs, but I couldn't get up. Ignoring the pain in my back, I continued to crawl along in slug fashion the few inches to where my lamp lay. Lorraine remained in the bed, screaming.

Just as my fingers reached the lamp, she suddenly cried out:

"My God! Kenny!"

As my pal jerked at the sound of his name, I grabbed up the lamp and brought it crashing against his head once more. He lost his hold on me, giving me the time to drag myself away from him. Dazed for only a second, though, he came at me again. I waited for him to get close enough and then stabbed with the lamp, crushing the exposed light bulb against his face. The fragile glass shattered instantly, a few pieces driving in and around his left eye and cheek. As he reflexively stopped, I pushed forward, driving the bulb shards deeper into his face with a twist. Then I swung the lamp two-handed as he staggered back, catching him on the side of the head, sending him tripping backwards.

He fell against the window, hitting it with a slam. Before I could step forward, even if I'd wanted to, the pane shattered and Kenny half-slipped, half-fell backward onto one of the thick, well-anchored shards, driving it through himself with his own body weight. Blood bubbled upward out of him, running over his sides down onto the hand-polished floor. Lorraine ran across the room to me while he continued to spasm, pinned to the window sill. I backed her slowly away, so the constantly reaching pool wouldn't ooze over her bare feet.

It was the only way to get both of us out of the room and to the liquor cabinet.

Once again, the NYPD acted better than their reputation would lead one to believe they would. They came in, collected our stories, collected Kenny, apologized for the commotion, and left. True, the same captain arrived in charge of things that had arrived at Lorraine's office, but there wasn't anything rare in that. Captains on the lookout for promotions generally try to keep the richer sections of the gentry in their precinct happy. At least those were the rules I'd always seen work in the past. Maybe Captain Phillips was an exception I didn't understand; I didn't know. I did know things were beginning to add up, though.

When my pal had been able to answer at all, he had answered to Kenneth Fenton. The police had surmised that he must have gotten a key at sometime in the past, since — no surprise after Lorraine's outburst — he was an old friend of the family. He'd been on the wrestling team with her brother and had spent several holidays with them. The cops'd said they would start checking on Fenton and his friends right away, to see if there was a connection between him, them, and any of the terrorist organizations who had taken credit for the bombing. I didn't laugh; I try never to be amused by one-track minds when I'm still standing in front of the locomotive.

By the time they left, the sun was just peeking up over the edge of the city. As I started to drag myself into the bathroom, Lorraine asked me, "What do we do now, Mr. Hagee?"

"Now I get cleaned up. If you want to, you can get cleaned up. After that, I could probably use a doughnut. You can have whatever you like. Before you get yourself cleaned up, or eat a doughnut, or whatever you might like, though, I want you to find me some more of your brother's handwriting — grocery lists, polo pony order forms, anything, I don't care. Just find me something with block letters on it."

By the time I'd shaved with Daddy's old razor and cleaned away the residue, I was beginning to feel a little bit better. Once I went over the papers Lorraine had gathered and the scrap I'd pocketed the day before, I started feeling a lot better. It was only a pair of letters from the back of an old photograph, but the shapes matched up well enough to convince me. From the look on Lorraine's face, I could see I wasn't the only one who was convinced.

She asked me, "What do we do now?"

"Now we go for a little family visit."

Lorraine begged time to get herself together. I didn't care. Another half hour wasn't going to make that much difference. Besides, she took the liberty of supplying me with a tumbler and a bottle of Gilbey's before she disappeared into the back recesses of her apartment; I was content. If anything, I felt she got ready too quickly, but such are the fortunes of war.

I stood up when she entered the room. As I screwed the top back on the Gilbey's, she asked me, "You didn't bring a gun, did you?"

"No," I replied. "I prefer to shoot off my mouth."

She smiled, but said, "Maybe you should take this then." She held a .38 out in front of her, butt first. Daddy's. I told her:

"No, thanks. I have the feeling you know how to use that as well as I do."

"Daddy did teach me."

"Fine. You keep it. If there is any trouble, whoever's dishing it out will go for me first. Best you have the hardware. I've killed enough people this week. Even cops as nice as the ones you seem to get have their limits."

She nodded, and we left. By the time most city dwellers were just catching their trains, we'd pulled up in front of Baby Brother's Upper West Side brownstone. Using her own key, Lorraine let us in the front door. We walked down the dark front hall, looking around for a trace of Richie. As I took in the decor, I began to realize why little Richie had joined the wrestling team. I had a notion it had more to do with bringing guys like Kenny home for Christmas and the habits Daddy'd frowned on than it did with school spirit.

I clicked on the lights, heading for the stairs. A sound came from the next floor, causing Lorraine to hold back. I moved forward, calling:

"Hey, Richie. Let's have a little talk." He appeared at the top of the stairs, dressed only in jeans and boots.

"You're an awfully little man to have beaten Kenny," he told me.

"What makes you think I beat Kenny?"

"Because," he sighed, "the plan was for Kenny to go and beat you. We all knew that silly bomb of his wasn't going to do anything — but he should have been able to dust you with ease. But if you're here and Kenny isn't, then that means you beat Kenny."

He talked with a faraway sneer, as if he'd spent time rehearsing it in front of the mirror.

"Do I get a gold star?"

And then, as he lounged against the wall glaring down at me, the reason for his fog became apparent. His eyes gave him away; he was tooted out of his mind — maybe on cocaine, maybe heroin, maybe anything — rich people can afford all sorts of fun. I moved forward one cautious step, testing the waters of his mood.

"Sorry, no gold stars until we know what's been going on."

He smiled at me. I got more cautious.

"Sister hasn't told you? Shame, shame, Lorraine. Ohhhhhh, I always did have to do everything. Now let me guess," he chuckled. "You want to know who killed rich old Ralph Morgan — right? Of course, right."

He started to move again, performing his way down the stairs.

"Well, that one's easy. I did. I clubbed Ralphie over his thick skull. Here, right here in this apartment."

He paused halfway down to the landing, indicating with gestures how it'd happened.

"Thud — boom — crash. That's all it took. Ralph didn't approve of some of my friends — or some of our habits."

Richie smiled again. It was not an endearing quality. He started moving again.

"Actually, you would have probably liked him. He was a fairly pedestrian fellow, just like you, like Lorraine—"

And then, as he said his sister's name, his hand snaked behind him, jerking a gun from the belt of his jeans. I leaped for the stairs, but before I could reach him, or he could aim at either one of us, a shot went off behind me, cutting him down. His gun sent a slug digging into the ceiling before he could drop it. I watched him fall past me, tumbling down the stairs, his life arcing out of him, gushing on the carpeting and the walls.

As I turned, Lorraine dropped the gun she was holding and ran over to me. I held her again, pulling her toward me instinctively, keeping my eye on Richie. He didn't get back up.

Relief shuddered through Lorraine; I couldn't decide exactly what kind of relief it was, but then, having another body to try and slide past the police without upsetting them too greatly could be termed as a reasonable distraction.

Deciding not to worry about it, I started guiding Lorraine toward the phone, hoping her rapport with Captain Phillips was still solid, and that her flowing tears were real.

Several days later, I found myself sitting in my office, having just finished collecting a retainer from my second New York client. Her name was Shayna Taylor; she was a friend of Lorraine's, a woman who wanted her husband checked up on. She'd seen my name in the paper, and Lorraine'd told her how ever-so-good I was, and so "take-my-check-and-help-me-send-my-marriage-down-the-tubes-and-my-husband's-money-into-my-account-oh-won't-you-please" was the battle cry of the day.

I took the case — phony insurance claims and bad marriages are what keep a large part of the private eye business going. Lorraine's check had been sizeable enough to not only give me the security to go after all three daily meals, but also to make snacks something more than a laughable notion. I knew, however, that nothing lasts forever, and so I accepted her friend's case with the assurance that I just couldn't wait to help her rake her poor jerk husband over the coals for the simple crime of having seen her for what she really was, and having gone somewhere else for what he really wanted. Life's tough in the big city.

As I sat figuring out just how I'd nail hubby, though, I found myself going over the facts of Ralph Morgan's death. Sure, Richie had killed Daddy, maybe even for the reasons stated. But he hadn't acted right; coming down the stairs, it'd seemed as if he hadn't felt he was the cornered one. Maybe that was just the drugs. Maybe. He'd certainly had enough in him; the police report showed that.

The police had been awfully cooperative. Maybe they don't like to give rich people a hard time, but Lorraine and I'd made a pretty big mess, the kind that doesn't usually slide under the carpet well without a good hand at the broom; they'd gone out of their way to help us clean things up and keep a happy face turned toward the ever annoying eyes of the media. Sure, I was glad to avoid getting jerked around over Kenny's death, and I was glad Lorraine's gun was legitimate, and that her permit had checked out, and that people can still justifiably homicide each other and not get huge hassles over it.

I was also glad to see that my part in things had been accepted, that the police had swallowed their pride and allowed the story to be printed as it happened, admitting their terrorist theory'd been wrong. I was also pleased as punch that Lorraine'd been able to show Carl Larkin Daddy's notes and get him to agree she should have a say in decision making, just as Daddy's wanted.

Everything'd tied together perfectly. Kenny had been in the army — had had demolition training. Phillips' team'd even turned up some of the bomb's makings in Richie's apartment. No, Kenny had definitely made the bomb, and Richie had definitely sent it. Richie had killed Daddy, and Lorraine had forced justice to be served.

The problem was, I couldn't help wondering at just how easy everything had been. Notes ready in the deposit box, matching lettering eventually, old family friend, brother's lover, father-and-son quarrel, dramatic confession on the stairs, detective saved by lover, et cetera.

Kenny's bomb hadn't stopped anyone, but why had Richie said we all were sure it wouldn't? Why was he sure Lorraine hadn't told me everything? Which "we all" and "everything" had he been referring to? Could she've been part of the plot? Could Ralph's death've been planned? Maybe Daddy hadn't written up his notes, or left them in his bank. Maybe he'd only written part of them, and some subtle additions had been made. Maybe he died just as stated, but she'd seen something in it for her, starting the ball rolling.

Lorraine'd been willing enough to tumble into bed with me before, but now there wasn't time to answer my calls. Not that I expected her to be head-over-heels — I understand desperation and the simple human arithmetic it can lead to — but her combination payoff/brushoff made me curious. I'd been wondering a lot of things, like had Kenny come to kill us, or had he thought he was only there to rough me up and run; just what had he been doing there? I was beginning to think his death was the only unplanned one in the bunch.

A letter bomb is one thing, but a letter gun is another. One might prefer a discriminating weapon when they know the script calls for them to be around when it goes off.

Unlike television, real life is never so neat. Crimes don't solve themselves every sixty minutes, and bought cops generally stay bought, getting done whatever job they've been paid to do. Captain Phillips sure had a way of popping up whenever he was needed. I wondered if he'd be campaigning the Mayor's office for police commissioner soon, and whether or not that campaign would be backed by Morgan Corporation funds.

Of course, I told myself, I could just be blowing things out of proportion. Some cases do simply open and shut. I could have all the gut feelings about being used I wanted — TV private eyes always get gut feelings. It's just that when real private eyes go up against crooked police forces resting comfortably in some millionaire's purse, they generally discover what a really good job crooked police forces can do of keeping cranks with suspicions and gut feelings away from their owners.

Pushing everything about the Morgan family out of my mind for a minute, I turned to watch the building painter put the last touches on my name. Unlike my wild conjectures about Lorraine, that was something I'd finally been able to do something about. All it had taken was solving my client's case, or taking her bribe, depending on which way I wanted to look at it.

It's funny how money that comes out of nowhere just in time to keep your life from going down the toilet can leave you feeling worse than when you were poised at the brink. I told myself I'd have to watch the Morgan Corporation, and probably soon-to-be Commissioner Phillips, and just wait for something that would allow me to either put them away, or know for sure I was wrong.

I told myself that especially loud when I cashed Lorraine's check. But then, it was like she'd said — nothing comes cheap.

Picking up the tumbler on my desk, I tossed off the last of my lunch and then went out into the hall, getting myself ready to do a job I could handle, like giving Shayna Taylor's husband trouble. As I left the office, I grabbed Daddy's hat from its resting place in the outer office and put it on. I'd decided to keep wearing it.

I figured I'd earned it.

All's Well That Ends Well

THERE WAS A touch at my shoulder, like a sudden cold breeze on an August night. I stared forward, holding my drink with one hand, steadying myself with the other, hoping that August would go back to being dry and miserable and familiar and that the breeze would drift back to whatever memory of winter from which it had escaped.

It didn't. It pulled at the edge of my arm again, pleading for notice. Whether I'd had too much to drink or not enough was academic. One or the other, I was in the right mood to give in to my darker nature. I slid around on my stool, one hand taking care to make sure I didn't spill myself onto the floor. The breeze fluttered at the edge of my range, small and tense and brown — wide-eyed scared. He was a Jamaican, too thin, too tall — willowy, like a ballet dancer, but without the muscle or the speed. His hair had been tightened in some way that gave his head the appearance of being covered with hundreds of black, Goldilocks curls. He was Uptown, Society, Connections, and a few other things I don't care for. He didn't like where he was, or whatever was on his mind, or me, either. Well, neither did I.

It was destined to be one of those mornings.

"Yeah," I growled. "Some reason I can't drink in peace without upsetting you?"

"Oh, no, no, no. Gracious...please, ah," he got hold of himself and started again. "You are Jack Hagee, the detective, no?"

"Nah," I told him, "I'm just the urn, waiting for his ashes."

The breeze stared at me, unblinking. I could tell I hadn't made much of an impression with my humor. Losing my patience as quickly as my balance, I growled, "What? What is it?! What'dya want from me now?"

I didn't know who he was or where he was from. I only knew I was tired and didn't want to be bothered by anyone else's problems. He answered:

"We need help."

"Yeah. Who doesn't?"

"Listen, my friend. This is a good thing. There is plenty of money in it for you. Plenty — all we have to do...."

It was the wrong time. I'd gone to the Holland bar to drink myself back into the abyss. I'd just come off a case which'd left me tired and nasty. It'd all been finished six weeks earlier, but I still felt grimy and used and not in the least friendly. The red lights started clicking in my brain, and suddenly, before the breeze or I knew what was happening, I was gripping his shirt front, dangling his meager frame with one hand, bouncing him off the wall with the other.

"Who cares?!" I screamed at him. "Who gives a good goddamn about you and your fucking problems? Leave me alone! You puking little shit — I ought to..."

And then, suddenly, my brain cleared as quickly as the tables around us. I glanced about the bar, looking at the people trapped against the walls by nothing more than their own fear. They'd overturned tables, spilled drinks, abandoned their coats, purses and dates, all in a mad rush to hide in the shadows. The bartender was coming for me, Louisville Slugger in hand. Not completely out of my mind yet, I dropped the breeze, holding my palms up to Matt, saying:

"I'm cool. This is bad enough. Let's not you and me get into it as well."

Matt wavered for a second and then blew his steam.

"You're a good guy, Jack," he admitted. "I like ya. But you'd better get your shit together. Go with this guy, will ya? Do some work. Earn some money. Pay your bills — mine first. You'll feel better."

Matt was right. I'd been moping around for weeks because of a feeling I'd been used. That never sits well with me. I had no proof...just the feeling. That always sits worse.

I turned to the breeze, checking out his nerves. He seemed to be calming down, but I still didn't think he liked me much. Testing out my theory, I asked him, "You still want to hire a private eye?"

"My boss does."

"And where's he?"

"In your office."

"Sure of himself, isn't he?"

"Fairly. So, shall we go to the limo, or do you want to dance around the room and terrorize me some more first? Men do it all the time. When I'm ready for it, it makes me smile like the sun. Do you want me to smile like the sun for you?"

"Let's hold off on registering our silver pattern."

He shrugged.

"Whatever you say, big brutal white person." Pushing off on one foot to get his hips in motion, the breeze fluttered out the front door, leaving his bruised dignity behind as if nothing had happened. My head was still spinning from having slammed him around, from too many drinks and too much self-pity. Anxious to see if I could make it to 'the limo' without throwing up I wobbled off toward the door. As I grabbed the front handle, I steadied myself on the jam, laughing inside in grim consolation at the fact that half the place was still on their feet.

Grateful to be one of them, I went out into the street. After all, it would've been a shame to miss seeing a limo pull up to my office. Especially with me in it.

I came into my office with the breeze. The driver had stayed with the limo. Made sense in my neighborhood. The boss was sitting in my outer room, scratching at a steno pad. He stood up as we approached, extending his hand.

"Mr. Jack Hagee…p-pleased to meet ya. Your door is fine. Maurice here is a real craftsman and the door's got a cheap lock."

We shook hands. He kept yammering. "I used y-your phone for a while. All local calls. Maurice, g-give the man a fifty."

The breeze peeled off a bill. I took it. Why not? My brain'd looked over all the angles around me on the way downtown and given up trying to get a handle on things. I'd figured meeting with the breeze's boss would clear things up. I couldn't have been more wrong. Willowy, smug, irritating Maurice had been a big enough mystery. His boss was a real puzzler. He was short and white and plain — a few years older than me, dressed in a neutral colored suit and a Hawaiian shirt, no tie, wearing black tennis shoes with red laces. His accent was tough to peg. It held a lot of New York, but it had traces of, and words from, a dozen other places, not all of them American. It also cracked and stuttered, making it a chore to listen to him talk. His face looked honest, though, so I figured I'd start asking some questions to see if I could find out what was going on.

"Okay — let's get down to it. Shall we go in my office, Mister…?"

"Hubert. Call me Hubert — everyone does. Let me tell ya, we've got someone else s-stashed inside. Just d-don't want you to be surprised." Sitting in the dark in my inner office was another black man. Hubert introduced us.

"Jack Hagee…," came the stutter as the lights snapped on, "m-meet Andrew Taylor Lowe…and visi-versi."

I shook hands with Lowe, my still clouded brain trying to force me to remember something. Before Lowe could talk, I said, "Look; let's face a fact here — you've got a drunk on your hands."

"A nasty one, too. Goodness," added the breeze.

"Yeah," I admitted. "Right. Anyway, I don't know who you people are, and I don't frankly much care. I'm going to heat up some coffee from yesterday afternoon that I don't really suggest any of you drink. I am because I need to punish myself into behaving."

"Sorta an unpleasant way of d-doin' things; ain't it?"

"Sort of guy I am."

"My, my, my..." he cackled. "An astonishing remark, me lad."

"I know what he means," said Andrew Taylor Lowe. "As Dickinson said: 'Anger as soon fed is dead; 'tis starving makes it fat.' She was right, you know."

I stopped for a second, listening. I had to shape up quick. The big boys were slumming again, shopping for muscle. Something was going on that was going to get dirty quick, and I was letting my stupid drunken ass get caught up in it. Damnit, I thought. Goddamnitheshitohellfuckingdamnit! Not again.

Mumbling some polite nonsense about needing my coffee and a cigarette it would only take a second clear the head understand better blahblahblahfucking-blah, I squeezed my brain clear, drying out the gin and the dope as best I could, refining the perceptions they both had to offer while pushing out the poisons. I studied the four I'd met so far. The driver was the quiet type — an efficient man behind the wheel — good, safe, quick, clean ride. He knew the streets — might have shoved in more than a few heads in his time — possibly dangerous. Possibly homicidal. Possibly. I opened the window for some air and to nonchalantly take his position. He was still with the limo. The rest of the street looked normal.

Maurice was a nobody — a hired gopher who made me want to roll my eyes...the kind of wimpy, whining artsie, strutting, 95 pound posturing homo that makes your shame for what men can become an unpalatable reminder you can taste like guilt. I figured if I could stomach him I could stomach the bilge I was boiling up in the pot on my hot plate.

Waiting for the coffee, though, I wished I could get a handle on what was going down. Fear was coming off Lowe like it does a second place man who loses the race halfway around the track and spends the rest of the meet trying to catch up. Knowing he won't. Like a fighter who's caught on that he's going to go down, but who'd like to do it with some dignity. Or without dignity, at least without too much pain.

By the time I could pour the coffee, I was studying Hubert through the steam. He was the focal point of all the characters. The driver was Lowe's man, Maurice was Hubert's. Hubert was keeping Lowe alive. It was as simple as that. He'd read about me in the papers. I knew he had. He'd read about me in the papers and was looking to tie two stories together and accomplish a goal. Six weeks earlier, I'd been involved in a case the media briefly picked up on. A murdered rich man's daughter'd come to me to find her daddy's killer. I'd done it, too. I'd put together the pieces like a kid's puzzle. Saved her life — twice. She saved mine killing the bad guy, who turned out to be her own brother. The case'd got me a bundle of publicity, and a number of clients. Friends of hers called me, some of them looking to sink their husbands in a divorce, some of them just wanting to scratch the balls of the big, bad plaything their fellow rich brat heiress'd introduced to the glittering side of New York City.

The reason I was so bitter was I felt I'd been used. I had the gnawing suspicion Lorraine had set me up — killed her father, manipulated her brother and his lover into trying to kill us so we could justifiably kill them, and thus get it all — the family name, property, business — the works. She'd said she'd come to me because I was new in town and that she could trust me not to be in anyone's pocket like the police were. I felt she'd know if the police were bought or not, for I was sure she'd made a major investment in them herself, just to cover the scratchier details of her plan.

The problem with all of it, of course, was that I had no proof. Not in the least. Just lame conjecture. Over the weeks I'd begun to doubt if I'd ever have any proof at all, which'd made me all the more depressed. As far as I was concerned, I'd sold out, traded my self-respect for some grocery, booze, and rent money.

The subsequent depression robbed me of any of the benefits the publicity could've garnered me. I'd been surly to the press, shoving them out of my office, hanging up on them, cursing a few, knocking a few around, breaking at least one camera. The booze told me I was a noble guy to throw away the chance to milk the papers and the television for a ride on the gravy express. The dope talked to the back of my brain when Lorraine's friends came on to me, forcing me to herd them out of my office. One after another. Good looking women, some of them diving for my zipper, biting at my pants as I pushed them toward the door, begging to wear my handcuffs, stripping in the hallway.

Poverty and celibacy — great ways to cheer myself up after Lorraine, great ways to put myself back to square one. When Lorraine had found me I'd been out of cash. I hadn't had a client since I'd arrived in New York or a meal in three days. She was my last chance and I'd have been an idiot not to take her case. Just like I'd be one not to take the case staring me in the face.

I replaced my coffee pot on my hot plate and sat back behind my desk. I sipped at its gritty, greasy, too-hot foulness with the same knowledge of my actions a Buddhist has when he strikes the match of his own immolation. And suddenly, the last month and a half made sense. I was scared. Scared and embarrassed. Maybe Lorraine had set everything up and used me for her own ends. So what, I asked myself. So bloody, fucking what? I wasn't upset that one millionaire had perhaps killed two other millionaires so she could steal their millions. I was upset that maybe Lorraine had made a fool out of me; I was embarrassed that a female, like my loving ex-wife, might have found me an easy mark. Might have stuffed my gut, spread her legs, given me a few bucks and sent me on my way so she could claim the big prize for herself.

As if a weight had crashed down from my shoulders, the rage I'd been crippling myself with for weeks fell away so quickly I couldn't catch it. I could still smell it; it was out there somewhere in the background, but it *was* in the background, waiting for me to lower my guard so it could rush back in, maybe, but put aside for the moment.

I forced more coffee, breathing through my nose, taking what I had left in my cup down in one long, burning, torturous gulp. The sludge tasted bad, worse each second, but once it was inside it was mine, energy I no longer had to fight, but could use. It was a little victory, but it was enough to give me control of my mood and partially clear my fuzzing brain. Okay, I though. Time to get back to work.

"All right, Hubert. What's the story?"

"I'll be b-brief. Andy here is the leading b-black candidate for mayor of New York. He's been gettin' some fairly dangerous sounding m-mail lately, enough to make him nervous about his health."

"With all due respect to Hubert's interpretations, Mr. Hagee," interrupted Lowe, "I'd say I was closer to panic. My campaign manager and I have both received threatening letters and calls. Both of our homes have been attacked. I've had windows broken in mine — Morris had his burned to the ground. The police haven't found a clue yet. I've had to send my wife and children out of town for their own safety."

"Doesn't it hurt a politician's image to appear in public without his family?"

"Not when he can tell the audience the reason they aren't present is because their lives have been threatened too many times for him not to take it seriously. It's bad enough I've painted a target on my chest for the lunatics — I don't need public office bad enough to sacrifice my wife or babies to the crosshairs of hatred."

"All right. Save the fancy rhetoric for the paying customers. What do you guys want from me?"

Hubert took over again.

"Andy's got a rally tonight. B-Big one. The real money maker. He has to be there, out front, for hours..."

"Wearing your target?" I asked, admittedly with snide impatience.

"Essentially," agreed Lowe, loving me more every minute.

"And so you want me to what? Cover an entire auditorium by myself? Put myself between you and every bigot in New York City? That could be more maniacs than even I could stop."

"Listen, D-Dick Tracy," answered Hubert, "don't get t-too cute for us, huuummmm? Right now, you're still a n-news item. You solved the Millionaire

Mugging. Releasing your name as Andy's bodyguard scares off the halfwits. Make's Andy's c-case look more serious. Might even turn a few votes if a famous white tough guy the morons saw on television s-seems to be saying the candidate is worth keeping alive."

"Hubert presents things so attractively, I find I cannot disagree," added Lowe. "Surrounding me with fifty police officers or even fifty obviously armed plainclothes thugs to satisfy insurance obligations makes people nervous. They forget to reach for checkbooks if they think they might get shot while filling in that last zero.

"Politics is a media event, Mr. Hagee. The only reason we are here is because you are a media event as well — the only recognized gladiator in town, as it were. After tonight, I'll know by the size of the contributions we take in whether I'm still in this foot race or not.

"Therefore, plain and simple, I'm willing to pay you a thousand dollars to be my bodyguard until the rally is over. There will be plainclothes back-up everywhere — Morris is handling that. But people will only be aware of you — the media hero. If there are any bullets coming my way, you'll be the only one the shooters think they have to worry about.

"Figure out whether or not it's worth your time."

Well, I thought, I finally had the whole story…a thousand bucks to shave and dry out and pose pretty for the cameras. They would use my image to scare off any amateur jokers, and my skills could sit on the shelf. Sure, I told myself, I was a lot better than they were giving me credit for — I was one smart, tough fish — worthy of better treatment than I was getting. But money's a great lure, and smart, tough fish get reeled in every day, dangling from a piece of steel that cut through their lower lip just because they nibbled. My pride whispered some nonsense about throwing them out of my office, but my common sense started screaming about my landlord's hungry bank accounts and how they hated to miss meals. My wounded pride had handed me enough damage. If these guys wanted to make me a media star, what the hell — why not? Maybe I could do Energizer commercials when we were done.

"Sure," I told them. "I'm in. Do I have any say in things at all, or do I just stand around and wait for my money?"

"You're being hired as my bodyguard. Do whatever you do when someone hires you to be a bodyguard."

"All right, then. First, I want a run down of where you have to be today and why. Before we do anything else, we map out the rest of the time you and I are going to be around each other — every minute. Then I figure out how to get you from A to B to C, and you do what I say."

Turning around, I told Hubert, "Go tell little Maurice to have Lowe's driver take him home. Actually, I don't care what you tell him, just as long as you shmooze the two of them out of here."

Hubert winked at me and gave out with a laugh that sounded something like a dying cartoon duck's. As he went into the outer office, Lowe asked, "And what is this all about?"

"This is getting rid of anyone we don't need. Trust me to know my job. You can never tell from what angle something's going to come at you. All it takes is a careless word from one person to another to another and before you know it, the man with the rifle knows where you're going to be even before you get there."

"I will not hide," answered Lowe angrily. "I am not a coward."

"Yeah, yeah. Whatever you say," I told him. "Let's clear a few things up. You want to run for mayor, run for mayor. It doesn't matter to me. But, please, save the speeches for people stupid enough to think their vote means something."

"What's that supposed to mean?"

"It means, if it was up to me I'd have all the lawyers and politicians lined up and gunned down as fast as the firing squad could reload."

"I suppose you'd line up all the blacks, too. And the Jews and the gays, the Native Americans and women..."

"All the ones that were lawyers and judges and politicians."

Lowe clenched his fists, almost ready to come out of his chair.

"You make me sick."

"Get real. You're a black man, a minority that's been on it's way up since the day you were born. My minority, it's been sinking fast since the same moment. Try waking up with that taste in your mouth every day."

"You son of a..."

"Je-zuz H. Kay-rist," shouted Hubert, coming back into the office. "W-What the hell is wrong with you two? Lost your m-minds, or somethin'? Cut the bullshit, already."

"Watch it, little man."

"Why, what're you going to do? G-Gun me down; beat me senseless? Step into the new millennium, Dick Tracy. People don't g-get away with that shit, anymore. Yes, except for the criminals, and yes," he turned to Lowe, "Andy, that *is* the fault of our esteemed courts and lawmakers. And, yes again, I know that's something you want to do something about. I know. And so would you," he turned back to me, stabbing a finger into my chest, "if you got your face up out of the booze long enough to read the papers."

"Now you're asking me to believe what I read in New York newspapers?" I joked. "You people want a lot for your money."

Hubert grinned, a wide, ear-to-ear affair leaking the cartoon duck sounds.

"Touche," he laughed. "Maybe I didn't make a mistake, after all. Listen, I c-can smell the bug up your ass. You t-think we only came here because of the headlines you generated. Okay; that's part of it. True enough. But, I'm not that big an idiot. Andy's my pal. We're from the dawn of time. I don't trust his ass t-to a gimmick.

"I checked out your background. Six years in the Army, four of them in Military Intelligence. Four years after that with the Pittsburgh Police Department — last year and a half of that d-doing undercover. You've got some interesting stuff in your bio. Enough to make it look like i-if you got that moron-sized chip off your shoulder you might be of some help here.

"What do you think?"

"I think maybe I'm not as sober as I thought. And maybe I sound off a little too much. Okay. Strike the 'maybe.' And the 'little.' Guess I lost control there. Sorry.

"But how the hell do you know so much about me? Granted, you might have read the Pittsburgh stuff in the papers, but I've kept tight-lipped about my M.I. days. Where'd you tumble to that?"

This time Lowe laughed. When I eyed him for a reason, he said:

"Sorry. It's just been a long time since I've ever seen anyone surprised at how much Hubert could tell them about themselves."

"Information is my business, Dick Tracy. If I can't find something out, it ain't happened yet. So when I say you're a good man to have on our side, don't go actin' like some g-goddamned shithead and ruinin' my reputation."

"That aside," interrupted Lowe, "I have to admit to having something to do with the extra heat in here, too. Strike the 'maybe' and the 'little' for me as well." He stretched out his hand to me saying, "I'm not used to knowing someone is trying to kill me, Mr. Hagee. I shouldn't have lost control, either. Hopefully you will allow me to chalk it up to nerves."

I shook his hand, asking:

"Is this just a politically correct handshake so we can get back to work, or are we kissing and making up?"

"A little of both, I suppose."

"Okay," I smiled, tightening my grip. "Honesty I can take."

We shook hands, and I tried to take Lowe's measure, feeling his spirit as our palms touched. The contact felt open, and I knew the fight was over. Good, I thought. Maybe it was time to stop feeling sorry for myself and get back to work.

"So," I asked as our hands broke contact, "any ideas on who's got it in for you this week?"

"No. Not really. I can name plenty of groups and individuals that might like to see me disappear, but no one I can point to and say, 'They're the ones.'"

"Too bad. Oh well, let me get a grip on this. Why's so much heat coming at you, anyway?"

Hubert took over.

"'Cause Andy's the perfect target. He d-don't want to play ball with the machine. He's runnin' on a clean record of good, solid, community service. Not like that tag-along, Jefferson."

When I looked at the pair for an explanation, Hubert added, "Forgive me, the Reverend tag-along Jefferson."

"John isn't a bad sort, really," said Lowe to Hubert.

"Oh, give it a rest, Andy." Hubert turned to me, saying, "The guy is a bum. Andy's logged plenty of public office hours in this town. He really could be on his w-way up. Jefferson's a two bit carny screamer and bible thumper — a civil rights authority whose idea of equality for all is everything w-white being divided up for all the blacks. W-Why W-Wortzman brought that nickel and dime hate monger into things I'll never know."

"Now, Hubert..."

"Awww, now, n-nuthin'. He's never held office, d-doesn't have a church — he doesn't even have a congregation. He's an opportunist bum!"

"Be all of this as it may," I interjected, "let's get back to the discussion at hand." Looking at Lowe with frank confusion, I said, "I'm sorry if I sound like an idiot, or at the least a cynic, but is this guy serious? Are you really running without any old boy support? I mean, no offense, but how'd you even get through the door?"

"They were looking for this election's honest face. Someone the downtrodden and the despairing and the unloved poor could vote for; that way when I lose the wretched masses can at least suckle comfort from the illusion that they had a chance."

"The big boys let Andy in knowin' he'll lose," added Hubert. "They w-were sure he'd be out of the race w-weeks ago. God only knows what they're thinkin' now."

I eyed Hubert carefully. A good information man has everyone in their little book. Why he didn't have any of the answers left me a little suspicious. I asked, "You're the info specialist. How come you can't find anything out?"

"Because there's a stone wall around this t-that makes the one in China look like a Lego set. Believe me, if one of the organizations in this town could drag one of its competitors down by releasing a little damning evidence — it w-would.

"But, no one's talkin'. Now, they could all know nothing, or the one that knows could be w-waitin' for Andy to be dead before they point the doomsday finger...two birds with one stone...or, it might be some loose nut case who doesn't want a black man with a conscience in Gracie Mansion."

"Have you thought that someone might be just playing with you?" I asked. "Looking to force you out of the race with some low level guerilla stuff?"

"Yes, I've tried to believe that, but I can't. The letters and attacks were great publicity — better, more consistent press than anything we could have paid for. I'd think it was one of my own people drumming up headlines, except...," His eyes broke from mine. The candidate was in his own world for the moment. Calling him back, I asked:

"Except...?"

"Oh, yes. Except that I don't think this is a game. I feel someone out there, waiting for their moment. Without trying to go voodoo on you, Mr. Hagee, I just know somebody is going to attempt to take my life. I have an itch at the base of my spine — it screams at me, warning me to take cover. It's that little voice inside your head that you don't dare ignore — the one that never lies."

"I know the one you mean," I told him. "I've spent a lot of time avoiding its advice lately. Explains my swell station in life. All right. Suffice it to say I believe you've got troubles. So tell me, what's our parade route for the day?"

Smiling, Lowe answered, "My agenda for today is simple. Tonight's speech is too important for me not to be in top form. Today's docket was cleared weeks ago. Nothing to do but memorize my lines and try to catch a few winks somewhere along the way."

"Swell. Then get Morrie what's-his-name..."

"Wortzman."

"Okay. Wortzman on the phone."

Lowe punched in the number and then handed the receiver over to me. After a few rings and a properly neutral message, I managed to get Morris Wortzman on the air.

"What do you mean, you have Andrew? Who the hell is this?"

"Calm down, Morrie. You'll live longer."

"Calm down? Fuck you. What the hell is this? It's...it's six o'fucking clock in the goddamned morning. Are you nuts? What is this?"

"Morrie — listen to me. I'm a private detective. Mr. Lowe and an associate have retained me to act as the candidate's bodyguard. For Mr. Lowe's safety, I'll be keeping him under wraps until tonight."

"Under wraps? My dick under wraps. Associate, my ass. It's that no good bastard Hubert. Where are you taking Andy? What's going on? I have to know..."

"Last chance to shut up and listen, Morrie. You have my word, Mr. Lowe will be at the fund raiser on time. No problem. I'm good at my work. Trust me, bubala. I'm not telling you any more because that way you can't accidentally get us all into trouble. Capisce?"

"Let me talk to Andy."

I ran the idea over in my head and then finally handed the phone to Lowe. I'd told him how I wanted to run things. If he wanted to blab what was going on and take an unnecessary chance, I figured, what the hell...it was his neck on the block. He played it cool, though. He calmed Wortzman down without saying any more than I had. Hanging up finally, he asked:

"So what now?"

I pulled my watch from the drawer I'd left it in the last time I'd needed to work by the world's hours, setting it to match Lowe's.

"Now," I told him, "we go to Tony's."

Tony's is a small time gym in the neighborhood where I have a standing arrangement; I don't tell Tony's wife Lisa about his girl friends and he doesn't charge me for the gym. She'd hired me to find out if he was cheating on her. It'd only take a few days to gather the proof that he was, but also to see what needed to be done. I could tell she didn't really want proof Tony was running around — she wanted proof he wasn't. Tony wanted more attention than one woman and a small life provided. Some people are like that.

The end result was that I confronted Tony and scared him into not being a good boy, but at least a better one. I reminded him that if his wife couldn't hold her head up in their neighborhood, she might repay him in the middle of the night with a turkey carver. He agreed with a nervous nod, begging me not to tell her what he'd been up to, throwing in a life-time membership to his place. So now, Tony and Lisa have a marriage not quite headed for the rocks, and I have a key to the front door.

I introduced him to Lowe and Hubert when he came in to open up, letting him think they were a mixed bag of pharmacists on the run. With his family background, it wasn't the first time his storage room'd come in handy. We all caught naps, improving our dispositions greatly. Hubert went out for Kentucky Fried later, warming up our dispositions even more.

Finally, however, we hit the road, needing a little air and sun and open places. It'd been a while since I'd gone outside during the day for no other reason than the medicinal benefits. I wasn't too worried about crowds gathering — Lowe had admitted his face wasn't very widely recognized, yet. In fact, he said most people, white or black, had little idea who the city's black politicians were. I was worried about staying too long in one place, though, so I kept us moving. It was a good day for once, warm, pleasant, almost quiet.

For some reason, the streets were fairly empty. Of course, 'fairly empty' on a Manhattan afternoon means being able to move for more than twenty seconds without bumping into someone. It made for an almost pleasant moment. Maybe that was why I missed the tail at first.

Something was nagging at me, worrying my complacency. We didn't seem to be attracting any attention, and yet I had the urge to check the crowd around us. Maybe it was only Lowe's speech on those little voices, but something had the edges of my hackles up, so I decided to follow through. Waiting for a good-looking girl to walk by, I used the excuse of checking her out to turn around and survey the crowd. I kept my head angled in her direction but moved my eyes over everyone until I spotted him.

He was good; there was no denying that. He'd kept a minimum of a half block away from us at all times, shielding his presence by not concentrating on us. There'd been nothing in the air to give him away, no heavy feeling of staring eyes on the back of the neck, no sudden chills or corner-of-the-eye glimpses to set me wondering. Actually, I felt not so much immediately threatened as I did scrutinized. As if he were looking me over and not the candidate.

Turning back to Hubert and Lowe, I ran our new playmate over in my mind. His stance, his carriage, at first glance, everything about him seemed almost frail. He looked like a divinity student, or an English Lit. professor — at least under a casual inspection. There was power in his frame, however. It was cloaked, masked off from those around him; perhaps purposely. Perhaps not. It showed if you knew what to look for, though. Especially in his face. His eyes were cut chunks of broken blue glass. Even from a distance they were a signpost for danger. Only a fool could miss the waiting trouble in them. Of course, the world's filled with fools.

His nose was sharp and decisive. There was a targeting sense to it, like a bird's beak or an ant's mandibles. The lines around it showed a sinister capacity for ferocity, like the ones around a woman's mouth that let you know she sometimes smiles.

Wanting a second opinion, I told Hubert, "There's a thin, bearded guy in a brown suit about four, five storefronts back. Check him out."

The information broker bent over to pick up an imaginary piece of change. Upon standing back up, he said, "D-Don't see anyone like that, Jack boy."

I turned. He was right. The divinity student was gone. But not the little voices. The back of my mind, although it couldn't explain why, was screaming at me that I was in big trouble. And, although I couldn't explain why either, I was willing to agree with it.

The dinner sounded like a big success. The noise coming out of the hall seemed to indicate Lowe was making a good impression. I wouldn't know. Morrie'd sworn by his plainclothed undercovers, sending them in to watch over the candidate during his speech. Me he had other plans for.

"No way we waste you standing around inside," he said. "I've got six guys in there. Andy's safe as my grandmother's ass. If you're here on our payroll, let's get something tangible for our dough."

After that he called over the roving press boys who could write their features without the benefit of actually bothering to listen to Lowe's speech. Introducing me as 'that guy you all wrote about you know the hero who saved the young heiress and solved the Millionaire Mugging oye how fickle is this press of ours a month ago he was your darling ask him why he's here…' That set them all off.

Before I knew it I was telling the microphones I'd been hired to protect the candidate, and yes he'd had death threats and no I don't have any leads yet and no well I don't really know the candidate's platform but yes I do think he's all right blahblahblahfuckingblah…

All's Well That Ends Well

The cameras did not make me comfortable. I'd been stuffed into a rented suit by Wortzman, a beauty of a Hong Kong three-piecer he figured would film well. In a way, it was a little annoying to know I couldn't buy one like it with the thousand I was getting at the end of the day, but that Wortzman could just call one up from central casting in my size. Poverty and celibacy were beginning to not look so ennobling. Or maybe I'd gotten as noble as I needed.

The media kept at me with the questions, digging to see if they could find anything new that'd happened to make the candidate afraid for his life. With a brainstorm I told them I couldn't reveal what had happened, and that it was probably best if they asked those questions of Mr. Wortzman. That sent them all back to Lowe's obnoxious campaign manager, getting them off my back, which is the way it looked Wortzman preferred it. He'd used me to get them all excited, but he wanted them returned so he could deliver the party line. He got all but one.

She was a reporter for one of the city's choicer news magazines. And a blonde. A real blonde. She had the looks and style and that New York attitude, the one from the movies and the television and the casinos and the lost dreams that looked bored enough to try anything. She was decked out in all black and white. A combination of silk and leather wraps and restraints that worked. Very few women have the legs to pull off black high heels and white stockings and make it look that good. She caught my interest like a dry sponge does water — slowly but completely. She was good enough at the game to make it look as if her interest was just a step behind mine. We talked through the typical press/victim stuff until she finally asked:

"So, you're really the detective who solved the Ralph Morgan thing?"

"Yeah; at your service."

"Are you a tough guy…'Jack,' isn't it?"

"Yeah, I'm one of the smart, tough ones, all right."

"You like being a detective?"

"Probably not much more than you like being a reporter."

"Oh," she said, half-coy, half-bored, "and this is where I say, 'well, why do you do it?' and you say, 'I could ask you the same question,' and then…"

"And then I say, 'look, I have work to do.'"

"I was getting to that one."

"Well," I told her, "I have to get to it now. Besides, as much as I'd like to kid this along into something, I might as well save us both a lot of time.

"I'm a flat broke bum trying to keep from falling flat on my face. Again. Flattering as attention is from someone who looks like you, in all honesty, I don't think I could show you much of a fun time right now.

"Hell, I don't even own this suit."

I winced slightly as I noticed Wortzman in the background, signalling to me that I had to get out of the rental suit. He'd wanted me dressed up to show off to the press, but didn't want to take a chance on having to pay for it. Regretting what I figured had to be the inevitable, I said:

"In fact, I've got to peel out of it and get back into my working clothes. I've done my little sidewalk monkey act for the press. Now it's time for the real world."

"Great performance," she answered coldly. "You charm a lot of women this way?" Digging into my wallet, I pulled out one of my business cards and handed it to her.

"Look," I told her sincerely, "you want to get together with me — I'm all for it. But, right now, I have to go to work. You want to drop in on me, feel free. Any time.

"I just don't think you'll like the address."

"I could surprise you," she called out as I walked off to the office where I'd left my bag. I thought of yelling back that nothing surprises me anymore, but then decided against it. Sometimes nothing surprises me; most of the time everything does.

It only took a few minutes to change into some comfortable slacks and a sweat and head back to the auditorium. From the size of the parking lot Lowe'd filled, it looked like his candidacy was going to get a hefty send-off. People had paid a thousand a head to attend his speech and be accorded the privilege of pledging more money on top of that. He'd held his rally in the wealthiest part of Brooklyn — a gamble, not holding his big night in Manhattan, but one which had apparently paid off. I was just getting smug in my assessment of how well things were going when the first gun shots went off.

I pulled my .38 and zigged into the parking lot, heading for the auditorium at a crouching run. A body burst out of the front doors, quickly tearing around the building off into the trees. I had a choice, try and find some back-up and risk losing him or head straight after him and risk wasting my time on some panicking citizen. Then, just as he reached the corner, he turned to check on pursuit. I saw his face. It was the divinity student. And I was the only one to see him. Waiting for anyone else to back me up could take too long. Damn, I thought. There was nothing to do but chase him.

Cutting across the lot, I disappeared through the same trees as Divinity. I knew no one'd seen me, either. Which meant if I didn't catch him, he got away. The back of my mind was reminding me I didn't know who I was chasing, or why. Maybe he was just someone who'd recognized the candidate on the street and had showed up at the rally…who sat near the back and panicked when the shooting started…and then ran through the trees and across the field toward the parkway. Yeah, sure.

Maybe. But not likely.

At the edge of the field he dodged across the four lanes of exit and entrance ramp traffic to head down a hill toward a small park tucked under the

Brooklyn end of the Verranzano Narrows bridge. Suddenly, what he was up to was clear. He'd left his car in the park's parking lot. He'd known a quick shoot & run would let him clear the auditorium before anyone could figure out what was happening. By putting his car over the hill, he made it fairly impossible for anyone to catch him. I knew the stretch of road he would be headed down. There were five exits all less than a mile apart from each other. If he reached his car, it was over then and there. I redoubled my efforts, realizing in an instant that booze and cigarettes were not helping my wind any.

By the time he hit the parking lot he was walking casually, waving to children. I kept running, straining to shorten the distance between us as fast as I could, trying not to make a noise which would cause him to turn. I was a hundred yards away when he reached into his pocket for his keys. Seventy-five as he selected the right one. Sixty as he slid it into the door. Seeing no choice, I shouted:

"Freeze! Move and you're dead!"

He turned as I skidded to a lower gear. Closing on him slowly, trying to get my wind back, I kept my .38 ready, watching him study me. Telling him, "Pull the keys out of the door. Toss them to me. Underhand."

He did. I picked them up cautiously. Very cautiously. Something about Divinity kept me watching him. His stance — his eyes. Especially his eyes. He was laughing at me. Amused. Something was going on I wasn't catching on to. I looked for possible incoming, but couldn't see anything. Divinity didn't have any back-up. No one was aiming a gun at me. I had the only gun. I had Divinity cold. But, his posture, his grin — those eyes — something was telling me he was laughing at me, maybe with reason. The little voice told me I was about to learn a lesson. My hands closed around the keys. School was in session.

I slid the keys into my jacket pocket and then barked at him to "assume the position." He spread his hands on the hood of his car. I told him "further." He obliged. I asked for more. He gave in again. I came in then, looking to pat him down. I reached under his coat; my fingers touched an empty shoulder holster and...bang, I was flying. The split second I was as off balance as I was going to be, his foot was in my side, bruising ribs and rolling me across the cement.

I hit sideways, rolling hard, coming up awkwardly. I still had my .38, but no target for it. Divinity had split. I scanned quickly, catching the tail end of him disappearing around the base of the hill we'd just come down. I stood rockily, testing my balance. I felt stunned, but unbroken. Trying to watch the hillside for any surprises, I started after him.

Divinity had things figured right. No one knew where we were. If I didn't go after him, he would get away. Rubbing my side, I wondered what was going to stop him even if I did. He was fast, rabbit snake fast, and limber, strong and self-confident. Not the best combination one could go up against.

I advanced carefully, trying to watch my step, and above me and behind me and, in the case of the sea wall, below me, too. The path I was following extended underneath the Narrows bridge, showing off its gigantic underside. Daring an upward glance, I took in the size of the thing. It was monstrous, built on a scale usually reserved only for science fiction novels — possibly the last grand giant the human race will ever build. Not that I'm knocking anyone — being alive in this era certainly hasn't inspired me to any projects of epic design of late.

My reflecting and upward glance had only taken a split-second — a moment in time so short they need special machines to measure it. Plenty of time for Divinity to make his move. He came out of the nowhere like the last car a child sees as their fingers grab at their runaway ball. I forgot to block and tried to aim. My .38 went over the rail and into the water below. My left side took it this time, a thudding beef punch that flattened me against the cement walling out of which the rail grew. I went for a breath; Divinity knocked it out of me by grabbing the back of my head and flipping me through the air. I landed in the brush, banging hard, the air flying out of me so fast it burned my throat.

I regained my feet slower than I did the first time. Divinity was gone again. I checked and found I still had his keys. He hadn't bothered to take them from me when he had the chance. Which meant he wasn't worried about making his escape. Why should he be, I asked myself. After all, I was the only obstacle in his path, and he'd already proved there wasn't much difficulty waiting for him on that road.

Pulling myself together, I started down the asphalt pathway again, looking for Divinity. What was going on was becoming obvious. I'd become sport for a bored athlete, fodder for a matched set of dangerous appendages all fueled by a massive storehouse of power and ego. It was rapidly occurring to me that since Divinity had little interest in escaping, he must be interested in something else. Rounding the bend gave me some insight into what that might be.

On the other side of the sea wall, a kind of cement dock jutted out into the Narrows, followed by a curving finger of breaker rocks. Divinity was in the middle of the dock, sitting cross-legged with his back to me — waiting. Part of my brain told me I'd stand a better chance of accomplishing something by running over to the beltway to try and flag down a police car than by facing the rail-thin Buddha on the dock again. The rest of my brain sighed as I busied myself with looking for the easiest way over the wall.

Hitting the sand below with a small thud, I stood straight and headed over toward the dock, saying, "If you don't mind me saying so, you've got me a bit curious. I mean, you could've taken off twice now. If you really wanted to, you could've left me dead. At least one of the times, anyway."

As I came up to the dock, I noted the close-set pillars and low ceiling of its underbelly. I wondered if Divinity's style would be at a disadvantage there.

After all, he was the one who'd picked the open area. Although, I thought, maybe he just liked having a stage. As I pulled myself up onto the dock, I said:

"Of course, both times you caught me off guard. That move at the car — real good. Haven't seen anything like that since the service. Second time, well that was just stupidity. I've been dealing with rummy thugs and wise guys so long I guess I've forgotten how really silly a gun can be at times."

Stopping about eight feet from Divinity, I kept talking, waiting for the show to start.

"Anyway, I got to speculating — why'd this guy get me down here? He doesn't look queer. Well, not a lot, anyway. And, if he'd been hired to kill me as well as Andy, he'd have done it already. I mean, it is obvious you're a hired killer — your whole attitude gives that away for...."

Divinity stood — quick, straight arrow, one movement. I'd hit a nerve — but which one? Turning, his face showed amusement. His thin lips were spread in a knife blade of a smile. He went into a familiar variation of the horse stance, giving me an idea of what was coming next. Without a word he came forward, crossing the distance between us in two close, balanced steps, looking to wedge his way inside my defenses. I stepped off to the left and ducked, neatly avoiding the second half of his one/two. Taking a couple of steps backward at the same time, I got some distance between us again as I searched for whatever it was I'd said that'd irked him before.

"Anyway, like I was saying, you being a hired killer and all, it doesn't make any sense that you'd do something like this just for sport. Good as you are, I mean, the cops could come swarming over us any minute. Granted, no one knows who we are, but we're still two guys trying to beat each other's brains out on public property..."

He came in again, faster. Too fast. I blocked his first blow, and the second, but missed the third. He was younger and apparently far less abusive to his body than I was to mine. I fell back hard, hitting the dock with the grace of an overturned garbage can. He stood above me, waiting for me to get back up. Comfortable where I was, I said, "Oh, man. Good one. Christ, much more of this and I'm going to feel like shit."

The chatter was getting to him. Not enough to make him careless — just annoyed. It was a start; we were in first gear. I baited him along, trying to get him to third.

"Maybe I'll just lay here and take my lumps. What'dya say? I mean, you seem to really have it in for me. Hell, why not just get it over with? What'dya think?"

His answer was to try and break my ankle with his heel. Perfect. Pulling my leg out of the way at the last second, I shot it back immediately, knocking Divinity off his pins. He fell next to me, catching himself with his palms. He made to push off again, but was too late. I had him. Before he could clear the ground I managed to wrap my arms around him from behind, pinning his to his sides, squeezing him with all I had in me.

Divinity thrashed madly, rolling us around the pier in circles, sometimes damaging me, sometimes himself. While we crashed around, I huffed:

"So…when did you start…killing people for profit?"

Divinity's answer was non-verbal. Reaching down with both hands, he dug his fingers into my thighs, tripping a nerve in each that sent me screaming. I couldn't help letting him go, but as he broke away from me I managed to catch the back of his jacket. Pulling him back to me as we struggled to our knees, I spun him around, putting everything I had into a roundhouse to the side of the head. Divinity spun around twice while still trying to stand, falling badly.

I tried to get to him to press my advantage but, he was on his feet again before I could regain mine. By the time I was standing he was in front of me. I got my arms up just in time for him to grab one. He twisted. I danced. Keeping me at arm's length, he kicked me twice, once in the side, once in the gut. I made to kick him but he caught it, trading his grip on my wrist for one on my ankle. Not that he kept it long. With a sharp jerk he pulled me toward him and then slammed me with his free hand.

I tripped backwards, stepped blindly, then falling. A second later I was staring up at the sky from the sand. My head was throbbing like a jack hammer. I could see stars and taste blood. Divinity looked down at me, smiling.

"God," I groaned, stalling for time, hoping for enough seconds to relearn how to breathe, "you're tough."

His smile widened almost enough to show teeth. A touch of a nod was the only answer he bothered to give.

"So," I croaked, sucking oxygen desperately, "you going to kill me, too?"

He raised one eyebrow and changed his smile enough to indicate 'probably.' I nodded back, saying:

"Well, fair enough, I guess." Coughing out a load of bloody phlegm, I added, "You know, though — it's funny. I don't even care who hired you to kill Lowe at this point…but I was wondering…who hired you to kill me?"

Divinity's smile faded. Bingo, I thought. Direct hit. I had no idea why he was so touchy about his occupation, but I was perfectly willing to keep needling him over it. Not at that moment, though. Putting all my energy into getting up, I threw myself forward into the dark recesses under the pier a split second before Divinity hit the sand where I'd been. Spying a soggy two-by-four the tide had washed in, I grabbed it up and leaned against one of the crumbling pillars, waiting for Divinity to come to me this time.

My labored breathing echoed in the underground retreat, coming at me from all directions at once. I'd positioned myself just to the left of the pier's center, hoping for a chance to use my newfound weapon and maybe even stay alive. Other sounds rebounded toward me besides my own, letting me know Divinity was in the underworld with me. I knew he realized I was stationary — knew he would be conducting his search looking for an unarmed man waiting to ambush him. Counting on his not expecting the two-by-four, I kept waiting.

Finally, his shadow edged forward toward me, black moving forward over the grey on the ground. Tensing, I gripped my board, holding out for the right second. He moved a half step closer, his shadow radaring his path, bringing him to me. I shifted my weight. The shadow inched toward me again, and then suddenly, it disappeared backwards. I whirled around quickly. Divinity was behind me already. I dodged wildly, letting him kick away part of the pillar instead of my ribs. Turning, I swung the two-by-four, missing Divinity, splitting the end of my weapon on another pillar. Divinity punched; I blocked with the board and then drove it upward, catching the ends of his left hand's fingers, tearing three of them open.

Following up, I swung again, hoping to catch him in the head. No chance. He caught the board with his good hand, stopping it cold. Before I could act he rammed it backwards, catching me in the gut. I staggered, but held on, refusing to let him wrest the two-by-four away without a fight. Divinity smiled. Setting his feet, he caught the board in both hands and twisted, tearing it away in one motion.

I stumbled back out to the beach as quickly as I could, running straight for the breaker rocks beyond the dock, hoping that reaching the high ground might keep me alive. A small arm I hoped was a doll's reached for my cuff. I jerked my way upward. Divinity abandoned the two-by-four to the sand and followed. As he started up the rocks after me, I wheezed:

"I'd have thought you'd had enough by now."

He kept moving, slightly slower than before, nothing that was going to be of any help to me. As he neared the top, I added:

"Man. Some guys just don't know when to quit."

Then I swung. He ducked. I tried to use my size to force him to stay at the lower position, but it was no good. He came in under my attack, pasting me two good ones in a row. As I staggered, he caught my arm and pushed, sending me dancing across the rocks. I almost slipped twice, but managed to catch myself. Divinity followed close behind.

He was forcing me out to the end of the breaker wall. The top of it was too narrow for me to get around him on either side. To try and climb down one of the sides, or even to jump into the water would've been suicide. To do either I'd have to turn my back on Divinity, and I knew that was what he was waiting for. I'd picked up on his style — he liked dominance, enjoyed calling the tune. As far as he was concerned, I'd decided to follow him, and now if I changed my mind, I had to be punished. Not that he planned to drag things out forever. I could also see in his eyes that the wrap-up was on its way.

Forcing dry air up to push the words out, I said, "You don't talk much, do you?"

He hit me. Hard. I fell against the rocks, slamming my left shoulder. The stars came to visit again and I lay where I'd fallen, just too damn tired to move. I'd never thought much about being kicked or beaten to death. Okay, I figured — this way it would be a surprise.

I tried to steady myself, to get ready for whatever was coming, but even that was beyond me — the rock I grabbed with my right hand was loose; trying to hang onto it had almost sent me into the water.

Turning my eyes back to Divinity, I watched him reach into his pocket and pull out a knife. I was shocked. After all we'd gone through, he was going to finish me off with a pig sticker. I went to look him in the eyes to find a clue as to what he was up to, but couldn't get his to meet mine. He was staring at my chest, smiling, leering, salivating. His tongue was working back and forth, sliding his frothing spittle across his teeth and lips. His mouth was so full he could've gargled with it. Instead he swallowed, coming up with the smile of a man who'd just finished a steak in the best place in town and was really looking forward to dessert.

He came at me in one motion, the knife working to carve open my chest, drops of blood from his fingers splattering me in the face. But, the little voice had screamed at me to move — fast. With everything I had, I jerked aside just in time, letting the knife slide past me to shatter against the rocks. He must've been sure I was down for the count, sure I wasn't capable of moving again. Luckily, he'd been wrong.

My right hand caught up the loose rock under it and swung it around. I caught Divinity behind the knees. He went all the way down. Sliding myself upward, I took the rock in both hands and brought it down on his spine. Twice. Twice more. His hands reached for me. I batted one away weakly, but the other caught my wrist. With strength I couldn't believe, he started dragging me toward him, my chest toward his face — his tongue licking, teeth snapping. He caught a piece of my sweat shirt in his jaws and pulled, dragging hair and skin with it. I howled and smashed him across the face with the rock, knocking him away.

Then, picking up another, heavier stone, I brought it down on his chest, hearing cracks and pops which made me think I might be the one to survive, after all. I brought it down again, smashing harder, bones breaking upward through his clothing. A rib scraped my hand open as I dragged the rock up out of his chest cavity. My hands covered with blood, I shoved the rock upward as high as I could, and then rammed it home again with every ounce of energy I could muster. Scooping the stone up out of his body, I had to pry it loose from the suction grip of the jelly I'd made out of his organs.

I smashed him over and over, tears of rage and pain and humiliation flooding out of me. Maybe it was fear — maybe just relief — I kept breaking his bones until I couldn't lift my arms anymore. I kept crying long after.

Much later, at my office, I sat waiting with Hubert for a visitor I was expecting. I'd gotten released from the hospital a couple of hours earlier. Hubert'd met me, sporting a new Hawaiian shirt and a Panama hat. After several phone calls which allowed me to put a few things into motion, we'd gone back to my office to swap stories and wait.

Hubert told me he had stationed Maurice in the auditorium, telling him to stay close to Lowe and keep his eyes open. He'd done both and topped it all off by throwing himself in front of the candidate when the bullets had cut loose. Divinity hadn't gotten Lowe, and hadn't even known it.

The cops had been pleased as punch to get his remains. They didn't like the shape they were delivered in, but admitted they didn't know of anyone who could have done a better job. Their admiration wasn't worth the beating I'd taken to get it, but it was good compensation nonetheless.

The media was awarding the lion's share of their attention to Maurice. After all, I was only the guy who'd done in the shooter in some back alley or something. Maurice'd had the sense to do his dance of death in front of the cameras. As Hubert said, though:

"Forget it. You need the right people takin' you serious if you're gonna l-last in this town. I'll make sure the story gets to the right people. I mean, you t-took out the Stone. One of the t-toughest hit men anyone ever heard of."

"Yeah, he was that, all right."

"So, don't sweat it. Let the TV monkey up Maurice's rep. I'll p-put your's in p-place for you." Hubert laughed and then took a nip from his hip flask. Wiping his lips, he continued.

"You know, the Stone had a nasty habit, too. Part of what made his r-rep. You see, he hated taking money for hits. W-Went against his trainin' or somethin', but anyway…to compensate for doin' a hit, right after one he would find himself a victim…a worthy opponent, not just some wino or anything, and then he'd beat them down and cut out their l-living heart and eat it while they watched. That was the story, anyway. You c-catch any of that action?"

"Saw the previews. Didn't stay for the feature."

"Yeah," said Hubert, "I was right about you. Another c-couple of weeks and this city'll know who the t-toughest son'va bitch around is. Don't worry."

"I ain't worried," I told him. "I hurt too much to worry. You got my money?"

"Yep," answered Hu. "Andy's still got reporters c-crawlin' all over him, elsewise he would've delivered it himself — didn't want to subject you to the media. Unless you want this place filled with camera-asses?"

"No, thanks;" I said. "I can't see any real trouble makers worrying too much about some guy whose rep got made by the tube. I'll take back alley whispering any day." Counting my money, however, gave me a question.

"This is five hundred dollars."

"Oooough, you can count."

"Yeah; I can. Where's the other five hundred?"

"In Maurice's bank account, with a nice note from you t-tellin' him to get better soon. You might not believe it, but y-you figured it was the least you could do." While I eyed him sourly, he added, "Don't sweat it, D-Dick Tracy. You can afford it. Classy guy like you's never gonna be hurtin' for m-money."

At that point a knock on the door cut off our conversation. It was Morrie Wortzman, Lowe's campaign manager. Hubert bristled, but kept his comments to himself. Wortzman didn't seem any happier to see him. After a few terse sentences, Hubert excused himself, shutting the door hard behind him.

"Okay," I started, "so you're here. What's on your mind, Morrie?"

"You called me, Jack. Mighty glad you did, too. Mighty glad. I wanted to talk to you. Yes, sir. Wanted to talk to you about the Stone. Heh. They say you killed him with a rock. Heh. Guess it takes a stone to kill a Stone. Heh."

"Get to the point, Morrie."

"Okay, you want this unsubtle, you got it. Fine by me. You called me. Remember?"

"Yeah," I told him. "I remember. We can lay this out short and sweet. The Stone tried to bargain with me. Told me you hired him to kill Lowe. Okay, I figure. This would be hard to prove to the cops, even if I let the Stone live to testify. So, I finished him off and gave you a call. I figured you and I could work something out. We're both real smart, tough fish, right?"

"Yeah," he agreed. "Whatever you say."

Getting up out of his chair, Wortzman paced a little, going over to the window first and then circling around for a moment until he finally came back to the front of my desk. Resting his palms on the edge of my blotter, he said:

"Look. Let's get this cut through. You don't have any proof of anything — right?" I spread my hands open in front of him.

"Right," I agreed.

"But, if I don't pay you off, you'll make trouble. You'll get rumors spread, you and that prick Hubert."

"No. No percentage in that," I told him. "Wouldn't make any sense."

"Yeah, sure, the fuck you say now. I know your type. I'd have you rubbed if I could, but after killing the Stone, your rep as a dangerous bastard is bigger than his was. Stone didn't have any friends I could turn to, so that makes you an uneasy man to kill at this moment." I leaned back in my chair, smiling as I told him:

"I won't argue."

"Yeah, I'll bet you won't. So — name it, already. What the hell do you want?"

"What...do...I...want?" I said each word separately, as if no thought at all had gone into my answer. "Well, I guess what I ask for will depend on what you tell me."

"What the hell are you talking about?"

"Why?" I asked. "I want to know 'why?' It made sense for you to burn down your own house. From what little Hubert and I could find making a few calls, you could never've sold it for what you had it insured for. But you were in the clear on the insurance scam. Why'd you want to go all the way and kill Lowe?"

"You want to know that bad, sure. Why not? You've got me on the hot rock. Big deal." Plopping back into his chair, Wortzman said, "I'll tell you why. Because he's honest. He really wants to become the mayor of New York City to try and clean it up."

The words came out of him in a laugh, one which set him to choking he found the subject so amusing. Wiping away a tear, he continued; "Yeah. I'm serious. Imagine, a jumped-up community service nigger cleaning out the NYC city hall. Oye, shit, that's a laugh."

Wortzman looked away from me for a moment and then stared, lighting a cigarette, telling me, "Yeah, he's serious about it. I fed him the notion that if a big time killer like the Stone was brought in to get rid of him that it must be the mob after him. Afraid he'll bust the unions and all. Boy, did that puff up the moron. He's really feeling important now."

Wortzman took a long drag, sinking into a comfortable mood. Sitting back in his chair, he exhaled, adding, "In a way, this could be the best thing that could've happened. See, I wanted to get rid of Andy, after tonight's dinner, of course, once all the contributions were in, and then move up Andy's second, the Reverend John Lawrence Jefferson. Don't you see; it's perfect."

He filled the air with smoke again, smiling a content smile. His look said that he had everything all figured out. I let him continue to educate me.

"You see, I had John all set. Andy gets cut down, the reverend runs in and grabs up the bloody body — careful to get handsful of red all over himself — and then declares that this foul deed, this terrible event, some such happy horseshit, must not go unanswered. Yak, yak, you know. So when we throw the whole campaign behind John — in Andy's memory — of course. We lose; we try again. We lose again; we go to other cities. John preaches and preaches, we raise lots of bucks, we keep running for offices and starting campaigns and it goes on and on and we stay rich for the rest of our lives.

"And so now," finished Wortzman, turning back to me, "all we need is for someone to finish off Andy and we've got it all set."

"Why bother telling me all this?"

"Come off it, Hagee. You know why I'm here. You want me to pay you off to keep your two cents to yourself. I have a better idea. Why don't I load you down with money, and you finish the job you fucked up?" I look at him in disbelief, smiling. Fighting back a laugh, I asked:

"You want me to kill your candidate for you?"

"Why not? No one would suspect you. No one! You're the man who damn near died saving his fucking life. Why would you turn around and kill him? How could anyone ever begin to think you had something to do with it?"

"B-Because," came Hubert's voice from the doorway, "the w-walls have ears, Morrie."

Hubert came into my inner office, followed by several detectives and a Captain Trenkel, head of the local precinct. It took some words and some doing to get Wortzman out of the room, but he finally left...half under his own power, half with the help of others. Trenkel thanked me for my cooperation and let me know he didn't mind P.I.s in his jurisdiction who played their cards right. I acted suitably grateful and sat by while his boys got their electronic taping hardware out of my office. Trenkel'd told me earlier that due to my injuries I could come down to the station house the next day. Banged up as I was, I could've begged off for a week.

As he left, Trenkel eyed Hubert and then looked over to me as if he wanted to say something. He didn't bother, though, and I didn't ask. Once he was gone, Hubert sat down and started another line of prattle.

"You know, there was once a p-politician no one could get a straight answer out of. He was a pip — no matter what, he never gave anyone a straight answer. So, at this one press conference, this smart guy gets an idea. He goes, 'Sir, we're all gettin' a bit tired of your refusal to be pinned down on a subject. I was thinkin', maybe the questions are too hard. So, I ask you, sir, what is your favorite color?' And the politician replies, "Plaid.'"

Hubert began laughing, hissing his cartoon duck noises about my office. I half chuckled, half groaned. Then, before either of us could say anything else, a voice called from the outer office. I directed its owner inside.

"This isn't such a bad place," she said.

"Well. Well...wellwellwell;" cackled Hubert. "What dainty little morsel is t-this?"

"Can it, you mutant. I'd introduce you except that A, if I did, the lady would never speak to me again, and B, I don't know her name."

She had changed into a pair of tan jeans and a yellow sweater, but she didn't look any the worse for it. Laughing, she extended her arm to Hubert.

"Hello," she told him, "I'm Marianne Kennedy. Don't listen to this guy; I'm very pleased to meet you."

"You'll be sorry," I warned her with a laugh.

"You hush up," growled Hu at me over his shoulder. "Call me Hubert," he told Marianne, kissing her hand. "Charmed to death, I'm sure. But, much as it p-pains me to leave you trapped here with this low class operator, I must be on my way. Got a date on Staten Island with a guy who thinks he understands the ins and outs of real estate. See ya in the f-funny papers."

Dropping his hat onto the back of his head, Hubert headed for the door, reminding us as he disappeared, "Don't take any wooden nickels."

And, after he had finally left, I asked, "So, you here as a reporter who wants to finish up the story of the century, or as a woman who doesn't know when she's better off?"

"Still strutting the glib words, eh? Surprising you don't have them lined up around the block with sweet talk like that."

"Yeah, well, what can I tell you?"

"A few things, I suppose."

"Like what?"

"Well, I was down at the morgue earlier...."

"Couldn't get a date there so you thought you'd try here, huh?"

"Can't help myself. Slumming is my nature."

I looked into her eyes and read what she wanted.

"It's time for me to shut up and listen, isn't it?"

The eyes didn't change.

"Okay, that puts me in my place," I admitted, pulling my Gilbey's bottle out of its hiding place in the big drawer of my desk. "So, what was so fascinating at the icebox?"

I tilted the bottle in her direction, asking. She accepted. While I poured us both a couple of fingers worth, she said, "One of those little men who doesn't get out much was in charge. You know the type, love to try and make all the girls screech by showing them something awful, or telling them some disgusting story about what he's seen in the past. Anyway, he had a story to tell me. About the Stone, that hit man you turned into a waffle."

"Yeah," I asked after a swallow. "What about him?"

"Seems you did a real job on him. Mashed him up pretty good."

"You asked if I was a tough guy."

"So I did. Well," she smiled, "he told me that there is something going on, and nobody knows what to make of it. Seems a piece of the Stone is 'missing.' Most of him is still there...not in good shape...but still accounted for. But, our little ghoul told me, a piece of the Stone's heart is missing."

"Do tell?" I said.

"Yes;" she confirmed. "And, interestingly enough, he told us it wasn't cut out, either. It was ripped out, as if some animal had done it."

"Well," I answered, pouring myself a few extra knuckles, "maybe one did."

She smiled again, and all my bruises hurt a little less. I smiled back at her, happy she'd come, happy for the company, happy for the chance to smile. Then, a thought ran across the far recesses of my brain; wouldn't it be nice if her underwear was black and white? I puzzled at what the back of my mind could've meant by that, but decided not to question it. Relaxing, I smiled back at her and lifted my glass in mock salute, deciding to finally start trusting the little voice.

"A toast," she said, clinking my hoisted glass with hers, "All's well that ends well."

"Yeah;" I half laughed, "I'll drink to that."

Bread Ahead

I'D GONE DOWN to Caesar's Bay to get away from everything. It'd been a foul, grey, humid day — one of disappointments — one I didn't want to remember. I'd solved another sad little case, brought another sniveling, cheating husband to ground like the big bad hero I am. I'd made the monthly office rent by ruining a family with pictures of daddy grunting in the back seat of their station wagon with a woman who didn't look anything like mommy at all. As a daily occupation, it was getting to me.

My name's Jack Hagee. I make my living, put food on my table, buy my toothpaste and subway tokens, by rooting through people's lives and their garbage, by turning over rocks for lawyers and crying spouses and tired shopkeepers and more lawyers. I'm a private detective and that day I was hating my job as much as anyone else. That's why, when midnight had passed and I still couldn't get to sleep, tossing in my bed, dying in the clogging humidity steaming in off the ocean, that I'd gotten dressed and driven down to Caesar's.

Caesar's is a shopping mall at the end of Bay Parkway, the main drag through the neighborhood I live in. Most people stay away from it after closing — with good reason.

After dark, Caesar's parking lot and the park adjacent become one large dark criminal carnival land. Dopers sell their wares, Johns pick up their ladies, kids strip cars, smoke dope, shoot craps and sometimes each other. And the worst thing about it all is, it isn't in some terribly seedy neighborhood. Not a home between my apartment building and the river would sell for under a hundred and fifty thousand. It's not a ghetto — just simply the same as the rest of New York City, bursting at the seams from too many people, all with painfully clear visions of the nowhere they are headed.

For those who haven't tasted the city, haven't felt the cold, leaden knuckle it digs into the backs of those who flock to it, let me just say that it is a hell — a black, indifferent hell, one which beckons to all types, the stupid and the arrogant, the talented, the cunning, the naive the hopeful and the self-destructive, to come from around the country to lick at the festering black syrup leaking from its million and counting wounds, begging them to call it honey.

Those who had begun to catch on to what the city had in store for them, however, sat in their cars, staring, or prowled the darkness of Caesar's. I parked my Skylark at the rail meant to keep people from driving into the ocean and got out to prowl. Lighting a cigarette, I walked down along the massive stone sea wall, looking out into the storm front crawling in toward me over the black, oily water. The Verranzano bridge was lost in the fog, as was the parachute tower at Coney Island, both usually easily visible from my spot. Not then. That night the clouds were hanging thick — waiting.

Ignoring the clouds and whatever they were waiting for, I threw myself up and over the steel railing in front of me, settling down on the foot and half of ledge on the sea side of the barrier. My legs dangling over the dashing waves below, I stared out at the ocean, my eyes not focusing on anything, my brain relaxing for the first time in weeks. I was tired. Tired and alone, dying of despairing old age while still in my thirties.

Leaning back against the rail, I pulled a cigarette and managed to light it in the wet of the surrounding mist. I sucked the smoke in deep, holding it down as long as I could, maybe hoping to choke myself. No such luck. The nicotine did start to relax me, however, which at the moment was good enough.

I'd left my apartment in a foul mood. I don't own an umbrella — ridiculous, effeminate props — but in my anger I'd slammed my way out leaving hat and coat behind. The thickening mist was soaking into my hair and clothes, drenching me. By the time I was ready for a second 'moke, the sky had started drizzling to the point where I could barely get it lit.

I downed its fumes one breath at a time, watching the lightning splash along both the far shores before me. The coasts of Brooklyn and Staten Island were illuminated over and over, the random split seconds of light revealing the increasing press of the waves below and the rain above.

The truth of the image depressed me. Even nature worked for the city. It squeezed people, crushing them, forcing them to huddle and shiver, always prepared to wash them away forever for the slightest mistake. Part of me railed at the image but a larger part spoke in calmer tones, implying that perhaps hopelessness was the only sensible feeling one could have living in New York.

I leaned back with eyes closed, the rain lashing, surf below pounding hard enough to almost reach my shoes. I thought of all the reasons people come to New York and wondered what mine had been. As a friend once said, "People don't pull up in covered wagons to the center of Times Square and say, 'here it is, honey — a good land, a strong land, a decent land where our children can grow strong and free.'" They didn't say it when people actually rode around in covered wagons, and they sure as hell don't say it now. New York is not a good land or a strong land, and it certainly is not a place to bring children. Not by a long shot.

New York is an aching scum hole, a never-closing maw always willing to let anyone — on matter how corrupt, or illiterate, or evil — call it home and hang up their shingle. It is a giant con, a government owned-and-operated money drain, constantly sucking the life and joy and wealth out of its inhabitants the way a dying man sucks oxygen — greedily, as if each breath were the last. It grabs everything in sight, using guilt and law and lies and finally thuggery, if nothing lesser will suffice, to strip those who can't fight it every single minute of every day, week in, decade out, of everything they have — their money their needs their dreams and wretched, desperate hopes — until finally it either gets the last juice left within them, piling their useless bones with the rest, or drives them away in pitiful defeat, frustrated and humiliated and wondering how anyone as tough as them could have lost — everything — so easily, to an enemy so impartial.

And, I thought, still they come. Every day by the hundreds — by the hundreds, they arrive by plane and bus, in rented trucks, old cars, on bicycles, motorcycles, or they walk and hitch if they have to — all of them desperate to follow some simple-minded plan they've mapped out for themselves that is just foolproof. One that shows how easy it will be to make it on Broadway, or in television, or as a painter, a broker, writer, dancer, restauranteur, publisher, actor, reporter, agent, or whathaveyou, willing to work hard now for their bread ahead, not realizing how many waiters and convenience store attendants and busboys, cab drivers, keyboarders, bartenders, store clerks, menials, drug dealers, hookers, homeless starvelings, and corpses the city requires for every you-have-made-it golden meal ticket passes out.

As the rain slacked of, I tried to get another 'moke going, ruefully asking myself what my excuse for being in New York was, knowing all along that I hadn't come to the city to find anything. I'd come to lose myself, to hide a person I didn't think anyone should see. I was tired when I did it, tired of corruption, tired of hate — of jealousy, pettiness, violence, and anger. I was tired of these things in myself and others.

So naturally, I came to New York, where all the above vices and sins were long ago renamed art forms, encouraged to grow with wild abandon like kudzu, or social welfare. It was the move of a desperate man — trying to hide in a sweltering sea of desperation — hoping the heightened insanity of those around him would make his own reflection look normal. It hadn't worked.

Not knowing what to do about any of it, though, I let the big problems rest and concentrated on lighting my cigarette. I'd just gotten my first lungful down when the city gave me something new to think about.

So skillfully I almost didn't notice, a pickpocket had reached through the railing my back was against, going for the wallet in my front pants pocket. His hand out with its prize, I managed to snag his wrist a split second before it could snake back behind the railing.

"Oh, no you don't!" I growled.

The pickpocket pulled hard, pushing with his feet against the rail, tearing my fingers at the knuckles as he scraped them against the steel rails. I pulled back, determined to keep my wallet, fighting for balance on the foot and a half of slick rock which made up my side of the fence.

"Let go, damnit! Let go o'me!"

Sticking his free arm through the rails, the pickpocket slammed me in the side, knocking me over the sea wall. I held his wrist in a death grip, feeling his shoulder slam against the rails as my weight pulled him tight. He cursed non-stop, his free hand tearing at my fingers around his wrist. I punched him away as best I could, hitting him sometimes, sometimes myself, sometimes the rails. My mind raced over my options, not finding much.

I could release my grip and hope to be able to catch a rail or the sea wall's edge, but the rain made my chances slim at best. It was possible I might survive the fall to the water, but it was only a fifty/fifty possibility. The rocks hidden beneath the violently pounding waves slamming against my legs and the sea wall were jagged and slimy with sea growth. Walking along the wall back to shore was impossible. So was swimming. The tide was too low for that, but quite ample to mash a man to death. I had no choice — I hung on.

"Com'on, man — let go o'me! I mean it — I mean it!!"

He shook at me, pulling back and forth, jerking my armpit painfully across the edge of the rock wall. I bit at the rain, growling in agony, but didn't let go.

"Le'go,le'go,le'go — you bastard — le'go,le'go!!"

"Just pull me up — fer Christ's sake!" I told him. "let me grab the rail so I don't have to die over five goddamned bucks!"

"No — shut up!! Let go o'me — le'go, le'go! Shit. I makes you le'go. I makes you!"

The pickpocket reached inside his coat. Bracing myself, I thought, okay, you want it — you got it, and then dug my heels into the wall. The pick-pocket's hand emerged with a straightrazor. My left foot slipped back into the water. The pickpocket's free hand came through the rails at me. My foot almost caught, but slipped again. The razor took my distance, cutting open my sleeve and flaying a fine layer of hair and skin away. My foot caught. I hovered into balance, finding my center of gravity. The razor waved above my line of sight.

"Now you let go."

"Not yet."

I threw my weight back, my legs pushing me out from the wall. The extra leverage broke the pickpocket's hold, bringing him slamming into the rails face first. The razor flipped out of his hand, arcing past my right ear. Blood splashed from his face, catching me in the eyes and mouth. Not slowing up, I leaned forward and punched, nailing the part of his face the steel to either side of my fist had missed. Blood arced again, running over his shoulder, down his arm to mine. The blow caused me to slip but, I managed to get half my body back up on the ledge. Releasing the pickpocket, I caught rails in both hands, dragging myself into a secure position as fast as I could.

Once on the ledge I turned to face the pickpocket in case he was going to be anymore trouble. He wasn't. He looked unconscious or dead. I didn't care which. Then I spotted it — my wallet still in his hand. Catching my breath, I reached over and pried it free. My playmate didn't stir then or as I slid back over to the landward side of the railing. I sat down in relief a few feet from the pickpocket, exhausted from my ninety seconds of past-event re-runs, glad for life and breath and safety. After a few minutes of being overjoyed with having remained alive, though, I noticed it was starting to rain harder. Tired of abuse for one night, I pushed myself to my feet and walked over to the pickpocket. Patting him on the back, I told him:

"Nice try."

Then I walked back to my car and drove home. When I got there, I had no trouble sleeping.

Dance

I'D SAT LOOKING at the place long enough. Parked in my Skylark across the street from the Big Sweet Ice Cream & Sherbet Company, I'd watched from quitting time until dusk, as fewer and fewer people left and more and more lights went out, until the place finally looked safe to approach. It wasn't that bad a dodge; a lot of guys lived in their cars in that neighborhood.

Technically, I wasn't doing anything illegal. My client was Cosentino Realty & Development; they owned the building. Nickels, the owner of Cosentino R & D, had been hearing strange things about his First Avenue property, things involving late-night comings and goings, and men whose attitudes didn't seem dedicated to the higher sales of Big Sweet Crunch Bars or Golden Song O'Chocolate Cups.

Nickels likes to keep his places clean — reasonably clean, anyway. He also likes profit, and there was a rumor the city was looking for a men's shelter site on the Lower East Side. The Planning Commission did owe Nickels one, and if he had proper cause to make Big Sweet vacate, with the eight-and-a-half percent increase he could charge the city along with the negotiable jump he could garner on top of that, he'd stand to make a fair increase in his next year's tax bracket.

But he also liked breathing, and several of the whispers that'd reached his ear involved those men with the bad attitudes, and gunfire, and the disappearance of a neighborhood woman with a knack for putting her nose in the wrong

What You Pay For

places. Nickels has a lot of money. I have a car and a P.I. license. So it stood to reason that that night Jack Hagee would be doing the sneaking around inside Big Sweet's downtown office/warehouse while Nickels Cosentino stayed home with a drink in front of his VCR. Life's swell that way.

I eased in the front door, first making sure no one was in sight. Keeping my ears open, I locked up behind myself and headed for the back. Nickels had given me the layout and told me not to bother with the front rooms. Their storage areas were all he wanted to know about. If there was anything going on he could use to lever his clients out of their contract, or into a steeper one, that was the logical place to find it. It was also the logical place for a private detective with more expenses than brains to get himself laid out for the count.

To be fair to Nickels, he had tried to see the back rooms for himself, but just like apartment dwellers, office leasers don't have to suffer the landlord's presence without a reason. And since he didn't have any reasons he cared to share, the next best thing to checking things out for himself in the daylight was for him to hire me to do it in the dark.

Normally I wouldn't take this kind of job, but I'd blown a bundle on the Jucha-Mayo bout. Even creeping through the halls, I couldn't get it out of my head. I'd been sure Jucha would dive in the fifth or sixth. Mayo was the favored contender, and a lot of heavy money was sure to be on him. But a lot of heavy money had been on Ortiz during the last big fight, and so I'd figured the mob would have Jucha pitch down so as not to have things looking too suspicious. I'd figured wrong.

Mayo dove just like Ortiz. Maybe the mob had double-guessed everyone, or maybe they were feeling too secure these days, or maybe I should just learn not to bother trying to second-guess guys with the imaginations of parking meters. Whatever; they'd called the tune, Mayo and Jucha had waltzed to it, and I was out twenty-five hundred bucks.

I was still speculating on the possibility of charging Nickels enough to cover my upcoming rent bills when I reached the back hallway. No one was in sight. Giving the door most likely to lead to the back a quick eyeing, I spotted the alarm. It was a double; an obvious first system to be easily disarmed, backed up by a more ingeniously hidden one. I didn't have any worries, though. I had keys. Or, at least, I'd thought I had keys.

I'd been afraid Big Sweet might have changed the inner locks. They had. My keys were for Corbins; I'd never seen the kind of lock I was looking at before. That meant circumventing two systems before someone came by, unless I tried the knob. It turned. I'd gotten in before they'd locked all the internal doors for the night. That meant getting around easier, but it also meant more people than just the janitor were inside with me. Pulling the door forward slightly, I sent out my radar, trying to "feel" if anyone was on the other side. It felt good. Pulling the door the rest of the way open, I slipped in and closed it behind me.

The back room of Big Sweet was one long series of walk-in freezers sided by row upon row of ceiling-high shelves. The shelves were covered with dusty, unfilled ice cream cartons, two-dimensional stand-ups of Uncle Creamy, the Sherbet Bear, and CoCo, the Chocolate Dog from Mars, and all the other Big Sweet characters, and a long trail of cardboard files, all of them crammed with old order forms and other paperwork.

Opening a few at the far end at random, I rummaged through a series of forms ordering the movement of hundreds of gallons of Big Sweet from one location to the other. Actually reading a few of the orders, I realized I wasn't looking at the movement of hundreds of gallons, but hundreds of thousands of gallons. That stopped me.

Before bothering to risk my license and life in as nonsensical a stunt as the one I was performing, I had run down everything I could on the company. Francis Whiting, a law student I use for research work, had checked out the business end of Big Sweet for me. They had a good little operation going, but "little" was the operative word. As best I could tell from what I knew, their operation was simply not large enough to be handling the volume of work their orders covered.

Before breaking and entering, even with the owner's consent, I'd also put my best legman, Hubert, on the case as well. Hubert checks the underside of things for me. The information he had uncovered was beginning to make sense. Hu had discovered that Big Sweet had two separate delivery systems. The regular, clean-cut, white-uniformed, smiling truckers from the company's commercials always seemed to be where the ice cream went. But another series of drivers, one sounding a lot more like the guys with the bad attitudes, had been observed moving material out of the Big Sweet warehouse on a regular basis in non-refrigerated trucks. Maybe they just delivered the ice cream cartons and posters and napkins and all the other paper paraphernalia, but I didn't think so.

Looking around, I spotted a copier. Turning it on, I waited in the shadows while it warmed up, and then made copies of the forms showing the impossibly large orders. Clicking the machine back into silence, I replaced the originals in their cardboard drawer and shoved the copies in my pocket. Before I could leave the file area, however, the door I'd come through opened. Slipping back into the darkness behind the files, I cramped down under a table, keeping my head where I could see who was coming, but not, hopefully, where it could be seen.

A chill ran across my neck as I put my hopes to the test. A large, bearded man moved into view, carrying a heavy machine gun. It was as stocky and single-purposed-looking as its owner. The man was dressed in drab colors, bulky clothing draped over a bone-breaker's body. He moved from area to area, looking here and there with the same bored sense of duty shared by all security guards.

The manner of his movements told me he wasn't looking specifically for me, just doing his normal job. The size and power of his weapon, though, told me his job was not one you got by answering an ad in *The New York Times*.

I waited for him to finish his rounds, motionless and soundless in my hiding place, prepared to stay there all night if I had to. Sweat beaded on my forehead, pooling inside my hat, making my head itch. I didn't move. The itching spread down my neck and across my shoulders, sending out signals to the rest of my body. My left foot fell asleep; my right foot followed suit. I ignored all of it. Guys like the one moving around the Big Sweet warehouse were great for inspiring discipline.

I jammed my teeth together tighter as he paused in the middle of the room to light a cigarette. A spasm started building in my right leg. I could feel the involuntary kick beginning. My eyes teared as I pulled in on myself, holding everything rigid. Machine Gun Kelly couldn't get his lighter lit. He tried eight times; I know. Each flick was an echoed cannon shot in the silent room. Giving up, he cursed in some mumble I didn't understand. Water from my body had started hitting the floor, thrown from me by the shaking I couldn't control. He didn't hear it over the noise of his own troubles. Jamming his cigarettes back into his pocket, he cursed again and left the room.

I dragged myself from under the table, crying freely, my leg jerking in wicked arcs in response to the cramps I'd forced to knot one atop the other while I'd been hidden. I punched myself in the forehead with doubled fists, hoping to distract my pain centers from the twisting agony lacing through my calf.

I rolled on the floor for two, three minutes-helpless as a runover dog. Having worked plenty of clock-watch security in my time, the back of my mind figured I had at least a half hour before anyone came through again. It also figured I'd never seen a place where the security carried machine guns, however, and kept urging me to get moving as soon as I could. Two, three minutes was as soon as I could.

Limping my way back to the center of the room, I decided I'd hit the freezers and then hightail it out of Big Sweet's life forever. Maybe the bills and the machine guns and the details on too-heavy security would give Nickels his added lever, maybe it wouldn't; I didn't care. All I was interested in was finishing up and vacating the premises.

Stumbling to the first freezer on my still shaky legs, I let my paranoia waste more time checking for alarms. Not finding anything, I jerked open the door; a welcome wave of frosted air struck me. Still a little wobbly, I slipped a Big Sweet Crunch Bar out of an open box and peeled it, biting down while I stepped back outside. Blessing the secure taste of white sugar, I made my way down the row of silver doors, dutifully checking each one, getting the same blast of cold air at every stop.

Feeling more confident with each door, I finished off the ice cream bar, ditching the paper and stick in a can brimming with trash. Reaching for the last freezer, though, I stopped just as my hand began to pull back on the handle. Something was different. As I studied the door, I noticed the insulating gasket had been partially removed. Waving my hand around that section of the metal jam, I couldn't feel any cold air escaping. Either this freezer wasn't working or it wasn't filled with ice cream. The answer to what might be in it made me curious enough to check again for alarms. This door had one. Wires ran out where the gasket had been cut.

Checking close, I traced them back to the same kind of double terminal I'd found at the storage room's entrance. The hairs on the back of my neck started to stand up again. I'd found what I was looking for.

Working as quickly as I could, I popped the alarm's outer box. Keeping an eye on the time, I backwired the systems, one into the other. It was a trick I'd picked up during my days with Military Intelligence. It only worked for a short time at best, but that was all I wanted. So far, Machine Gun Kelly had been gone a little over ten minutes. There was no telling when he'd be back. I planned on being long gone before whenever that was. Crossing my fingers, I pulled open the door.

The freezer was larger than the others. It went up higher and back further. It also didn't have any ice cream in it. What it did have was a confusing array of crates and bales I couldn't make heads or tails of. Clawing out my pad and pen, I started scribbling as fast as I could. One stack of boxes from Motorola were listed as Portable C3: Satellite.Line-of-sight.Manpacks; some cartons from Rockwell were merely stencilled Collins AN/ARN-139(V) TACAN. A stack of computer tapes stood awkwardly on a shelf labeled only with the names of countries.

None of it registered. I didn't have the faintest idea what I was looking at. An entire half wall seemed to be lined with nothing but crates from some place called AAI, all labeled SEWT. I stopped bothering to try and guess what I was looking at and set to copying as many names and places as possible before time ran out. I filled two pages working my way around the room as quickly as I could.

When three minutes was up, though, I headed for the door; I had to get back outside and dismantle my handiwork before it gave me away. That was when I spotted the suitcases, neatly lined up on shelves toward the front, harmless but intriguing. Hooked, I pulled one down carefully, surprised at how heavy it was. Its weight wasn't the only interesting thing about it. The arrangement inside it was as unidentifiable to me as everything else in the room — but not its warning label. Screwed to a metal box in the corner of the apparatus in the case was the international symbol for radiation.

Quickly, I reshut the case, fastened its snaps, and slid it back onto the shelf. Whoever was behind Big Sweet was playing at something beyond me, and I aimed to keep it that way. I ran for the freezer exit, numb with the thought of what might be within the innocuous line of suitcases and what exactly someone might be planning to do with them.

As I reached for the door handle, however, I thought, what *was* the goddamned Big Sweet Ice Cream & Sherbert Company doing with those things? Shutting my eyes, I slipped my fingers around the handle of the case I'd opened, thinking *in for a penny....*

Then, turning quickly, I grabbed one of the tapes from the stack in the back — East Germany — and stepped out into the warehouse. Hoping for a little bit of luck, I set about restoring things to the way they were before I arrived, including getting myself out the front door as quietly as possible.

I made my way to the front, lugging my booty with me, trying to not alert anyone to my presence. Creeping in silence, I ignored recurring visions of machine guns and the damage they can do. By the time I was back in my car, my shirt was plastered to my body, the sweat trickling into my shorts and down my legs. Sliding the ignition key home, I gunned the Skylark's engine and headed uptown for my office. There was a half-full bottle of Gilbey's in the large drawer of my desk. It wasn't enough, but it was a start.

I woke up wondering who had emptied their ashtrays into my mouth. I made to stand up out of bed and found myself laying on the floor. Whatever was wrong, it was going to take more than a hangover to explain it. I felt weak and nauseous; muscles all over my body were twitching slightly, including my eyes, making focusing on anything a major chore. I was sick, sick past my stomach, in some way I'd never experienced before. Groping my way to the bathroom, I spun the shower into life and pushed myself under it. The cold water opened my eyes for me, but brought the shakes on with more intensity. I slipped in the tub, nearly falling. I kept my hold on the faucets, though, bringing the hot water up as quickly as possible. Clinging to the wall, I fought the shakes, burning them from me, praying for a little steam to breathe.

A hundred years later the shower was over, and all the strangeness had passed, but only for me. Walking barefoot in the apartment, leaving splotchy footprints behind, I toweled off as best I could, looking for my dog, Balto. I found him stretched out underneath the living room table. He looked to be suffering from the same thing I'd had. So did the roaches. They seemed to be everywhere, stumbling in dizzy circles, dying or dead. At first I'd been scared, thinking somehow I'd picked up some kind of radiation sickness before I'd ditched the case. But even if I could have absorbed enough radiation to affect Balto as well as myself, it wouldn't have mattered; radiation doesn't kill roaches. As I thought about it, another possibility came to mind — one from my intelligence days.

I finished drying off, looking around the apartment for anything that might be out of place. I dressed quickly, throwing on the first clothes I could find. As

I buttoned my shirt, however, I noticed something in the mirror; the second bedroom window, the fire escape window — the one I always leave closed due to the constant possibility of the break-and-enter boys, was open a crack.

I hadn't opened it in so long, the last time the painters had come to my place they had painted it shut. I checked the edges — the coating of cheap latex they had sealed it with was split and broken. Someone had opened the window. Somehow, I didn't think it was Balto.

Things were wrong. Slipping on my shoulder holster, I checked my .38 over quickly, clipping a set of half-moons to my belt, shoving more into my pockets. Then, figuring I might be in something deeper than I realized, I went to the closet with the loose board under the heap of my shoes where I hide my old .45. Whether the people who had rummaged through my life during the night had found it or not, it was still there.

I pulled it and its spare clip and their holster free, checked them over, then secured the whole assembly to the back of my belt. Hiding it all beneath my jacket, I grabbed my hat and headed for the hall. I knocked on the apartment of Elba Santorio, catching her just before she headed downstairs to do the family laundry. She's only twelve, but she watches my apartment when I'm gone, making sure Balto gets fed and I have groceries — that kind of stuff. I told her our favorite pooch was sick and asked her to take care of him. I told her to air the place out with fans, keeping her nose covered while she did. Then, knowing there was nothing else I could do at home, I headed for my car. I had all the questions I could use.

It was time to get some answers.

It didn't take me long to realize the Chevy with the load of goons in it was tailing me. It didn't take me long to shake them, either. The myth of being able to follow someone without either their catching on, or losing them, is a popular one, but a myth nonetheless. In fact, in New York City traffic, tailing someone without their knowing it is virtually impossible. I ditched them on the Prospect Expressway heading into Manhattan. While my new found friends hopefully kept circling around scratching their collective heads, I pulled off at Hamilton Avenue looking for a phone, deciding to use the one in the McDonald's a few blocks along the exit. Parking off a side street, I hid my car from the main road and then went over to the phone. Thumbing in my change, I called Hubert.

"B-Batcave; Alfred speaking."

"Can the crap, Hu. I got trouble."

"Hey, hey, Hagee. W-What's up, Dick Tracy?"

"Last night I checked out Big Sweet. I found a whole lot of nuthin' that made any sense, and a guy the size of a tank with a machine gun guarding it. I ditched everything I took from there, including a lead suitcase with a slug of plutonium somewhere in its guts, at Freddie's. I'm pretty sure my apartment got gassed last night, and I've got a carload of guys in a Chevy trying to figure out how the expressway swallowed me."

"Sw-sweet shit, Jack. What's goin' on?"

"That's what we're going to try and figure out. Do me a favor."

"Jesus, Jack-what?"

"Get down to my office. Call me back at this number." I read him the McDonald's number and told him I'd explain when I heard from him. After we broke the connection, I fished out more coins and called Nickels at his office. His secretary told me he hadn't come in yet. Using the last of my change, I dialed his home number. He answered on the second ring.

"I-I-Hello?"

"Nickels; Jack. What are you still doing home?"

"Oh-ah, I just thought I'd stay home for the day. Why, Jack? What's wrong?"

"Who said anything was wrong?" Nickels was scared. His voice was filled with the nervous innocence of a guy who's just been pulled over for doing ninety. You could hear the sweat in his voice. He knew something, or had been told something, or was talking with someone listening. Someone who might be taping, or even trying to trace our conversation. Not wanting any company while I waited for Hubert to call back, I wrapped up quickly, reporting that I hadn't been able to find anything special.

At that Nickels stalled for a moment, most likely to get instructions from whoever was with him, and then suggested I bring everything I had found over to him. I agreed, telling him it would take me a couple of hours to go over to my cousin George's to pick the stuff up and get it over to his place. I knew I had no intention of going over to Nickels', but I wondered if he did. I also wondered if whoever was pulling his strings did. Thinking like that started making me nervous. I tried to cut the conversation, but Nickels stalled me again. Fighting the urge to simply hang up, I said:

"Look, Nickels, I got a lot to do today. If I'm going to get this junk over to you, I have to get moving. We can talk about everything when I get there. But I'm not getting caught in rush-hour traffic for anybody."

"But, but, Jack..."

"Hang up the phone, Nickels."

I hung up. I wondered if doing so pulled a trigger aimed at his head. I thought about it while I stood in line at the counter, while I ordered, while I waited, while I ate. By the time Hubert called back, I'd thought about it enough.

I asked if my office had been searched. It had.

"Christ, Jack; I t-thought hurricanes only hit the shore. This place was dumped on b-by someone with a real creative sense of trashing. Who does your decorating — the Three Stooges?"

That news didn't add up. Why do my apartment with kid gloves if they were going to ironball my office? Not having the time to think about it then, I told Hu to go across the street to Freddie's. Freddie is the toughest woman in New York City — possibly the world. Pushing sixty years and 250 pounds, she's run her newsstand without any help since long before I ever took my office on 14th Street. The way things were running for me at the moment, it was beginning to look as if she was going to be there long after I was gone, too.

I'd left everything I'd carried out of Big Sweet with her the night before, a practice I've gotten in the habit of whenever I have something on me I don't want to have on me. She's held everything for me from a Girl Scout knapsack filled with malted-milk balls and uncut diamonds to a human arm chewed off at the elbow. To her a little plutonium was no cause for panic.

I had a feeling that after all the trouble people were going through to get their hands on what I'd taken, that someone would have to be watching my office. It seemed doubtful, however, they'd be watching the newsstand. Not wanting to waste anymore time, I told Hu:

"Bag the stuff to keep anyone from spotting it. You're going to get a computer tape as well as the suitcase. Think you can get it printed out?"

"What language?"

"How the hell would I know what language?"

"N-Never m-mind. I'll get it d-done. No problem."

"Ah, yeah. Sorry," I apologized, remembering that snapping at the help like a South American dictator never works unless you actually have despotic powers. Catching hold of myself, I explained, "Nerves. You get it done and then bring the results to Central Park. I'll meet you there."

"Where?"

"Where else? At Grampy's."

Grampy is an old friend from my service days. He's handled more explosives than anyone else I know. If anyone was going to be able to explain what was in the American Tourister Hubert was bringing, it was him. He'd left Military Intelligence before I did, fed up with the whole system of the government owning the key to the jukebox, gifted with the opportunity to get out by way of a shrapnel wound in his leg.

These days, Grampy and three other guys make their living in Central Park, entertaining the locals and the out-of-towners. Their constant location is the Alice In Wonderland statute off the boat pond near the 72nd Street entrance. They've been there for years now, pulling in money with their routine. His partners, Kriss, Mark, and Darin, are a trio of the hugest men I've ever seen, one bigger, wider and larger than the next. Unbelievably, their act consists of the three of them dancing while Grampy blows harmonica. I guess with television the way it is these days, people will pay to see just about anything.

Outside of shoes and Grampy's mouth organs, the only equipment they use is a hat for people to throw their contributions into, and a sign reading:

THROW YOUR MONEY
IN THE HAT
WATCH THE FAT MEN
DANCE!

In the distance, I could see the sign, partially hidden by the dust its owners were kicking up. I wandered over toward them trying to be as inconspicuous as possible. A small crowd was present, as always, and the boys were doing their best to send everyone's hands to their wallets. I waved to catch Grampy's eye. He saw me and started raising the tune's pitch, signaling the dancers to start wrapping toward the big finish.

Moving through the crowd, I waited for the right moment and then started cheering and clapping, dragging the rest of the crowd with me. Before they knew it, most everyone was fishing out their change or a single, filling the battered Stetson. Hubert showed up with the suitcase and a second bag I figured held everything else as the crowd began to thin. As we approached, Grampy said:

"Goddamn. Don't seein' the two of you mean some form of deep shit."

"Thanks. We love you, too, farthead."

"So let's see it. What brought you peckerlips here this time?" Hubert handed him the case. While Grampy opened it, Hu whispered to me.

"We couldn't get anything off the tape."

"Nothing?"

"N-Not yet. I didn't want to take too long, so I just got up here quick." Hu smiled weakly. Worried I might blame him for the tape not turning into something, he added, "Oh, in case you were worried I ran a Geiger over that thing. It's sh-shielded good. No leaks."

I involuntarily sighed with relief. That news was more welcome than anything the tape could have told us. Before I could tell him that, though, Grampy exploded, "Jesus Fuckin' H. Bloody Christ — what the hell is goin' on here?!"

"What's the good word?" I asked.

"The good word is you're an asshole. Where in hell'd you get this thing?"

"In an ice cream freezer, on a shelf with a few dozen more just like it. Now, the old $64,000 question. What is it?"

"What the flying fuck do you think it is — it's a goddamned nuclear bomb, you shit-fer-brains . . ."

I calmed Grampy down, reminding him it wasn't proper etiquette to yell at the top of one's voice about stolen nuclear devices in a public place. Hubert gave me his patented scared-rabbit look; I told him to leave everything and take off. He did. Then, with Hu safely on his way, I filled Grampy in on what had happened. Once he knew everything I did about the situation, he said:

"Figure they hit you during the night with a two-hour compound — just enough to keep you asleep while they went through your place."

"Right," I answered. "Can't explain why they trashed my office, though,"—then it hit me—"*unless* there are two different groups after me."

It was the only thing that made sense. Maybe Big Sweet only searched my office, not knowing where else to find me — after all, Nickels doesn't know where I live — most people don't. Nor can they find out easily. The phone's not in my name — neither is the apartment or the mailbox. Of course, even if Big Sweet did grab Nickels and do in my office, I still didn't know who did in my home. Not that I wasn't going to find out. At that point, Darin threw us a warning:

"We got citizens. boys."

Grampy and I glanced up; what looked to be a real team of pros were gliding into a circle around us. We stood, but it was too late. The back-ups were already in position, the front men moving. Hoping no one wanted to cause a scene at a children's boat pond on a sunny day filled with witnesses, we held our ground and waited for the approach man to make his move. He didn't hesitate.

"Jack Hagee." It wasn't a question. He ordered, "Tell your friend to close the case and slide it forward."

Grampy followed through without me having to say anything. The stranger was in his late twenties, tall, white, clean-cut, sporting an Esquire casual look. Something told me whose badge he carried. When I asked for I.D., he showed more than enough. It made sense; I was in the middle of just the kind of mess the CIA loves to play in. I asked:

"You want to tell us what's going on here?"

"Yeah." The agent slid the case back to another in his team. "You've shot the shit out of a two-year operation — that's what's going on."

"Care to elaborate?"

"Sure." Esquire indicated a place where we could sit. His team closed in, herding us to our seats. "Big Sweet is a KGB operation. Oh, the employees are American for the most part — the place does manufacture and sell ice cream and sherbet as advertised. Here and abroad. It's just that some of their overseas shipments haven't been made up entirely of Rocky Road. You name it — car and truck service manuals, I.C. chips, pocket knives, home computers, government printing office pamphlets, all the little stuff. Lately, though, in light of the crackdowns we've been running on a lot of the leaks in this country, their operation has been forced to step up what they help move out of the country."

"Stuff like this?" I asked, showing him my notes from the night before. He whistled.

"Exactly. This TACAN — that's a highly restricted piece of equipment — designed to take the guesswork out of airborne rendezvous for tankers and jets, or Pathfinder programs." His eyes moved over my scribbles. "Some of this stuff is radar components; this ARINC 600 — that's a symbol generator. Nothing here that can't be bought over the counter in this country — if you have the right approvals. You're just not supposed to be selling it to the Russians. So, what's happening is, some sleazy son-of-a-bitch is getting this stuff together and selling it to the Big Sweet KGB."

"Great," interrupted Grampy, "but none of that explains a fuckin' nuclear bomb now, does it?" Esquire got a little green around the gills. It wasn't a look that suited him.

"No," he responded, "not at all." The agent got a little greener. I wasn't sure why he was letting us in on so much in the middle of a park instead of having us all cuffed and driven to a back room somewhere. He seemed nervous, as if he wasn't quite sure what decision to make. With everyone staring at him, he decided to keep talking.

"I'm going to explain something to you five because you already know more than you should, but not enough to allow you to realize the magnitude of what is going on here." Esquire's sextet of helpers turned around, scanning the area to make sure no one was going to overhear us. "Short and sweet — the Russians don't like our nuclear capabilities. They're not happy about the Star Wars program — neither is a lot of the rest of the world. They don't like our solitary super power status. I'm sure you've noticed some of this in the papers."

Stopping for a second, as if his throat had gone momentarily dry, he patted the case at his feet, saying, "If we have things pegged correctly, this is their next step. If they can't be sure of getting missiles to us while stopping everything we might send at them, then the hell with missiles — period. We're not sure, but we suspect that these bombs are slated to be hidden throughout the country, cutting their attack time of twenty to sixty minutes down to as many seconds as it takes to push a button."

Even Grampy got quiet for that one. It made the frightening, hideous kind of sense spy novels do when the last crucial clue falls into place — except this was for real. I swallowed the lead ball in my throat to break the silence. I wanted to ask him if he was serious, just in the hopes that it could all be some kind of insane joke told in extremely bad taste, but I knew better. For my own piece of mind I changed the subject.

"How did you know where to find us?" Seeming grateful for something else to talk about, Esquire told us.

"Obviously we have Big Sweet staked out. We take down the license number of anyone who goes in there. About an hour after you came out, KGB started pouring in and out of the place like maniacs. They're pretty clever about not giving anything away on the phone, but it was pretty obvious from the conversations we were able to listen in on that someone had made off with something — something pretty damn important.

"You were the only person who had come or gone lately we didn't recognize, so we ran your plates, got your I.D., and looked you up. As to how we followed you today, especially after that little driving lesson you gave my boys, well…,"

Esquire reached around to my shirt collar, pulling a pin the size of a small fly from behind the store lapel. "Stuck a number of these in the clothes it seemed likely you'd walk out the door in."

"So. You were the ones who hit my place last night."

"Yes. But we're not the ones who did the two-step on your office. That mess was there when we got there. Blame that one on the Red Menace."

"Fuck you!" shouted Grampy. Shoving his finger in the CIA agent's face, he yelled, "Who gives a shit how you found us? The important question is what the hell do you want with us? You ain't bein' this nice without a reason."

"Well," drawled Esquire, "you're right about that. Let's look at the facts. They're easy enough to get into order. The Russians want their bomb and their tape back. Have you been in touch with their building's owner?"

I told him I had, as well as my suspicions as to who else might have been in touch with him. He assured me I was correct. Their taps on Big Sweet had allowed them to piece together that one of the approaches the Russians had planned to use was the questioning of their landlord. After I told him of my conversation with Nickels, Esquire's face lit up. It was a smile with trouble written all over it.

"Okay. You told Nickels you were going to go and get the stuff you took and bring it to him — right?"

"Yeah, so . . .?"

"So that's just what you'll do. Look, this operation is blown wide open. The best we can do is hope to scoop up as many of these creeps as we can. Now, you said you were coming over with everything, right? That explains the lack of withdrawal we've noted on the part of their people. You must be a hell of an actor. We'll get you over to this Nickels guy's place, you give the Russians their stuff, they calm down for a minute, and then we can sweep them safely."

"And if I think my chances of getting myself and Nickels killed are too great…?"

"I'll remind you just how many laws you and your client have broken and just how sharply and neatly and finally the correct agencies can prosecute the pair of you if you think you can stir up a toilet like this and then not help flush it."

I looked over my predicament, mentally cursing my bookie and his great odds. Thanks to him I was caught between the KGB and the CIA, just for not knowing how to bet on the fights. If I ever caught up to Jucha or Mayo, I told myself, they'd go down for more than the count of ten. Taking a deep breath,

I looked Esquire dead in the eye and told him how pleased I'd be to walk into a house filled with Russian spies gunning for me with a nuclear bomb under my arm.

He and his men walked Grampy and his boys and me to their vans. I called Nickels again from their mobile phone, telling him I was coming right over. His voice told me he wasn't very pleased to hear it. I wondered what my voice told him.

Our two vans pulled up in front of Nickels' estate. Esquire asked if I was armed. I told him.

"Sure, all the way to the shoulders."

Grampy gave me a look. I flashed my jacket open, giving our host a peek at my .38. Pulling a small machine pistol from the glove compartment, he offered:

"Trade you. Where you're going, if anything goes wrong you might need more than six bullets."

I made the switch. His pistol just fit into my holster. I asked, "Got another?"

"Yeah, why?"

"Give it to Grampy. I could probably use some back-up on this play and you and your boys all look too Fed. He can be my cousin George, helping me make this delivery."

Esquire agreed, pulling another lethal little weapon out and handing it to Grampy. All that out of the way, I drove the first van up the drive to Nickels'. The second van, with two of Esquire's men and the dancers, stayed out on the street. The plan was for us to take the Russians' merchandise in to them, distract them for a moment, and then wait while Esquire and his men swooped in and clamped down. They were to be inside ten minutes after we went through the front door. I thought to myself that Custer had had a plan, too.

Once we were parked in the vehicle circle, Grampy and I got out, carrying the goodies. I spotted someone watching us from an upper bedroom window out of the corner of my eye. As we walked to the front door, Grampy whispered:

"All the way to the shoulders?"

"All the way," I whispered back.

"Fuck."

I rang the bell as we stepped up onto the threshold. A man answered the door, looking as much like a butler as Hubert does a prima ballerina. When I told him I was Mr. Hagee and that we were expected by Mr. Cosentino, he told us to follow him to the main living room. I said fine and slammed him over the head hard with the bomb casing the second his back was turned. He crumbled, going straight down. Blood oozed from his nose and one of his ears. Grampy relieved him of the gun under his left arm. I slid the bomb to Grampy, telling him:

"Arm it."

"Bad as it looks, huh?"

"Yeah," I agreed. "Just that bad."

He had it set in seconds. I was surprised how easy it was. Two small red lights were the only clue that the weapon was operational, but they held one's eye like a city in flames, or a baby being eaten, or any other image that ever stopped someone in their tracks. Sliding the detachable cover off, I stood holding the bomb in front of me. Grampy covered me with the "butler's" gun as we moved forward. We found the main living room on our own.

Nickels was there, along with a few friends, all with smiles and guns. The smiles dropped when they saw the bomb. I advised they do the same with the guns. They hesitated. I moved my finger for the detonation button. A couple of them started to follow along. Some didn't.

"This place is going to be crawling with CIA in a minute," I warned. "Give it up now, 'cause easy or hard — you lose."

"You threaten to kill yourself," asked one, "yourself and millions of others — destroy New York City — just to capture us?"

"No. To stay alive. We all know what happens to me if I turn this thing off. Look in my eyes and see if you think I care what happens to this world if I'm suddenly not a part of it."

Some of them thought about it harder than others; the younger ones weighed their chances for long minutes I could only measure in sweat, but in the end the guns ended up on the floor. I told Nickels to gather them. Then I made the Russians drop their pants down around their ankles and stretch out on the floor at the far end of the room. Sweating out the time before Esquire and his boys broke in, I told Grampy to disarm the bomb, setting Nickels to watching the Russians with one of their own guns. I wanted to go out to the vans, but I knew there were still other Russians in the house. Taking my chances, I stepped out into the hall and headed up the stairs.

I reached behind my back for my .45 and then hit the top landing with its muzzle leading the way. The door from one of the bedrooms opened. Before I could offer any choices, the men coming through raised their weapons. I fired at the one in the lead, sending a slug through his face, splashing the man behind him with bloody grey matter and bone chips. The second one, the security guard from Big Sweet, fired blind, sending a rush of lead into the wall beside me.

Dropping to one knee, I sighted quickly and pumped two shots through the man's chest, spinning him backwards into the room he'd come out of. Grabbing his machine gun, I spun around to cover the front door.

Two of Esquire's men came through it at a run, their automatics out. One spotted me before I could aim at either. Tired of dodging bullets, I sent a burst in their direction to throw them off balance and then jumped back out of range. More shots dug into the plaster around me. Somewhere downstairs, glass was breaking and someone else had decided to shoot guns off, too. Swell.

Inching my way to the stairs, I surprised one of the pair, taking off the top of his head with another burst from my captured weapon. The other took a wild try at me, spraying my face with splinters. He'd been close, but not close enough. He'd also given away his position. I flipped over and fired in his direction, creasing his left leg. It wasn't serious damage, but it was enough to send him stumbling off balance. By the time he'd righted himself, I was at the bottom of the stairs, bouncing his head off the heel of one of my size elevens.

Hearing Grampy's voice shouting orders from the main living room, I gambled on his and Nickels' safety and headed out the front door running. Esquire lay down a pattern of fire which would have tagged me if I'd come out any other way.

Not waiting to see the results, he slipped back into his van and started it up. I sighted up its front end and emptied the machine gun, ribboning its motor. Esquire started back out, cursing, but I threw myself into the door, knocking him back inside. Then, before he could bring his gun around, I dragged him out into the driveway, slamming him against the side of the van. I rammed him into it a second and third time, waiting for his gun to fall free. Once it did, I clubbed him to the ground with my automatic. He snapped back up, though, putting everything he had into catching hold of my gun hand. He twisted — hard — and my .45 slid out of my fingers, bouncing off under the van.

Reaching around with my other hand, I caught hold of his neck and dug my fingers in, forcing him to drop his hold. As soon as he did, I stepped back and then swung, rocking him across the jaw. He took it and stepped in, jabbing at my side. I swallowed the pain, tried to push him away — missed. He stepped in and jabbed again, sending me staggering.

His fist smashed against my face and then into my gut. I tried to dodge, but he was too fast, too good, too young. The only thing I had on him was weight. Figuring I'd better use it against him before the possibility disappeared, I blinked through the blood in my eyes and locked on him coming in at me again. Bracing myself, I took his punch and threw myself into him, sending us both to the ground. We rolled over several times, each of us struggling to gain the advantage.

One of his hands caught my chin, pressing my head backwards in an attempt to snap my neck. My fingers clawed up over his face, digging into his flesh. We tore at each other's heads, trying to be the one to inflict the most damage first. His teeth snapped at my fingers, but I managed to keep them out of his mouth, digging into his eyes instead. He screamed, making a last surge at breaking my neck. I resisted and then pushed forward, feeling a sickening wet rush as one of his eyes scooped free. I managed to drag my aching frame atop his while he howled in pain.

He punched up at me, but I stayed on top, pinning him to the ground. Then, pulling back my fist, I slammed him in the jaw as hard as I could, bouncing the back of his head off the cobbled bricks beneath us. That staggered him, but I didn't stop. Knowing what he was, what he had done, I punched him again and again, cracking his head against the rock under it until his skull softened and splintered. Police sirens came at me from somewhere in the distance.

I rolled off my opponent — stopped pummelling him — not because it was finally over, or even because he was dead. My body simply hurt too much for me to lift my arms anymore.

Grampy and I gave the feds the story later at the hospital. Esquire had told the truth about almost everything. Big Sweet had been shipping illegal merchandise to the Russians. But he and his men hadn't been on a KGB stakeout; they were the Russians' suppliers. I'd realized it when he'd told me the Russians were so clever about not giving anything away on the phone, and then slipped up about the tape. It was understandable that he might know what the bomb was, but I'd never told him what was in the other bag. He'd mentioned the tape to me when he shouldn't have known I had it.

I'd given him my .38 for what I'd known would be a worthless weapon because I knew I still had my .45 for back-up. I took Grampy with me because I knew I'd need more back-up than just a .45. I'd tipped him off to the fact that things weren't kosher with our old "up to the shoulders" code from our M.I. days. Sometimes being older than your opponent can have its advantages.

It was risky, but it was the only chance we'd had. Esquire had wanted to get us out of the park quietly, and off to where his KGB pals could do his dirty work for him. Nickels, Grampy and his boys, and myself would've all been dead while he and his crew would only have to explain a little missing time from their schedules. Luckily, things didn't work out quite as he planned them.

Grampy and Nickels took care of Esquire's last man when he stormed the house and the Russians I'd left on the floor, all without getting a scratch. The police managed to corral the agents in the other van and free the dancers without anyone on either side getting hurt. Actually, even I didn't get banged up too badly.

The feds and the police cooked up a story for the press about a foiled robbery at Nickels' estate. Nickels was happy to cooperate. Considering some of the things they could lean on us for, we were all happy to cooperate.

Big Sweet was cleaned out and the public never heard Word One about nuclear weapons being planted around the country in basements. The Russians disappeared, and nothing was ever seen in the papers about a Soviet protest over any missing citizens.

Grampy and the dancers went back to the park, Nickels went back to his million-dollar business, and I went back to my trashed office to try and put it together, all of us with the same strong "suggestion" from our government to try and forget the last couple of days.

I billed Nickels five grand just because I felt like it. He didn't complain. Just said he'd send a check. I knew he would. I slated the money for paying the back rent on my office and apartment, and to buy some new, used furniture to replace what the Russians had wrecked. I also went out and got a case of Gilbey's, just to celebrate having lived through such a mess.

I think Esquire's team went the way of their boss — I hope so anyway. I'd wanted to believe that they'd been moles planted in the CIA by the Russians, twisted idealists willing to sacrifice their lives for their principles, but that wasn't the case. A friend of Grampy's and mine still in M.I. was able to get his hands on the results of the Agency's follow-up investigation into Esquire and his boys. It'd all been for cash. The lot of them turned out to be sitting on savings too substantial to have come from their weekly pay. The Russians taken in the Big Sweet sweep could report down to the last ruble how much it had taken to buy seven Americans. Apparently, over a half dozen government officials can be had for the grand sum of $250,000, paid out over nearly six years. A little math breaks that down to around fifteen dollars a day. Keep that in mind the next time you want a parking ticket fixed.

Every time I think of them, selling their country out for money, inviting us all to step up into World War III, not for any ideology, but just for some dough, I reach for one of those new bottles of gin. I also reach in the same direction every time I think of my finger over the button, and how easy it would have been to do the same thing for revenge just because I couldn't protect my own life. My finger isn't over the button anymore, but a lot of other people's are.

Somehow I don't think one case is going to be enough.

A Game to be Played

I WASN'T LOOKING forward to getting up to my office. The day before I'd been lucky enough to live through its trashing by a single-minded squad of Russian agents looking for some of their property. Nothing in particular, just a nuclear bomb I'd been forced to borrow for the day. With more than a little trouble, and a few deaths, I'd managed to round up all the nuclear bomb-owning Russians in town and turn them over to the CIA, along with the bodies, wounded or otherwise, who'd decided to supplement their salaries with some traitorous blind-eye-turning.

Truth to tell, I was in a good mood — glad to be alive and not in trouble with the federal government. A few years back, I'd spent most of my time scampering around the Far East practicing my technique for our Military Intelligence forces; I know the kind of grudges people with a flag behind them can hold. Some of them can hold one for a long time — a *long* time.

It wasn't enough of a good mood to cheer me completely, though. The office behind the sign: JACK HAGEE PRIVATE INVESTIGATOR holds only one employee — me. There was no one else to had a broom to, or to help clean up and cart away the smashed furniture and wrecked shelving; the ruined filing cabinet — no one to help replaster the walls and nail the floor back down and fix the ceiling. At least, no one was supposed to be behind the sign.

"Supposed to" wasn't working that morning, though. Someone was inside, sitting on the remains of one of my chairs, reading the *Post*. He'd propped the three-legged remnant against the wall, bracing it upright by planting his feet firmly on the floor. The fact he looked at ease doing so was my first clue that he was worth watching. I studied him through the shattered glass of my front door, wondering what he might want. He had "Fed" written all over him — hard-edged, no nonsense Fed — in big, upper case, grief-filled letters. Looking up, he spotted me and called me inside. I went in. What the hell, I thought, it's my office. What was left of it, anyway.

My new pal folded his newspaper as I came in and then stood away from his seat. It fell sideways into the rubble. He extended his hand, saying:

"Good morning; David Metticap, Mr. Hagee. Hope you don't mind, I let myself in. The door wasn't locked."

Locked? It wasn't even intact.

"No," I told him. "I don't care."

Righting a chair fragment of my own, I slid it behind my desk and sat down. Pulling open the large drawer, I was happily surprised to find the half-full bottle of Gilbey's I'd left in it unharmed. Setting it on the desktop, I asked, "Can I offer the government a drink?"

"Maybe not quite this early."

"Can you offer me some I.D.?"

"Certainly."

He smiled the big, "#3 Trust Me" smile while he handed it over, the one so popular in teenage movies these days — the first one they taught me in Intelligence. I unscrewed the top of the Gilbey's and took a long pull, stretching out an imaginary cramp in my left shoulder at the same time. Continuing to stretch after I put the bottle down, I tried to gauge Metticap for any clues he might be giving off as to what he wanted. Nothing gave. I was a bit worried. The day before I'd broken a lot of the conventional rules. The time might have already come to pay the piper and frankly, I didn't think I had enough in my checking account.

"I have a feeling," Metticap said with adjustable sympathy, "you're a little nervous about this business."

I put my cards on the table and agreed he might have a point. He smiled me the #3 again. I tried not to look as worried as I was.

"All right, let us get everything out into the air." Metticap uncrossed his legs and spread his hands, indicating he was being open and honest with me. They taught us how to do that convincingly, too.

"You had a lot of fun most people don't get to enjoy yesterday. While you were at it, you did your country a great service — you uncovered a nest of Soviet agents planning to nuke our major cities, and you cancelled a large leak in our network. As you might suspect, we are, of course, extremely grateful to you for these services."

"Don't bother with a medal," I told him. "I'll pat myself on the back while you're on your way out the door. Otey?"

"It isn't quite that easy, Jack."

Somehow I'd suspected as much. I let him pace in front of my desk, his calculated hesitancy showing how much he cared for me, and how difficult it was for him to say what he had to say. I took up my Gilbey's bottle and knocked back a double slug, showing him how much I appreciated the effort. Finally, he told me:

"Let's nutshell, Jack. We have a problem — a serious one. Ever since you exposed the rotten apples in our barrel yesterday, the top brass have had their asses screwed up tight and dry. 'No one can be trusted.' 'Double all security checks,' et cetera. Everything is grinding to a standstill. Our department heads can only assign work to people with top-top clearance until the simmer cools off."

"This is as fascinating as it comes, Dave — honest. But what's the point?"

"I want to hire you for a job."

My eyes caught his and held them. He seemed serious. More than that, he was desperate. I let him lay out the last of his sad story.

"I have a delivery that must be made. The importance of it is beyond the time I have to make clear. It is information too delicate to risk interception. No faxes, satellites, nothing. My superiors insist on hand delivery. They also insist on a courier above reproach. Right now, that means the President, my boss, or myself."

"What'd the President say?"

"He's lunching with my boss."

"Well, have a nice trip."

"Actually, I was thinking the same for you."

That'd been obvious for a while, but there was a game to be played, and since I was in no hurry to start cleaning the mess in my office, I went along for the ride. Apparently my former security clearance, along with my years of government-sponsored infiltration and hand-to-hand training were enough to qualify me for the job. Metticap gave me the details.

Things were going badly for his South American division. The CIA was being forced to make some fast changes. They had a new list of instructions for his Latin operatives that they needed — pronto. What they also needed was someone to get it there. The job entailed driving to Miami in less than two days — not easy, but do-able. Link-up had to be made with a team of advisors who would be docking at a place called The Shark's Lair just outside the city. All I had to do was drive down, identify the team, give them their orders, and split.

"Of course," admitted Metticap, "there is an element of danger involved."

"Yeah, of course."

"All that's meant is, despite this precaution it is *possible* for the enemy to mark you as our ringer. It's unlikely. I've made this move on my own initiative;

no one else is involved — this contact exists strictly between you and me. On top of dismissing any charges that might be brought to bear on a man who decided to run around town with a nuclear bomb under his arm instead of giving it to the authorities, or who guns down government agents because he has a 'hunch' they're not on the side of the angels, et cetera, I'm also prepared to make a substantial contribution to the Jack Hagee retirement fund."

"How substantial?"

"How substantial would you like it?"

"Appeal to my greed."

We settled on ten thousand dollars. We had each other over a barrel, but I had more time to waste getting my feet back on the ground than he did. He gave me the exact location of the meeting place, the team leaders code name, the exchange phrases I'd need, and a sticker for my car window that wound make bending the speed laws between New York and Miami more than a bit easier.

When I asked why couldn't I just fly down, he told me the method used to disguise the list was metal detector sensitive. It made flying too risky, especially since the airports were under enemy surveillance due to the short delivery deadline.

"In fact, that being the case, perhaps you should be on your way."

As he said it, he handed me a magazine, *Hogtie* Vol.4 No.5. The cover showed an attractive blonde, Debbie Harris in 'Strapped Heat,' modelling a black leather strait-jacket jumpsuit affair. She was straddling a little-girl bed covered with a blue satin quilt. Resisting the urge to thumb through it, I asked:

"For my late night enjoyment?"

"One of its functions. It also holds the instructions list magnetically encoded on foil sheets in between some of the pages."

I thumbed through the magazine trying to determine which pages had the extra weight. I couldn't find them. Dropping the hunt, I rolled Debbie up for the moment and slid her into my inner jacket pocket. Metticap looked pleased until I told him there was one more problem. When he asked "what," I reminded him that, as he could plainly see, my office needed someone, or a group of someones, to take out all the debris, replace my ruined furniture with some government standard issue, and fix the walls and floor and ceiling and door, all the way down to the repainting of my name on a new pane of frosted glass. With an exasperated sigh, Metticap asked:

"Do you think you might've bled enough out of this situation now, Mr. Hagee?"

After agreeing that things now were looking just fine, I took another slug of gin, just to annoy my new best pal, and then stood up, put on my hat, and swept along to the remains of my door in a much better mood than when I'd arrived. I had a client, ten grand in my pocket, and a real milk run of a job that basically ended in a Florida vacation. Best of all, I'd gotten out of cleaning up my office.

Smiling as I headed down the stairs, I laughed to myself over the thought that I should tangle with subversives more often. I should have known my chance was coming.

When I picked up the tail I wasn't sure. I first noticed it a few hours out of Manhattan. I was moving at a good clip down I-95; so fast, in fact, I thought I'd attracted an unmarked car. Always looking to avoid a hassle, I took my foot off the gas so I'd slow up without showing any tail lights. They kept moving at the same speed. I watched them as they shot past, checking to see if they looked like a state police team. They didn't. I couldn't catch much, but too many things were wrong.

There were four men in the car. Two were bearded. The right rear passenger was too short to be on anyone's police force. They went by quickly, but I did get the impression they were watching me — that driving by with everyone noticeably not looking in my direction was a ruse to throw me off — and that if I kept my eyes open for a green, three-year-old Chevy, sooner or later I would find one...with the same smiling faces inside.

All of a sudden, the game that needed playing seemed less of a holiday. Circumstances had forced me to make the best of a bad situation and take Metticap's offer. I'd convinced myself that he was misleading me, that everything was going to work out perfectly, that I was going to earn my outrageous fee and clear myself with the government all in one easy motion. As I drifted along at a more respectable speed, my mind flashed back to when I was seven.

Playing with the wrong kids and opening my mouth in the wrong way had put me in a bad situation a lot in those days. The worst time, however, I thought for sure I'd bought the farm. There were twelve, thirteen of them chasing me. We crashed through the woods behind our little neighborhood, splintering the small, lower branches, trampling the brush, destroying a straight line through the forest. What I'd done to bring such a massive welt of wrath on me didn't come back — just the running, the aching sides, wet-faced, torn clothes panic dash that carried me from our fort of the day to the edge of the woods in half the time of the others because they were the ones who were laughing, and I was the one who was scared.

Unfortunately, fear had driven from my mind the memory that the edge of the woods was created by a sloping cliffside, one that, despite its lack of steepness, still had to be climbed. No one could simply walk up or down it; you had to hug it for safety. Just like Fatty Borra had done the week earlier when the gang had chased him to its edge. They'd bombarded him the whole way to the bottom — rocks, branches, beer cans, large clumps of dirt and weeds — anything handy had gone over the edge, all of it combining to put Fatty in the hospital for two months. Somehow I didn't think the bunch of them had gotten any more civilized in just seven days.

Desperately, I looked about me for a better plan than Fatty's. Not seeing anything, and hearing the hunters behind me coming closer, I suddenly flashed on the lessons the nuns'd been drumming into me. Tales of believers being delivered out of the hands of their persecutors reminded me of what I'd momentarily forgotten — the power of the Lord God. Without hesitation, my child's mind knowing He would save me from the evils on my trail, I threw myself off the edge of the cliff into His invisible, waiting hands.

I fell thirty feet before the first bounce. I flew up and out again, hard, a dying stone slammed against the Earth over and over until my upward arcs lost all altitude and I was merely rolling.

When I reached the bottom, I lay flat and bruised as a cat who'd lost an argument with a panel truck. I was mud and tears and bloody scrapes bound together by one long, wailing scream soaked with fear, but I was alive and unbroken and not headed for the hospital. Nothing was cracked or splintered, except my belief in the god of the quiet, fanatical women in the black cloaks. Dragging myself to my feet, I bit my lip against the pain of moving and began walking home. On the way, I swore to myself I would never, ever again, hang around with guys I didn't know or play games I didn't understand.

Flowing along with the rest of the cars on I-95, I wondered what had happened to make me forget those very important lessons. I ate up the miles thinking about a lot of things, like why Metticap trusted me and no one else, and why hadn't I seen him the day before when the CIA had been thrashing out the details of what had happened with me, and just who were the smiling faces in the green Chevy? Russians? CIA guards? CIA traitors? Innocent bystanders with whom my imagination was running away?

I thought about the Chevy a lot, which was most likely the thing that saved my life. If I hadn't been concentrating on it, I might've missed it when it pulled out of the rest stop behind me.

The car barrelled out of the merge lane at fifty, doing eighty by the time it lined up behind me. It angled for my rear end, trying to knock me off the right-hand side. I shot forward fast, forcing them to slice back to compensate. Cutting across lanes, I jumped ahead a few car lengths and pulled my .38 free of its holster, wedging it between the base and back of the seat where I could get it in a hurry. A rear view check showed the smiling faces were just as prepared; muzzles were sticking out of two of their windows as they wove through the other cars trying to close with me.

Of course, as always, no cops were there where they were needed. The Chevy and I balleted back and forth across the lanes, cat-and-mousing away the miles. I hit the top of my speedometer after the first two minutes. The Chevy had no trouble pacing me. We continued zigging in and out of traffic, angering some, terrifying the more observant ones, forcing several of each off the road. And then, it finally happened; a clear stretch. Suddenly I had nothing left to hide behind.

Before I could react, a blasting slam crashed against my trunk. I swerved to the far right quickly, watching as the other barrel of the shotgun took off my side-view mirror. It vaporized into cracking metal and rips of chrome, flying ahead of the rest of the car for a moment then disappearing.

The Chevy began pulling alongside of me. I swung to the left, cracking my rear end against their front. They gassed hard, digging into my fender while I kept pushing the other way, hoping to send them into the median. Their left tires hit the shoulder and slipped over the edge. Dirt churned instantly into clouds of filthy billow, choking us and sending more of the drivers behind us into each other. We roared down the interstate together, sparks rocketing from the heat of our grinding metal, paint burning away.

The shotgun barked again — my rear window spit breakaway pellets over my shoulders — lead shot bounced my hat off the windshield and tore a bloody layer of skin off my ear. I ducked low, counting on the headrest to cover me for a while. Playing the wheel harder, I pulled to the left with all my strength. The sweat on my palms made it hard as the wheel's plastic coating greased from the slickness. The shotgun tore through my car again, eating up the warm leather of the headrest and exploding the windshield.

We hit the curve at a hundred plus, bouncing back and forth against each other, forcing another set of cars from the road. As the other driver wasted time straightening out from the turn, I made my move. Pulling my gun free, I mashed the brakes at the same time. The Chevy hit me like hail in July, bouncing me off the steering wheel, but sending its occupants flying as well. Before they could recover, I emptied my .38 at their driver, seeing at least two new holes open in his face. Then I lunged desperately at the wheel, jerking it hard to the right, trying to disengage us.

We both skidded forward, jammed together, but then broke apart — me skidding completely over the right lip of the interstate, them 360'ing forward into a flip. Road surface tore and splintered as they hit. Glass and blood splashed across the highway, the screams of car and men folding over each other unnoticed as the other cars coming behind us braked madly in spinning confusion.

Pulling some tissues from the glove compartment, I pressed them to the side of my head, feeling them drink. They stuck to the smear dripping out of the raw flesh, letting me know they would be painful to remove later. Ignoring all my pains, however, I keyed the ignition, hoping the stall I'd gone into wasn't permanent. It wasn't.

A Game to be Played

The Skylark kicked over, its tires biting their way up over the shoulder and back down I-95. Looking in the half a rear view mirror I had remaining, I checked the Chevy for any signs of life. The nothing I saw made me smile.

I knew I had a decision to make quick. It was fairly certain the smiling faces had some friends somewhere. It was also fairly certain I was highly recognizable due to all my car's recent streamlining. The only way I could make my deadline was to keep tearing up the miles ahead of me. If I got off the interstate and onto the back roads I'd never make it on time. All of which meant I had to change my look and fast, before the opposition brought in the second team.

I had to change vehicles. The only question was, how to get someone to swap cars with me for a while. The only answer seemed to be that the swap would go a whole lot easier if I was the only one in on it. That decision made, the next question was where to do it. The Southern Tourism Board provided the answer.

Up and down most of I-95 are signs for a place called South of the Border. It seemed I'd started seeing signs for it a few miles outside of New Jersey. At first they were staggered fairly far apart. After a while, however, they started showing up every twenty miles — then ten — then five — then every other one until they were everywhere, extolling the virtues of good ol' South of the Border. According to its advertising, you could buy everything under the sun there, ride any kind of ride, play any kind of game. As I pulled off on the exit for this wonderland, I only had one kind of game in mind.

The place was even duller, more commercial and cheaply depressing than I could have imagined, which was saying something. Large, wildly painted stone men in sombreros stood about guarding the area. Oversized cement-and-plaster animals with equally garish paint jobs helped them. The loose-knit collection of tacky stores which made up the place were a joke — sucker shops banded together hoping to eke out their living by trapping saps roving down I-95 toward Orlando and its more substantial attractions — hey, kids, let's start the vacation fun right here. Yeah, right.

Music filtered over everyone, even those of us skulking around in the parking lot. I'd left my car in the back corner of one of the parking areas and fanned out from there, looking for a likely bit of new transportation. And then, the flickering crawled into my stomach, the jumpy, juice-mixing combination of stress, nerves and intuition I hadn't felt to that degree since I'd left M.I.

It comes from trying to second, third and fourth guess the enemy. Some guys tear themselves apart with the feeling, plotting and replotting their next moves, looking for every possible contingency until the time comes when they get up in the middle of the night to hustle a snack in their own kitchen, and suddenly find themselves frozen with fear at the thought of opening their own refrigerator because the light might signal a shooter outside, or because a bomb might have been planted in it, or any of a dozen other wild ideas that ulcerate them whether they're asleep or awake.

Taking a deep breath, I pushed aside such worries and resumed my search for a swap vehicle. I must've been too obvious about it. After another few minutes, I found something that looked do-able. The problem was it appeared someone had spotted me. Once he noticed me noticing him, he walked straight over. My .38 beckoned to me, doubling its weight to remind me it existed. I passed over the urge to pull it. The mood wasn't right.

My new friend lived in a heavy black beard and near-shoulder length hair. His mouth was big — wide like a jack o'lantern grin, but the nose over it was classic enough to drag his face all the way to handsome. It hardly mattered, though. The first thing anyone was going to notice in his face were his eyes. They were stark chunks of blue rock that could nail a bug to a wall with their intensity, and yet somehow still managed to seem faraway. The kind of eyes Jesus must have — and Charlie Manson.

He smiled wide and stopped a few feet away from me, asking, "Hey'lo, brother. See anything you like?"

"Don't catch your meaning, pal."

He grinned. "Evasive and unfriendly. No bullshit but no 'give,' either. Northern — northeast. Could be New York. Wrong accent — East Coast mixed with something else."

He stared at me for a moment, then asked, "Pronounce p-o-l-i-c-e, would you?"

I was still jittery, but Bugeye was just amusing enough to tolerate, so I answered, "Police," saying the "po" as "puh."

"Ah, ha," he nodded to himself, then snapped back, "do you know what 'chipped ham' is?"

"Yeah," I told him, "it's ham sliced real thin, like paper."

"I don't know where you live now, but you grew up in the Western Pennsylvania area, didn't you?"

I nodded. He cackled.

"I knew it, I *knew* it!"

I didn't know what to make of him. He had an air of authority, but not any of the kinds I dealt with on a regular basis. If he was a cop, I was Isadora Duncan. As always, I figured the best way to get some information was to ask for it. When I questioned what he was up to, he answered:

"Savin' your soul, brother. You look too decent to get messed up in stealin' cars. Not from such a damn fool place as this, anyways."

I looked at him and almost matched his grin. I'd played out bizarre scenarios in my Intelligence days, but nothing like Bugeye. Everything about him screamed out that he was genuine. Deciding to roll with it, I offered, "You want to save my soul, give me a ride to Miami."

"Surely — if that's what it takes to keep you from poppin' the lock on this Toyota wagon, or that Buick overtheres, or any of the fine vehicles on this lot."

"I get the feeling you were in the sales game at one time, somewhere back before you started saving souls."

He smiled again. "Playing loose — I can appreciate it. Yes, true, true to God. I had the material world sewn up sweetly at one time. Interested in the story?"

There was something about Bugeye that was hard to resist. Maybe my run in with the smiling face had rattled my nerves a touch, or maybe the smells of a thousand and one different fast foods were taking their toll on my long flattened stomach — whatever it was, I felt more like listening than driving, so I nodded again and told him, "Sure, as long as you can tell it on the way to a hot dog stand."

"As good a stage as any — a better pulpit than most. Let us away to the nearest doggery, to swap chatter, and to prepare for the pilgrimage to distant Miami."

The gravel of the lot crunched under our shoes. The carnival din of South of the Border's half a million loudspeakers rained down on us, drowning all superfluous noises except our own voices. As we walked, Bugeye told me:

"A salesman I was — true, indeed. Satellite dishes. Oh, I'd sold the world everything else previous; shoes, toys, men's suits. Salesmen move up and up if they're good, better and better merchandise if they're good, and I was good. Good enough to save the money to buy my own lot. I bought up a used car spot that'd gone under and brought in the dishes. Lots of little ones, lots of big ones, too. I mean *big* ones. Pull in Japan if you wanted — Mars if they were sendin' from up there, but they aren't, but if they were, huuuuuu-boy...

"Anyway, I was doin' pretty good. Wife happy, kids happy, salesmen I had to hire happy — life was sweet. Then, boom. Crash. All over. They change the laws and suddenly everyone's paying for the right to use their dishes every month. Boom — crash — no more sales. No way. No how. None. Salesmen first to go. One at a time. Gone. Then the business. Couldn't pay the lot rent, couldn't sell off the merchandise, couldn't hold onto the material side of life. It just took off on me. Gone. Then my wife and kids disappeared. Boom — crash. Gone. Probably with one of her relatives, but nobody's talkin'. Won't tell me nothin'. Anyway, gone is gone, and it's all gone."

Bugeye drew in on himself then, going abruptly quiet. He was moving alongside me at the same clip as before, but suddenly all the life that had been spilling out of him dried up. The air couldn't have changed more if he'd disappeared. I didn't prod him, and he didn't offer anything. Stopping at the first food stand we found, I ordered six dogs, three with mustard and onions for me, three plain for him. Gratified to see that they not only had Diet-Rite Cola, but that they had it in bottles, I got a sixteen ouncer, knocking back the first four in one gulp. Bugeye got a Coke, no ice. Then, he squirted a fat line of ketchup on each of his dogs, saying:

"Always got to have your vegetables with every meal."

I nodded in agreement and kept eating. The dogs quieted my stomach while perking up Bugeye's mood. Once we were down to one apiece, we started walking back to the parking lot. I recognized his depression and knew letting him take his own time was the only way to handle it. My wife'd walked out on me a few years earlier — I don't care anymore, but I did for a long time. I let it eat me up inside, let it redesign me into someone different…someone who didn't take chances with women, who didn't rush into relationships and get his ass burned off every other day, who didn't get hurt. I've never been sure if the new front I'd put up then was better than the one that got torn down, but at least I don't drink as much these days.

When we reached the lot, I told Bugeye, "Look, pal, let me level with you best I can. I'm a private detective, and I'm working something very important. I have to get to Miami, and because of certain details I can't go into, I have to be there soon, and I can't take public transportation.

"Now, I don't see how anything can happen to you if I get in your back seat and stay out of sight, but things've been hairy already, and I have to be honest — there could be trouble. This could be dangerous."

"Well," he said, grinning, "Well, well, well. Man comes to me and says, 'Sure, I'd love a favor, but I have to tell you, it's dangerous.' Don't worry about it. Maybe riskin' losin' my life is what I need to make it worth livin' again."

I started to protest, but he cut me off.

"Quiet. Don't say it. I know what I'm doin'. And although I can't say I know what you're up to, my friend, I can say I trust you. You need a ride, I need someplace to go. I say, let's get on with it, shall we?"

Minutes later we were on the road, heading for Miami and The Shark's Lair. Bugeye kept a good, steady pace. I flopped out in the back seat, keeping my head down, grateful for the way things had turned out. Being forced to team up with someone else'd given me the chance to calm down and work on the puzzle, something I hadn't been able to do since the morning.

I'd started out thinking I'd picked up a real milk run. Until the smiling faces I hadn't worried about anything. After them, I'd done nothing but. Now, however, I had a chance to just think. I started quick.

What was Metticap after? Was I being set up? If I was…then, why? If I wasn't, then how'd the Chevy find me? Was what I was carrying *that* important? And if it was, was I actually the most trustworthy man in the country to get it through?

Everything I thought of led me around in a circle. It was true they could've put the papers on a military plane and flown them down, but it was equally true that the Russians have spies everywhere. When I'd been with M.I., we'd weaseled traitors up out of every branch of the military.

My problem was that nothing'd happened yet to trip my trust meter. I simply had no solid reasons for trusting or not trusting what I knew about the situation. I also knew it wasn't likely I'd have anything more to go on until we got to Miami, either. That fact safely assumed, I pulled my hat over my eyes and let myself get comfortable. Although I didn't know it in detail, deep down a part of me knew things were going to get worse before they got better. If only I'd known how right I was.

The Shark's Lair was a dive, a lone business on the end of an aging dock catering to locals only. Wharf bums and long-haul fishermen made up the majority of their business with a sprinkling of neighborhood toughs, wage workers and petty gamblers for color. Decades of smoke and old fish grease hung in the air, waiting for something new to light on. The walls were thick with the smell and the feel of them.

It was a beer joint; it held no pool table or dart board, no television or juke box. It was a place for tired, angry men to go and drink until they got enough down to push them over the edge to either sleep or violence. No women were in sight; not even the hardest prostitute would find it worth her while to work a place like the Lair, if for no other reason than the fact no one inside was likely to have her price to spare.

I been waiting inside for two hours which felt like fifty. I'd nursed a few beers along while I waited, keeping to the shadows and myself, watching the crowd for any sign of my contact. I didn't want to appear as if I were waiting for anyone because the simplest motions attracted attention. People moving up to the bar for another drink drew stares; people talking to their friends got stared at, as did those who were sleeping. I stared at the ceiling while waiting for the door to open. A lot of people were doing that, too.

I'd left Bugeye at a motel nearby. He'd said an extra day in Miami was no bother to him, and that he could wait for me to finish my business before going back. I was glad for that because it gave me an anchor — finish my business, walk back down the dock, collect Bugeye, get in the car and get out. I hadn't yet spent a full week dealing with the government and its plots again, but I was already feeling the old neuroses creeping out of the woodwork.

The tension of not looking behind me was beginning to cramp my neck and shoulders. I caught myself digging my thumb into the flesh between my shoulder blades, trying to break up the muscles knotting there. The "worry" was setting in.

Playing the espionage game teaches one to wait, but it also teaches one caution. I was starting to feel set up, like I'd been maneuvered into the Shark's Lair for some reason sleep depravation was keeping from being obvious. It was also in my head that after the past few days I was understandably paranoid, and that all I had to do was stay calm and everything would be fine. If the CIA people who had to meet me'd been put on as short notice as I was, they could simply still be en route. They might also've had the same kinds of troubles I did, and not've been as lucky. Their set of smiling faces might've held a better hand than mine.

Deciding, however, not to worry about "mights," I went up to the bar for another beer. On the way back to my table, a man moved out of the corners and crossed to intercept me. Putting out his hand, he asked, "Doug? Doug Straker?"

It was the cue I'd been waiting for. Feigning recognition, I replied, "Ray, Ray Hunter. Jesus, man; I didn't think I'd see you here."

"Well, like we used to say in Munsey, 'cameras take pictures.'"

"Spoken like a true son of democracy."

A look in his eye let me know we'd completed the exchange to his satisfaction. He was convinced I was the courier he'd been expecting. We sat down at my table, laughing a little, mumbling about our imaginary past together for the benefit of the leaden crowd passing out around us. Finally, 'Ray' whispered, "Are you ready to make the drop?"

Sure; the sooner the better."

We got up together and headed for the door. Once outside, I steered us down the dock back in the direction of my motel. The boards of the wharf were spongy, thick slats of wood begging for a chance to send the unwary to their knees. The smell of rotting fish mixed with other less pungent odors of decay to make the sea night sadly revolting. As we walked, Ray asked:

"Where's the packet?"

"My motel. Didn't want to take chances."

"Which motel? How far?"

"Calm down. It's the ugly one at the end of the pier. Everything's in my room."

"That's great," answered 'Ray'...too happily. I caught the edge in his voice, the dropping of the character he'd been showing in place of someone my instincts screamed at me to watch out for. I turned, backing away at the same time, just avoiding the knife coming for my throat. 'Ray' stumbled a few inches from the missed stroke, but regained his footing quickly. I planted myself carefully, waiting for his next move. There was no time for guns — we were too close. We watched each other, him keeping his body between myself and the shore. It was soon clear why.

A pair of men came into sight, moving down the dock from the Shark's Lair through the darkness, obviously coming to help one of us. I figured I knew which one of us that was. Forcing things, I feigned for my gun. 'Ray' leaped forward, looking to make contact while I was off balance — just what I wanted. I caught his knife hand's wrist in my left; a twist sent the blade tumbling. He tried to swing but I blocked and then released his wrist so I could grab his shirtfront and pull him forward into my waiting right. I bounced his nose off my fist — twice. The light went out of his eyes for the count. I let him fall, stepping over his slumping body to confront his friends.

They weren't ready to use guns any more than I was…than 'Ray' had been. Everyone was trying to keep the cops and the locals out of things. My mind flickered toward the fallen knife, but I ignored it. What I wanted was a few feet ahead of me leaning against the dock wall — a set of oars. I grabbed one up just as my two new friends arrived. One came in quick, not thinking about the sloshing timbers beneath his feet. As his blade extended into my circle, I held for the right second and then went after him.

I could see in his sideways dance he expected me to try and club him. Reversing my grip, I ran the oar blade into his stomach and then pivoted, coming in closer. He hadn't begun coughing before I slammed the oar's meaty end against his left ear, sending him tripping away.

His pal cut the air near my head, not touching me as I stepped past him. I caught the back of his neck with the oar, bouncing his face off the dock. Standing away from the trio, my back to shore, I watched the three of them straggled upward. Only one had managed to hang onto his knife. Muttering to each other quietly, they stepped forward, hoping to surround me.

I tricked them by stepping forward into their midst and then attacking those to either side of me. Two quick slashes sent each reeling for the sides of the pier, slipping and cursing all the way. The one in the center grabbed my oar, looking to pull it out of my hands. I released it instantly, letting him fall backwards from the force of his jerk. From the screams he let out when he hit, I figured he'd landed the wrong way on one of the fallen blades.

Pulling my gun then, I ordered them all to get up against the railing. Only two of them got up. I checked the one who stayed down. The only movement coming from him was leaking out in trickles. I hooked his wallet, then cleaned the other two. They were all carrying a low caliber weapon, but none had any ID that told me anything.

On top of that, I now had three prisoners for which I had no use. The situation smelled as bad as when Metticap'd first walked in on me. Thoughts flashed through my head, like did these guys have more pals coming after me and who were they anyway and what was really in the magazine I'd been carrying, and did I care nearly as much about any of that as much as I did getting off that dock and the hell out of Florida? I let my playmates handle the answers.

"Who're you guys?" I asked.

"We will tell you nothing."

"Look, moron; I'm not the government. I'm not going to start torturing anyone, or calling newspapers or policemen, or anyone…as long as I get some answers. If I don't get any, though, then I'll just shoot the lot of you and blow, so — for your own good, spill — what is it you think I have?" After a moment, one answered.

"The code books."

"What code books?"

"The submarine code signals used to direct our submersible traffic in the West."

"The West? Russian submarines? You guys are Russians?"

One of them turned, looking me in the eye. Even in the dull light reaching us from the Shark's Lair, we could search each other's faces, looking for signs of trickery. As we sized each other up, I told him:

"Listen; I want you to understand what I'm going to tell you. I think you were tricked by the same people I was. For what reason, to what end, I…don't…know. Do you understand that? I…don't…know. I don't have any submarine codes. I don't know anything about them. What I was given to carry supposedly has nothing to do with submarines. Somebody's playing us all for chumps, and I think the miserable way this's all turned out proves it."

I slid one of their weapons into my belt and then threw the other two over the railing into the dark water below.

"Now," I told them, "first, I'm going to put my gun away. Them I'm going to drop your fake wallets back on the dock. Then I'm going to walk away — all after you do one little thing for me." The turned man's face told me he was willing to listen.

"I want to know whose side you're on."

The two against the rail chattered to each other in low, grunting whispers. The one on the dock continued to snore. Finally, after a handful of very long seconds, their spokesman turned back to me and said, "You like truth, American — we give you some. Yes, we are Russian. We are KGB — Seventh Directorate."

They were with the 'NN,' the branch of the Kremlin guard entrusted with the secret observation and shadowing of both Soviet citizens and visiting foreigners.

"If you're NN, what're you doing pulling a stunt like this? Enforcement isn't your usual line."

"The team entrusted with bringing you down was killed — I imagine by you. We were reassigned to intercept you because we were the only team in the area. We, as you must have noticed, did not succeed." His eyes confirmed he was telling the truth. Tossing their wallets on the dock, I backed away from the scene. Moving off slowly, I told them:

"All right, take your wallets, and your pal, and go back in the bar. You can do whatever you want after you've gone inside — all I want is a moment to put some distance between us."

As their spokesman picked up his wallet, he asked, "And what are you going to do?"

"Me? I'm going to nail the son'fa bitch who set us up."

I made it back to the motel in under a minute. Hurrying to the room where I'd left Bugeye, I went in quick, not for a second expecting what happened next. Bugeye had company.

There were three of them, all powerful-looking, well muscled. Not the weight-jerking, gorilla-boy, mutant-monster "well muscled" we always see, but the comic book hero/decathlon winner kind of "well muscled" look we all want. They were powerful little gods, whittled down to a mere six foot something apiece with iron fingers and rock-hard stomachs and a mentalities which knew how to move correctly and efficiently. They were a team of somebody's killers, and they had me covered before I even knew how many of them there were.

In a different voice that the one I was used to, Bugeye told them to take my gun. I looked at him and laughed. Finally, things were beginning to make a little sense.

"Okay, Jack," he told me, "here's the story. Everything I told you about myself is true. The only part I left out is the fact that the whole time I was losing my business and my family, I was also the only thing I still am, a federal agent."

He flashed me a badge identical to Metticap's, as he continued.

"You offer us a problem, Jack. We're on a hunt and we don't know if you're the quarry or a setter pointing the way. So, I guess what we do next depends on the story you have to tell us. Any questions, or would you like to dive right in?"

I dove. I had no reason not to. They were government agents, their IDs were as good as they come. So were their guns. Besides, I could see how I'd been made without asking. Having heard that someone'd busted up a carload of Russian agents on I-95, they stalked out the most likely places in the area where someone might try to swap a suddenly marked car for a merely stolen one.

I told them everything — my troubles from before Metticap had walked into my life and after. I told them about the Central Americans I couldn't find, and about the Russians who'd found me.

"That's it, really. After I got on the interstate, I had the tussle you apparently already know about, went to South of the Border for car swap — met you — came here — went to the Shark's Lair — got into another tussle — got tired of tussling — came back."

I handed over the issue of *Hogtie* I'd been carrying around and finished, asking, "And, that's the whole ball o'wax. So — your turn. What happens now?"

"We leave."

"'We' us all, or 'we' you four?"

"I'd suppose you'll want to leave sometime, but I was only referring to us."

"You going to let me in on what's been going on, or do I have to guess it all for myself?"

Lifting the copy of *Hogtie* from where I'd thrown it on the table, Bugeye tore it down the middle, tossing the two halves into the wastebasket in the corner.

"No metal centers," he said. "Nothing. Just a gambit to start the game. Metticap lied to you — set you up. My guess is he was afraid you knew more than you thought you did. He sent you on your way, then leaked word to the Russians you were carrying their submarine codes. They kill you, he gets away clean."

"But what the hell did he think I knew that was worth killing me for?"

"The agents you rounded up the other day were his men. Under his section, anyway. We've been expecting Metticap to do something to either clear him of suspicion or sink himself permanently."

"You mean you knew he was dirty and you let him waltz me out into all that shit — you let me go down to the pier, knowing I was headed off into another trap?"

Bugeye stayed cool. His mutant gods held their poses. We might have all joined the same side, but I noticed they still had all the guns.

"No; we didn't do anything 'knowing' he was dirty. We only suspected. Sadly, for cases like these, this is still America — being 'pretty sure' isn't good enough. We had to give him enough rope to hang himself. Obliging son-of-a-bitch that he is, he did. I'm glad you survived, especially since we'll be needing your testimony when it comes time to finish nailing his ass to the barn door — but for all we knew, you could have been his go-between. He could have set up clearing out all his men with you the other day, and then paid you off and iced you, too.

Don't get steamed. It's a perfect scenario. It all makes sense."

"Then why don't you cuff me and drag me away?"

Bugeye sighed. Shaking his head, he answered, "Because I believe your story. I've talked with you — gotten a feel for you. I trust you."

"You trust me — yeah; given' what's happened, and the whole dirty situation, and the fact you want to ice Metticap a hell of a lot more than you want to ice me — sure, you trust me."

"Glad to see you catch on quick."

Bugeye made a hand motion to his man holding my .38 and the Russian's .45. He threw them on the bed. While I replaced my gun in its holster, I asked, "So, does this get you guys off my back finally?"

"We were never on it. This is America, Jack."

"So you keep telling me."

"Think about it. Think about what's been going on. You've just spent the last two days breaking every law you could run up against. Technically, you're a top drawer murderer. What's your punishment? A ruined fender and ten grand to spend." As the quartet filed out, Bugeye finished, "Capitalism been 'bery bery' good to you, Jack. The rest of the world should have it so easy."

I listened to his laughter as he and his men disappeared down the hall. Sighing, I put a call through to Manhattan to my friend Freddie. She runs the newsstand across the street from my office. I asked her to check my place to see what my new furniture looked like. She called me back ten minutes later, letting me know everything looked drab, but fine. We talked for a few minutes more then I signed off, promising to bring her a fat bag of oranges.

I hung up the phone. Finally, I knew what was going on.

Sitting in the darkness, I counted off the minutes. I'd waited for hours, knowing what was going to happen, just not when. Bugeye and his men had left before 11:00. I was impressed he could wait so long. The doorknob finally turned, though; quietly, as I knew it would.

Bugeye came in, gun out, staring straight ahead at the form I'd sculpted in the bed. After he pumped three silenced shots into it, I called out his name, giving him a chance to put his gun down. He spun around shooting instead, trying to get me. His bullet tore up plaster. Mine shattered two of his ribs. He went down hard.

"Good guessing, Jack," he coughed.

"Not so hard."

People were already gathering outside in the hallway. I shut the door on them and headed for the phone, saying, "Metticap was right — there was more dirt in his department...someone giving hot papers out to the Russians. I take it your three bruisers are part of the good guys."

Bugeye nodded. The motion made him cough, a reflex which bubbled blood out through his clenched lips. I felt real sorry for him.

"Figured. Elsewise you would've taken care of me when you were here before."

"Couldn't take you out with them around. Had to...wait."

Talking made him cough again — violently. Crimson mixed with what looked like fried sea food splattered the worn carpeting. While I worked at getting a line through to Metticap, I told Bugeye:

"You almost had me conned. Only a couple of mistakes. You knew I'd gotten away with only a dented fender, but you'd never seen my car. What made me suspicious, though, was the fact you knew the Russians thought I had their submarine codes. I didn't even know that until after my scuffle on the dock. After that, I called my friend Freddie and asked her to check my office. Metticap delivered the new furniture I'd bartered out of him. He wouldn't have bothered if he was expecting me to take the deep six."

Bugeye moved his hand from his side to look at it, or at least at the blood covering it. It dripped from his fingers like water from a porch roof after a rain. Closing his eyes against the pain, he said:

"It's a shame you…left M.I. You're very…very good, Jack. You must get…a lot of practice." As the line to Metticap finally opened up, I told him:

"Hey, like you said, this is America. The place is full of maggots to practice on."

Bugeye died before I could finish filling Metticap in on everything that'd happened. I'll leave it to your imagination as to how many tears we shed.

The Piper's Tune

I PEEKED OUT from behind a sand-leaking pile of rubble someone once called a wall. A .45 in hand, I scanned the dunes, watching for those of Mulask'tar's tribe who'd followed us through the night. The handful of survivors from our party who'd made it to the oasis alive, along with the few who hadn't, lay behind me in heaps, all except for Bomber. I was grateful he'd made it. I haven't known many tougher guys in my time. Although our escape across the desert proved I was a much better shot, I had a healthy respect for Brannigan's ability with his fists or a knife. And, though I didn't like thinking about it, there was little doubt the trouble we were in was going to end in the kind of confrontation where such skills would be an asset.

"Bomber, see any of 'em?"

"Some." Brannigan wasn't much for conversation when there was trouble. It didn't matter — I knew what he meant. Spotting one Arab on the desert means at least twenty or thirty hidden from your sight. I'd spotted four or five myself, which probably meant that between every weapon in camp we didn't have a third as many bullets as we did enemies. Sweat beaded on my forehead — despite the chill night wind, the whipping cry of the slashing air around me — the soak dripped off my head freely, muddying the sands below briefly only to then dry and disappear, as if it had never been.

Swatting at the sand gnats buzzing around, nipping my ears and neck, I realized that our hiding in the ancient oasis was just a stall — sooner or later we were all going to have to pay the piper. I didn't mind that, actually. I just wished I'd been there to hear his tune.

Things had all happened too fast. I didn't belong in the picture. My name's Jack Hagee. I'm a private detective, the kind of guy who usually makes his rent by tailing people who can't find their way to their own beds at night, or by reporting on people who don't know how to accurately fill out an insurance claim. A friend had come to my office with a news clipping about his son's death and a tale of killers with thick accents. Darnell Lowe had died merely for being in the wrong place at the wrong time. His father wanted it proved. I was the only person he knew who might be able to help him.

Never do business with friends.

The trail of clues led me from back alleys in the Bronx to poppy fields in Turkey. The men who had punched Darnell's ticket disappeared in an explosion, one the local police in Diyarbakir were willing to ignore as part of the constant drug wars that tear apart their city. The killer's employers were not so open-minded, however. I'd posed as a federal narcotics agent to find the pair I wanted. Unfortunately, my act must have been good enough for Broadway because my targets weren't the only ones I fooled. Instead of a Tony, however, my performance netted me a beating that felt like it was administered with baseball bats.

I woke in the desert. The horizon was a flat line of heat and sand in every direction. I lay where I'd been dropped until I passed out again. Once it got dark, I managed to stagger off in who knows what direction until I fell over again, this time for good. I lay on a dune wall, blistering in the next day's sun when I was spotted by members of a British archaeological expedition. They dragged me around with them, taking care of me until I was actually able to help out a little.

When they took me in I became bottom man in a part of forty-two men and women, ten camels, three horses, two trucks and one jeep. Now I was somehow second-in-command of eight men, four camels and two horses. When the British had departed Diyarbakir, they'd had nearly four tons of supplies; looking around through the faintly cracking dawn, I figured we had maybe two hundred and fifty pounds of that left. Twelve pounds of that was ammunition. Maybe seven was food.

"They're movin'!"

I looked up, searching the desert for the Arabs Brannigan had spotted. I saw three of them crawling forward, bellying their way across the sand.

"Kulkai — get over here."

The half-caste boy ran low to get to me. Eyeing the circle of stones and trees behind me, I told him, "Tell 'em to get back or we'll poison the well!"

Nodding, Kulkai screeched out toward the advancing Bedouins. Barely in his teens, the boy's voice cracked several times as he stammered out my warning. While he did, I yelled to Brannigan.

"Bomber, drag a body over here — quick!"

While he sprang to the far end of the wall where we'd first dragged the dead, I ran to the well. Loosening a length of rope, I rigged a lasso as quickly as I could, then threw it up and over the ancient bucket brace. Brannigan was next to me a moment later, a corpse dangling from his powerful left hand.

"Get his feet in the noose," I told him. "I'll tie off the end."

Others of the survivors swarmed around us while we worked.

"Here, Hagee," snapped Palmer, the expedition's leader. "What's this all?"

"Shut up," I snapped. Turning back to Kulkai, I shouted, "Are they listening to you?"

"Yes, sir; this they are good for, sir."

Brannigan gave me a high sign, indicating he had the body tied off over the well. Running back to the wall, I scanned the early morning for myself, checking to see if the Arabs had really stopped coming at us, even if just for the moment. Brannigan hurried back to his own end of the oasis, doing the same. We didn't see anything. Palmer came up to me while we continued watching.

"See here — I want a word with you."

I turned, waiting for him to close the distance between us. Sir Jeffrey Fenton Palmer was the archaeologist who had put together the expedition that had found me. It was his belief that a year earlier he'd located the undisturbed burial grounds of some previously unknown pharaoh. At the time he'd made the discovery, though, he'd been short on men, money and supplies, let alone any kind of government sanctions for digging up the local real estate. It'd taken him a long time to get the whole thing together, tensions being what they always are in the Middle East. My guess was he was about to blame me for whatever the hell was going on around us now. Fine, I thought. Let him try.

He rooted himself behind me as I continued to watch the desert, staring at my back. "This, I suppose, is your idea of a rational ploy?" He sputtered for a moment, then added, "You — you've *trapped* us here."

"I've trapped us here?" For a moment I thought the heat might've softened his brain. "What's your problem, Palmer?"

"We should have continued to run for it. Surely we could have reached some better sanctuary than this."

"Surely we could've been cut down one by one like every other body that's out there on the sand starting to blister." I mopped at my head and brow. The rising sun was making short work of both my chill and my patience. "We stopped running *here* because *here* is all there is. We're fifty miles from anywhere else. Any*thing*! The only chance we have is to swap our freedom for their water."

"Our only chance vanished in gray smoke when your nerve ran out and you raced us into this hell-bound way station. If I hadn't set the alarm and gotten us all moving," the older man snapped, "as many of us as did survive would already be dead."

"What I don't seem to be able to puzzle up at all," said Nash, another of the Brits, "is what set all this madness to whirl in the first place."

"Good question," added Brannigan as he joined the rest of us. "You think these bedsheets have some legit reason for bustin' our chops, Jack?"

I didn't know what to say. I'd asked myself the same question a hundred times since the first of us had been cut down. I'd studied the whole thing a dozen times, but I couldn't find any sense in it. When we'd first come across Acbai Mulask'tar's tribe, they'd seemed genuinely pleased to see us. They weren't part of any oil-fat herd; these were simple tribesmen who spat on the rest of the world with a set of emotions ranging from hatred to indifference. To them, the only things that mattered were those found in the desert.

We traded with them, bargaining under the sharp eye of Allah's laws of hospitality. When the Bedouins discovered what we were there for, they were eager to become a part of things. A number of the younger men volunteered to hire on as diggers, interested only in securing a part in history. The older men saw it as an opportunity for a celebration. What their women saw the chance meeting as was unknown. They remained out of sight during the trading, their voices unheard, nothing seen of them but their completely draped and bundled forms. Maybe not wanting to lose their hold over their women had turned these Arabs away from the wealth the area offered. I knew a lot of guys who'd give up something as simple as unimaginable wealth for the mastery of their homes.

That was beside the point, though. The Arabs hosted a wild party for us, setting was sure seemed as all their best forward. We "Europeans," as they insisted on calling all of us, were given the finest of everything in sight. Tents were filled with fiery dishes of mutton and goat, desert puddings, and curries. Mulask'tar provided wrestling matches, jugglers, a magician, and even a sort of Passion Play that brought tears to the eyes of the faithful and keenly captured the interest of the archaeologists, while not boring we of the grunt caste too much.

We responded with howled choruses of popular songs and a drunken dance around the central campfire. One of the students along on the dig told a tale of vampires and maniacs, hamming things up worse than a made for TeeVee movie. The necessity of translating things didn't overly seem to bother either the teller or his audience, however.

Not to be outdone, Mulask'tar set about winning our unspoken contest by calling for his daughter. She came without a word, wrapped in long thin shreds of black fabric, laced and stitched in patterns too delicate to read in the firelight. She was young, a child really, barely in her teens. Probably the only reason she was permitted to dance in front of us was the fact that she was too young to be considered a woman in the first place. I wasn't so sure, though. She moved across the sand around the central fire, gliding in the footprints of our drunken dancers the way grass fills in the scars of a bombed-out field.

She raced everyone's breath, keeping our eyes like a miser's purse does pennies, even the usually stiff and proper Palmer's. Bone flutes and goatskin drums helped weave her magic, but only slightly. The movements, the wild kicks and turns and leaps, were hers, borne from an inner urge to express what was within her before approaching womanhood cut her off from the freedom she could only exhibit as a child.

But then, after laboring every man's temperature more severely than the desert's hostile noonday sun, she disappeared into a tent beyond the firelight's edge, the slightest of giggles the only sound she made the entire time. I had to force myself to remember she wasn't a child of the New York streets, a product of the fast and ruthless era of greed and shameful knowledge that had its hooks so deeply into the West. She was innocent — totally. The thoughts she gave us were ours alone, and not of her conscious devising. And suddenly, I realized just what the rest of the world means when they call us decadent.

The Bedouins, pleased with their chieftain and themselves, insisted we share their camp that evening. As stuffed and drunk as we were, we didn't have the slightest urge to offend anyone's kind gestures. If that was what they'd been.

"Maybe we were set up," I told Brannigan.

"Yeah," he answered. "Maybe they didn't want us diggin' up their holy dead and just suckered us in."

"Seems unlikely," responded Nash.

"I pretty much agree," I told him. "But what makes you think so?"

Prentiss Nash was one of the directors of the museum sponsoring Palmer's expedition. He had accompanied more than one British team into the Middle East, and seemed to know what he was talking about.

"It doesn't have the proper feel." His hands swept the horizon. "These are not a subtle folk; we are talking about a people unchanged in their ways since before the coming of Moses. You've got to forget the outside world when you're here — Christian ethics are nothing more than a confusing nuisance when trying to understand the nomadic mind. If these people wanted us to stay away from something, they would have simply told us to stay away from it — period."

"And I think you're being far too naive," interrupted Palmer. "Mulask'tar is unfortunately no fool. As much as you do not wish to subscribe to your own theory, Mr. Hagee, I am afraid you are correct. We are not the first to enter this region in search of her treasures. The fact we wish to uncover history to put it on display for the world does not diminish the fact that much of that history is fashioned from hand-beaten silver and gold.

"You know nothing, Nash. I've lived most of my adult life amongst these people, dodging their insane Jihads and persecutions — sifting the dunes around us for bits and fragments that make your gloomy, grey-stoned royal sideshow the attraction it is, and I've done it with a spade in one hand and a Webley in the other."

The archaeologist lifted his sun helmet and wiped his forehead. "They meant to kill everyone except those of us who knew where to dig. And, I leave it to your imaginations to decide how long those kept alive would have retained that condition once the tomb had been unearthed."

Nash tried to calm Palmer down, but the older man wheeled in the sand, pointing his finger at the museum director and myself, cursing, "Damn both you fools. This affair will end in death. Everyone pays for their mistakes eventually, Mr. Hagee. Everyone.

"We shall all pay dearly for yours."

Palmer turned then, retreating toward the palms growing around the well. No one else said anything. The day was becoming uncomfortable, both from the heat, and the hostile glare of hundreds of unseen eyes.

I looked at the watch I'd borrowed from one of the dead for the thousandth time. It let me know there wasn't much time left before the last of the sunlight disappeared, leaving us in the weakly lit grey of the desert night. There were no clouds to mask the stars and the moon, but their feeble light only made the shadowy web of dunes around the oasis that much more unreadable. Brannigan crawled across the encampment, joining me near the well. He asked:

"Think they'll come at us?"

"They might. We probably won't know it until it's too late."

We sat with our backs to the rapidly cooling stones of the well. While I checked my .45 again, making sure no sand had crawled inside since the last time I'd broken it down, I asked Brannigan what had brought him into our little mess. I knew some of his career, but couldn't figure out what might have brought him to the Middle East.

Bomber Brannigan is a name known to most older sports fans. At 6'6", weighing over 300 pounds, he isn't an easy man to forget. He'd been a decent heavyweight in his prime, once going the distance with a pre-champ Sonny Liston. He'd lost the decision, but I knew an old timer who'd seen the fight, and he said it was so close they must've tossed a coin to see which guy's career they were going to toilet. On top of that, Bomber chipped a bone in his knock-out right during the ninth with Liston, the piece of bad luck that finally took him out of the boxing ring and landed him in pro-wrestling.

Knowing all of that, however, still didn't give me a clue as to what had landed him in the Middle East. When I asked him, he told me that eighteen years on the grunt-and-groan circuit had been enough. He'd settled down in Rockford, Illinois, where he now owned and operated a popular bar called The Bomb

Shelter. What had stirred him from his comfortable nest was the interesting part.

"Kinda hate to admit it," he said, twisting his mouth in a way that showed he was uncomfortable, "but I'm here because of a damn woman. Not just any woman, mind you, but the kind of dewey-eyed, bubble-busted blonde that's been drivin' guys like me bugfuck since Adam first peeked under Eve's fig leaf. Well, this one was no good — not for me, not for anyone but herself. I had a lot of people try and tell me that, but I wouldn't listen. Even took a poke at my best buddy when he tried to set me straight — guy named Hannibal, who, by the way, you sorta remind me of."

"Hope it's not enough of a resemblance to start you taking pokes at me, too."

"Nahhh," he grinned. "I'm over the tramp now. Once I finally wised up to what a fool she was playing me for, I sent her packing. But then, well, I had to get away for a while, you know? Get it all sorted out in my head. Had to get away from things that reminded me of her and away from people who either felt sorry for me, or were snickering behind my back.

"Anyway, I always had a hankering to see the Pyramids, so I decided that was just about the right distance to do the trick. After I'd been over here a few days — long enough to get bored but not enough to go back — I saw an ad in one of the English papers stating that Palmer and his bunch were looking for some real roughnecks to keep the sandbugs digging. I figured what the hell. I got good people takin' care of The Bomb Shelter for me — let's go play archaeologist for a while."

"Yeah, sure," I agreed. "But what makes you think we're gettin' out of this mess?"

Brannigan looked at me as if seeing me for the first time. "Hell, Jack," said the older man, "don't tell me you're worried about all this?" When I admitted the possibility, he said, "Let me tell you something I learned when Liston and I were pushin' each other's mushes in. I was worried before that fight. He wasn't the champ or nuthin' yet, but the Bear was undefeated — he was the toughest man in the world — and he knew it. It showed on his face plainer than his nose or eyes. He was a thunderer, a wreckin' ball, a big black monster that just dared anyone to get into the ring with him. He wasn't arrogant about it — he was just the best, and he knew it. A lot of guys lost to him just because they couldn't get past their fear. I knew some of them; I knew they were beat even before they got in the ring with him, just because they thought they couldn't beat him.

"Well, maybe there *are* too many bedsheets out there for us to put a dent in 'em. Maybe Palmer was right and we're all goin' to end up payin' a heavy price for bein' here at that. If we do, though, I don't see any reason in over-tippin' the sons-of-bitches."

Brannigan smiled. I joined him. Our throats stung too much from swallowing sand all day for us to laugh, but we could still smile. Exposure had started taking its toll. Although we had all the water we wanted, we couldn't afford the luxury of tents or lean-tos. The first of us to try and hide from the sun died as gunfire leveled at us riddled the canvas sheet he tried to hide beneath with lead.

The Arabs might be keeping their distance, but they weren't about to let us "infidels" relax. Throughout the day, random bursts had strafed the camp, keeping the last of us hopping. With that thought coming to mind as the sun disappeared, I suggested we post some guards. "Two of us at a time — two hour shifts."

"Sounds good to me," said Brannigan. "I'll take the first with Beardsley."

"Okay," I agreed. "I'll second with Nash." Pulling my jacket down from the edge of the well, I wrapped it around myself while I asked, "What kind of signal do you want to use?"

"If I see any bedsheets, I'll start shootin'. Good enough?"

I pulled my hat down over my eyes. "Terrific."

Branningan didn't see anything to aim at during his two hours, though. At his watch's end, he sent Beardsley to get some sleep and then woke Nash and me. After making sure we were both fully awake, the ex-heavyweight curled by the well and dropped off quickly, falling into such a deep sleep he was actually snoring in minutes. With nothing better to do, Nash and I picked spots and began watching the desert.

I cautioned the Brit to unfocus his attention. Staring in one direction too long, listening to the sound of the wind over the sand, would be the easiest way to fall under the desert's powerfully hypnotic spell. I kept myself alert by whistling under my breath, varying the melody from time to time. Concentrating on a tune was just enough to stop me from thinking on anything else that might prove too distracting. Men with girlfriends and wives must make lousy guards.

Thoughts of our situation, of the numbingly hot day past, or of our collective chances — all had to be driven away. Emptying my head of worries, I just kept whistling, constantly eyeing the sand, listening for anything beyond the range of my own noise. Five bars into "Puttin' on the Ritz" I heard what I'd been waiting for.

It was a slugging sound; a short, scattering noise like the winter breath of a small child. My ears perked, my eyes searching for the source. Not moving my head, I shifted my eyes from side to side, looking for whatever was crossing the sand toward the oasis. My hope was to find whatever was headed toward us without letting them know they'd been spotted. Finally getting the direction, I stared intently, watching the crest of an unbroken dune from which the noise was coming. Nothing happened. I waited. Sliding my .45 slowly from my belt, I flicked the safety off and then slipped it atop the well wall behind me. Still watching the horizon, I reached down to my left and grabbed up my rifle, careful to remain silent.

Suddenly a hand inched up over a small dune only a few dozen yards away from me. Slowly bringing the rifle to my knee, I aimed, waiting for more of a target. My forefinger wrapped around the trigger. A burnoosed head followed the hand. I waited, letting the Arab come completely over the crest of the dune. After several more seconds, another Bedouin followed. Cross-hairing the second man, I held my breath and squeezed off my first shot.

Instantly the camp erupted in confusion. I fired again, exploding the head of the first Bedouin. Brannigan was awake and heading toward the well, firing his revolver from the hip. He dropped two running forms with six shots, cursing his misses, reloading while still on the move. I heard Nash's rifle blast over everyone else's shouting.

"Kulkai," I screamed. "Call 'em off — tell 'em we're not bluffing about the water!"

As the half-caste cried into the night, Brannigan leapt atop the well, his knife reaching for the rope still holding the corpse we'd suspended earlier. I stood and fired again, trying to draw the attention of those Arabs headed for the well. Bullets flew through the camp from all directions. I fired again and again, emptying my rifle before I knew it.

A scream went up behind me. Beardsley was flopping on the sand, trying to hold back the blood leaking between his fingers. As three Bedouins came over the ruined wall only yards from the well, I grabbed up my .45 and fired, the first's throat bursting in a splatter of red, the second knocked backwards by lead ripping through his ribcage. There was no time to sight up the third one, however. He fired twice; one of the bullets whistling past me by inches, the other digging into Brannigan's side. The ex-heavyweight grunted, almost losing his footing. Blood jerked from his left side as he finished slashing the hemp. Holding the corpse with one hand, he dangled it over the mouth of the well, shouting:

"Shoot me again, you bastards — go ahead! *Now* kill me!'

Kulkai screeched more entreatments, telling the attackers to pull back before the only water for fifty miles was contaminated. All movement stopped. The Arabs considered their next move more silently, the only noise to be heard coming from the flies slowly buzzing around Brannigan and his threat.

Then, finally, the Arabs turned and disappeared back into the night. As those of us left in the oasis gathered around the well, a lone voice broke through from the darkness. Kulkai translated.

"He says they were fools — serpents sleep with open eyes. But Mulask'tar's hell is wide enough to crush the largest fangs. He says Mulask'tar is coming and that in the morning, he will kill us all very thoroughly."

I took a long look at our situation; I probably wasn't the only one. Brannigan had saved our asses for the night, but had gotten himself shot doing so. Beardsley was a red smear on the sand, the hole through his chest empty and unmoving. That left me with Palmer, two useless paper pushers, a cook and a boy. I had to admit that if Mulask'tar wanted to kill us all very thoroughly he certainly wouldn't have to try very hard.

Dawn came and passed without any more trouble. Nothing moved on the sands. Those of us that were left clung around the well, breathing the scant shade of the miserable scrub palms next to it. Brannigan was in tolerable condition, the bullet having passed cleanly through. Nash had patched him up without too much trouble. The ex-heavyweight's side was too sore to allow him a great deal of movement, but he was in no danger of dying — from that bullet, anyway.

"Pretty funny," said Brannigan. "Nash says I'm fine. Guess that means I'll live 'til they kill us."

"That sounds about right," I agreed.

Leaning against one of the palms, I waited for the inevitable, watching the others. I hadn't slept after the attack, unable to get the wrongness of our situation out of my head. I still didn't have a clue as to what the Arabs wanted. Palmer was certain they were after the treasures most likely to be found at the site of the discovery; Nash believed him wrong. Fine — but if he was, then why *did* the Bedouins attack us? I asked myself, did we do something to offend them, and if so — what? They'd seemed pleased with us all through the celebration. The tribe didn't impress me as that good a bunch of actors; I was hard pressed to believe they'd set us up to be slaughtered in our sleep. Hell, why bother wasting the goats to feed us? But, if that wasn't the case, what was? It would have to be something that happened during the night — but what? What could have been done to draw the wrath of the entire tribe down on us?

Another thing that disturbed me was the warning that one Arab had shouted during the night, that Mulask'tar was coming to take care of us himself. That might have meant we'd only been contained in the oasis, awaiting the chieftain's pleasure, that they wanted us so bad they were willing to risk our contaminating their only water just to get us.

I stopped puzzling over things, though, as my eye caught some of the others. Nash had gone off with his assistant, Pickering, to root through the remaining supplies. They were going to each box, one at a time, tearing them open and unwrapping whatever was inside, usually tossing the contents about, whispering between themselves all the time. They'd glance back and forth around the oasis and across the desert in between their exploring, alternating between silently staring and cackling like a pair of old women in Atlantic City who'd just hit it big on one of the nickel machines. The expedition's Arab cook sat with Kulkai, the pair praying while they eyed the sand around us vacantly. I had no idea where Palmer was.

Suddenly, though, Nash threw a jar high into the air, letting it crash against one of the camels. While Kulkai and the cook rushed over to calm the animal before it started kicking, I ran across the small stretch between myself and Nash as he threw another jar into the air. I grabbed his shirtfront and then shook him hard as glass shattered behind us — the smell of ammonia reeking across the dunes.

"Get a grip!"

"No need, old chap; none at all."

"Don't hand 'em out, ''cause nobody's buyin'." I shook him again. "You and this bad check here better pull yourselves together before the fun gets started."

Nash tried to break my hold. He bounced around, trying to swing at me, but he couldn't hit me, or escape until his shirt ripped, his thrashings sending him toppling.

"Pull ourselves together," he screamed. "For what?! So we can straight-spine-march into a thousand rifles? So we can let them take us and—"

Before he could cry anymore, though. Palmer came rushing up to where we were, shouting, "What is this? What in the Crown's name is going on here?" Seeing the ruin Nash and Pickering had made of the expedition's supplies, the archaeologist screamed, "What in God's Great heaven has possessed you all?" His hand swept over the ruin of scientific equipment laying about them on the sand. "Have you lost your minds?"

Nash laughed at Palmer, a chokingly bitter sound that disturbed everyone.

"Shut up," ordered Palmer.

He practically shrieked the words, scaring Nash into silence, but the effect was of the moment only. The museum director looked to his assistant in silence but then suddenly, the pair broke out in even greater hysterics. Palmer grabbed for Nash, but the latter dodged away, screeching insanely, his eyes rolling.

As the archaeologist moved forward, Nash clambered atop the well, tottering on its lip. Palmer chased him around it several times, but couldn't catch him. Nash was around the far end, his eyes wild with whatever nightmares he'd given himself thinking about our fate. Finally, as he and Palmer faced each other from opposite sides of the well, Nash grabbed hold of the swaying corpse and shoved the decaying weight at the archaeologist, trying to hit him with it.

"For God's sake, stop it, man!"

Nash screamed back at Palmer at the top of his lungs, his words making no sense. Batting at the dangling body, he sent it reeling back and forth, its arms cutting the air. "Death, Palmer. Death, Sir Palmer. Look it deeeep-ly; smell it deeeep-ly. Mummy's come to nip you home, Palmey."

Palmer drew his Webley. His arm came up, but before he could shoot, I grabbed the pistol away from him, backhanding him with my left, sending him stumbling into the swaying body over the well.

"Hagee!"

Palmer snarled, then threw himself at me, only to get struck again, harder. When he began to rise I hit him again, harder still, sending him face down into the sand, his nose and eyes filling when he hit. I didn't care that he was an older man — if he'd stood up I'd have hit him again. He was crazy from the tension and the heat. Maybe we both were. Turning my back on him, I walked over to the wall where Brannigan sat sweeping the horizon with a pair of field binoculars.

"See anything."

"Yeah." He handed me the glasses. I turned the center to pull the distance closer. What had seemed a blur to the eye became hundreds of rapidly approaching riders. I handed the binoculars back to the Bomber. He was already checking the rounds in his rifle.

"Time for the main event," quipped the heavyweight.

I snorted for reply and looked about for the rest of our crew; they'd spotted the Arabs, too. Kulkai and the cook were prostrate toward the East, lamenting their lives in loud wails. Pickering was behind a packing crate, crying. Nash continued to play with the hanging body. Palmer lay where he'd fallen.

Checking the chambers in the archaeologist's revolver, I slipped it into my belt next to my .45 and then looked down at the man. Something had begun to click in the back of my head. I knew the only way to get us out of trouble was to find out what kind of trouble we were in. That meant asking the people who were mad at us. I pulled my hat down over my eyes, then yelled to Branningan.

"Watch our pals here, Bomber. Try to keep 'em away from each other's throats. If you feel like it, anyway."

"Sure thing, Jack." Brannigan wiped a bit of sand from his rifle saying, "Been nice knowin' ya."

"Don't worry about me. I'll be back."

"Glad to hear it."

Brannigan smiled and then sat back to watch the cloud of approaching riders as I walked out to meet them. I measured each step, moving across the sand at an easy pace. I had to keep a steady rhythm, which meant ignoring the Bedouins closing in on me. It wasn't easy. The rising cloud in the distance had begun settling, dispersing about the oasis at what seemed a half mile distant. The Arabs were no longer looking to hide themselves. They knew as well as we did there was no longer any point.

Shots rang out, slugs speeding past me from several directions. I knew they were only toying with me, trying to make me jump or run. I could hear them yelling one to another. As the shouting increased, so did the number of bullets dancing in the sand to the sides and in front of me.

Once I figured the Bedouins could see me clearly, I drew my .45 from my belt slowly, carefully holding it away from my body. My arm extended, I opened my fingers and let the weapon fall to the desert floor. The shooting continued around me. Ignoring the closeness of the flying lead, I reached into my belt for Palmer's Webley.

Again I extended my arm, letting the second weapon fall into the sand. Never breaking stride, careful to keep the same pace so the shooters could match, I moved beneath the broiling sun, step after step through the waves of bullets and curses and heat. I wasn't too worried; I knew I had them curious. If I hadn't, I'd have already been dead. Getting them curious and keeping them that way were two different things, though. Reaching up, I grabbed the brim of my hat and pulled it away from my head, letting it drop away behind me.

The heat struck my scalp like a sledge; the unchecked light scraped at my eyes, blinding them down to slits. At least I wasn't sweating; I'd lost all the extra body water I had the day before. My hands started shaking a little. I put them to work unbuttoning my shirt. The rifle fire around me started to slacken. When my shirt touched the sand it stopped altogether.

The sun tore at the suddenly exposed white skin, sending burning itches throughout my body. I ignored the sensations as best I could, as I had the bullets — as I was the thought of dying. Stiff-legged, shaking slightly, I marched toward the largest body of the Bedouins, totally exposed. Pushing my teeth together, I sucked in the warnings screaming in the back of my mind and marched up to within a few yards of their horses and camels. Then I stopped — and waited.

The tension between us continued for long minutes, both sides unsure as to what to do next, until—

"European...."

I turned my head toward the speaker. "Mad to die for sin of sin? Kneel down."

I ignored his question and his order, growling one of my own.

"Mulask'tar."

"Give no order. Speak to this one. Do as told. Answer question. Kneel."

"Mulask'tar."

Stepping down from his mount, the Arab walked over to me, breathing into my face. "You do not speak to the prophet. You speak to this one. Do as told. Understood?"

I understood. Smiling, I took a half step back from the man and then brought my fist up, driving it into his middle like a hammer into bread. The Bedouin fell backwards as if I'd shot him. I continued standing and staring beneath the constant sun, trying to control the heat itches ripping across my body, waiting for the tribal chieftain to come forward.

"*Mulask'tar!*"

That shout brought results; the shuffle of horses and whispers of men grew and fell as the assembly parted to allow Acbai Mulask'tar to ride through their midst. Stepping down from his horse, the man walked forward, coming to within inches of me. Reaching up, he took my face in his hands. I stayed as still as I could, feeling his calloused fingers, waiting. Bending his head, the desert leader kissed me on one cheek. Then, moving to the other side of my face, he spat.

I let Mulask'tar step back, and then spread my arms, trying to signify a desire to understand. The chieftain grunted, calling the man I'd punched to my side. As the still-groaning Arab hobbled to his master, Mulask'tar spoke in a rapid string; the other interpreted.

"You are not he of sin. But you shield he of sin. This not be."

Sin, I thought. What sin?

Staring at the old man's face, I probed his darkly burnt features through the heat and the silence. Mulask'tar stared back at me. Pushing things as far as I could, I told the interpreter, "I know of no sin. This is no argument. This is truth. If I am to understand, I must be enlightened."

The chieftain never broke off his stare. Through the entire exchange he stood silently, watching my skin bake to crimson. He was probing me, looking for something I couldn't quite fathom, keeping at it until suddenly, he decided to believe what his instincts were telling him.

Clapping his hands, he screamed an order to those behind him. Again his army parted, allowing another rider to come forward. I stared at the figure. It was small — a woman or a child. The rider's robes hid a lot, but I could tell that much. The interpreter, still fairly bent over, wheezed as he announced, "Shenra — first born of the prophet. She who is all good."

My mind raced. She was the ticket; but what did a girl, even Mulask'tar's eldest daughter have to do with anything? Unless...my eyes raced back and forth from man to child, and suddenly, the jagged lines of rage and shame, mixed in the eyes of father and daughter made a horrible, sick sense. I knew. I'd seen that look before. The eyes had been blue and she had been half a world away, but the look was the same, and I'd piled bodies like bags of trash because of it.

The Arabs had been coming at us with hatred and death like a whirlwind, but not for all of us — just one; the one stupid enough to chance forgetting where he was and what he was doing. The one without the control to stay away from a child's body — the one who woke us in the middle of the night and told everyone to run because, unlike the rest of us, he knew what had happened, and what was going to happen.

"Palmer."

Mulask'tar's eyes glossed over with a hate and a desire beyond description. I understood. He knew it. The sheik spoke through his man once more. "You had no understanding of this sin, did you?"

I shook my head numbly, still trying to understand the stupidity of it all.

"You have no children, do you?"

I shook my head again. That part of his anger I could not match. Taking the edge of his own caftan, Mulask'tar wiped away the spittle still slightly damp on my cheek. As he spoke, his interpreter said, "Your idea to ransom our water — yes?"

"Yes."

"Very good. Intelligent. You force all leaders talk. Mulask'tar held by desert law. All forced wait."

I stared at the stretched lines of riders disappearing to his left and to his right off around the oasis. Bitter, hard men, astride equally rough animals, they'd come far and waited long for one thing. I figured they had a right to it.

I looked the chieftain in the eye. He understood. At a hand signal from the warrior leader, two horses were brought forward. Another man brought me a caftan to wrap around myself. Once we were mounted, the chieftain slipped his own burnoose onto my baking head. He shouted a few orders to his men to which they roared agreement. Then, Mulask'tar and I rode for the oasis alone.

As we reached the crumbling wall, I could see Palmer, being held by a freshly bleeding Brannigan. The ex-heavyweight shouted, "Crazy bedbug took my rifle when he saw you comin'. Tried to shoot the two of you. When I took it, he hit me and tried cuttin' his own throat. I stopped him."

"Good."

I unknotted a length of leather stripping from my saddle, carrying it with me as I dismounted and crossed the sand to where Brannigan held Palmer.

"No," he screamed. "Don't give me to them. Please, For the love of sweet Lord God Jesus Christ — you're a white man — don't give me to them! *Please!!*"

I wanted to tell him to shut up, but I couldn't speak. I was too angry, too crazy from the heat and from thinking of what Palmer had done to trust myself to stop at simply cursing the man. Knotting the leather around his wrists, I then dragged him across the oasis to the horse I'd ridden where a coil of chain-threaded rope hung from the saddle horn. I threw Palmer to his knees and then reached for the rope, pulling its lariat end open just wide enough to fit his head. When I went to put it on the archaeologist's head, he thrashed back and forth, staring at it wildly, begging for mercy. I only smiled. Grabbing him around the neck with one hand, I slapped him across the face with the chain-woven rope, once, twice, and then again, until he was almost senseless.

"Oh, God," blubbered Palmer. "Oh, please — please. I'm so sorry."

I ignored his meager repentance; it was too little, too late. Still smiling, I slipped the noose over his head and then jerked him roughly across the sand to where Mulask'tar waited. Filigree strands cut into Palmer's neck, blood smearing from their urgings, leaking slowly into his shirt.

"Why? Why must you do this? Why won't you kill me?"

Handing the end of Palmer's leash to the desert chieftain, I told the archaeologist, "Because, just like you said, Sir Palmer — everyone pays for their mistakes eventually — everyone."

Mulask'tar wheeled his steed, dragging his prey behind him. Watching them leave, I told Brannigan to gather everyone together. Nash's mad laughter mixed with Palmer's burning howls, but I paid no attention to either of them. While Brannigan lumbered toward the well, trying to favor his wounds, I walked back out into the desert to fetch my automatic.

It was all I needed. Nothing else mattered.

Change From Your Dollar

IT ISN'T OFTEN one picks up their draw and finds their attempt to fill an inside straight has been successful. Especially when they need two cards to do it. I had thrown away a three and a seven, holding onto a nine, a ten, and a Jack. Picking up an eight and a wild two was the highlight of my morning. Hoping I'd masked my excitement and gratitude to the gods, I eyed my hand, carefully adjusting my bluff mask. My only hope of winning lay in convincing everyone else at the table that I was bluffing. It wasn't going to be easy. They were a sharp bunch of guys.

To my immediate right sat Grampy. He wasn't old, it was just a nickname his wild, pepper-gray beard had earned him when we were both with the Special Forces. That and the ever-present beer bottles he hid behind kept his raw features unreadable. He was by far the most dangerous player at the table, with a steel hard poker face and the nerve of a Russian cavalry officer.

Next to him sat Rich Violano. The only one at the table who didn't drink, Rich used the chewing of a constant stream of munchies to keep his face too animated to read. That, along with the rigid, fact-seeking expression he'd created for himself over his ten-year career as one of the city's top crime reporters made him no pushover, either.

The Lil' Doc was to his right, running his hand through his hair, worrying at his ever-expanding bald spot. The Doc was not a great player, but he had learned to read the rest of us over the years. If the others sensed a winner at the table, he could at least pick it up from them.

Finally, to my left was Hubert. Hu's main tactic for baffling the competition is to continually crack wise. His never-ending string of jokes, sarcastic comments, and insults has won him plenty of pots, mainly by annoying the concentration out of those playing with him.

I had this pot, though. When we lay our hands down, I reached forward and swept the careless pile of bills toward me without waiting for anyone's approval. The circle of groans around me was all the confirmation I needed. Grampy threw his cards down in disgust.

"That's it," he cried. "I'm callin' a time out."

As he lumbered off toward my bathroom, Hubert called out, "D-Don't fall in, f-fatso."

"You," Grampy threw the words over his shoulder, "I kill later."

"Geek murdered in New York detective's apartment," shouted the Lil' Doc. "Film at eleven."

"Hey," added Rich, stretching his round body, "let's have a little respect for the world of print, here."

"Okay," grinned the Doc. "Extra edition at your local newsstand at eleven."

"Thank you."

"You're entirely welcome."

"C'mon, you guys," I said. "Let's clear away some of this debris before we get started again."

"Ah, my highest f-fuckin' goal in life...to clean up J-Jack Hagee's dump of an apartment."

"Up yours, mutant," I told him, bouncing a wadded paper bag off his head. "You help make it a dump, you help unmake it."

The bantering continued, but work got under way. We had started playing around ten o'clock on Friday night. It was now almost three on Saturday morning. We were surrounded by empty bottles and garbage-stuffed paper plates. The ashtrays were filled, even though only three of us were smokers, and everywhere around the apartment lay open pickle and mustard jars, microwave brownie packages, potato chip bags, and the hundred other scraps and tatters we'd strewn about us while we'd played. As we puttered about, emptying the wastebaskets and reorganizing the grease and crumbs, Rich yelled:

"Okay; how about a round of 'Stupid Crook Tricks'?"

"Sure," responded Hubert. "I g-got one."

"Shoot," I told him.

"H-Heard about this one last week. The c-cops c-called up the last known residences of a bunch of crooks — petty guys, but d-dozens of 'em, right? Anyway, they tell whoever they get on the line that the g-guy they're lookin' for has won Super Bowl tickets, okay? So then, they tell 'em where and when to send the 'winner' to get his prize. Then, then they…"

Hu started laughing at his own story to the point where he almost could not continue. Catching hold of himself, though, he managed to quiet down and finish.

"Whoosh. Anyway, then they deck out this w-warehouse with 'Superbowl Contest' signs — wait for the crooks, and then arrest the lot of them when they come in. For the price of a few signs, some coffee and doughnuts, and the phone calls, they netted over two thousand guys."

We all chuckled.

"Well," I said, deciding to take a turn, "I must admit I heard a good one the other day, too. Some guy robs this bank once. Then he goes back and robs it again. Then he goes back and robs it again. And then, again. And then, like an idiot, for the fifth time in two weeks, he walks in again. By this time they have an F.B.I. man behind the counter. So, of course, before the guy even gets up to the window, the fed spots the moron and arrests him. Then, honest, while they're taking him out, the guy has the nerve to ask how they'd caught on to him."

We all laughed again. After the noise died down, Rich offered another true tale of criminal stupidity.

"I saw this one on the wire. Guy walks into a bank, gets up to the teller, points to his belt buckle, which has the handle of a gun sticking out from behind it, and tells the woman, 'You know what to do.' She did, all right. She gave him the money, and then told the police to watch out for a guy with a big silver belt buckle that said 'Greg.'"

"He wore his name to a robbery?" I asked, half-disbelieving Rich.

"Scout's honor. They caught him before he could even get home."

We all laughed long and hard at that one. Agreeing Rich was the hands-down winner, we went back to clearing out some breathing room for ourselves in the midst of the debris we had created. While we did, the Doc asked, "Hey, Rich, you're a legendary connoisseur of fine food, right?"

"Yes, I am. Yes, I am," agreed Rich vigorously. "Pass the Ding Dongs, will you?"

"Seriously, I wanted to ask you a question."

"Okay; shoot."

"What was the best hamburger you ever had?"

"Can I ask, for curiosity's sake, why you would want to know this?"

"Sure," answered the Doc. "I'm seeing someone new and they're a real beef patty fiend, so I'm just trying to get an idea of good recipes or settings, or, well — you know," he grinned sheepishly. "Anything that'll help the ol' cause along."

"Huummmm," replied Rich, stroking his chin, his eyes lost in some other world reviewing the great ground beef platters of the past. "There's always Dunaier's, down in the Village. They have a real good burger menu."

"Yeah...?" The Doc's eyes lit up.

"Oh, yeah," assured Rich. "They fry, char, or broil — your preference — and all their toppings are the best. They only use good garden tomatoes and lettuce, no hothouse stuff. And if you want cheese, they pile it on. Real cheese, too. No imitation, cheese-like, processed cheese-food substitute — cheese. Real cheese."

"Kid," yelled Grampy from the bathroom, shouting over the roar of the flushing toilet, "if you've got a date to impress, do yer cookin' at home." Coming back into the living room/kitchen area of my apartment, he wiped his hands on his shirt as he continued.

"Last time I was out in Jackson Hole, I came across the world's best hamburger. Ya cook this up fer yer new sweetie's dinner an' ya'll be cookin' again fer breakfast, too. Now lissen up. First ya take bacon, already half/three quarters cooked, and some of them little green jalapenos, and grind 'em all up into yer beef, right? Then, ya fry the suckers up, no other way — ya gotta fry 'em — then, just hit 'em with a little salt and pepper. When they're done, melt down some mozzarella on 'em, and hat 'em with a thick slice of raw onion — don't cook the damn thing — and you will have yerself one class A demolition derby of a hamburger; guaranteed to rope you an evenin' a'romance."

While I mentally agreed that Grampy's recipe sounded like it would make a damn fine hamburger, the Doc turned to me, asking, "What about you, Jack? What was the best patty melt you ever gobbled down?"

"Seriously?"

"Yeah, sure."

"Well; in all honesty, the best burger I ever ate came from McDonald's."

The predictable groans and boos echoed through my apartment. I reminded everyone that it was three in the morning, quieting them down for the sake of my neighbors, and then told them:

"Look, I'll happily admit I've had better hamburgers than the average McDonald's burger but, the Doc is asking for stories about the best burgers we ever ate, and the best burger I ever ate was in a McDonald's."

"I sense a story here," said Rich, sitting back as if someone had just popped a top movie in the VCR.

"I thought we were gonna play cards," growled Grampy.

"Ahh, piped in Hubert, "g-give it a break, ya big turd. Haven't you w-won enough of our hard-earned cash tonight?"

"I can never get enough of your cash, dick-face."

"Well, I've had enough cards for a while," said the Lil' Doc. Flopping onto my couch next to Rich, he insisted, "So, c'mon; tell this story. What made this one burger out of the billions and billions they've fried up so special?"

Putting down the ashtray I'd just emptied, I looked around the room to find myself suddenly the center of attention. Even Grampy had parked himself with a Coors, waiting for me to explain. With a sigh, I got my own drink and chair and told the story.

I'd received my discharge from the service a week earlier. I'd been assigned to Military Intelligence during the last two years of my tour of duty — where I'd first met Grampy. Neither one of us were the college man/ROTC type they liked to put in charge of things. But we were clever at killing people and blowing things up, so they put up with our obvious lack of breeding and utilized our talents for the good of America's goals around the world.

Two years of sneaking around in Southeast Asia and Central America were enough for me. Grampy left long before I did, fed up with the whole system of the government owning the keys to the jukebox, gifted with the opportunity for early retirement via an intense shrapnel wound in his leg.

At the time, I had no idea of what I wanted to do with my life. I had a girl back home I thought I should probably go marry, as if that would somehow clear all the confusion out of my system. It didn't, but I wouldn't discover that until later.

Taking stock of my feelings, I realized that the service had wrung me out — used me up. I felt as if I were in my sixties, tired, useless, feeble. Death's grin hunched over my shoulder often in those days, whispering insanities in my ear, calling me to join it on the other side of the cold divide.

At that time, the first answer that came to me for every situation was a violent one. The checkout clerk is too slow, slap her silly; waiter doesn't get the order right, gut punch. Cop handing over the speeding ticket — kill him. Kill his partner. Car's rented under an alias...no way to trace me...tracks covered. Clever as ever. Don't take shit. Don't take it — kill anyone who presents a threat — remove every obstacle.

Not that I actually slipped. I kept the rage and the laughing whispers bottled inside, fighting the pressure with logic and hard-won self-control. But my discharge'd put me out on the street with the rest of the civilians, and it was a disturbing set of circumstances. I had about three hundred pounds of souvenirs and junk I'd dragged around the globe from post to post with me stashed in the trunk of my rental car, and a hefty bankroll, but that was it, all my worldly goods.

None of it amounted to anything that spoke of a life of even modest proportions. It was just bric-a-brac, photographs of people and places with little meaning, junk picked up on street corners and novelty shops. Toys and clutter and the garbage of youth, bundled up and shoved in the back of some corporation's car.

I decided to drift for a while, not able to think of anything better to do. After my discharge I had no real place to go. My home life had always been a withering, callous joke to me. My C.O. had some influence in the real world.

He said he could pull some strings, get me on a police force somewhere, which of course meant more uniforms, more orders, more death and killing, and all the rest of the pain that had driven me from the service in the first place. When the voices had started I'd almost panicked; the little whispers in the back of my head, urging me to violence at any opportunity, towards others or myself, were too tempting.

Deciding to try something else, I rented a car in San Francisco, the first place my feet touched down in the country. After that, I bought a sleeping bag, some basic supplies, and food for a few weeks, tossed it all in the trunk with my cardboard-boxed mementoes and got out of the city, quick.

I needed to get away from people — away from the cars and their noise and dirt, away from the screeching and the whining, the never-ending lights and cement and shuffling mobs. Stopping at the Grand Canyon'd seemed like a good idea at first, but it washed out quickly. I couldn't take the tourists, asking questions, being too cheerful, too friendly. You can't get angry at someone for being decent to a fellow human being, but I wanted to, badly, so I got back in the car and kept moving.

I finally ended up in the Rockies. I found a dirt turnoff, what appeared to be an abandoned logging run, that left the back road I'd been following. It was nothing more than a trail through the surrounding trees, one filled with rocks the size of garbage cans and ruts deep enough to hide a dog. It was a slow drive, one which did my renter little good, but didn't bother me. It was perfect. When the forest finally fell away on both sides, it emptied out onto an overgrown plain of tangle brush and young trees. There was no one in any direction. Which was just what I needed.

Setting up camp took fifteen minutes. Fifteen minutes after that I was a mile back in the woods, wandering. I had a lot of questions to work out, and a lot of anger with which to deal. I wasn't even sure what I was angry at or about. I just knew I was, and that I had to do something about it before I tried dealing with people again. Figuring that being alone out in the country would help, I kept walking. I hiked until it was dark, and then made my way back to camp. The next morning when the sun woke me up, I went out in a different direction, again not returning until nightfall.

I followed the pattern for the next few days — eating a little here and there, sleeping on the ground under the trees, swimming in freezing mountain lakes, barehandedly scaling the few cliffs I found — trying to put the destructive voices in my head aright. The air was fresh and biting, the lake water clean and brisk. I didn't see another soul, or wish for one around. For most people it would have been a dream vacation. For me each day was worse than the one before it.

My mood grew darker, my vision clouding over in a red haze for hours at a time. I started talking to the countryside around me, threatening, imploring, begging answers from the sky and the trees — answers to questions I did not know — all of which only served to make me angrier. I'd removed myself from society to allow my bad mood to blow over, but it hadn't worked. Now I was spoiling for a fight, looking for any excuse to employ the tricks of my recent trade and beat the living hell out of something. It was the worst time possible for what happened next.

On the fourth morning of my little wilderness holiday I went out again, but returned in the early afternoon. Frustrated with the results of my 'cure,' I had decided to pack and leave, not knowing or caring where I went next as long as it was away from the quiet of the mountain top. As I approached my camp, I heard something larger than the rabbits and chipmunks I'd been seeing for days moving ahead of me. Curiosity dispelling my anger for a minute, I glided through the trees, eager to see who was poking around my site, and what it would take to provoke them. I found more than I'd expected.

The noise was coming from a bear, nosing my car, breaking the windows and digging at the trunk. I came into the clearing shaking my fists and screaming. The bear paid me scant attention. Picking up a rock, I threw it beanball hard and straight. It came in smoothly and bounced off the bear's noggin. Smiling to myself smugly, I shouted at it again, warning it away from my possessions, less angry with life merely because I'd had the chance to inflict a little pain.

As I neared the car, still shouting, the bear came around the front end, exposing its full size. It was a grizzly. A large one. A very large one.

Suddenly, my self-destructive mood cleared a bit. I held my ground, but didn't advance any further. The bear stared at me, swinging its massive head from left to right, trying to get my scent. Luckily there was a slight breeze in my face, keeping me upwind. The grizzly, not knowing exactly what it was facing, kept trying the air, growling deep in its throat, challenging me.

Its growls turned quickly to roars. It didn't take a Rhodes scholar to figure out that my companion was mad, and for some reason about more than getting banged in the head with a rock. This grizzly was spoiling for a fight, looking for something to smash just for the fun of it. The damage to my renter vouched for that. Coming all the way around the car, the bear stretched up onto its hind legs and then roared again.

I roared back at it, bellowing with all the hate I had in me. It roared again, slapping at the air with its claws, showing me it meant business. I picked up a thick branch near my feet and swung it over my head, growling back, letting it know I felt the same. The grizzly took another step forward, continuing its challenge. So did I. As we drew a tiny fifteen yards from each other, the danger I was in began to dawn on me. The animal in front of me was not a simple black or brown bear — it was a grizzly, one standing nearly nine feet tall, and looking as if it would tip the scales at well over a thousand pounds. Any one of its claws weighed more than the knife on my belt. Its teeth, long, curled, and jagged, were dark with the tartar of many years.

Suddenly, the tiny part of my brain that still cared whether or not I lived or died began to get that fact through to me; I was facing a monster. A giant monster, one that could run thirty miles an hour. A monster fast enough to knock fish out of a river with one swipe, and strong enough to kill a horse with one blow. It was not a cub, nor on its last legs; it was a tremendously powerful brute in the prime of its existence, filled with rage and looking at me as a place to deposit it.

As it stepped forward I roared again, loud and long, reaching down into the bottom of my lungs for every bit of air I could find. The bear hesitated. Whatever was driving the animal choked for a moment, instinct cautioning it. Caution ruled only for the moment, though. Its rib cage expanded as it sucked down a breath. Leaning forward to keep its balance, it roared back, a howling threat that shook the trees. The challenge went on and on, shaking branches and the air around us. It was not a bluff; I was not facing an animal that was going to be cowed. I had squared off with a demon, one that then decided the pregame entertainment was over.

Still roaring, it took its first step forward. I roared back, shaking my branch, kicking dirt in its direction. It continued on its way. I hefted the club in my hand, checking its sturdiness. It was a good three feet long, sure and solid as a baseball bat. The grizzly continued toward me, not measuring its steps but merely walking forward — no longer challenging; just closing distance. I spread my feet, planting myself firmly.

We were down to the last few yards. The beast came closer, still thundering its rage. I screamed back, daring, taunting, waiting. It stepped up in front of me and reached down, massive arms and paws grabbing for me. I swung from overhead, bringing the branch down on its closing paws. The branch broke, splinters filling the air. The grizzly howled and swatted at where I had been. Bouncing away from the swinging paws, I threw the piece of wood still in my hand, catching it on the snout.

The raw edge of the wood tore open its nose. Blood sluiced into its mouth, giving it a taste of the damage I had done. It lunged again, cutting the air with its claws, missing me by inches. Dancing away, I speculated on my chances of getting back to my renter, wondering at what good it might do me. True, my rifle was there in the trunk, but it was only a .22 Long, good for small game and deer if the shot was well placed. Even if I could get to the car and get the trunk open and get the rifle free, assembled and loaded, it still wouldn't be enough weapon to handle the bear.

It came at me again — charging on all fours. I leapt to the side again, but it turned and followed me, quicker than the last time. I dodged it and then kicked, bringing my steel-toed boot upward into its throat. It did no good. The bear was too well-muscled, protected by too many layers of fat and fur. It was a blow that would have killed most any human being. The bear shrugged it off as one would a luck punch on their birthday.

Taking advantage of my surprise, the grizzly stood and turned, closing its arms, nearly catching me in its powerful grasp. I ducked and punched it in the side, searching for its kidneys, twice, three, four times. Annoyed, the monster clipped me with a backhanded slap, sending me reeling.

I stood clumsily, like a drunk getting up off the ice. Nothing was broken, but where the beast had connected, my left shoulder was a knotting slice of pain. I stumbled back several yards into the trees with no strategy in mind, not even the beginning of a plan forming. The bear, already having forgotten whatever damage I might have done it, turned and followed. It was slower, more cautious now, but just as determined. Blood dribbled from its muzzle into its mouth, mixing with its frothing juices, creating a scarlet saliva that splashed freely on the ground as it stalked me.

I picked up the occasional loose rock or branch and hurled it at the following monster, but to no avail; there was no deterring it now. I had started something and it was going to see it through to the end. I had caused it grief and it wanted me dead. It was as simple as that.

We moved uphill through the trees. The grizzly had learned its lesson. It no longer charged or took to its hind legs. Staying low to the ground and always on a straight, closing angle to me, it pushed its way closer, confident that sooner or later it would have me. For my part, I had to keep one eye on the terrain above me and one on the bear. I couldn't turn and make a break for it; the grizzly was too fast; it could've run me to ground in a matter of seconds.

Taking too many backward steps while watching the beast, though, almost finished me. Before I saw it, my left foot went down deep into a tiny, marshy pool. Sticking for a second, it came free only with effort. The lost moment became the monster's chance. Throwing its head back with a roar, it charged forward full force.

I broke into a run then, slopping through the mud, tearing through the trees fast as I could manage. My brain cleared, leaping back to basic training — remembering twenty-mile marches with full packs — ten-mile runs — days of exhaustion that pushed me far further than I'd ever dreamed I could be pushed. I ran uphill, trying to keep my wind, dodging trees and brush, setting a jagged pattern in an attempt to keep the bear off balance and unable to gain speed. I wanted to look at the monster on my tail, but I forced myself to remember the words of my C.O., Major Rice: looking back wastes time and energy, throws you off your track, and gets you killed. If things get to the point where you have to run, then run, and don't look back!

I ran. Moving across the side of the mountain, I dodged left then right then over again. I circled large rocks and tore straight through brush; if I approached two trees close together from the left, I would cut to the right upon exiting, anything to slow up the bear and hopefully extract myself from the mess I'd put myself in.

After ten minutes my chest began shrieking the strain of the chase to the rest of my body. Running uphill in weighted boots over bad terrain, for those who haven't tried it recently, is quite an exercise. Holding back the pain, though, I kept running, ignoring the lead spreading down my legs, the thin, slicing folds of agony pistoning through my arms and shoulders. I begged out further yards, ignoring the throbbing red agong stabbing through me, forcing my feet to keep pumping, up and down, up and down, up and down, constantly pushing myself away from the bellowing thing on my trail.

Then, rounding a small corner of rock, I spotted a bramble tangle a couple of hundred yards down the mountainside. The only problem was it doubled back toward the direction of the bear. If I made for it, there was a chance the grizzly might cut me off if he caught on to what I was doing. Checking over my shoulder, I saw the beast had decided to try a tactic of its own. He was actually ranging up the mountain behind, but above me, working upward so he could force me down.

"Well," I thought, "you want me down — you got it!"

Turning suddenly, I jumped from a small bluff, dropping ten feet in a second. Hitting hard, my feet skidded on the surface leaves and loam. I tried to stop but couldn't, my slide continuing unabated until a tree finally loomed into my path that I could not avoid. Slam! I hit it with a stunning thud that shut my eyes and showed me stars. My right arm went numb, hanging useless as I tried to stand. Shaking my head, I slid my back up the tree, working slowly to stand until I remembered. . .the bear.

Reality came back to me in the form of harsh, guttural roars. The thing had spotted me quickly and changed its course to come charging down the mountain after me. Forgetting my pain, I rounded the tree and fumbled off for the bramble tangle I'd spotted before. I closed the distance in stumbling leaps, half-jumping, half-hobbling. Behind me, the grizzly's steps came in precision thuds. Front paws hitting the ground — bang. Back paws pushing off — boom. Bang, boom. Bang, boom. Closer and closer behind me, thundering down the mountain.

Reaching the brush, not bothering to look back to see if I would be followed into the thicket, I dropped to all fours — face in the dirt — and crawled forward as fast as I could. Thorns tore at my face and hands and neck, spikes gouged and bled me. My legs and arms, sides and back and head flowed freely, none of the clothing I wore heavy enough to protect me. I was thirty feet into the mess when the monster hit the edge.

I'd hoped it might be tired of our game and leave me alone within the den of pain I'd chosen as a hiding place. I might as well have hoped for peace in the Middle East. As I watched in horror, giant, outfield's glove-sized blurs of fur and claw tore their way into the tight-knit jungle of needling pain. Whole bushes and saplings flew through the dirt-choked air. What it couldn't knock out of its way it trampled underfoot with complete indifference.

I'd entered the thicket in a fear run, ignoring the agony of advancement until I could go no further, hoping I'd gotten far enough back to protect myself. Now, seeing that I had to move out again, every new pain was immediately realized. I stayed as low as I could, trying to go underneath the majority of it all, but it was no way to make speed. Behind me, the grizzly tore forward, vines and branches pulling it back, tearing its skin and fur away in noticeable chunks.

It closed the distance between us — fifteen feet, another lunge — twelve feet. I scrambled further, it threw itself forward — ten feet, step — nine feet — eight — five — three—

The monster's bleeding jaws snapped at my retreating feet, crunching, tearing the brambles away between me and it. The grizzly was thoroughly entangled now, creepers and branches wrapped around its neck and front paws in a criss-crossed mess that simply wouldn't allow it to move any further. Barely aware of the monster's restraints, I continued to drag myself away from it, my arms smeared with blood and crushed leaves and mud. Then my hands hit rock. Lifting my head, I could see I'd hit a small boulder. Taking a chance, I pulled myself atop it hoping for a view of some way out of my predicament. Looking off to my left, I saw a tall, easily climbable tree not too far away to reach. The only thing separating us was a few dozen yards of open space, and ten more feet of the thicket.

I felt the shape of the rock below me with my feet, trying to find a position that would allow me to jump without slipping. Behind me, able to now see as well as smell me, the grizzly redoubled its efforts to free itself. I could sense the strain on the vines holding it in place, feel the ground loosening around their roots. The beast's nightmare roars washed over me, panicking my attempts to straighten myself on the rock. Then, suddenly, as my feet found their perch, the bear tore free.

I launched myself instantly, landing in the last two feet of brambles. I came down harshly on my side, a number of the thick, inch-long spikes and scores of the smaller thorns breaking off and sticking in me. Rolling my way free, I regained my feet and hobbled for the tree I'd spotted earlier.

Behind me the grizzly pressed onward, ripping its way through the rest of the thicket. Thorn saplings were pushed aside or broken in half. The monster crashed free a moment after I did, angling across the swath of ferns and grass toward the same destination as me because it was where I was headed.

Reaching the sizable oak, I grabbed the lowest strong branch and began pulling myself upward. Heedless of the noise behind me, I inched my way up the thick trunk, dragging myself higher as quickly as I could manage. My hands were punctured and sliced to the point where the blood flowed freely any place where skin showed through the dirt. By the time the grizzly reached the tree my fingers had stopped working. Using my wrists like hooks, I pulled myself to a spot some twenty feet from the forest floor and then hung on as best I could as the monster started its assault.

Rising up to its full height, the bear stretched its inhumanly long arms upward, trying to reach me. Seeing it couldn't, it tried to come up after me. Digging its claws in, it tore free chunks of bark and wood the size of door stops, but could not manage the climb. Like most grizzlies, it wasn't built for it.

Giving up the attempt, it threw its head back and roared, letting me know it was by no means giving up completely. It howled again, and then scarred the tree further, stripping away large areas of bark with each swipe. Then, suddenly, it reared back, coming forward in a rush, slamming its massive weight against the tree. Branches shook; leaves fell. I almost joined them. Not pausing, the grizzly threw itself forward again, and then again. The tree vibrated hard enough to hurt my teeth.

It crashed against the oak repeatedly, tangles of bramble vines whipping behind it, still stuck in the fur of its legs and back and neck. I hung on tight in desperation, scarcely able to believe the monster was still after me. My brain raced, trying to figure out 'why?' What could have I have done to make the howling thing below as determined as it was to finish me off? Then, suddenly, staring down at the beast told the story.

Sticking out of the thick fold of muscle behind its neck was the broken shaft of an old hunting arrow. Its edges were smoothed; the blood crust circling it dark and hard. Now I knew why the bear below me hated the smell and sight of man and his things — and why it was determined to kill me. And, I knew there was no chance it might tire and leave me alone. Which made it all clear — only one of us was going to walk away from our confrontation.

I had to get clear of my perch, and only one way out presented itself. Steeling my nerve, I sucked in a deep breath, held it, then replaced it with another. As the monster below continued to slam itself against the tree, I caught hold of my nerve, calming my runaway pulse. The bear backed up again, getting ready to crash against our tree once more. Go ahead, I thought. I'm ready for you.

As the grizzly began its run, I changed my grip, ready to release my hold at the right moment. It hit the tree again with a jarring smash. Absorbing the blow as best I could, I took a fast aim and then leaped. Falling fast, one steel-toed boot held straight down as my weapon, I landed on the bear's neck, cracking the splintered arrow lodged deep within it.

A roar cascaded out of the grizzly. It shot up and over, dazed and maddened with pain. Blood broke free in rivers, splattering through the air in response to the animal's crazed gyrations. I hit the ground awkwardly on one foot and the opposite shoulder, the newest pains heaped on with the rest, all of them begging me to lay still and just let the fight end. Dragging myself to my feet, though, I headed away from the bear as quickly as I could, determined to play every card I had.

By the time the grizzly had gotten its own pain under control and remembered me, I had a sizable lead on it. One I could not maintain, however. Following my trail, it came through the forest in bounds, sniffing the ground on the run. It sighted me in minutes, howling in triumph when it did. It no longer mattered, though. I had dragged myself as far as I needed to. I was in position to make my last stand.

Without care or subtlety, the bear lowered its head slightly and charged up the slope I had planted myself atop. Despite the damage I had inflicted on it, it came at me fast, determined to take me with it. I held as still as I could, leaning to the left, trying to signal the beast that that was the direction I would dodge toward when it arrived. It gobbled up the yards between us, snorting and panting its rage, only a moment away.

Finally, when we were only a second apart, I pushed off with all my strength hurling myself to the right. The bear, angling left as I had hoped, skidded forward as it tried to correct its attack. My plan had worked. Before it could stop itself, the grizzly slipped on the thick grass of the cliff edge I'd chosen, tumbling forward and over in a howling scramble, tearing free two clumps of sod as it went. I lay on the swath where I'd fallen, panting uncontrollably. I was tired and aching, bleeding in dribbles and spurts from a hundred spots. My lungs ached as fire rippled through them, each breath an unstoppable, shooting pain. I wanted to just curl up and sleep where I'd fallen, but I couldn't allow myself the luxury — not yet, anyway. After what I'd been through, my mind refused to let me relax until I confirmed that the bear had finally been disposed of.

Dragging myself to the edge, I stuck my head over, and then stared in disbelief. The bear was coming back. My eyes opened to the size of saucers. The bear was coming back. With my mind screaming at me to move, to run away shrieking, I remained frozen, head hanging in the air, mouth agape — the bear was coming back. It hadn't flown outward far enough to fall to the rocks I'd hoped to smash it against. Somehow it had twisted in mid-air and landed on a slope some thirty feet below. Watching it lumber upward toward me, I realized it probably hadn't even broken any bones. I searched quickly for a stone or log big enough to do some damage with, but nothing lay at hand. Another glance over the edge showed me the monster was halfway back to the top.

Pulling all my remaining strength together, I turned and hobbled back for my car. No escape was possible through driving; the road was far too bad to allow any speed. There was a gun in the trunk, though, and as small as it was, it was the only hope I had left.

As the car came in sight, I could hear the bear behind me, pulling itself up over the cliff edge. By the time I reached the renter, the beast was a mere fifty yards distant. I fumbled the trunk open, amazed I'd been able to retain the keys throughout my struggle, and pulled the rifle free from its hiding place. The bear was forty yards away. By the time I had it assembled and my box of shells in hand, it had covered two thirds of that distance and was picking up speed. Knowing I had no time to load and aim, I did the only thing I could; jumping into the trunk, I pulled the lid down and locked myself inside.

Trapped in the darkness, before I could even begin to get my bearings, the bear attacked the car. Its massive paws came down on the trunk over and over, the noise of each blow echoing in my ears. Then, suddenly, sunlight hit my eyes. The bear had managed to puncture the trunk lid with its claws. I had scarcely register this new threat, when another set of holes pierced open above me.

Realizing I had to do something quickly, I kicked at the back seat with all the fury I could muster. Hitting as hard as I could with both legs, I felt the side restraints snap. I kicked again, pushing it free, opening the crawlspace for myself as the monster's claws snagged in the metal above my face. Working my way forward, trying to retain the rifle and shell box as I did so, I started through the narrow aperture.

I got no further than halfway, however, when suddenly the car began to shake violently. Trying to hold my position as well as my weapon, I suddenly lost everything as the left side of the renter was hoisted off the ground. Before I could even register shock, the car crashed to a thud on its roof. The force of the impact flattened the vehicle slightly, the walls of the crawlspace pinching me sharply at the waist. Gasoline splashed down my back, transforming each of my cuts and scrapes into wells of flaying agony.

Desperate to escape the burning cascade, I twisted violently to the side where there was more room, finally making my way into the back seat. Laying on the roof, I held my sides, the skin over my ribs rubbed away from my struggle, gasping desperately to hold back the screams. I had lost the rifle and the shells and hadn't even noticed. Without conscious thought I crawled for the left side of the car for no better reason than that side was the closest. The random action saved my life.

Just as I began to pull myself through the broken window, the grizzly's head came through the one on the right, its spring tight jaws snapping at my feet. I pulled myself through and rolled free over the twisted metal and broken glass just as the door frame around the bear collapsed. It pushed its way in up to the shoulders, still desperate to catch hold of me. Stumbling to my feet, I discovered that the trunk had spilled open, retching my belongings across the grass. I pulled the rifle butt toward me, only to find the barrel had been bent in the overturning. Dropping the now-useless .22, I searched for the only other weapon I could think of. The car shook and bounced as the grizzly tried to extract itself. Seconds later, I pulled one of the flares from the rental company's emergency kit. It was soaked with gasoline, just like the car and everything in it and myself.

Without thinking I yanked the ignition end free, tearing a fingernail in half, the pain causing me to drop the flare. It exploded into life, flames dancing up and down its petrol-soaked length. The grizzly howled with rage in the background, almost disentangled from the ruined car. Knowing I had no time left to think, I reached down, grabbed up the burning flare, and threw it into the gasoline-drenched trunk.

"And...?"

I had drifted away from my audience for a moment, lost in the lateness of the hour and the memory. Responding to the Doc, I asked:

"And what?"

"And," answered Grampy, "what happened next?"

"Oh. Well, that was pretty much it. The bear'd cut its neck open on the car window. Between that and getting set on fire, and whatever might have happened to it when it went over the cliff, it just gave up the ghost. Never even pulled free from the car."

"That isn't what I meant," said the Doc. "I want to know about the McDonald's burger."

"Oh, that. Well, I had to get off the mountain on foot, then. I'd lost everything that'd been in the car, all my money, except for a loose dollar I found in the grass. It took me until the next day, but I finally got back to the bottom. The first civilization I came to was one of those long stretches of road hemmed on both sides by a hundred stores. I dragged myself into the McDonalds, lay down my money, and got a cheeseburger."

"And c-change from your dollar. You t-took that with ya, right?"

I thought about the bear for another second, something I hadn't done in a long time. I thought about how senseless our whole battle had been, again wondering if it had been the rock I'd thrown that had started it all, or if it would have attacked any man because of the one who'd maimed it.

And, once again unable to reach any conclusion, I stored the memory back in its usual resting place and told Hubert that I had indeed taken my change. Why not, I thought; at the time — not counting my life — it was all I had.

Nine Dragons

THE OUTLINER HAD struck again. New York City's police were still baffled over their newest serial murderer, a seemingly actual random killer who drew chalk outlines around the bodies of his victims. Why he did it was apparently as big a mystery to everyone on the force as it was to Chet Green, the *New York Post* reporter who'd made the city's latest freak his pet follow-up story.

So far, the red-ink rag informed us, the Outliner's score was holding at eight. The first had been an unceremoniously white-chalk-surrounded knifing on 116th up in Harlem. The next two had gone down in Brooklyn, one in Flatbush, the other in the Heights. With the fourth he switched from white to blue chalk, and came off the back streets to leave his prey in the dairy aisle of a Queens Key Food Mart. Pulling that one off during business hours stunned a lot of people. The fifth he left on the observation deck of the Staten Island Ferry, sketched around in pink chalk, budding out at all the appendages in crude but recognizable roses. The sixth became his first female victim. No rape, just the familiar slash across the throat and a five-color rainbow made up of four lines of chalk and one of blood.

The latest was his masterpiece, though. In an Empire State Building men's room, he left two known homosexuals locked in anal intercourse nailed to the wall with railroad spikes. Again, no one had a clue as to how he'd pulled it off. Police estimates insisted he would've needed a minimum of forty-five minutes, even with the dearly departed's cooperation. The suspicions of cooperation came from the fact the purple chalk surrounding the couple was underneath the blood which had flowed from their individual stigmata, along with the suggestion of the jockey's penetrating genitalia, a detail impossible for the Outliner to have arranged if his subjects had already been dead.

The Post had run the photos available to it, the chalk outline, the scab-like pool of crusting blood, the smear-covered body bags being wheeled out of the room, et cetera…all part of the people's sacred right to information.

Weary of the people and their sacred rights, I folded my newspaper, shoved it behind the counter I was leaning against, and turned to look out the window. Reading newspapers was how I'd wasted the better part of the previous seven days, and it was wearing a little thin. I'd spent the time in a small-aisled, packed-to-the-rafters grocery store on Mott Street, one of the busiest in Chinatown. It was a guard duty job, and I was not, what you might call, enjoying myself. Not by a long shot. I'd been foxed neatly by an old dog who must've seen me coming six miles off. He was a Chinese who called himself Lo Chun. When he'd padded into my office I'd figured some easy coin was ahead. Of course, in my time I've figured the government was my friend and that my wife would love me forever. Sometimes it's depressing to see how little my intuitive boundaries have stretched over the years.

It was February outside the window — the worst part of the year in New York City. By that time of winter, everything is cold; everything hurts. Every inch of stone in the buildings and sidewalks and streets is frozen through, solidly bitter to the touch, or even to be near. Manhattan snowscapes may look pretty in the movie theater or on TV, but walking just a few blocks in the reality of its biting canyon winds can take the romance out of the scene quick — as can just looking out the window.

New York in winter is ugly — monstrously so. The snow reduces to slush on contact, immediately shot through with the gray and black of the city's soot and grime. Grease from the town's million and one restaurant cooking vents combines with the salty, cold blasts of wind that screech in off the ocean to turn the dark ichor into a freezing, slippery mess that does nothing for the soul save hinder and depress. The vision of it grows especially bleak once the fine folk who live here finish decorating the heaping piles of cinder-rough slop with chicken bones, styrofoam cups, used tissues, diapers and condoms, pizza crusts, urine, bottles, cans, and every other scrap and tatter they don't feel like bothering with any longer.

Looking out the window got me through another five minutes, but it wasn't enough. I was bored. Straight through. Bored down to my ass and still upset with myself for being jerk enough to take such a boring job in the first place. Laughing at me, my memory replayed the meeting Lo and I had the day he came to see me about guarding his store.

"Mr. Jack Hagee, sir...?"

He asked everything as politely as he had my name. A fellow detective, Peter Wei, had given the old guy my address. To make a long story short, the street gangs were getting out of hand in Chinatown. The mayor's office had released the story that they were all trying to raise cash to finance the making of Black Dreamer, a new synthetic opium that was flooding the city, funneled through the major oriental neighborhoods. To gather capital, they were planning to hit each other's territories on the Chinese New Year, demanding as much revenue from each other's pigeons as possible. As Lo told it:

"I no care about pay gang. You keep shop, you pay Tong. Always been. Always be. No one get rid of Wah Ching. Not for thousand year. That okay. But now, big trouble. Now, all gang fight. All kids go crazy. Want each other dead, take each other space. Now, gangs no can keep store safe. Store all my family have. I not lose it. No care about pay gang who rule when New Year come. Fine okay. No problem. But won't pay loser and make winner mad."

I ventured the mayor's explanation about the drugs, but Lo wasn't hearing it. He insisted the whole thing came down to territory and that it would all be over after New Year's.

"Pay you thousand dollar. You stay all New Year's. Keep bastard kids away from store. I pay good, you protect store. Make deal?"

I tried to tell him he was offering too much money, a lot more than double my daily fee, but he wasn't hearing it. Peter Wei had said I was the best, and that was what he wanted. We argued back and forth for a while, and then I figured 'what the hell,' if the old man wanted beat out of his cash so bad, I was as available as the next guy. Shaking his hand, I told him:

"Okay, pal, I'm yours for New Year's."

"All New Years. Whole time. You no leave store. I pay good. You protect store all New Years."

"Yeah; you got it. The whole thing. I won't budge. When you want me there?"

"Tomorrow. New Year's start tomorrow. Finish next Tuesday."

I looked at him for a second as if I'd missed a beat, and then I remembered. The Chinese New Year is a ten-day celebration. Peter had told me that before. And I was willing to bet the old man knew I knew. For the first time since he'd walked into my office, I looked him over carefully. That was when I realized he was older than he looked, when I stared into his happy dark eyes and saw them waiting for me to catch on, saw them smile when I did.

"So," he asked, "now you want to say something about deal?"

I bit at my lower lip, running things past in my mind. I had no jobs on the docket, but a thousand bucks for ten days of risking my life against who knew how many bands of highly efficient young murderers was not the best deal I'd ever made. There was plenty of dough in my bank account, but on the other hand, a lot of money there had come from Chinatown, and Chinatown referrals. Not that I'd miss them much. I'd reached the comfort zone where dirt jobs weren't nearly as attractive as they'd been when I hadn't known where my next burger was coming from.

The worst part, though, was that I'd known the difference between European and Chinese New Years before Lo had come through my door. A guy with scruples would've refused point blank to take so much money for one day's work. The old man had maneuvered me into the position where it was up to me to call myself a cheat or a coward.

I asked him for his address instead.

And that was what brought me to closing time on day eight, looking out the window wishing I had something better to do than read the paper I was reaching for for the fiftieth time that day. So far I'd had no trouble, but the news was getting so boring I was beginning to wish for some.

I'd read the story of the court battle over "Tan Fran" twice. A white girl with a great tan, she's gotten a job in a law office because everyone there had assumed she was Puerto Rican, and they needed someone good looking and Puerto Rican or Black or something to prove what good left-wing liberals they were now that it appeared a Democrat could end up as President on top of the one we had for governor.

At her first promotion, they found out she was white, and thus useless since they already had a few women around to prove they weren't sexist. The result: she was fired. So she sued them. And on it's dragged for two months.

I'd read the tale of the guy who spotted his ex-wife in a department store six times. I liked that one. Seeing her just drove the poor bug-fuck nuts; he killed her by breaking her head open with a bottle of ammonia, which he then emptied into the crack he'd made. Then he just sat back and smiled and watched her scream as her brains boiled up out of her skull.

He didn't run away or resist arrest. He just smiled and watched, even after she was long dead, even after the cops cuffed him and took him away. Once they got him in the squad car, though, he suddenly came to life and slammed his head through one of the passenger windows, purposely tearing his throat open on the jagged edge left. Nice family entertainment, *The Post*.

I was rereading the latest exploit of the Outliner when I suddenly found myself rolling the newspaper back up, tight and solid. Looking around the store, I saw what my subconscious radar had spotted. Two youths, heavily bundled against the cold, had entered the store, looking at items their body language said they had no interest in whatsoever. Finally they walked over to Lo and began a high-powered sales pitch in Chinese. I walked over, too. One of them greeted me.

"Back off, qua'lo."

"Why, boys? What's the problem?"

"No problem white shit whore-licking maggot sucker. Go buy a vegetable. Get a big eggplant and take it home to sit on while you dream of my dick."

The second youth gave the first a nudge and a whisper, probably a hint that most likely I wasn't some daffy Good Samaritan.

"What're you? Cop? You got some reason to fuck with us, shit bastard?"

"Yeah." I slapped the talker across the face with the rolled up newspaper. "I do." Another slap in the opposite direction. Hard. Cracking. "I work here." Two more, one on each ear, sharp and stinging. "I'm the trash man, you see." A reverse sent the hard end into his left eye. "I gather up all the useless crap and put it out in the street."

A blunt end shove to the gut sent the talker flying, bouncing him off the counter behind him. A dozen or so cans fell on him, slowing his responses and adding to the confusion. Grabbing him by the hair, I jerked him to his feet, ignoring his screams and the blood running from his nose.

The other hadn't moved yet. He was clearly the bag man, the negotiator. Without his strong arm, he was terrified. I tossed the first out the door, making sure his back would hit badly and hard against the Ford parked at the curb. It crunched. So did he. Good, I thought. I don't like Fords much better than I do punks. Turning to his partner, I asked:

"And what do you want?"

"Nothing. No, no…nothing."

He was scared. No one had thought collection was going to be much of a problem. If someone refused, the gang would just come back later and take care of things. But fighting back — defying their goof shit little band of thugs — his eyes told me that such a thing had never crossed any of their minds. Not even for amusement.

"What do you mean, nothing?" I asked the question with angry suspicion. "You came into a store for nothing? I think you must be with that real tough guy out in the street."

"No! No I'm not. I'm not!"

"Then what are you here for?"

The sweat was beginning to break out on his forehead. He was carrying the money they'd already collected. He was a runner, not a fighter, but I was between him and the door. If he lost the money he had, he'd be in for even more trouble than the talker outside.

"I mean no trouble. I, I — I came in for…," — his eyes darted in every direction, finally hitting on an idea— "…for some candy. Yes! Candy!"

"Well, then…, buy some candy."

As the runner dug into his pocket, I told Lo, "Sell him a crate of candy." As the punk's eyes came back to me, I said, "A big crate. Something expensive."

Lo disappeared into one of the back aisles and then returned with a large cardboard box on a hand truck. Total cost: four hundred and fifty four dollars. I asked, "This is what you came in for, right? Candy?"

The runner kept his eyes on the newspaper still in my hands and nodded vigorously. I opened the door for him after he paid for the box, watching him struggle his purchase out behind him. Just as he began to pass through the doorway, I slid the paper under his chin to catch his attention.

"Now; you collect up your future cellmate out there and you go tell the rest of your crew that this store is off limits until after the New Year. You tell them this…Mr. Lo will happily pay his respectful fees when you kiddies have sorted out your boundary problems, but not before. Go shake down someone else. Anyone else. But not this store; not until after the New Year."

He nodded vigorously, keeping his eyes away from mine. I pulled the newspaper away from his throat and let him pass. As soon as the door shut, he abandoned his crate, running over to the tough guy still pulling himself up off the sidewalk. They stared at the store for a long time. I lit a cigarette and waved. Finally they walked off down the street, leaving the candy behind.

The box sat in the snow, abandoned like the Japanese gun emplacements along the beaches of Okinawa the day after the Marines landed. It sat in view as a marker, commemorating the winning of a battle before the war had actually started. With a shrug, I went out and fetched it back inside. Then I helped Lo pull the steel shutters down over the window and door.

Satisfied we'd secured our bunker as well as we could, we went upstairs to the second floor where the old man and his family lived. I took my by-then familiar place at the table and started in with everyone else on Mrs. Lo's spread. As usual, it was terrific. The food sat in colorful bowls on a large lazy susan; celery and crab meat, bamboo shoots and peppers, freshly roasted cashews, pork ribs and chicken wings crusty with barbecue sauce, two different kinds of steamed fish, bean sprouts and hamburger heavily doused with black pepper, and a bowl of large, batter-dipped shrimp flash-fried so evenly you could eat them shell and all without even noticing the crunch.

The food wasn't the best part of dinner, though — it was eating with Lo's family. It'd been a long time since I'd eaten a meal with other people at the table. My own childhood hadn't had a family that met at the same time every day to eat together. My own childhood hadn't bothered with a family much, period.

Lo and his wife had five children, as well as a few brothers and a sister who gathered every night to eat and discuss their businesses and jobs and school. The first few nights I made the mistake of filling up on whatever I saw in front of me, forgetting the dessert to come. I remembered that night, though, and left some room for the peaches, apple cakes, coconut rolls, and oranges which followed.

Keeping the pounds off wasn't easy under Mrs. Lo's watchful eye. She'd figured out what kind of eater I was the first night and made sure plenty of what I liked was on the table every night after that. She didn't speak more than a handful of English, but so far we'd had no trouble communicating. I'd been made to feel like an adopted son, and what loving mother can't communicate with her little boy?

Lo told the assembly what'd happened in the store earlier, the end of the story meeting with everyone's approval. The general consensus was that more of them would be back the next day, but I'd known that when I'd started in on the tough guy. Lo'd known it before he'd come to hire me. But we were in it now, with no turning back. Figuring I might need some extra beauty sleep, I excused myself from the table and headed downstairs to my cot.

I thought about the family as I lay in the cold aroma of sawdust and dried fish, trying to figure them out. They were proper people, loving people, happy people — the kind I don't spend much time with usually. They all had their own chair around the table, and their own place in the living room for watching TV. They even changed clothes for bed, wearing pajamas, or nightgowns, one of the smaller girls even sporting a little tasseled cap. As I scratched at my underwear, the same I'd worn all day, I had to admit a lot of their lifestyle was very appealing.

In their home, which was in effect their own little world, they had so far managed to keep the rotting decay of progress out of their lives. True, they dressed in Western clothing, owned stereo systems, televisions, a computer, and a garbage compactor. The girls wore makeup and the boys had Walkmans. The travel pictures we went through one night showed me they'd seen a lot of America — a lot more than most of the people born here.

And yet, somehow they'd managed to work and live here for years, in the heart of one of the country's dirtiest, nastiest, most corrupt and violent cities and not be overly affected by it. They had a set pattern to their lives, and the backbone to hold them erect against any kind of outside interference. Every day as we worked and ate and lived together, the time seemed to go faster. Actually, I had to admit the eight days we'd spent together had practically flown by.

Closing my eyes, I scrambled toward the back of my mind, searching for sleep. Day eight was going to be day nine before I knew it.

The morning *Post* was its usual treasure trove of laughs. "BACKYARD BODIES SURFACE THROUGH AIDS CONFESSION" was the field day they picked to go after to catch the commuter crowd, reporting on the activities of a pair of lesbian dominatrixes and their male slave. One of the women had posed for a number of bondage magazines. The dutiful reporter on the story only had room to list *PUNISHED!*, *HOT n' HELPLESS* and *WHIPMASTER*. The other had made a splash for a while in a variety of HOM, Inc. videos.

The gist of things was that slave would go out to bars, pick up girls, bring them home, and then turn them over to his mistresses. They would then 'punish' him for 'seeing' other women, getting around to the women he brought home a little later. His punishment would be to get his plugs and rings lovingly replaced, along with a short whipping and perhaps a few maternal kicks and punches, just to let him know what a good puppy he really was. His date would be beaten, slashed, burned, urinated on, and in other ways abused for as long as she could be kept alive and enjoyable. Then the slave would bury the new victim in the wooded hillside behind the house and go shopping for his ladies fair once again.

The whole thing broke up when the neighborhood dogs nosed up one of the shallower graves for a late-night snack. That brought some human bits and pieces to the back porches of a few of the neighbors. It also brought the slave forward to confess, something he'd wanted to do ever since he'd discovered the three of them had AIDS. "God's punishment for their evil ways," as he'd put it. The story then let the public know how many graves'd been uncovered so far, and what'd been found in them.

They had a string of other fun tidbits as well; the man who cut off three of his toes in the lawnmower, more on the ex-Miss America who'd been embezzling from her company, updates on the attack-dog situation, as well as the search for the hit-and-run driver who'd tagged out a cop and his baby daughter, the continuing crackdown on Black Dreamer, and the never-ending indicting of city officials.

True, there wasn't much on the national or international front, but what the heck? It was just the kind of quality reporting one expected from the newspaper established by Alexander Hamilton in 1801.

Quality reporting or not, though, the paper hadn't managed to capture my complete attention. I'd been keeping my eyes open, watching the door, who came through it, and when they left, as well as the front window, who went by it, and how often. Which is why I was ready when the friendly foursome came into the store.

They arrived quietly, without any rude fanfare, but everyone in the place knew what was coming down. The majority of Lo's customers vanished in less than a minute. Some remained long enough to check out, hurrying away with their plastic-bagged purchases. Most of the others simply abandoned their baskets in the aisles and fled.

Two of the quartet were big, each bigger than the previous day's tough guy. Then came a medium-sized one with a joke of a mustache and a look in his eye that dared me to find the punchline. The last one was a runt, but one with "shooter" written all over him. It was obvious that at least one of the others was armed as well. I sized up Mustache as their leader and moved on him; positioning myself between them and the back of the store, I kept two stacks of heavily crated canned fish nearby in case I needed the cover, then pulled my .38 and said:

"Far enough, boys. Give out with your message and slap pavement."

"What's the gun for? Need something to suck on, faggot?"

"History lesson, kids. Bernie Goetz only got six months for gunning down his punks with an unregistered weapon. My gun's got a license. So do I. I'm on the job. I'm protecting my employer's property and life. They'll slap my wrist.

"You children are only someone else's voice. So, just give me your message and get back to kindergarten."

"You know, you talk real big for a dead man — but, you've got guts. Not much gray fuel in the upstairs — no; brains are your short suit all right — but guts…yeah, that you've got."

"Thanks for the anatomy lesson. Get to the point."

Mustache pulled a joint from his pocket and lit it. It burned slowly, leaving thick, purple-grey billows of smoke, indicating it was laced with coke, or crack, or hash, or Black Dreamer, or something else even newer than Dreamer that I'd never heard of. Stabbing it at me, he said:

"The point, Caucasian, is that the Time Lords have secured this territory. The war is over. The old man isn't your concern anymore. His store is ours. You should be on the last train back to white pig happy land."

"Do tell." Mustache and one of the giants took a step forward. I warned them off. "Step it easy and backwards. If you're in charge now, the word'll be streeted soon enough. So, go back and tell the king of the Time Lords you did your duty and let's all get out of this the easy way."

The midget and Mustache looked at each other, judging the percentages open to them. For a moment I thought they were going to rush me, but then good sense broke them off in the direction of reason. Mustache pointed the others toward the door with his reeking baton, laughing as he told me:

"Okay, ghost; why not? We got nothing to prove here. Too cold to bother with you now, anyway. But tomorrow, collections go back to normal. We'll be back — all of us. And you — we will not want to see. So, put away your little gun, Caucasian, and book passage back uptown to the mainland. You'll be a lot happier that way."

As the four left I slid my .38 back into my shoulder holster. The wind howled coldly as they passed through the door, its bark cut off sharply as wood and glass slid back into place. Lo looked at me with a question on his face. I tried to pull enough confidence into mine to answer him. Finally, he asked:

"You think it all over?"

"Don't know — could be. It'd be nice to get out of this without getting my clothes dirty."

Tossing me a crystal pear, the kind that are all water and sugar, but with no substance to them at all, he said, "I don't think things so easy. Gang boys all too young to be so reasoning. Too easy you believe their words and forget their pride. They be back tomorrow, all right.

"Tomorrow be big trouble."

I shrugged and kept on chewing, not really having an answer. Feeling a little up-against-it-all, I went to the back of the store to where Lo's tiny office was to use the phone. I wanted to call my main information broker, Hubert, so I could get my mind onto something else. He answered in his usual manner.

"Hey, hey, Dick Tracy. W-Where'd you park the squad car?"

"Can it, mutant."

"Oh, in one of yer surly moods, eh? Oh well, what's on yer mind?"

"I'm still stuck in that Chinatown gig and I'm getting a little bored. Thought I'd give you a ring and see what was doin'."

"Not much. I have that videotape we need for T-Thursday. Outside of that, t-though, I was thinkin' of skippin' town 'til then. Why? What's up?"

"Ahhh, nothin'. Not really."

Hu went quiet for a second and then asked, "You okay, Jack? You need a little backup or somethin'?"

"Nah," I told him. "I'm just bored. This job's a piece of cake. If I can't handle this one, I'd better get out of the business."

"Well," he answered, slowly, "Okay. Guess I'd better get movin', then. Maurice should have the car downstairs waitin' for me. I've got t-to hustle out to the airport. Little job to oversee down southwise. Yes, sir — it's B-Bermuda fer me fer the next couple days."

"Don't get sunburned, ya little weasel."

"Yeah," he laughed. "I'll try real hard not to. Don't you freeze yer balls off up here in the Ice Age."

We laughed at each other for another minute. Hu made sure to remind me not to take any wooden nickels, and then it was quiet again. I hung up the phone and went back to finishing my pear. For pieces of fruit with no weight to them whatsoever, those pears sure lay heavy in your stomach. At least that one did.

The whole week had been a continuing racket of mortars, bottle rockets, and pin wheels. Nothing, though, in the first nine days of that Chinatown New Year's could have prepared anyone for the tenth. Tiny, bright colored bombs went off constantly in every street and alley. Rattling strings of explosions peppered the din — two, three hundred at a shot. The air hung dark with burning gunpowder, new plumes rising from every corner to further choke those in the frozen streets. Explosives dropped out of windows and off of roofs; missiles flew upward, lit the sky, and then dropped back to earth.

The perfect time for a mob of punks to stalk the neighborhood and empty machine guns at each other and the rest of society if ever I saw one.

Lo and I opened the store at the regular time, not wanting to encourage the gang to perhaps torch the whole building just to get at us. Most every other place around was closed for the holiday, which sent Lo's business through the roof. While we worked, the old man told me the story behind the ten day tradition.

When the farmers in China celebrated the coming of a new year, since they couldn't really put any work in at that time of year anyway, they just got in the habit of partying longer and longer. The traditional length is actually fifteen days, which was easy to pull off two thousand years ago; just shut the country down for two weeks and let everyone get shitfaced. Not possible in our enlightened age, of course. Thank heaven for the legion of bloodless, leeching old ladies who run this nation. Without them to protect us from ourselves, God only knows what kind of fun we might have.

Anyway, normally the biggest night of the festival is New Year's Eve, just as it is for us. This year, though, the mayor's office planned events throughout the city to show how in touch he is with the minorities. Unfortunately, the boob's people got everything backwards, not realizing the ten days of Chinese New Year's worked like the twelve days of Christmas, with the biggest day of the holiday first. And, of course, they got all of their media coverage lined up before anyone could straighten them out. So, doing the only thing the fearless leader of a city hall can do, he had the police street the news that people who celebrated on the tenth day instead of the first could expect no tickets for illegal fireworks, or broken arms, but that those trying to celebrate before then could expect major hassles. He even arranged for the side streets to be blocked off — no traffic to interfere with the festivities.

Which explained why on what should have been a business-as-usual day the streets were raining explosives, and most of the stores were closed, their owners trapped between their fear of the gangs and the mayor's indifferent stupidity. Welcome to New York.

Lo's business, of course, was the best it'd been in ten years. That brought half the family in to help. At lunchtime, Mrs. Lo and the youngest granddaughter brought down two trays of large bowls filled with noodles and pork, as well as fishballs, fried rice, shrimp toast, and tea with cakes, cookies, some mixed pastries and a large platter of orange slices — just to keep us all from starving before dinner, you see. While everyone else was eating, Lo's youngest came over to me.

"Mr. Hagee, sir?"

"Yeah, Git'jing; what's up?"

"Will things be bad today?"

"They could be," I admitted. Telling the truth to their offspring seemed to be a routine matter with the Los. Besides, this was one of those kids to whom you just couldn't lie. At least, I couldn't.

"What makes you ask?"

"So far you have been very lucky. But we can't ask you to use up all your luck for us. So I have brought you this."

She handed me a chain with what looked like an ivory dragon on the end of it. Closer inspection showed it was actually one large dragon with eight smaller ones crawling all about it. I wasn't sure if they were supposed to be playing or fighting.

"Thank you," I told her. "Is this supposed to bring good luck?"

"Nine dragons in the home always means good fortune. Every home needs nine dragons in it somewhere to bring good luck. They don't need to be the same, or in the same place, or anything like that. You just have to have nine of them in your home somewhere for the luck."

"But I'm not in my home," I joked with her.

Quite seriously, she told me, "You do not have a home."

"Sure I do," I replied. "I live in Brooklyn, in Bensonhurst."

"No. You may eat and sleep there," she let me know, "but it is not your home. Your home is still within you — you have not yet begun to bring it out. That is why you can carry your dragons with you — because you have only a place to stay, not a real home."

That said, she smiled politely and then ran back to her grandmother when the old woman started to collect up the dishes. I wanted to argue with her, but didn't see the point. She was right. I lived in a barren apartment that I kept clean by keeping it empty. Half the time I slept on the couch in my office instead of going home. If it wasn't for Elba, the girl from downstairs who takes care of my dog, the poor mutt would've probably starved to death by now.

The thing that made me wonder was how Git'jing could tell all that just by looking at me. After all, everyone hates being obvious. Figuring it wasn't worth the questioning, however, I slid the chain over my neck and hung my dragons inside my shirt. I feel luckier already, I told myself. Besides, the way things looked I was willing to take any advantage I could get my hands on.

The morning paper had given an update on the situation in Chinatown, one so wrong I wondered how it could've been printed, even in *The Post*. Not that the other New York rags were ever any more accurate; *The Post* might be the most flamboyant of the main quartet of papers keeping the city 'informed,' but it has no monopoly on inaccurate reporting — not by a long shot.

Luckily, for all the news that mattered to me that day, I had other resources. In Chinatown, as in all real neighborhoods, not fancified motel parks for the rich like Sutton Place or Park Avenue, the vocal grapevine is as strong today as it was in the first grove of trees that ever knew human congregation. Sadly, it was not carrying good news.

Despite the message the Time Lords'd delivered the day before, the word on the street was that they were bluffing. They were still in dispute with the Angry

Ghosts and Mother's Blood Flowing over three prime real estate areas, one of which was Lo's block of Mott St. They had given the same message to a number of stores looking to see what the popular reaction was. Most everyone else locked their doors to see who got picked to be made an example of; you can guess who got picked.

I thought about calling in help, but decided against it. When the gang showed, another gang waiting for them wasn't going to slow them down. They'd picked Lo and me to teach a lesson to, so we were the ones who were going to get it. Face demanded it, which meant there was little hope of stopping it merely with force.

Actually, I couldn't imagine how much muscle it would take to back down the Time Lords. I'd been able to send the first two packing because they hadn't expected me. The next bunch had only been sent to deliver a message. But this time...this time was for all the marbles and they would move forward no matter what.

As we waited, Lo told me:

"No worry. I know this first day talk to you. What else to do? Take chance they no burn store, kill me, wife, children? Hope not to be a dead man? Crawl on floor, beg for mercy from animals who kill just for chance to laugh? No thank you bullshit very much not. Standing better way to die than kneeling.

"What you think?"

"I think you've got a point," I told him.

"Good," he answered, slapping me on the back. "Damn good. You get ready. Trouble come soon; be sure. I go sell rice."

Lo sold rice for another four hours before our troubles finally came home to roost. There was no mistaking what was happening. You could feel the attention focusing on the store before our playmates were even in sight. Lo could feel it; so could his wife. She came downstairs to chase all the kids back to safety while I was still putting on my coat. I hit the sidewalk just as the evening's entertainment came into view.

There were at least two dozen of them; hard muscled, impressed with themselves, young — the oldest couldn't have been more than twenty. Some were carrying ball bats, some had bricks. God only knew what was hidden from sight. I could see all my old pals from the previous two days intermingled with the fresh troops. Their leader was a new face, however.

At best he was seventeen. The way he walked, the power in his step, the way he ignored the blasting chill killing its way through the streets showed he held his position by being the toughest animal in the pack. His eyes were what betrayed him. They were plainly etched with privilege. He was a child used to snapping his fingers for whatever he wanted — money, women, drugs, police protection, transportation, invisibility — whatever. It had all come too easily to him until now. He was more than sure he was in charge, more than *aware* that his word was law — he was certain. If he believed in any gods at all, it was only so he could rest assured they'd appointed him master of all he surveyed.

Looking into the master's eyes, even from a distance, I knew he was the reason for all of Chinatown's current troubles. It was his needs, his desire and greed that were tearing the neighborhood apart, setting the gangs at each other's throats, killing a total of twelve so far in the last three months.

Expectedly, there wasn't a cop in sight. No one knows the grapevine like they do. I could count on them not showing up until things were long over, one way or another, using the mayor's stupidity as their excuse. Hard to blame them, really. Pulling out a pad and scribbling with a Bic are a hell of a lot easier than taking on a drug confident wild ball gorilla-rough teenaged killer. Or two. Or who knew how many.

A hand signal, fingers over the left shoulder, stopped the gang's advance. The leader took three more steps toward me and then planted himself between me and his boys, playing the scene for all the drama he could remember from the last WWF match he'd seen. I leaned against the stone of the next building, lighting a cigarette, waiting for him to start it. Things were beginning to fall into place for me. All of Chinatown'd known trouble was coming for New Year's. The residents and the police'd all prepared to the best of their abilities to stay out of the gangs' ways, hoping a lot of winnowing might befall the ranks. Lo had decided on protection instead of prayer.

The gangs had knocked the crap out of each other, and now the top three were ready to divide up the remaining plums — and the Time Lords were the ones making the first move. Maybe they were the strongest gang after all — they'd made all the moves I'd seen. Word had it they weren't, though, and I was betting the word was right. Their strategy was wrong; it lacked finesse. It was blunt, broken bottle, dull-eyed slugger stuff. The kind of planning that always springs into the minds of children.

I've never liked that aspect of childhood. It's necessary, I suppose, but there's something about the way people think until they finally go mad and reach adulthood that is almost tragic. The smug condescension of youthful righteousness is almost unbearable to watch. Whether it is unbearably funny or painful depends on the child putting on the exhibition, but no matter how much sympathy one has for them, the end result is that they make an ass out of themselves and there's no way to warn them off from it. Adults know this because they can remember the things they once believed from which no one could warn them away.

Because, no matter what one might think to the contrary, there are certain things which make the world run, and that make human beings tick. Those who play by these rules are called grownups. And those who think the rules can, even for a millisecond, ever be broken, are called children.

Children.

"So," cried the leader, "how's the night watchman of the North Pole?"

Christ, how I hate children.

Letting my lungful out, I answered through the smoke.

"Tired of playin' jacks with you and your boys, Sonny. Take 'em on out of here. Get smart, juvenile. I'm more trouble than you ever saw in one place in your short, possibly soon-to-end life."

Sonny cracked his innocent prankster's look just slightly, his eyes narrowing as he forced himself to consciously take my measure. Rechecking his footing on the ice, I caught another secret hand sign directing two of his troops forward on either side of him. One of the giant's I'd seen the day before. The other, bigger one, was new to me.

"You were told to go home, Kojak."

"European powers were told to stay out of this hemisphere. Nobody listens."

Conversation stopped with a snap of the fingers — the shorter giant's cue to attack. He was a rusher, sweeping forward at me like a runaway train. I took another drag, waiting for the right moment. When his foot touched the walk I sidestepped out of his way quick, letting him ram his fingers into the bricks I'd been leaning against.

The second giant was already moving. Him I took more seriously. He came in calmer, with a sharper idea of what he was doing. Waiting for him to swing, I stepped inside his arc, throwing him off balance just by being so close. He stumbled for a second. I bounced the back of my fist off his nose and then pivoted, catching his ear with my elbow. He staggered off, but by then his partner was up.

He was more cautious this time, but I couldn't afford to congratulate him. Before he could overcome his hesitation over doing his fingers any further damage, I reached out to the point of being off balance, something he never expected. Grabbing his left hand, I jerked him to me, crushing his fingers together while I dragged him across the ice. He howled. I let him.

He swung at me blindly, swatting to stop the pain. I dodged him with a chuckle and spun him around, letting him fly into his partner, bouncing his head off the other giant's back. They sat on the ground together, shaking their heads, wondering what had happened.

Crossing to the street, I stepped on the first giant's hand, drawing screams so loud you could hear them blocks away despite the fireworks. Stopping ankle deep in the growing slush, I asked:

"Got any more acts you want to audition before you go home?"

Sonny's waving hand brought forward a quartet, two with baseball bats, two with knives. The first to try his luck was a knifer. He stabbed, danced back, stabbed again. I stayed out of reach. This bunch was better — not in each other's way. The blade came at me again, but only as a feign. He was setting me up for the batters. Noting that in time saved me from getting my head splattered. They'd moved forward together, not swinging, but stabbing as well, limiting their range but keeping their distance. Almost worked.

I ducked the first blade again and then grabbed out, catching the punk's wrist. Twisting, I got him to lose the knife; then I got him jumping. As long as he was hopping around in pain, no one else could close in on me. He tried to swat me away, but was in too much agony to connect.

Reaching down then, I came up under him, getting a good enough hold to hoist him over my head. The others back off as I knew they would, thinking I was going to throw him into them. Very dramatic, but hardly ever workable. I threw him over the curbed cars into the sidelined giants. The others got the idea. I had forced them to flinch needlessly — bad loss of face. Then I showed them I was going to take them out one by one and stack them like firewood.

The batters came forward again, rising to my challenge. This time they were swinging. I tried to time my catch but I was off. One caught me in the side. Hard. I slid on the snow and rammed into a parked car. The second batter stepped up, the cheers of his fellows making him reckless. Swinging down, he went for my skull — took out the Toyota's windshield instead. I kicked sideways burying my foot to the cuff in his side. Bones cracked. His. Good, I thought.

The first batter came back again, stabbing. I sidestepped twice then faked a slip. He struck again, too quickly. With better timing I grabbed out and took his bat from him, sliding it out of his gloved hands with a twist. He turned to run, but I put everything I had into a spinning return hit and broke his ankle, sending him rolling through the street, screaming for mercy.

The second blade carrier debated facing me on his own for a second, then stepped away, melting back into the ranks with his head hung. Smarter than he looked. The gang stood their ground, silver breath mixing with the burning gunpowder and smoke wreathing through the air. The night continued to hammer noisily around us, the constant explosions becoming our silence. I'd lost my cigarette in the slush. Lighting another one, working at keeping my bare hands from shaking too badly, I questioned the boy in charge.

"Had enough, Sonny?"

His eyes bored through me, heating buildings on the other side of the street. Spitting into the slop at our feet, he growled:

"Full of tricks, aren't you, ghost man?"

"Oh, cut the crap." I exhaled smoke at the gang. If he was an adult, I was dead. He'd have someone gun me down and that would be it. I was gambling I'd figured him right, though. If I acted like I wanted everything to end then, I was sure he'd misinterpret and go for me himself. Which was, of course, the only way out I'd seen since the gang'd first arrived.

"I'm tired, and you're scared," I told him. "You can't afford to lose any more face, and you don't know what to do about it. My advice is 'give up.' Take this band of rejects to whatever flop you throw yourselves into at night and get out of this the easy way. No one's been hurt too bad yet — especially me."

Without hesitation he began to shrug off his coat. "So you haven't been hurt too bad yet; eh, ghost? Well, let's see if we can't change that."

He'd taken the bait. Now, if I could just live through another fight with the toughest beast in the pack, I might be able to get through the night. Winded and trying not to show it, I shrugged off his attitude, sucking as much nicotine down as I could before I had to start moving again. Sonny stared at the baseball bat in my hand and then picked the fallen one out of the frozen mess it lay in, wiping it off on his sleeve. He pointed at a large construction dumpster and walked away toward it. I followed. So did the gang.

"Emperor of the mountain," he sneered. "Winner decides what happens."

"Yeah; doesn't he always?" He looked at me; smiling. I pulled down a last lungful and said, "Okay, Sonny. Let's get to it."

The dumpster was filled with the guttings of an apartment building in the icy throes of winter gentrification. Ten feet wide, thirty-five feet long, six feet deep, it was filled with old wiring, rotting pipes, broken plasterboard and bricks, and nail studded splinters of wood. One corner was a stacking of old-fashioned windows. The top layer was one of garbage, some in bags, most tossed in loose or torn free from its wrappings by hungry cats and desperate humans. A wonderful little arena.

Sonny was already coming across the field by the time I got to the top. Bracing myself, I swung up to take the first hit, barely able to shift positions to take the second. He slammed at me unmercifully, swinging at me from the left to the right to the left, on and on, waiting for me to fall into a rhythm so he could break the pattern and paste me. I matched him, blocking hit after hit, feeling the numbness starting to climb my arms.

Knowing I couldn't keep taking such punishment, I waited for a weaker strike and then pushed, putting our bats off to the side and our faces up against each other's. Letting my weapon go, I caught his bat arm with both hands and threw him off balance, unfortunately only into some soft garbage bags. He started to get up, but I threw myself on him, forcing him back down into the trash. He thrashed about, trying to stand, but I kept the pressure up, pushing him down as deep as I could into the bulging plastic sacks. His raking fingers tore several open. Our bouncing around freed more.

Snow started to mix with the frozen grease and decaying pus from the bags, making it impossible for us to hang onto each other. Sonny slipped away from me, clawing his way across the arena, gasping for air. I tried to grab his ankle but sunk to my knee in the trash, suddenly finding my leg trapped in the bricks and debris below.

"Now," came Sonny's rasping voice, "I'm going to kill you."

I jerked at my leg, tearing pants, skin, and muscle, but freeing it. Sonny came forward, swinging one of the bats at me so violently he almost threw himself from the dumpster when he missed. I dragged myself out of his path just barely in time, grabbing up a couple of broken bricks as I stood. He came at me again. I lobbed the first at him — missed — only denting a parked car's door. Weighing the second in my hand for a moment, I let it fly; he hit it away with the bat. It fell to the street, almost clobbering one of his followers.

"No more jokes, ghost man? No more tough talk?"

My breath was scorching my throat. Blood was sluicing from my leg, the pain filling my eyes with tears. My side still hurt from the first batter's swing in the last inning.

"Naw," I admitted. "No more jokes."

"Well then — if you can't amuse me anymore, faggot, you know what that means, don't you? It's dying time!"

He stepped across the trash gingerly, watching his footing, coming with a smile to dash my brains out. Too tired to dodge or resist his attack, too close to the end of my resources, I pulled out my .38 and gut shot him, sending him thudding into the street below.

Instantly five of the Time Lords started to clamber up the sides of the dumpster. Two in the background began pulling out guns. Conserving ammo, I grabbed up one of the stacked windows and flung it at the first three heads coming over the side. One ducked; one got a broken chin; the other lost an eye. I pitched two more windows into the crowd, catching one of the marksmen, sending another backpedalling for cover. A knifer came over the wall, tearing through my coat and nicking my side before I could get hold of him. I slammed him across the jaw with all I had left, sending him falling into another behind him. That one's screams told me he'd fallen onto something sharp and nasty. Too damn bad.

As more guns came loose I readied my .38 again. My head was empty of thoughts except for how many of the enemy I could take with me and which ones I wanted the most. I'd hoped to bring things down to just their leader and myself — to take him out and then bluff the others into leaving. Hadn't worked. A hail of automatic weapon's fire gouged at the metal of the dumpster, sending thick sparks and ricochets off into the surrounding fireworks. A couple of slugs went by me. I took aim at the main shooter and was just about to fire when I suddenly spotted dozens of figures moving through the gloom at both ends of the street. A bull horn sounded, orders barking at us in Cantonese. The Time Lords lost interest in me immediately, looking to the left and right, sizing up what was happening. A Chinese youth in a good suit with a sharp-edged haircut came up to the dumpster. Offering me his hand, he called:

"Come on down, Mr. Hagee. Join the party."

The newcomers were armed to the teeth, not looking for anything except cooperation. After a second it dawned on me what was going on. Shoving my .38 back into its holster, I answered:

"Ah, I'm going to have a little trouble getting down from here, and — um, well…as gracious as it is for someone of your importance to offer his hand, I wouldn't want to ruin your suit. Sir."

The newcomer smiled an expansive, dangerous smile and turned to Sonny. Roughly nudging the still howling gang leader with his foot, the smiler told him:

"You see — respect. This warrior knows how, and when, and to whom to show respect. Too bad you never learned that, William."

Turning back to me, he answered, "Don't let it trouble you. What are clothes? An artificial shell. A dozen suits are not worth what you have done. Take my hand."

I did more than just take his hand; I slid out of the dumpster like a mouthful of spit going down a bathroom wall. Smiler caught me and held me up on my feet. Whispering, he asked:

"You're not going to die on me, are you?" When I assured him I wasn't, he said, "Good. You hang tough for two minutes — let me gather up the face to be gained here and you'll come out happy."

I nodded. He turned to the crowd. His speech was simple. I knew he was the head of either the Angry Ghosts or Mother's Blood Flowing. Both gangs had known the Time Lords would move first. They had waited for the best moment to stage their takeover and then moved in in unison. Probably planned for days.

His offer was straightforward — the Time Lords were too wild, too undisciplined, too much of a troublemaking organization. They caused more discord than harmony, and thus had to be disbanded. When someone countered that you can't disband a gang that had a leader, Smiler answered:

"Why, you are right. Debbie, my sweet queen. If you could oblige us."

A dazzling oriental girl, possibly Korean, in an expensive-looking gray fur coat came forward and pressed a sawed-off shotgun over the hole in Sonny's stomach where my bullet had entered. Pulling both triggers, she splattered the asphalt with meat and bone. Sliding home two more shells, she retriggered and splattered the street some more.

While she worked at her repavement operation, Smiler told me, "This way no one will bother to look for any stray slugs from some unnamed private detective's gun, eh?"

I nodded again, with as much strength as I could. My job'd been to protect the store. I'd done that. In the end, since it matched their own interests, the Time Lords' rivals had come in and finished what I started. After Sonny was put out of his misery, none of his followers had anything more to say. The rules had been followed; honor had been satisfied. They split ranks and joined one or the other of the two gangs surrounding us like the last kids to be picked for a stickball game.

Smiler walked me over to the Los' store. I'd played down to him because he was the king of the moment. There was no honor to be had in provoking him into getting rid of me like he had Sonny, and little sense. He'd come in at the last minute and pulled my bacon out of the fire because he wanted to show he was friends with the toughest man on the street. He could have just as easily waited until I was dead to make his move. I've made worse friends in my time. Check out my ex-wife if you think I'm lying.

"Okay, pal," he suggested, "why don't you go inside and get put back together before you croak or something?"

While he helped me over the curb, he quietly shoved a wad of bills into my pocket. When I looked at him, he whispered again, "Look, gangbuster, don't get all proud on me. I've been waiting for someone to do what you did for a long time. Now, I know who really shot Billy Wong, and you know who had him finished off. I could kill you, and one of Billy's relatives might go to the cops with that to get me, and on and on it could go. Who needs it? Revenge is as ugly as greed. I like you, Big Hagee. You understand the basics. Billy...he was crazy. Kept trying to throw balance out the window.

"He had to go."

The Los managed to break through the mass of gang members surrounding us then. As I fell into their arms, Smiler said, loudly enough for plenty of people to hear:

"Everybody — know this. The Lo family, and their property, is under my protection. This noble warrior, Chinese or not, has shown us what must be done with those who upset the old ways. He is under my protection as well for he is a great and honorable figure, and too much a man to be my friend for things as small as money or his life. For this, I owe him favor — for this, everyone in Chinatown owes him favor."

Taking in a harsh breath, Smiler's face suddenly grew dark as he added, "So all who hear me and know how far my words travel, remember only of this night that the fireworks were wonderful, and that you all watched the skies from your windows and saw nothing of the streets."

The few onlookers took their cue and disappeared. Most of the gang members followed them. A cleanup crew restuffed the dumpster, finding room for Sonny somewhere in the middle. By the time the Los helped me hobble back up to their apartment, the streets were empty save for the black snow and the never-ending explosions. My leg and side were messy, but not nearly as seriously hurt as they appeared. The girls burned my clothes in a barrel on the roof while the boys scrubbed me down and treated my wounds.

Smiler had paid me five thousand dollars for eliminating the Time Lords. Less than I would have charged if he'd asked, but more than anyone else was offering once it'd already happened. I wasn't quite sure at the time I'd ever get the chance to call in the marker he claimed I was holding on him, but I figured it didn't hurt to keep it in mind. I've never been one to pass by money in the street just because some people think it's undignified to stoop in public.

Mr. Lo made a big show out of paying me while I held court from his easy chair, answering the continual barrage of questions about the fight. I laughed most of it off, only playing up the dangerous parts for the youngest children.

I also added a corny bit about grabbing the dragons around my neck and praying to the gods for help. I didn't really care who else bought it; Git'jing's face lit up at the mention, and that was all that mattered.

After that, Mrs. Lo chased us all to the dinner table where the food was so deep you'd have thought the rest of the neighborhood'd been invited to join us. The family chattered about the fight, and the whole of my New Years' visit, and the excitement of it all. For a while, at least.

Before dessert, however, the conversation was that of shop and school and business and dating and homework and babies and all the other talk that fills a happy home. Something that, come the morning, I'd be leaving behind.

Grabbing for the last piece of lobster, I pretend rage at the baby who snatched it out from under me, just to see that innocent laughter one last time. I thought, what the hell...even if you can't go home again, at least sometimes they'll let you visit. Besides, I had my dragons now. Who knew what would happen next?

Outside the snow continued to fall, dodging its way around the explosions.

All the Money in the World

THE NOISE OF a cartoon duck yodeling in the hallway let me know Hubert had arrived. I'd come in early in the hopes of finally knocking off the Iliad, but had only managed to get through another fifty pages. Knowing I'd get no peace now that he'd arrived I slid a 3x5 card in place as a bookmark. Then, leaving the women on the beach to moan and wail and pull their disheveled hair over the death of Achilles, I reshelved them with all the other half and three-quarter finished books on my wall and braced myself for Hu's opening barrage.

"Hey, hey, Hagee…what's doing, Dick Tracy? Got a great one for ya. What's the difference b-between a refrigerator and a faggot?" Admitting I didn't know got me the answer. "A refrigerator don't fart when ya pull the meat out. Hahahahaha — ha, oh god, I love it — ya get it, right — hahaheeheeha — right…"

"Yeah; honest. It didn't go over my head. You want some bean?"

"Not that sludge you make. I plan to make retirement age with a f-functioning set of kidneys, thank you very much."

"Everybody's a critic."

Taking another long draw of coffee out of spite, I kept myself from grimacing at the taste while making a mental note to clean my pot the next chance I got. Peeling out of his dripping duster, Hu waved a VHS tape at me, saying:

"Here it is. And, b-boy, is it a riot."

I looked at the black cassette without much excitment. The case it would be wrapping up was one of those usual sorry state of affairs. My client was a wife who more than suspected her husband was cheating on her. The main reason she was quite sure was he had admitted it. He had also made it fairly clear to her he was not about to change his ways, or grant her a divorce.

He was a minor D.A.'s office official, one who didn't want the aggrevation and trouble of a scandal. He was also a slap-'em-up artitst who'd first knocked his wife around a bit, then bullied her with threats of legal maneuvers that would keep her poor and away from their children, which he'd smugly felt would keep her sufficiently in line. Luckily for my ability to meet the rents of March, he didn't know his wife as well as he should have. She'd come to me for proof that would carry her through any court battle. She wanted more than a few black & whites snapped through a hotel window. She didn't want a show that could be decried as a setup — she wanted something raw, ugly, and final. From what Hubert'd told me on the phone, she'd gotten her money's worth.

Abandoning my coffee for the moment, though, I asked Hu:

"So, where'd you finally catch up to our roving romeo?"

"Where else? At the Buck."

I wasn't surprised. Mrs. Sinnott'd listed it as one of the places her husband used for business. When I'd seen that I'd asked her how long she was willing to wait, knowing that if he frequented the Buck we just might be able to snag him up easily. She was more than willing to give him enough line with which to hang himself.

The Buck is an interesting place. In most respects it's a normal, wooden-barred, brass-railed, big-mirrored drinking joint. What gives it its name, though, is its linoleum's pattern. The floor is covered in money. The design is made up of American coins and bills; pennies, dimes, fifties, singles, tens, nickels, silver dollars, twenties and all the rest. You can find most of the styles of each denomination as well; Indian Head and Lincoln pennies, Liberty and Mercury dimes, et cetera.

What brings people in, however, is the Buck's habit of putting real money down on the floor amid the fake. The tradition is that the bar puts money on the floor and the customers, if they find it, put it on their table as a tip for those hard-working Buck girls. The rumor runs that those who generously put something large on the table would get taken to the back room for some fun by the grateful table-hopper who benefited from their generosity.

The truth, however, is that the Buck is actually a clever little sex club. The bar maids, mostly doubled-out hookers working side hours, use the Buck to meet Johns they want to keep private. They really do wait tables; rubes are let in all the time to keep the respectable image up, but just as large a percentage of the profits come from the back rooms as they do from the front. Sometimes it makes me wonder if all the interesting little places in New York have truths just as ugly hidden underneath their colorful myths.

Today, however, with everyone looking for safe sex, the Buck has become an exhibition club — a place with a lot more show and tease than the old days. From what I'd heard the back rooms were practically gone, but not the sex. That was out in the open, the patrons as entertainment, everyone wink-and-nodding each other into the happy carnival spirit of things, creating a new mythos so they can more easily accept the vulgarity of their needs.

Since it might easily have taken months for things to fall into place, I'd arranged a sliding fee scale for Mrs. Sinnott that would charge her only for the actual time involved rather than my daily fee. After that, I'd put one of Hubert's people I use a lot, Carmine Cecolini, a tail man good for long jobs, on her husband. Carmine worked with Mrs. Sinnott, watching her husband's schedule, following him on those nights it was possible he might be headed for a rendezvous with some cutie. After eighteen days, he struck pay dirt.

"So," asked Hubert while he checked over my office TeeVee and VCR, "when you goin' to break down and make a real agency out of this dump?"

"What? With lots of people on salary and elevator music playing in the waiting room and charts to show clients statistics on crime?"

"You could do worse."

"I could piss blood, too."

"You may need to s-sell it if you k-keep goin' on this way. J-Jesus, Jack — the detectives in paperbacks have better operations than you do."

"Yeah. They've also got big-titted babes waiting for them behind every door and sixteen-inch skulls. They get shot and run off to play tennis, and they don't ever have to worry about digging up dirt on guys like Andrew Sinnott to make ends meet."

"Com'on, Jack. Steppin' into the n-new millennieum w-wouldn't be nearly as painful as you make it sound."

"The hell it wouldn't." Draining my coffee, I banged my cup down a little too hard, saying, "When the hell are you going to get it through your head that I like being responsible for just myself. I had enough of sending people out to do dirty work in the service.

"I like things the way they are."

"Things the way they are are g-goin' to get yer ass blown off one of these days."

"Promises, promises."

The arrival of Mrs. Sinnott at that moment kept us from discovering how morbid we could get. She came in wearing the face I've seen a thousand times — knowing and expecting the truth, determined to see everything through to its inevitable conclusion, and yet still hoping against all reason to be proved wrong. Praying for it. Her hope faded fast. Simply looking into my eyes told her she didn't have a husband worth keeping. Pushing aside the useless, she said:

"Well...it certainly didn't take you very long."

"No, ma'm. We were pretty lucky right out of the gate."

"Yes. Weren't you just so fortunate."

"Mrs. Sinnott," I interrupted, knowing where she was headed, "you knew what you were after when you came to me. I can appreciate how you feel, but I don't think it will help us any if you decide to take your anger for your husband out on me."

"Oh, you can appreciate how I feel, can you? And what gives you all the insight? Have you just grown so used to the parade of pathetic women that can't keep their men that the sight of us just bores you now? Is that it?"

"No, ma'm," I told her. "A few years back I tried marriage myself but...," I sucked in a long breath, letting it out as I talked. "After seven months my wife figured she could do better than a police detective and moved out on me while I was laid up in the hospital. I came home to find her drawers empty and a letter blaming me for everything from her monthly cramps to the trouble in the Middle East.

"I'm not saying this to upset you, Mrs. Sinnott. I just thought maybe I should let you know you're really not as alone as you think."

Steeling herself, Mrs. Sinnott slipped into one of the padded chairs in front of my desk, wiping at her face with a rolled-up tissue. My guess was her eyes were a fairly nice shade of green when she wasn't crying as much as she had been recently. Also, stripping them of a little of the suspicion, anger, and hate she was feeling toward men in general wouldn't have hurt, either.

"I'm sorry," She apologized. "Obviously I'm not really mad at you."

Wives apologizing to me — I think I hate that more than any other part of my job. They try to sound sincere; they really do. Somehow, though, they always sound like a real estate merchant trying to convince a black family the agency really doesn't have any properties in the nice sections of town. I never blame them for it. Truth knows I've done the reverse and hated everything female in sight because of the actions of only a few members of the species.

Shoving it all out of my head for the moment, I concentrated on my client, waiting out her lament. "It's just that I've tried for so long. I tried to be a good wife. I tried! After that I tried to be a good politician's wife, and then..., later... then I just tried to stay — to keep — to..."

She looked away for a long moment, not really in the office. Abruptly she began to root around in her purse for something and then, just as suddenly, she snapped it shut again without pulling anything out. Looking back up, she continued.

"I thought for a long time," she said, "that maybe, maybe he'd grow up, realize what he was doing to us...to our son and daughter...I don't know... that maybe, somehow, he'd think about what he was throwing away."

She laughed at herself then, turning her eyes away so she could hate herself for a moment without the burden of someone else's pity taking any of the sting out of it. The moment passed quickly, though. She looked back at me, fixing her gaze on mine, her eyes pleading for understanding.

"But, that didn't happen. And...I don't think it's ever going to happen, either. What do you think Mr. Hagee?"

"You might be right, ma'm."

I said what I did because it was what she wanted to hear, and because there was nothing else to say. Once before I'd collared another cheating husband, but one whom I'd sized up as partially reformable. Taking a chance on my instincts, I told him what was going down, giving him the choice of either going headlong into the inevitable divorce his actions were dragging him toward or, cleaning up his act. He'd straightened out enough over the years to not cause me to regret my decision to bend the facts I presented to his wife.

But Andrew Sinnott was not in that category. From what Hubert and Carmine had told me, he was more than just a womanizer. He was foul, miserable, dirty water — the kind of drink you wouldn't trust if you were dying in the desert. Reaching foward for the VCR, I switched it on, splashing Mrs. Sinnott full in the face with her husband's antics.

The tape started with a few establishing shots cueing the audience in to where the action was taking place. Hubert took charge of the narration.

"Okay. Here he comes now. T-That is your husband..., right, ma'm?"

She studied the screen carefully, finally admitting, "Yes. That's him."

"Okay," responded Hu with enthusiasm. He rubbed his hands together to show he was just getting warmed up and then dove back in. "Well, now — here you'll see the film take a break. Watch that wall clock jump. See there? First it's a little after eight, then it-it's almost nine. All he did was have a few drinks. And t-talk with a couple of guys. We have it all on tape, but we duped out this s-shorter version for today because..., oops — t-there he goes.

"Look there."

Hubert aimed an index finger at the screen, making us aware of Sinnott's movements.

"See," yelled Hu, still pointing with one hand, directing us in closer with the other. "See? He's pulling three, one hundred dollar bills out of his wallet, there — right there. And now he's pretending to pick them up off the floor. See. Did ya see?"

"Yes, Hu," I told him. "We can follow the story."

"Huh? Oh, yeah; s-sorry. Anyway — now watch — here he goes, calling the waitress over. Now see, he shows her the money. Puts it on the table — and now — the moment of truth."

At that point I asked Mrs. Sinnott if she wanted to view the rest of the tape in private, but she told me "no." She didn't elaborate past that point, either.

She merely sat in front of the television, her legs crossed tightly at the ankles, hands gripping the arms of her chair, waiting. I half-watched the screen, half-watched her, waiting for her reaction. Over the years I've seen a lot of different ones — from men and women.

Nobody wants to find out they aren't enough to hold their mate — that they're no longer attractive enough, or intelligent enough, or stimulating, interesting, or whatever enough. People raised on Snow White and Cinderella often don't understand that marriage is a tight-fisted battle of two people against the world. It's a partnership where love is important, but trust is the most highly prized ingredient. Once a husband or a wife forgets their principal duties, usually, that's pretty much the end of things. Whether or not the couple remains together — for the children, or from a lack of financial options or imagination or courage, or out of the fear of being alone rather than departing from the hateful stranger they've saddled themselves with — does not matter. Once trust is gone, in all but the rarest cases, that's the end of things. From the look on Mrs. Sinnott's face, I could see that, sadly, there was nothing very rare about her case. Nothing much at all.

Carmine had aimed his mike as narrowly as possible, but only one word in ten from Sinnott's table came through to us. It was enough. First he indicated he'd found the hundreds on the floor, and that he was leaving them as a tip. That got him a rousing kiss of gratitude. The waitress wrapped her arms around Sinnott's neck, pulling him half up over the table while she manuvered herself in closer. Continuing the kiss, she slid his jacket off his shoulders and started on his tie and shirt buttons. Mrs. Sinnott's eyes grew wide. I was a little surprised myself. Hubert had to clamp his teeth together to cover his snorting laughs. While we watched the straight-on camera shot, the blonde continued tearing at Sinnott's wardrobe, dropping some of the pieces she got loose to the floor, tossing others over her shoulder.

Not at all nonplussed, Sinnott responded like a man who knew what he'd paid for and expected to get his money's worth. I wondered at why the pair had even bothered with the pretense of the tip. Maybe it was a rule of the management to keep the owner's legal hassles to a minimum. Watching the screen made such questions unimportant.

Sinnott was not built like a porn star, but he made up for his lack of musculature and penis size with an over abundance of determination and joy. Balanced on the single legged table, he grappled his partner from above like a man clinging to the face of a mountain. The pair slammed against each other repeatedly, the slapping noise of their violent contacts loud enough to reach Carmine's mike. Each crack made Mrs. Sinnott flinch just a bit more than the one before it.

The edges of the screen showed the other couples around their table. All eyes were on the pair. They weren't waiting for the table to collaspe or admiring technique — they had become an audience, using the bouncing couple on the table as a surrogate release. Sweating faces, all with unblinking eyes and restless mouths, crammed up body on body against one another constantly jocking for better views…

By this point Sinnott had stood up on his table, the waitress straddling him in a locked-leg position. His thrusts were choppy, showing his concern for the strength and balance of the table, but his face showed only that he was in his element. He had not paid merely for sex; he'd paid for the chance to entertain, to be admired, respected, perhaps to generate envy.

Regardless of my personal feelings, I had to admit, anyone who came on a night Mrs. Sinnott's Andy did was sure to get their money's worth. He whooped with glee, laughing and shouting, giving out with Tarzan yells, all the time dancing and rocking his willing partner. At one point she released her leg hold and Sinnott flipped her upside-down. She locked her legs around his head then, arms around his waist, and then caught his still hard member up in her mouth, sending a new look across his face.

With greater dexterity than I would've imagined him capable of, Sinnott bounced down from table to chair to the floor without shaking his partner's grips loose, and then began to stride about the club, showing off his prize. He stepped out of camera range, and all the heads of other patrons still visible to us followed him. They were the main show, after all.

Due to Hubert's editing, Sinnott came back into the picture almost immediately, but I reached out and turned off the tape. I didn't see any need to explain my actions. Mrs. Sinnott knew the tape wasn't over. She also knew if she wanted to view any more of it with us present that we would oblige her. But, like myself, she saw no purpose to it. I asked her if she would like anything, a cigarette, a drink…there was no answer. I searched out the rewind button and pressed it. I told Mrs. Sinnott I was reversing the tape, checking to make sure that was what she wanted done with the same apologetic whisper a funeral parlor director uses to ask the widow where she wants the latest flower arrangement placed.

She made a quiet mumble that sounded like a "yes," but then found she couldn't let it go at that. Still frozen harshly in place, her head down, legs rigid, fists tight, she said:

"Yes. Rewind the tape. Yes. Rewind it and give it to me so I can take it home and get on with this…this — Yes. Yes. Rewind it. Take it back to the beginning, take it all back to the beginning — take everything back to the beginning—"

She was crying now, reaching out to me in an unconscious, desperate grab from the center of the black loneliness that had surrounded her for so long, but that she had only that moment admitted actually existed. Her tears streamed, her sobs echoed. It was a death wail — the death of her mate, her partnership, her future, her life. Mrs. Sinnott wasn't a woman who had lived for herself. You could see it in her eyes; I could feel it in the pain with which her agony filled the room. From birth she'd waited for her chance to be 'Mommy.' She found herself a marriage, a husband, children — she'd done everything she was supposed to, when she was supposed to — and now it was all disappearing.

"What am I, I mean, what am I going to do? Oh, dear God Almighty… what am I going to do?!"

I held her, patting her back, trying to project a feeling of fatherly concern, mumbling niceties, hoping the developing scene wouldn't grow too messy. I refrained from saying anything of substance. As I'd explained to Mrs. Sinnott earlier, it had nothing to do with any "parade of pathetic women." Having been in her shoes, I knew there was no cure for what she was feeling but time. Even if I'd understood her position perfectly, even if I'd had all the answers she needed — which I didn't by a long shot — I wouldn't have bothered to say anything. After all, who ever listens to good advice when they're howling with pain? I never do. No one does.

While I quieted Mrs. Sinnott, Hubert retrieved the tape from the machine, replacing it in its plastic case. After that he put it on the desk in front of us with the full-length version and then gave me a high sign that he was going to go out and get something to eat. I nodded, knowing it would make things easier on all of us if Mrs. Sinnott was allowed to pull herself together without an audience. He managed to shut both doors without any noise.

It only took another minute for her to get a hold on herself. Pulling away from me gently, she apologized for her behavior and then took quick stock of herself in a compact mirror. Wiping her face down, she drained away the last of her tears and ruined makeup, leaving behind cooling skin and hard, chilled eyes. Silently, she pulled out her checkbook so she could clear up our account. I gave her a receipt along with the number of the best divorce attorney I knew. She took it all and then she put on her coat still without a word, picked up her evidence and headed for the door. Suddenly, though, just as she was on the threshold, she stopped and turned back toward me.

"He's going to wish he'd kept that three hundred dollars," she said. "He's going to wish he had all the money in the world."

Then she left, silent and alone. I sat quiet for a moment, not thinking, just shaking off the effects. Finally I sighed and reached over to my hot plate for the coffee pot. Hubert returned as I started to pour.

"S-So," he stuttered, "Wanda Waterworks finally got her little seizure under control, eh?"

"Can it, ya mutant."

Crossing the room, his familiar limp dragging only slightly, Hubert set his own coffee on my desk as he pulled his drenched overcoat free. The rain was getting worse. While he piled it in the chair next to the one he usually likes to sit in, he cackled, "Oh, come on, man. She was flake city. What'd she really expect?"

"Jesus, Hu. We didn't give her an envelope of 8 x 10s taken through the motel window shades, you know. We delivered a Ken Russell special. That was a hell of a rough trip for anyone."

"Awwww, bullshit. Christ, b-b-but you can wimp it up with the best of 'em. That miserable bitch — what else did she expect? Trust me, Dick Tracy, her husband ain't the only one at fault in that marriage."

"And what makes you say that?"

"Were you lookin' at that tape? You saw how our b-boy likes it. Wild and dirty and public. You're right. That was no b-back road motel room…it was a fancy club in the middle of one of the world's b-biggest cities that all kinds of people go to all the time."

Hu snorted at me, waving his arms as he continued, saying, "You wanta bet hubby tried to get her interested? More than once, even? In fact, I'll b-bet there was a time she was willing to indulge little Andy in his fun and games.

"But then," Hubert paused to gulp the top layer of his coffee down. "After that sweet ol' piece of paper made them legit, my money says that's when she got morals."

"And people call me a cynic."

"Fuck that. All that guy wants is some g-good, clean healthy fun, which you can b-bet your rent money dried up in his house a long time ago. So now, just because he goes out for a little partying, his whole life is going to c-cave in. Now he loses his j-job, home, p-place in the community — everything — all 'cause he went to a hooker to put a little more fun in his life, and 'cause you wanted more cash in your till."

Sitting back, sipping at my own brew, I answered Hu wearily.

"You're so full of shit, I can't believe it. First off, you and Carmine are making almost as much off this as I am, so I resent the insinuation that I'm the big bad ghoul here. Second, I don't care if you're right or not. Marriage is marriage…period. You take a set of vows, you're supposed to respect them. You got problems, you work them out."

"Thus speaks the expert."

"Hey; okay," I told him, "I'll be the first one to admit my marriage did not happen, and that I was just as much to blame as she was. But I didn't cheat on my wife."

"Why not?" He leered. "No opportunity?"

"No, you little weasel. Because it's not right. Plain and simple." I knocked back a half a cup of coffee in one slug, and said, "I'll tell you the truth — guys amaze me. Every time you turn around, some movie star or politician or preacher or athelete or your neighbor is getting caught with his pants down — with some whore, or some animal, or some grandmother they knocked down, or their baby daughter or their best friend's baby daughter — and they defend themselves with all the same stupid speeches you just made. And all because they just had to go on and on, trying each new bit of sick nonsense that came into their heads, because they can't control their cocks long enough to think about anything but themselves.

"Hey, that one's got nice high heels — oh, that tingles my favorite fantasy; better call the wife with an excuse — wonder if she takes it in the back door — wearing heels like that? Sure she does. Bet she likes it rough, too. Bet she'd just love it if I followed her home and slapped her around and made her blow me. I mean, look at those shoes will you? You know she's dying for it. No wonder so many women think we're all dirt."

Picking his coffee up, Hu drained it in two fast pulls. Then, getting back into his foul weather gear, he said, "Well, it's always a pleasure to visit you when you got a b-bug up yer ass. Remember to invite me around the next time you haven't been laid in a while."

I could tell he was inviting me to launch off into another tirade, but I was too weary. I settled for mumbling an appropriate goodbye while watching his back as he headed for the hall. He made it all the way to the outer office, but then turned in the doorway and cautioned me:

"All this worrying you do about the rest of the w-world — that's what causes you all your grief. Do what I do, Dick Tracy — tell the rest of the world to go fuck itself.

"You'd be a lot better off."

As he left, I went back to my desk, grabbing down the Iliad as I went by the shelves. Pulling my Gilbey's bottle and a glass from their resting places in the bottom drawer of my desk, I poured myself a good handful of ounces, leaving the bottle out when I'd finished. Mrs. Sinnott and her husband had put me off the idea of lunch.

Then, going to my place marker, I picked up reading where I'd left off. The women were still wailing on the beach. I finished my drink before I got off the first page, wondering if all the money in the world would have made them feel any better.

Woolworth's... For All Your Defensive Needs

The New Jack Hagee Story

"THERE HE GOES!"

"Don't just talk about it — get him! Shoot him! Kill the bastard for Christ's sake."

As distinctly as I could hear their voices echoing through the trees, I could hear the following shots even better. A lot better. That's when I started to move. Let me tell you, all pretenses of stealth disappear when people start aiming and pulling triggers. I could feel the wind from their bullets whipping past me. It gave me speed I didn't know I had. Thank God for small favors.

I'm willing to admit things did not look good. I was being chased by four armed men over rocky, muddy, mostly unfamiliar terrain. They were burdened by trying to get their rifles and shotguns through the heavy foliage. I was burdened by trying to do the same with my own equipment without leaving a trail they could follow.

Getting through tangle brush with a long bore weapon is always tricky. You either hold it barrel-to-face, trigger-to-groin, or you move real slow. You lose good shots or you lose ground or you end up getting your weapon knocked out of your hands or back into your eye — whatever. From what I could tell, two of the men following me were going for good shots, keeping their weapons to the ready and doing a slow stalk. The other two were crashing after me as fast as they could.

I heard one of the ones who was going flat out with his weapon to the ready go down hard. I've seen it before — men running scared through the trees, ramming their own weapons into their chests, sides, faces because they were in a panic or sometimes just a stupid hurry. The one behind me had gone down screaming. The heights his choir tryout was reaching made me think he might have broken some ribs.

Good, I thought. First goddamned smile I'd had all day.

Never gloat, my old top kick, Major Rice, used to say. It's bad for character and it's bad for business.

I should have listened. In the split second it took me to relish the thought of the guy rolling on the ground screaming like a stuck pig, I let my foot come down on a slopping wet piece of rock-top moss. Bad move. The moss tore away from the slick chunk of granite beneath it and sent me flying.

My first instinct was to grab the camera bag hanging from my shoulder and curl myself around it. If anything happened to what was inside it, even if I did survive I would be back to square one with nothing to show for my troubles — an idea I didn't relish.

So, instead I took the fall as best I could and prayed for some luck. Twigs tore into my face, snapping from the pressure. Blood flicked up into my eyes. My shoulder caught on another piece of granite sticking up out of the ground. It was solid enough to stop my progress which only meant that while my shoulder stayed where it was the rest of my body kept travelling.

I hit the ground badly. My chin dug into the mud. My legs flipped up over me, crashing down through a thorn bush, one breaking a low hanging branch. The air rushed out of me with a whamming bang. I could hear the loud *woooooffffff* of air running out of me, could hear the gasps and coughs that followed. I prayed to God I was the only one who could hear them.

My mind begged my body to shut up and control itself. It couldn't. Not immediately, anyway. All the thinking part of my brain could do was hope no one could hear me over the still screaming crybaby who'd wracked himself up a minute before I did. At least, I thought, as I shut my eyes against the automatic onrush of tears, he was making a hell of a lot more noise than I was. It was grim satisfaction, but as I lay on my back in the mud with the wind knocked out of me and the taste of blood in my mouth, it was the only kind I had.

My name is Jack Hagee. I'm a private detective working out of New York City. The way things were looking then, I remember thinking maybe I should've stayed there.

It all started the day I picked up Carmine Cecolini's VW bus from his widow, Marie. Before he'd shuffled off his mortal coil, Carmine had been one of the top freelance tails in the business. One of the reasons for his success had been the remarkable equipment center he'd put together. Carmine had been on the verge of joining up with my agency when an explosion killed both him and Francis Whiting, a young law student I'd used on occasion. I didn't feel anything back then. I'd been too mad, too set on finding Carmine's murderer to worry about anything else. Afterward, well...afterward it was too late for emotion. I helped make sure Marie and the kids would have some money coming in. Then, I bought the van because I knew Marie had no use for it whereas I certainly did.

Carmine had built a hell of a surveillance shop on wheels and I was happy to be the one who got it, if not happy about how it came on the market. He'd built a police scanner into the front dash along with CBs with upper and lower sidebands which the cops use for communication between units. A thousand other things were built in as well, all within intelligent reach — note pads, cameras, a cellular phone, handcuffs, metal detector, portable crime lab, camcorder, flashlights, binoculars, first aid kit, electronic tracking equipment and a ton of other stuff.

He'd even put in a folding bed, a chemical toilet, and a mini-refrigerator. It was, without a doubt, the best piece of equipment like it in the business. I'd given Marie the $47,000 she asked for it without batting an eye. I knew it would be worth it in the long run.

A few hours after handing her the check I felt for sure fate was agreeing with me. No sooner did I get back to the office than I found a message from Mike Ogden, a claims adjuster I know over at Bigelow Mutual. He had a surveillance assignment for me that promised to pay back a nice piece of my recent investment, a fact that made me very happy. He was sitting on an obvious case of compensation fraud. His only problem was he couldn't prove it.

Bigelow had been disputing the workplace injuries claims of a Mr. Dennis Forenti for nearly three years. Forenti had been working as an asphalt spreader for an upstate construction company. He took a tumble off his machine — an action most of the witnesses swore was his own fault. That hadn't stopped him from suing his company for workman's compensation, however.

When they went to court, his claim was that his injuries were of such a severe nature that he could no longer hold down his job, or any other job for that matter. He listed it all — the inability to lift over thirty pounds, constant migraines, blurred vision, back pain, neck pain, trauma, anguish...I was surprised he hadn't tried to claim the fall had given him AIDS.

To make a long story short, the ultimate outcome was that Bigelow was down to its last appeal. If they didn't come into court with something better than they already had, they were looking at paying out six to nine hundred a week to Forenti until he hit retirement age. Or, as Ogden put it:

"That's about forty-two years in the future, Jack. How's ten grand sound to rustle me up some proof that'll get us off clear?"

"That's on top of expenses — right?"

"Right. Your daily and expenses for taking the case...I'll give you four days on salary...you cop the ten if you can snag something that'll hold up in court."

I told Ogden he was a gentleman and a scholar and that I'd like to spend some more time dishing up compliments to him, but that unfortunately I had to run out and spoil the opportunistic plans of one Dennis Forenti. I could feel Ogden's smile over the line. He faxed me a few pages of pertinent information to get me started, promising a messenger would arrive within the hour with everything else I would need, including a good faith retainer to get me motivated.

I told him the chance to earn ten grand had me plenty motivated, but that I'd accept the retainer because I wouldn't want to insult any of my good friends at Bigelow. As soon as I hung up I got my Chinatown partner on the phone, told him to plan on taking over the operation of both our offices for the next few days, then explained what had happened. His smile put Ogden's to shame. After that I poured myself a cup of coffee, collected the pages I could hear rattling out of the fax machine, and sat down for a study session. It was, to say the least, illuminating.

Dennis Forenti sounded as typical as they come. A high school drop out who could only get a job through friends and the upstate Democratic patronage machine, he had a sheet that made for interesting reading. His pre-adult list went from shop-lifting to school ground muggings. After eighteen, he turned to other creative activities, like cultivating marijuana as a cash crop, moving stolen car parts, skirting the law to bring cigarettes, guns and fireworks into the state for untaxed resale, and a host of others.

Thanks to a half-brother in the local assembly, he hadn't served any time yet. As Bigelow had put it together, the only reason Forenti had taken the road job was that his half-brother had arranged it as a keep-your-nose-clean final favor. Forenti had managed to avoid the local law for the time he was on the job and ever since. Which meant he'd either actually wised up, or had at least decided to keep clean to avoid blowing his case. Studying the packet Ogden's messenger brought me didn't give me any indication that Forenti had brains enough to actually wise up. Which, of course, gave me hope he would be easy to put away.

Or, as my mother used to say about hope, foolish boy.

Forenti lived on his share of the family farm just outside of Dormansville. His parents were both dead and their property had been divided amongst three brothers and a sister two years earlier. The map Ogden sent me showed part of the problem with catching our boy doing anything he claimed he was physically incapable of. Forenti's property was in the middle of the family land. That meant he was surrounded by kin on all sides.

With only one road leading into the area, it meant an investigator was going to have to cross a lot of private property to get to Forenti. Ogden's report admitted that several attempts had already been made and that all of the people sent in so far had been run off at gun point. There was also little doubt that the clan wouldn't be expecting another try in the last weeks before the final trial.

Suddenly that bonus didn't seem so firmly in hand. But then, since nobody ever gives anybody something for nothing, I figured if I wanted it badly enough, I'd get my ass in gear and go out and earn it. So decided, I changed the message on my answering machine, grabbed up Ogden's faxes and my new set of car keys, and headed for the door.

My strategy was fairly simple. Since it was already late on a Friday afternoon, I decided to get out of town before rush hour. I headed home, threw a bag together, left word for my neighbor Elba to feed my dog Balto until I got back and then hit the road. From there I figured I'd get a two-night in a nearby motel, then see how close I could get during the weekend. What should have been a four hour drive was dragged out to almost seven thanks to a rain storm that started a half hour out of the city and dogged me the entire way.

Drying out in my motel room, I balanced the idea that a weekday might be easier. If any of the family had jobs, that would be one less set of eyes to spot me. On the other hand, a stranger in the woods could explain himself away as a goofy lost city geek a lot easier on the weekend. Ogden's files didn't show the Forenti clan as one that much believed in working for other people — or at all, for that matter — so I decided to just jump in and see what happened.

You'd think I'd learn.

The next morning I had breakfast at a roadside diner where they almost knew how to give a person enough food, even if they didn't know how to prepare it very well, and then headed off to see what I could accomplish. I'd studied a map of the area the night before. My first couple of hours of driving around helped focus my alternatives. I finally decided to join a group of fishermen near the local lake.

Parking seemed permissible in a field off the main road simply because there were twelve vehicles parked there already. My van wasn't going to draw any undue attention sitting there with the others — not until dark, anyway. That gave me a good ten, eleven hours of daylight to hike through to Forenti's property, get a better idea of what I was up against, and get back out.

My best calculations made it look like a five mile trek. Having to move through mountainous woodland and open fields trying not to be spotted meant I would have to figure on about three hours each way. Undaunted, the sound of cash register bells still in my ears, I moved into the back of the van and grabbed up what equipment I figured to need.

Luckily I'd brought my own hiking boots which would see me through whatever kind of mud might be waiting. Trying to go as light as possible, I kept things to a bare minimum — canteen, some jerky and a bag of unsalted nuts, the video duffle, a rain pauncho just in case the cloudless sky overhead was as big a lie as the day before's, and Carmine's Woolworth special.

The last was a cheaply made survival knife modeled after the one carried by an adventure movie character back in the eighties. Carmine had bought it in a moment of weakness. It had a lousy blade on one side and an almost useless saw-ridge on the other, but it was filled with silly do-dads like a compass and other gimmicks which had made it irresistible to him.

Knowing it was quite possible I might have to use whatever knife I took along for some real hack work, I figured it best to take the worst one I owned and just beat it into the ground. I also grabbed up a small box of Slim Jims Carmine had left in the van. I chuckled as I noted a Woolworth's sticker on the back of the Slim Jim package. It made me wonder if Carmine did all his shopping there.

As I packed the bag, I thought back to eating Slim Jims as a kid. Back then they were a really good snack. Nowadays, though, they're made with so much grease they're hardly worth the eating. But, they're light and, I figured, if I got desperate they might not be tasty but they were still edible. Then, with that decided, I set off and made my way into the forest.

The trip was worse than I thought. The day before's rain turned the ground into a humidity magnet calling every fly, mosquito and gnat out in force. Sure, the jungle tours I'd done had prepared me for such duty, but nothing ever makes it enjoyable. I slogged up and down the mud hills, slithered in and out of the trees, and basically had a miserable time trying to find my way to Forenti's property without being seen.

Obviously I was looking for the most out-of-the-way route possible. The going was hellish until I stumbled on a thin shallow that bottomed out and circled the more treacherous terrain. I'd almost missed it due to a well-placed length of camouflage netting. Interestingly enough, it turned out my playmate and his family were still in the marijuana farming business. They'd planted the shallow because, as best I could tell, once they'd netted it over, it was impossible to see what was growing in it unless you were standing directly in it.

It made me laugh. I'd figured from his rap sheet that he was probably still involved in something shady, no matter how clean an appearance he'd been keeping up. Finding a half acre of ganja on his property was no surprise. Stopping to take a good sniff told me it was fairly low grade dirt weed. Considering what a class act the Forenti clan seemed to be, that wasn't much of a surprise either.

I videoed the whole set-up figuring evidence of any kind of wrong-doing couldn't hurt. I kept my guard up, even after I found my way out of the crop line and back into the forest. Later, by the time I finally traced the best route in, it was pretty much time to turn around and head back out. I spent more of that night scraping off mud and trying not to scratch bug bites that I care to remember. Being able to snicker at Forenti's low grade grass took some of the sting out of things.

Sunday I simply repeated my Saturday itinerary without the mistakes. Getting an earlier start, I ate a larger breakfast faster, headed straight for the fisherman's parking lot, doused myself in insect repellant, grabbed the same supplies — including the untouched Slim Jims — and then dodged straight back to the trail I'd marked the day before. A lot less heat and humidity and far more cloud cover made for a much better day.

I was moving along the boundary of Forenti's property before ten o'clock which had me feeling pretty smart — a feeling destined to not last long. I found what looked like a good scout hole — twenty feet of cliff wall to my back, thick ground scrub for camouflage, and a clear shot of the target's house and a good bit of his grounds. Unpacking the camcorder again, I checked the range and then sat back to wait for my target.

He came into sight with two other men after about forty-five minutes. I took some tape of him standing around having a cigarette just to get warmed up. Ogden had said that anytime Forenti had been seen off his property he was the soul of pitifully slow movement — his every public action a thing of agony. I figured if nothing else the animated way he and his pals did even the simplest things might make good viewing for the new jury.

Then came the moment I'd been waiting for, but couldn't believe had fallen into my lap so quickly. Slapping his pals on the back he moved them over toward an old Dodge flatbed parked next to his house. Before I knew it, the three of them were jacking up the front end and stripping off its tires. Forenti was changing the brake pads on his truck just for me.

Within an hour, I had tape of him pumping a hand jack, wrenching off lug nuts, carrying truck tires and moving around underneath the truck on his back. The trio even obliged me by have a water fight with the hose, slipping in the wet grass and knocking each other around like school boys.

When they stopped for their fifth cigarette break, I decided it was time to pack up. I figured I could always come back if Ogden needed more, but I didn't like pushing my luck anymore than I already had. Besides, I'd left my cigarettes and lighter in the van so I wouldn't be tempted to give myself away with a smoke trail. To be honest I was getting tired of watching them have all the fun. I'd just finished packing the camcorder away when all the good luck I'd been patting myself on the back over finally ran out.

"And who might you be, asshole?"

The voice came from above me, down from atop the cliff I'd been using to shield my back. Looking up, I saw a face I recognized from Ogden's files as one of Forenti's brothers — Thomas, I thought. Whether I had his name right or not, I knew the name of what he had in his hands. It was an M16 fitted with what looked like a twenty round magazine. From the way little Tommy was pointing it, I had a feeling he wasn't about to believe anything I had to say.

How? my mind demanded. Unarmed, except for Carmine's Woolworth special, caught in the crosshairs by an opponent with the high ground. How had he gotten up there without me hearing him? How did he know to get up there in the first place? With no better defense in sight, I screwed my friendliest "Oh, gosh" expression on my face and waved, saying—

"Oh, *hi.*"

And then dove into the side brush as low and fast as I could. Shots tore into the ground where I'd been standing. If my opponent had been a professional I wouldn't have stood a chance. But, he was just a normal guy, not used to the idea of killing people without at least knowing he had some justification.

I crawled as fast as I could, smashing my way through the underbrush. Heavy slugs blasted into the ground behind me, throwing clumps of soil and forest growth in every direction. Voices started shouting somewhere off in the distance. Not that I could understand anything they were saying — not that I cared. I was too busy elbowing my way through the bushes, crawling for my life with a camera bag bouncing against the small of my back with every move.

The explosions stopped as suddenly as they started which I figured only meant my playmate had emptied his clip. I spit a prayer over my shoulder and risked rising up into a low crouch. Then I started running, heading for the deepest cover I could remember. As I moved, I started picking up snatches of what Tommy was yelling to the others.

His shooting up the countryside had made all of us a little deaf, but I finally caught on to what had happened when he yelled, "The tracks in the back field — the ones we found yesterday. The motherfucker's back! We got him!"

"Don't talk about it! Get him! Go on! Get the som'bitch!"

Moron, I told myself. Goddamned moron! No. These hicks won't check their crop. They won't notice anyone's been through. Of course not.

I couldn't believe I'd been so stupid — couldn't believe I could start tripping up like an amateur just because there was more money to be made if I worked fast and careless. I'd known the second I'd stumbled onto the Forenti family's inflation hedge that I should have backed off and scrubbed the day's effort.

Asshole, I cursed myself, pushing to move faster. That's what he called you. An asshole. Notice how well the word fits.

I cursed myself a few more times, trying to get it out of my system so I could start figuring my way free of the mess I'd fallen into. A part of my brain started taking stock of the situation. The Magoo on top of the cliff face had tried twenty times to hit me, but hadn't. I've seen guys run out of a battle with an arm blown off they hadn't even realized was missing, but I was sure I hadn't taken any hits.

Slowing a bit, I reeled my mind in, forcing it to assess the situation. Beating down the panic burst that had saved me, I looked for my best way out of my fix. Not knowing how Magoo had found me narrowed my options. It was certain he had stumbled across my tracks from yesterday. If he'd been able to retrace them to their point of origin, then he knew where I was parked. Heading back for the van could be a big mistake.

That meant I had to strike out over unfamiliar territory in the hopes I could reach safe ground before the Forenti clan could catch up to me. I slowed down a bit more, trying to watch where I stepped. I had to avoid muddy areas, avoid breaking any stems or branches. With the ground so wet, I also had to be careful of leaving dull spots behind me. As Major Rice used to say, "Step in the dew, they see you."

Moving uphill, trying to make only dry steps over a granite outcrop, I slowed to nothing more than a fast walk. I was moving carefully from piece to piece, trying to fade away into the forest. If the quartet behind me headed back to their precious crop, or even straight to the meadow parking lot, I had it made. All I needed was a bit of a head start and I could stay ahead of them all day. Sadly, I wasn't going to get it.

Before I knew it, one of them was screaming, "There he goes!"

"Don't just talk about it — get him! Shoot him! Kill the bastard for Christ's sake."

That was when shots began ringing out from more than one source and I started running like a scared pig again. I heard their man go down, had my laugh at his expense, and then went down myself. Laying on the ground, more than slightly stunned, I fought with myself to get moving.

Get up, Goddamnit! my brain screamed at me. Get up — get up! At least make it a *little* difficult for them to kill you.

I forced myself up off the ground, testing my legs one at a time before I tried to start running. Bruised but not broken, I moved off again, forcing the best speed I could manage. Subtlety was out the window. What I needed was distance. I ran all out, pushing myself poundingly hard. I could feel my head cooling as the wind chilled the sweat building in my hair.

Finally, after a solid five minutes, I began to feel myself growing light-headed. Spotting a small grouping of wide bottomed pines, I threw myself forward and slid underneath the largest one. I lay there for a moment, trying to get my breath back. I'd used up a vicious amount of energy by that point. I had no choice — I had to rest and take stock before I just ran in a circle, or worse, ran back into the Forenti boys. Glancing at my watch, I gave myself ninety seconds.

First I checked the camera bag. The camcorder seemed in one piece. Pulling the canteen, I treated myself to a long drink and a short head dousing. Then, my hand closed around Carmine's Woolworth special. In desperation I unscrewed the pommel and emptied out its cache of treasures. That turned out to be a good length of fishing line, two weights, several fish hooks, a bit of sandpaper and two water-proof matches. It wasn't much, but it did give me some ideas.

My ninety seconds stretched out into several extra minutes, but I felt it was worth it. When I was done tinkering with the stuff I'd gotten out of the handle I gathered up the camera bag and all my new toys. Then, after a careful inspection of the surrounding area, I moved out again.

I had one advantage in that three of my pursuers were in their street clothes. None of them except Magoo was dressed for running around in the forest. It gave me colors to watch for. After a while I spotted a lone blur of white and blue moving off through the green. That was the bald one in the T-shirt and bib overalls, which meant a shotgun. Sliding carefully along an intercept angle, I kept one eye on the blur, one eye on every other direction.

As we drew closer, I saw what I needed — a long, clear break in the trees. If I was going to have a chance at Baldy, that was going to be it. Picking up speed, I arrived at the stretch before he did. Unshouldering the camera bag, I pulled free my canteen. Back under the pines I'd packed it with dirt and then tied a three foot length of fishing line to it. Now I got it spinning over my head, waiting, watching for Baldy.

He stuck the end of the shotgun out first, then his head. I let go my bomb a split-second before he showed himself. The canteen slammed into the side of his face, knocking him sideways. He went down screaming. He also went down hard. When he hit the ground his trigger finger tightened. Both barrels let loose, bringing me the unexpected bonus of more screams.

Another brother staggered into sight, then flopped down next to Baldy, grabbing at his leg and his side. Since only his leg was bloody I thought maybe he was the one that had taken the bad spill just before I did. The pair of them were yelling so much I couldn't decide which of them was screaming louder. My mind spent a split-second debating trying for one of their weapons, but the sound of more rifle fire changed my mind. A quick scan showed me Forenti and Magoo as blurs of color coming through the trees.

They had started shooting as soon as they had a hint of me, which meant their shots had been blocked by the forest. I started moving again before they could get to the clearing. I could hear them questioning the two on the ground — what happened, are you all right, can you move, and so forth. They didn't know, they weren't, they couldn't, et cetera. Eventually Forenti and Magoo just left them and moved on.

In a way I was glad I'd seen Magoo again. It gave me an idea. He was the one that had trailed me from the marijuana field. Getting my bearings, I headed back there, figuring that if the Forenti clan were as worried about their crops as they seemed to be that might be the best place to finish things. It took a bit of crawling and a lot of dancing around the two brothers to make it back to the patch without being seen. Actually, I'd needed more patience than anything else — sitting on my hands, telling myself to keep still and wait more than once when I sensed one or the other of them nearby. Eventually I arrived back at the shallow where the crop was planted. Lifting the edge of the camouflage netting, I rolled under and moved to the middle of the patch.

Some of the bushes had reached upward over six feet already. I smashed a number of them down and broke them up into campfire sized pieces. Once I had a three foot tall pile, I hollowed out a rough hearth center and prepared to start a fire. My hope was that if anything could make the last two lose their cool it would be their precious ganja burning down.

Quickly I searched my person for every scrap of paper I had. It wasn't much. The Slim Jim box, the peanut bag, and a handful of dollar bills. Worse than that, I only had the two matches. They weren't going to be enough to light the entire pile. Although the marijuana had dried out enough to burn, everything close to the ground was still too wet from the day before to use as kindling. Then, desperation gave me a strange idea.

Grabbing up the Slim Jims, I stuck them into the mud of the hearth one by one. Then, praying I was right, I used the sandpaper to strike the two matches together and tried to light the pyramid of greasy, processed meat. It worked, the Slim Jims sputtered like miniature Roman candles. In a minute they were sending flames several inches up into the pile.

I shoved the paper I had into the marijuana in the path of the flames, shoved my money back in my pocket, and then got back out of the shallow. Hiding myself in between a thick pair of bushes, I sat back to wait once more. My last weapon in my hands, I watched the gray violet clouds climbing up through the netting, wondering how long it would take the smell to reach the brothers.

Not long. After only a few minutes, I heard Magoo shouting.

"Oh good fucking night — the bastard done set fire to the damn back field!"

In seconds Forenti and his brother dodged out of the trees, heading for the shallow. As they moved past me, I stepped out from the bushes, twirling the last of the fishing line over me head. I'd tied the weights to it, as well as several small rocks and the three fishing hooks. Whipping it out, I got it around Magoo's chest.

I gave it a sharp pull back as it began to wrap around him. The fish hooks dug into his chest and arm. He went down screaming. Before he could hit, before Forenti could turn, I charged forward. My target was so intent on trying to save his dope I was halfway to him before he realized anything had happened to his brother. By the time he began to turn I was only a yard away. He tried to raise his shotgun, but I threw myself at him, putting a fist into the side of his head so hard I closed his left eye with the one punch. Spinning away from him, I turned on Magoo and kicked, snapping his chin back with my size twelves. His rifle spun out of his hands.

Then, whipping around again I got my hands on Forenti. Knocking his shotgun out of his limp grasp, I doubled him over with a solid gut hit. He went down hacking and spitting. He didn't bother to get up, either. Actually, after that none of them were any trouble. I tramped out the grease fire in the shallow and then walked the two back to where their brothers were still laid up holding their own guns on them to keep them docile.

After I got them back to Forenti's house I sat them all down on the same couch and called the state police, telling them to bring a couple of ambulances and plenty of handcuffs. The troopers didn't have any trouble finding the shallow — they just followed the smell of burnt dope back through the trees. Later, as I gave the officer in charge my statement, he got a good laugh out of the burning Slim Jims.

I thought about that once I was finally on my way home. I'd laughed at them before, too. I'd laughed at Carmine's gimmick knife, as well, but it was the knife and the Slim Jims that had saved my life.

Bored and tired, I decided enough was enough. As I continued to speed along the New York State thruway, I fumbled underneath the dash for the bottle I knew had to still be there. Sure enough, I found a pint of Jack Daniels taped in place right where I'd remembered Carmine always kept one. Breaking the seal, I threw back a healthy couple of inches. Then, I toasted Carmine and did it again. The JD rolled down my throat taking away the taste of the fearful bile that had dried there earlier.

Feeling the warmth roll around in my stomach, I smiled widely. And then suddenly, I was laughing. As the back of my mind finally realized I was no longer in danger, it joined in, flashing every silly thing Carmine had ever done or said through my brain, making me laugh all the harder. Finally, at the height of it all, I hoisted the bottle upward and toasted:

"To Woolworth's...for all your defensive needs."

Putting the bottle to my mouth again, I just let the smooth sour mash keep flowing until the bottle was three quarters empty. And then, finally, my grief caught up to me and I mourned my friend, barely able to keep his van on the road for the tears in my eyes and the pain I could finally feel.

Toothpick

TUESDAY

The heat of the wires was fading; slashes of skin stuck firm, however, where wrists and ankles met the now cooling metal. The girl had stopped crying. He didn't like tears. She didn't move now, holding herself tight, fighting the jerking sobs crawling against her terror, seeking to cough their way free. He didn't like noise, or movement — he didn't like anything, except cooperation.

And fear.

Her good eye circled the darkness, searching for something to focus on, something of hope, or similarity. She could only see his tools: the things that had burned her, nipped her, prodded and bruised and sliced and reduced her. She could see bits of her suit, torn shreds with charred edges. The only other thing she could see was the yellow glare of his kitchen light. He was cooking or preparing to cook.

Like everyone else, she'd been reading the papers, watching the television. She knew what was coming. Maybe, she told herself, maybe she could please him, be afraid enough, good enough, be whatever it took so he would just end her quickly and grant her peace. His shadow brushed the door frame and she felt her legs and the floor beneath her growing wet. She smelled the urine, saw the sharp reflection, and then upset him with tears.

SATURDAY

The day'd started no worse than any other of the thousands I'd woken up to in New York. I'd slept in the office the night before, grinding myself into my couch, twisting my legs into a shape that would fit it. Sweat, wet and dried and wet again clung to my shirt and back and face in ripening layers making me itch. My stomach hurt; I'd fallen asleep without undoing my belt. Dragging myself upright, I staggered into my inner office, heading for my hot plate. There was still some coffee left on it from the afternoon before. I clicked the burner on under the pot and fell into my chair, waiting for the heat creeping through the window behind me to either finish waking me up, or put me back to sleep.

Sleep won out. My eyes glazed over, my head sagging back across the top of my chair. I was probably snoring when the knocking came. My left eye cracked, scouting the room. When I came to enough to realize someone was looking to see me, I croaked out a 'wait a minute' and staggered to the door. My back and shoulders ached with cramp and boredom. I stretched on my way through the office, dog-dragging my legs one after another to try and shake the stiff fingers of night still curling through me.

Reaching the door, I flipped the deadbolt and welcomed in a short, dark-complected, balding man. I judged he was Italian, southern, bad temper, family pride, dark connections somewhere around grandpa — the eyes that knew about truth but pretended to respectability. He looked at me, standing in the doorway, dripping morning heat like stale rain. Evenly, he asked, "You want to kill somebody?"

"A lot of people," I told him.

"Good," he answered, walking past me. He pointed inside; "Let's talk."

"Yeah," I answered. "Why not."

Pacing each other, we chose our sides of my desk and settled in. The coffee was steaming over. I clicked off the burner, asking what I hoped would soon be a client if he wanted any. The dark brown staining that'd leeched to the inside of the glass and the strength of the coffee's smell was enough to make me think twice, but he took one. As he thanked me, taking his first sip, I figured I could be as tough as a balding middle-aged man and poured myself one. Then we got down to business.

"Okay, I take it you need a detective."

"Yes. You are the Mr. Hagee?"

"Right. I get two hundred a day plus any reasonable expenses. I don't like getting shot at, and I don't like getting lied to. Try not to do either until I've finished my coffee."

"What are you — a funny guy? I don't need a funny guy."

Something was wrong. This one didn't want a cheating wife tailed or a stolen truck found. "I came here for a man, not some snot bastard who gives me jokes. Me!" There was blood in his face. I saw him more closely as his anger focused my finally waking attention.

"Maybe I came to the wrong place."

"No," I told him. "You came to the right place, you just didn't find the right guy." He stayed in his chair. "Look," I told him, "you came here looking for someone off the TeeVee, and I opened the door expecting another nuisance. Maybe we were both wrong. Let's find out. You tell me what you want, and I'll see if I can help you."

He thought for a second, hard, painfully. Something was tearing him apart slowly, the way the tide does a grassless shoreline. Looking into his eyes shook me. I realized I'd allowed a crazy into my office, one who was going to detour off into tears or swinging fists or worse any minute. Trying to postpone the moment, I asked him, "You've been to the police, haven't you?"

He nodded. His right hand balanced his head above his knee, his fingers sliding back and forth across his face, up and down the side of his head. He looked at me. His eyes rolled upward and then dropped back down to lock with mine. With visible effort, he asked, "You have heard of this man in the newspapers, on the radio, the one they call 'the Chef?'" I knew what was coming. Suddenly the bitterness of the coffee disappeared from my mouth, replaced by something less tangible but a lot nastier.

"I've heard of him, too. You know when I heard of him — I heard of him about three in the morning. Three o'clock in the morning, my wife and I got to hear about this monster. We got to hear about him, and we got to take a ride in a police car to see our daughter…," he stammered for a moment, gasping for air.

The fury within him started his shoulders shaking. He closed his eyes as his fists clenched; he'd have drawn his own blood if his nails hadn't been trimmed. The redness of his face spread down past his shirt collar, darkening like storm clouds unable to release their burden. Eyes tight, fists curled, he spurted words through grinding teeth.

"I want this man. I want him dead in the longest way. My Antonetta, she sits lost and tired. She is a black shape for the rest of her days because this monstro, this bastard coward—"

I sat and listened, letting the little man in the black suit rage to my walls. I wouldn't have tried to stop him even if I'd thought it possible. I'd heard of the Chef; everyone on the eastern seaboard had heard of the Chef. He'd gotten his nickname from a disreputable New York paper with a particularly clever knack for turning the mindless horror of other peoples' lives into a sort of daily disgust fix for the masses and profit for themselves. For them, and the rest of the city's information peddlers, the Chef was a dream come true.

In six weeks he'd practically brought the city to a standstill, at least at night. Once a week, he murdered a woman. He found one alone, or with someone, and he took them somewhere and then he raped and killed them. Raped and tortured and killed them. The papers and the radio newscasters and the evening reports were having a field day. They broadcast every guess about him, every hint, every rumor.

They hounded the police, and the families and friends of the victims. They badgered people in the streets about where they thought he might strike next, what they thought he was after, why they thought he was doing it. One station brought in Madame Tarna, a psychic they claimed would predict the type of woman he would go after next; when and where and how he would strike. He performed exactly as the woman said. Then he sent a letter to the network that had run the swami, and to their rivals, thanking Tarna for all her great suggestions. No one else put on a psychic.

But they kept up the coverage. Before they talked about the elections, the Middle East, prices, taxes, or any of the run-of-the-mill murderers and thieves and wild-eyed fanatics, they all updated the public on the Chef. Because everyone wanted to know what he was up to. They kept their radios on and they watched the news channels, and they waited in silence or blanketed in the jaded, joking manner of city dwellers, surrounded by their fear because the Chef worried them. Because he took women, once a week; because he took them and tortured them and raped them and slaughtered them and then ate them.

Slicing away select pieces, he saved fingers and ears and breasts and haunches and vaginas and ribs. He dumped his tired eyed choices in back alleys in broken heaps, going home to the freezer his letters claimed was stuffed with hearts and kidneys and brains all shiny in Reynolds Wrap, labeled in magic marker on masking tape — date, name and contents.

The man in my office was Johnny Falcone. He had buried his daughter at 9:00 in the morning, driven his wife home, charged his sons to keep any more reporters from getting at their mother, and come to see me on a recommendation. Staring at me with black eyes, he set the distance between us distorting with the heat coming off him. He sat in front of me waiting for vengeance, not even beginning to suspect there was nothing I could do for him.

"Mr. Falcone," I started, "You know there's not—"

His hand slammed my desk. He rose like a wave, threatening to wash over me in his fury. "I can pay. Whatever it is — whatever it takes! You are bought for $200.00 a day — this you said. I buy you then." As I looked back at him, he shouted, "what's your worry? Find him. Kill him! That is all you need to do. Now *do* it. Do your job. Take your money and find him!"

I didn't get angry. It wasn't his fault. Some self-important, manic ghoul had sent him to me. The madness crippling the city had jagged its way into Falcone's life, dragging at him like an anchor caught in dark water. He saw me like a shipwrecker's flames on the reef, mistaking the beacon for a lighthouse. I tried to explain that this was a job for the police. They were embarrassed; somebody who couldn't be satisfied by television had decided to find both their bread and circuses elsewhere at everyone else's expense. This made the police look worse than usual — and they never like that.

"The cops have every man they can spare, every dollar they can free out, tied up in finding this guy, There's no reason to hire me. I can't compete with them. You go to a private when the cops ignore your case. That happens — all the time, that happens. But this is different. This is their honor. They'll catch this guy."

"And do what — get him a psychiatrist? Put him on a couch so he can boo-hoo his terrible childhood? My father — he worked all the time — we don't see him. My mother, she beats us every day. I worked dirt poor from the age eight. My father died when I was ten. My mother when I was fifteen. I didn't live on 'Leave It to Beaver.' My life was tough enough — my brothers, my sisters, everyone in our neighborhood...we had it tough enough. But this bastard is allowed to kill and kill and kill and everyone jokes. They joke in the streets. They laugh at how this one will get out of jail — they know this before they know anything about him. Everyone knows he's going to get away from this, simply because he is a beast. Because he is an animal, he will be the safe one.

"When did we start treating the animals like people, and the people like animals? Can you tell me that, Mr. Hagee? And before you explain again how much the police are going to do for me, explain why one of these noble men, so concerned with his honor, asked one other if he had heard the newest Chef Joke. Have you? Do you know how many Chefs it takes to screw in a light bulb? My Antonetta knows. God Damn them forever. She knows."

He was wrong. It wasn't the latest Chef joke. I'd heard four since then. I sat with my mouth drying, my legs suddenly tired and weak. He stayed in his chair as well, suffering, I suspected, from the same weakness. For once in my career I didn't need a case. I had cash on hand enough to make it for the next several months. I'd even been thinking of taking a vacation. Nothing big, nothing fancy, just a couple of weeks out of the city, away from the dirt and the noise and the incessant red shriek of traffic and people and daily disaster that drives everyone here just a little crazier with every passing morning.

Mentally, I closed up the travel folders and filed them away for later. Falcone had known since he'd come in that I would take the case. He'd told me so. I couldn't see any point in arguing any further. With as few words as possible, I told him I was paid for. He agreed, writing me two weeks worth of checks. As I walked him to the door, I thought about getting something to eat, but scratched the idea. My stomach still hurt. I had the feeling it was going to keep hurting for a long time.

I sat, sometimes thinking, sometimes not. Long after Johnny Falcone had left my office, long after my coffee had gotten cold again. I sat staring out my window, glass in hand, watching the city's mobile parts shoutingly crawl over and past and through one another. I was happy to stay inside out of it. The gin I'd pour before lunch-time seemed no more appealing hours later, but I held the glass anyway. Never know when you might change your mind on something.

To pretend I was earning my fee, I'd made two calls, both to people who might be able to help. To challenge the legion of police working on the case I'd just taken, to try and solve the riddle their battalions of fingerprints and sweepers and probers, their scientists and psychiatrists, had been attempting to unravel, I'd called in a little talent of my own. The first call I'd made had been to Dr. William Norman, a friend who runs a free mental clinic in the village. The second had been to Hubert, a leg man I use a lot, known on both sides of the fence as reliable, top-notch, and an irritating nuisance. Both of them had been out. I'd left a message with the little doc's assistant, and one on Hubert's machine, and then started to wait for call backs. When the phone finally rang, I got two surprises, who it was, and who it wasn't.

"Jack Hagee, Investigations."

"Mr. Hagee…" It was a woman's voice. Calm, even, young, or at least youngish, but basically nondescript. It was a bland voice, the universal kind of drone one got from soap commercials. That should have been my hint. When I admitted I was myself, she started in. "Hello; Sally Brenner, WQQT News — I'd like to talk to you for a minute if I might."

For some reason I missed the connection. Without thinking, I asked, "What about?"

"Mr. Hagee, we've been given information which suggests you have been hired to track down and apprehend the criminal commonly known to the public as "the Chef?" Is this true? Could we get a statement on your plans? We'd like to send a crew out—"

As she droned, I stared at the phone, seeing her face from the evening news, the plastic features mouthing the words squirming about me. I held the receiver away from my head, looking at it, watching her words curl out of it. Without bothering to comment, I let the receiver fall off my fingertips back into the phone cradle. Before I could react, it rang again.

I stared at the phone wondering how they could know — how they could have found out so soon? The phone kept ringing. It didn't seem like it planned on stopping. Annoyed, I picked it up.

"Mr. Hagee? Sally Brenner. We got cut off somehow. This phone company — I tell you…anyway, listen; I'd really like to get that crew over soon. If we could make our 6:00 lead—"

Somehow, I found my voice. "Let me make this simple for you lady."

"Excuse me?"

"First — we weren't cut off. I hung up. Second — I don't care when your lead is; I don't want to see your crew. Send them here, and someone will have a camera repair bill. I don't know how you found out about this, or what you think you could possibly do except ruin any slim chance I might have of finding this guy, and I don't care. Don't give me any of your sanctimonious nonsense about the first amendment, or 'the people's right to know.' Don't talk at all. Leave me alone."

"Mind if I use my tape of this conversation?" the voice turned less bland.

"Yes. Don't."

She turned up the frost control, cutting the conversation the way ice water does a steam bath; "And just what is supposed to stop me, Mr. Hagee?"

"The fact that if you do," I told her, "not only will I *not* talk to you, but that I will talk to all the other stations, and I'll tell them that I suspect WQQT's reporting to be responsible for egging the Chef on. We've got no other use for each other, cunt. Trust me on that."

I hung up. Staring at the phone, I tossed off the gin I poured earlier. I continued to stare, challenging little Sally to call again. She didn't. Unable to stay in my seat, I got up and crossed the room, no purpose in mind. Walking back to my desk, I doubled back to the far wall, and then crossed to the outer office. It didn't take me long to realize I'd be pacing. I kept at it, moving about the office as I did.

Something in me had changed my liking for my surroundings. Before I knew it, the wastebasket was filled with newspapers and old files. Candy wrappers and juice cartons came down from the bookshelves, along with a few old beer bottles and a shoe. I didn't know whose shoe it was, or why it was on my shelf. I ran my finger through the dust on it, worrying the patterns, trying to decide how something as obvious as a shoe could have sat on my shelf long enough for the sun to change the color on one side — long enough to blanket itself in filth, without me noticing it. I didn't come up with any answers. I didn't need any. The shoe dropped into the wastebasket, followed by more papers, more cartons, more debris. When it was full, I stomped on the pile and filled it again. When I couldn't stomp on it anymore, I lugged it to the hall and emptied it in the building's trash chute. The phone started ringing again while I was in the hall; I didn't rush back. Whoever it was could call back. I was busy.

I'd always thought of my office as a neat place. Maybe not always clean, no cover of *Better Homes & Gardens*, but neat, proper. All it had taken was opening my eyes to see that wasn't the case. I continued to work, moving faster and faster, ripping open drawers, examining their contents, deciding the fate of each object that came before me. Going to the hall water fountain, I dumped yesterday's coffee. Filling the pot with water, I swirled it around, trying to get the brownish-gray haze it wore to fade away. It wouldn't. Admitting that stains that deep don't fade away with a shake of the hand, I headed for the bathroom at the end of the hall.

By the time I returned to my office, my shirt was wet to the elbows, and my pants were soap and water spotted from the waist to the knees, but the pot was clean. It looked clean; it smelled clean. In fact, the whole office was clean. The phone rang again. This time I answered it. My luck was improving; it was Hubert. I asked him if he was busy. He rhymed:

"Not today, D-D-Dick Tra-say. What's shaking — 'sides my b-bacon?"

Hubert's jokes have been known to leave more than one person cold in their time. Not bothering to comment, I told him, "Meet me at Billy's in an hour."

"Y-You got it. Little doc N-Norman need a hand scrubbin' down the loonies?"

"No;" I told him, "I do."

Hanging up on Hubert, I called Billy's again. He hadn't returned. The voice on the other end of the phone was curt, letting it be known that I should be asking for "Doctor William Norman," not Billy. I was curt, too, letting it be known that receptionists, whether they were boyfriends or not, should try to stay within the parameters of their jobs. Otherwise someone might take some accidental offense and mistakenly send them to the dentist. Then I told him to find Billy, and tell him I would be there in an hour. He was less curt.

Hanging up, I dialed the local precinct house, getting my closest thing to a pal on the force, Ray Trenkel. I asked him to stay put, telling him I'd be right over. He agreed, warning me he wasn't in his best mood. I said 'fine' — neither was I. As I hung up, I rolled down my shirt sleeves, checking to make sure I'd finished drying out. Taking my note pad and clip pen from the top drawer, I stashed them in my pocket on my way to the door.

Grabbing my hat from the pole, I went out into the hall, locking the door behind me. On my way down the stairs, I came across two eager newsmen in blue blazers going over the building directory. While the one figured out my office was on the third floor, the other asked me:

"Excuse me sir; do you know this Mr. Jack Hagee?"

"Yeah," I told him. "Prince of a guy."

"Do you know if he's in right now?" asked the other.

"Naw," I answered. "I was going to take him out for a drink, but his secretary told me he was over in Brooklyn; she said he was closing in on the Chef." Getting excited, they asked who I was and where the capturing was taking place. I told them I was Teddy London, and that the capturing was going to take place in a diner on the corner of Nostrand and Lafayette Avenues. They hopped out to their little news wagon and took off.

Teddy London is the name of my favorite paperback character — believing that one could make them look pretty silly. Nostrand and Lafayette cross in Bedford-Stuyuesant, a black neighborhood so tough the cops walk their beats in quartets — believing that one could get a pair of pretty blonde white boys dead. I wasn't worried about them, though. I was sure like all good newsmen they'd check their sources before they rushed into something foolishly. And, I smiled to myself as I walked down 14th street, if they didn't, the world had all the bad newsmen it needed.

The fan atop the standing file behind Trenkel rattled the cabinet drawers with each swing to the left. The metal complained the further indignity, adding one more noise to the assortment of groans and swelters making up the background symphony of the station house. I'd learned not to complain a long time ago. I didn't complain to Ray when he was in a good mood, and this was not one of those days. He stared at me through the beads of sweat dripping into his eyes. Checking his paper cup, he snarled to find it empty. Crushing it, he tossed it not his wastebasket without looking, asking me:

"Proud of yourself, Jack?"

"Most of the time. Why?"

"Shut up. Don't get cute and don't give me shit. I've got no time for either. You care to guess why?"

"Probably 'cause you're busy."

"God F.A. I'm busy. And you know what's got me so busy, don't you? You must. That's why you volunteered to help me. When do you think you'll be turning him over to me? Soon, I hope."

"What'dya mean, Ray?"

"What do I mean? Son-of-Sam-with-a-knife-and-fork, The Gobbler, Jack the Diner, The Galloping Ghoulmet, your playmate. You son of a bitch; you know who I mean. Aren't you over in Bed-Sty picking him up right now? That's the word from our communications post."

I sighed quietly. Ray reached into his bottom drawer, pulling out a nameless fifth. He had what I consider to be a strange habit of pouring the ends of whatever bottles he has around into that one fifth. Over the years, the color has ranged from nearly clear to purple. That day it was amber, with little eddies of a heavy brown swirling near the bottom. He took a short plug and offered it to me. I took one to be social. He asked, "Why'd you do it? Don't I have enough troubles on this one without you in my way?"

"I'm not going to be in your way, Ray."

"The fuck you're not! You already are. This thing's been with the media for less than an hour, and already you're the great something-or-other hope; Private Eye Jack Hagee, brought into the case by bereaved parent — already on the trail of the Chef, worst mass murderer the city has ever known — Christ, you sound like some sort of cheesy addition to the ABC fall line-up. Where were your goddanmned brains?"

I told him. I told him about Falcone, and his wife, and his daughter. I told him about the feeling the old man had given me, and how I couldn't refuse him. I also reminded him that I was a working man, and that working men have to keep working to survive.

"It's in our genes."

"Fine," he snapped, taking another plug of his unidentifiable slosh, "go for it. Try to conduct an investigation with those bloodsuckers hanging off you, giving away the details of how you take a goddamned crap at six and eleven every goddamned night. try catching a jaywalker with the restrictions we have to contend with for a change."

He stood up, beginning to circle his desk, his voice taking on a sarcastic tone. "Did you know a group of concerned citizens has already hired a lawyer to go after any officer who uses too much force against your boy?" He pounded his desk, making the fifth jump. "*Too* much force?!"

Sagging back into his seat, he caught his breath, looking old for a moment. The world had broken through and touched his shoulders for just a second, robbing him of his steam and thunder. With a shrug, he muttered, "As if shoving his balls down his throat ten times and hour for the rest of his life would be 'too much force.'"

He grabbed for his fifth again, staring at it, not quite letting it reach his lips. It made sense, if any cop took a drink every time he wanted to, even every time he needed to, the force would have a lot more alcoholics than it already has. The bottle sank back to the desk.

"Shit." His tone softened. "I know you didn't have any choice.

"I've seen those fathers every day for fifteen years. Back when it starts, you always listen, and they always win. 'Cause they have something you think they should have, and when someone takes it away, it seems wrong, somehow. After a while, though, you just learn how to skip past their emotions, their tears and the high school photos, and what's right, and what's wrong — skip straight to the facts."

Ray's hand tightened around the bottle. His fingers drummed its unlabeled belly, but he didn't pick it up. "Hell," he finally sighed, "you're a big boy. You know all this. I guess all I really want to do is warn you about the newsboys."

"Warn…?"

"Don't fuck with them, Jack. They got no sense of humor. They'll turn on you as soon as you stop being good copy. Once they feel you've had enough time to catch your boy, they'll start to 'wonder' about what's taking you so long — and you'll start to catch the kind of flack we do every election year. I knew you were going to take the case — I just wanted to make sure you handle the media right."

He eyed his fifth a last time, and then returned it to its place in the bottom drawer. With another sigh, he asked me what I needed. I told him.

I was late getting to Billy's. Ray had had more information than I'd thought. When I got there, Hubert was in the back room, waiting where Billy chased him. His jokes had probably been upsetting the patients. The little doc was in a session, but had left word to be called whenever I arrived. He was curious. He knew I never came down officially without something interesting. I figured this one was as interesting as could be.

Hubert spotted me and hurried over, his limp more pronounced than usual. "I'm shakin', boss — heh, heh ha — I'm shakin.'"

I could tell from the way he was favoring his bum leg we'd be having rain soon. I hoped it would be the kind that washed the city down, taking the heat and stickiness and the muggy bad tempers with it. The kind that just increased the humidity we didn't need.

"What's up, D-Dick Tracy?"

"Trouble, Hu. I got a bad one."

"Knew that. W-Wouldn't want to see the lil' doc and me b-both if it wasn't."

Billy came out. "Hi, Jack." He pointed toward Hubert. "I see you found Quasimodo."

"Don't start on each other," I sighed. "I need the both of you. Give it a rest this time." Hubert grinned. Billy nodded. They disliked each other only as a hobby. They could postpone it for a while. Pointing toward the back, I asked, "someplace private?"

"You got it." Billy motioned us back to his office. Inside, Hubert sprawled on the couch. "It started when I was a c-child, doc. I think it's b-because I hate your mother…"

"Can it, Hubert," I growled. I wasn't in the mood. He sat up, looking sheepish. I didn't care. It had just begun to dawn on me what kind of deadline I was working under, and just how impossible my task was. I didn't need the distractions. While Billy took his seat behind his desk, I took the armchair near it. Tossing my hat on the desk, I said, "I've taken a case that can't be solved, so I thought I'd let you guys help me not solve it. You both heard of 'the Chef'?"

"Heard of 'i'm; hell — I can give you his phone number. O-I-C-U-8-1-2. Heh, heh; g-get it? O-I-C—"

I cut him off. "Shut up, Hu. I already know Chef Beer has lots of body but no head, and that he keeps Lady Fingers in his cookie jar. I've heard all the jokes about this sick bastard I care to. Am I printing in a language you can speak?"

Hu nodded, pulling in on himself as if I'd tried to bite him. Billy asked, "You have a plan?"

"Yeah," I told him. "I'm going to tell you guys everything I know, and you're going to tell me how to catch this pervert. Sounds simple, doesn't it?" Neither of them said anything, waiting for me to get started. "Okay, here's all of it. Like you know, the Chef came to attention about a month ago. The press is playing up the fact he's killed six women, one a week, for the past six weeks. Truth is, the police think he's actually responsible for about twenty-two murders over the last eighteen months."

Billy sat back, flipping open his memo pad; Hubert's eyes got wider, his grin dragging back from wherever my sour mood had chased it. I continued to talk, giving them the facts. The cops had found too many similarities in a recent series of violent homicides to rule out connections. The killings had occurred over all five boroughs. When the Chef had announced his threats to the papers, claiming credit for two murders which had taken place in the previous two weeks, the cops had already tied them to the long files they'd been keeping.

Just to refresh our memories, I read the first letter he had sent the press aloud:

Folks,

This is by way of informing you that the sky is falling
I have arrived and my appetite is large
You are all in it for now
Little Linda was a good fuck but did not know when to be quiet
Nancy tasted yummy
Do you
Does your mother
I am going to try and find out
Once a week
Do not stop me
Let me kill again
your best pal

Linda had been Linda Ann Wright; Nancy was Nancy Reid. Over the next month they were joined by Unera Ujaque, Prisilla Morley, Rita Sumoki and Anna Falcone. The police had compared them on the surface; then they had dug — deep, hard and long. There were no uniform similarities. Going back and including all the women they were reasonably sure had been killed by the Chef, they could find no lines — not even unconscious ones he might be following without knowing it. Some of the women were black, some Spanish, most were white; there had been one Oriental. Most of them had been city workers — not surprising in a city. Two were housewives, though one was a hooker, two were college students. No lines.

Most of them had been alone when they disappeared, but one had been with her boyfriend in Central Park, and another had been with an entire group of people. they had disappeared, though and no one knew how. Some were blondes, most brunettes, et cetera. Some wore heavy make-up, others none, et cetera. Some were overweight, some were pretty, one had been a model. Et cetera. No lines.

"No fucking lines."

"Maybe that is the line, Jack." I prodded Billy for more. "I mean, don't whip the expired stallion. Maybe it's just women…period."

"Then why no little girls? Why no older women? Why's everyone been between twenty and forty?"

"Because that's how we think of women. Most of us don't see our mothers until mom is twenty or older — not see so we remember. And most of us move out by the time mom is forty. To most men, women are twenty to forty years old. Everything else falls into some other category."

"Okay, great. Super. So he just kills to kill? No go. There has to be a 'why'."

"'Cause he likes to." I got ready to snap at Hu again, but Billy interrupted.

"No; he's right. It's just the 'why'? What does our Mr. X think he's doing when he does all he does? Is he getting back at mom; is he striking back at an ex-wife, a current wife, a girlfriend? What? What do the police think? Did they find any ex-husbands or boyfriends in the—"

I cut him off. The cops had tried every angle on every guy ever connected with any of the victims. They'd found a few hot leads, a few brooders, but no one off base enough to be our boy — certainly not when they tried to start connecting them not only to one murder, but over twenty. No lines. Billy started again. "All right; let's say for the minute it's random. What we have to do is try and narrow down what kind of problem Mr. X has. He likes a lot of things. He tortures; he sexually abuses. He's left sperm in the mouths of severed heads. He's mutilated, and, if we're to believe his letters — he's cannibalized human bodies. He even claims to have cooked and eaten parts while his dying victims have watched."

"So," I said. "He's the sickest guy in the city — how does this help us?"

"What will help us is determining what kind of sickness he has. Strong possibilities; if we can narrow him down, there are clubs you could check, people you could talk to, types to check for. You have to remember, we've already cut half the perverts in town off the list.

"This fellow is a top; a dominant top." Billy gestured dramatically. "There's a swagger to his walk — force lives in him. You, you're a dominant fellow, Jack. But when the tension gets to be too much for you, you down a shot of gin. This boy, when the screws are too tight for his forehead, he goes out and does real damage. We're talking a very self-assured kind of guy."

"Meaning what?"

"Meaning, I think in all probability, You're never going to find this guy. My bet is when he's not performing for the 11:00 news, he sits at home, glued to the telly. He's hit on a way to get his rocks off, supplement his menu and feel important all at the same time. Figure out what he's striking back at, you'll have him." Billy's fingers came together, snaking in and out of each other.

"H-He's right. Something about these girls sets this guy off after them. M-Making that connection is the only way y-you're going to get 'im."

We tried. We looked over every fact Ray had given me, working off into the night to find what he and the rest of the force had missed. Our luck was no better. Whatever it was connecting the bloody string of corpses our little maniac had left behind together, nothing jumped out at us any quicker than it had for the cops.

No lines.

We watched the late news over pizza and doughnuts. Billy's little black & white glared at us in the shadows of his office. A smiling man in a greyish blazer assured everyone that a hero had entered the arena, and even though they hadn't had a chance to talk with me in person, he was sure the Chef would be stopped shortly. For some reason he said my name as if I was going to be able to do something. Hubert wasn't the only one in the room to make jokes about that one.

Grabbing another doughnut, I put my feet up on a chair and watched the smiling mouth open and close; it was almost midnight. Soon it would be Sunday, and the clock would be ticking. Somehow I wasn't as sure as the grinning mannequin leering out of the screen that everything would be okay.

A week later, I found out how right I was.

TUESDAY

The blood had rushed to her head long ago. She had tried to plead, to whimper — not for herself, but for the other life in his hands. He laughed at her, tittered with the amusement of a bored child once again approaching his household pet. She struggled against the wires, her tongue pushing against the ball of his underwear he had taped into her mouth. Nothing moved. He had lashed her too firmly, too thoroughly. She could not even stir the chair — nails held her legs secure.

She tried not to look up into the mirror. The bites had stopped bleeding, but the ragged ovals showed red; she could not look at them, or watch his fingers sliding in and out, rubbing the unresponsive flesh away shred after shred. He stood behind the chair, smiling, in and out, watching television, one hand holding an unidentifiable strip of meat to his chewing face, the other hand working its way deeper.

He laughed at the anchor man; he found the actor's concern not nearly as convincing as the woman's from QQT. He liked her. Maybe they could get together for lunch. That would take planning, of course. An offer she couldn't refuse. Her and Jack both. He would have to give the media and Mr. Avenging Angel Jack fucking Hagee both their shots at him.

Later, after the blood and the mess and the satisfaction, he found the means to start his plan into motion.

THURSDAY

Hubert and I were sitting in my inner office when the eighth Chef showed up. He pleaded with me, swearing he'd committed all the crimes, including Mindy Freeberg, the girl they'd found yesterday morning, the one with the fetus cut out of her. This one's name was Paul, and he was as sad and confused as the first seven.

We finally got rid of him by convincing him Hubert was the Chef, an act which had worked on number three also. As Hu shoved him out the door, I muttered, "Why don't you just confess to Ray and end this show?"

"S-Sure; think he'd b-believe me?"

"Naw; not really." Hubert came back into the room, carrying a small package. he tossed it to me saying, "F-Found this in the hall, outside the d-door. S-Santa musta come early." He grinned as I caught the package, saying, "You know, D-Dick Tracy, I bet I know w-where you should look for ol' Cheffie." When I didn't answer, he sputtered, "C-Check the places that have skeleton crews."

He launched into his cackle. I tore at the wrapping of the box he'd brought in, looking to change the subject. Thinking of the trembling slob he'd just escorted to the hall, I said, "God, I'm coming to hate the press. I'll never give Ray grief again. These guys are too much. I mean, Billy says they keep confessing because they want to relieve society's guilt, but what's wrong with them? First they go to the cops, and the cops get rid of them, so they start coming to me."

I threw the wrapping in the trash, barely aware of what I was doing as I talked. "These phone calls, from the jokers and the cranks, and every grandmother who's seen a shadow go by her window; it's getting to be—"

The conversation stopped like cars in an intersection crack-up. Unaware Hubert was out of his chair standing next to me, unaware of anything, I held the contents of the box and stared. I looked through the green water, my eyes searching a constant path through the floating pickles inside, following the small, near-human body bobbing with them. I continued to stare as Hubert left the room, and as I reached for the phone. I stared while I talked to Ray Trenkel, and while I waited for his men to arrive. I sat the jar on my desk, not moving from my seat. Hubert came back in. Taking his handkerchief out, he went to cover the jar. I grabbed his wrist.

"No," I told him quietly. When he protested, I pushed him back toward his chair. "No. Just look at it. Look at it and get it through your head what it is we're up against."

Tears were rolling over Hubert's cheeks. He made to turn away. I reached across the desk, slapping the side of his head. He cried, "I, I, I don't wanta, Jack!"

"Look at it, Hu, or so help me I'll break your arm." He stared. He cried and stared, the snot dripping from his nose. He wiped at his sobbing face and my desk where he'd gotten it sticky. It wasn't long before he got his reprieve. Trenkel arrived, with enough people in tow for an elephant to get lost in the confusion. The door opened with a crash, the flood of curses and shouts waving in at us like a war. Uniforms and plainclothes had to keep people out physically, pushing bodies backwards out of the door to the sound of clicking shutters. Ray came into my inner office, spewing dark attitude.

"You're quiet; good — stay that way. Goldberg," Ray shouted to one of his detectives, directing him to Hubert, "take this model citizen here in the next room and get his statement. Gerella; in here." He pointed at the wastebasket, asking me, "That the box and all?" When I shook my head, he started Gerella in on pawing through my trash for things to lift prints off of. Pointing toward the jar, he growled, "You open this?"

"What for?" I asked, feeling insulted. "The deli always sends me a pickle with my lunch."

"Go to fucking Hell."

I sat and watched the circus roll from one ring to the next, drumming my fingers in the heat. The breeze I'd been using for an umbilical cut off far too early, leaving me and the sixteen other people jammed into my office to swelter. Ray hurried his boys; they took the jar, the box, the wrapping, the string and the last of my good humor. After I'd told Ray's right-hand, Mooney, all of the hardly anything that'd happened, they packed up, bracing themselves for the tight-lip back through the wall of Sonys and Nikons outside the door.

Ray turned to me, grinning. He loves to grin when he's causing trouble. "We're out of here." He pointed toward Hubert. "I'll leave Porky Pig here in your care." And then, as he headed for the door, "oh — one last thing. We won't be saying much on our way down the stairs, so get ready for the onslaught."

I hadn't had much trouble with the press, yet. I knew this would be different, though. They'd spent most of their time so far waiting outside my door while I avoided the office, getting hung up on, or digging through old police and newspaper records, looking for anything worth screaming to the world seventy three times a day about my life history. Since I wasn't a public official, they couldn't stop me from hanging up phones or walking the other way when they found me in the street. Besides that, despite what most people think, the media really isn't that stupid. They knew as well as I did the chance of my catching the Chef. Up until now. Most of them didn't even bother to follow Ray and his crew. As soon as the police line went down, they started through the door. Hubert slammed the inner office door. "I — I c-c-can't…"

Crossing the room, I held the door, waving him to the window. "Take the fire escape, Hu." In a job like Hubert's, having one's face plastered all over the newspapers and the tube was not the wisest of career moves. He scrambled out the open window, taking the rusting rungs three at a time. He was lucky I had a corner office off the alley, But then, I'd rented it with that in mind. It was about the only advantage the dump had.

Once I figured he'd had time to hit, I stepped away from the door. Two from the front of the crowd were thrown to their knees as the herd began to move. I stepped back to my desk, replanting myself. Some of them tried for the windows, but I stopped them, asking if they wanted me or the hired help.

They stayed, figured they could find Hubert later. That showed how much they knew about Hubert. I started to answer their questions, looking to see how much they knew me.

They had details on some of the cases I'd been involved in, but most of their questions about the past got shouted down by the majority who were only interested in the now. They wanted to know who the man was I'd let out the window; what he had to do with the case; what I has doing to track down the Chef; why he had sent Mindy Freeberg's unborn child to me, et cetera. They didn't get a lot. I didn't bother to dispute that he had sent the package, or that the fetus was hers. There was no other answer. I was sure of it — I couldn't see any reason why they shouldn't be. After that, though, things got tougher.

"Sally Brenner, Mr. Hagee. Tell us, why do you think your adversary sent you the 'container,' and not the police?"

"I don't know. I'll ask him when I find him."

That started an avalanche of when-will-that-be's, are-you-close's, do-you's, will-you's, can-you's, and the such, all spewing at me in an impossible jumble. I sat quietly, letting my amusement at their eagerness show until they got the point. Brenner managed to clamp control again.

"Do you think that he might be seeing himself as your 'foe,' an opponent? Moriarty to your Holmes?"

I was beginning to like Brenner a little. At least she knew she was just doing a job. Some of her more irritating peers didn't seem to have figured that out yet. Besides, every detective likes to think of himself as Sherlock Holmes once in a while. Trust me on that.

"Anything's possible," I admitted. Although, I didn't really like the thought of some cannibal lunatic singling me out for a one-on-one, nothing else made much sense. She followed up, asking:

"How do you plan to respond?"

"By tracking this maniac down. Let me try to explain something to you people."

Cameras hummed. I welcomed myself to show biz and then settled in to the ugly process of dealing with the press en masse. As they smeared against one another, bayoneting their spear mikes at me, I told them, "Let's try and get things straight here — there's no telling what's going on in this joker's head. He may be thinking of himself as Jack the Ripper, or the next Christ; he may feel what he's doing is paying women back for the Lib movement. He may hate mom, the ex-wives, or all women, period. Whatever his reasons are, they aren't really important. *He* thinks they are, of course, but—"

"What do you mean?" chirped a faceless voice.

"I mean anyone willing to actually kill people has to think they have a good reason. His thinking his reasons are good, though, doesn't make them good. This twerp is a coward—" That one caused a lot of gasps. The air got hotter from the flash bulbs and the sudden excitement. I waited for the quiet to slip back into the room, and then answered the how-can-you-say's and what-do-you-mean's as best I could.

"You're right," I told them, "he has killed a lot of people. In fact, he's killed more people than you give him credit for."

Tension split the silence again. As they yammered questions about what I meant, I forced myself to go slowly. I'd been teasing them along into doing something. Now we were all at the brink. Keeping my voice calm, my hands from shaking, I began talking them into jumping first.

"As best we can tell, the Chef has killed some 23 people over the—" The shouting ballooned. Some of the stringers raced for the door, heading for telephones or cars; I told those who stayed everything I had. I gave them figures on the body count heaped at the Chef's door, one of the few things the cops'd been able to keep quiet. Ray was going to go through the roof. I didn't care. It made good press, and I needed some.

As quickly as I could, I told them of how the Chef had started killing some time back, and how it had only been recently he had made a show of it. I laid out for them how extra attention had goaded him into trying to top himself.

"He's trying to provide good copy, because he loves to play it back. This boy's got a scrapbook, and a VCR, with all your by-lines and faces."

"All well and good," chimed in QQT's Sally, "but why do you call him a coward?" I wondered if she's caught her cue. Hoping so, I let her keep talking. "He's taking on an entire city — its press, its police — every citizen in town is watching for him. That's a coward?"

"It sure is," I assured her. The guy's not Robin Hood; he's a deranged little worm. He isn't taking anyone on. He hasn't the guts. He kills in secret; he hides in darkness. Shadows are no threat to the people smart enough to stay out of them. His victims have all been people with 'it-can't-happen-to-me' stamped on their forehead."

Looking straight at little Sally's cameraman, I told everyone, "You call this guy my 'adversary.' He isn't. An adversary is someone threatening you — they're someone to worry about. This pathetic little moke, he may kill a hundred more women but, he'll never get up the nerve to come knocking on my door. This isn't some psychological ploy to bring him to me — I'm not a guy who looks for trouble. It's just the truth. The Chef is a terrified little fungus — for whatever reason, he's killing women to feel powerful, important, not realizing how much smaller such acts make him. I doubt we'll ever be adversaries, mainly because I don't have time to turn over all the rocks in town."

The house came down with that one. Before anyone could even begin to quiet down all the shouters, suddenly Ray was back with Mooney, and someone larger that I didn't know. They didn't look happy. The press was dismissed — quickly. I was told to lock up and come along — also quickly. As I triple-timed down the stairs to a waiting squad car with Ray and his pals, I crossed my fingers and hoped for the best. Ray's rapid return showed me just how angry he was. He was hungry to get this case off the public monitor, and I'd spilled the only beans he had. I was shoved into the back of a patrol car and rocketed to the station house through the afternoon haze and heat.

Before Mooney had finished parking, the large stranger grabbed a handful of my collar and yanked me out onto the street the way he might a sack of potatoes. Managing to land on my feet, I showed up with both hands, breaking his hold. He came at me; I stepped back, fists up, snarling.

"Listen, melonhead; I know how to walk — I've been doing it since I was eight. I'll go in under my own steam and not give anyone trouble. Don't give the Press the excuse to make me more of a hero than they already have."

Ray came around the car, his voice venting in ragged snorts through the heat. "You bastard — you big-mouthed shit—" He swung at me; I ducked. "I'll tear your goddamned head off and feed it to you." He lunged again, missing again. I danced out of his way, warning him:

"Why don't we take it inside?" I pointed at the news van pulling toward the curb. "I mean, with company coming, and all?"

The trio calmed themselves and we all wired for the door. I was ushered to Ray's office and pointed toward a chair. Melonhead pushed against my back. I stumbled a couple of steps towards Ray's filing cabinet. As I hit it, I grabbed the swinging fan atop it and stepped around quickly, slashing with it at Melon. He leaped back, slamming into Mooney, knocking him into the hall.

Ray grabbed Melon's jacket, screaming, "That's enough, goddammit!"

"C-C-Charges, C-Chief." Heads turned; It was Hubert and Billy, running down the hallway to Ray's office.

"Don't rough Jack up too much," cooed Billy. "It isn't the politically correct time for such antics." The little doc indicated the noise coming from the front lobby behind him. "Flashbulbs, incrimination — 6:00 shame. Don't chance it, Cappy."

"W-W-What's bail, C-Chief?"

Ray cooled. He had to. Then he grinned — that surprised me. With a wave, he dismissed Mooney and Melon, sending them back to doing whatever they did when they weren't pretending to be intimidating. With a growl, he told me, "Okay, Jack — you're on your own with this one, now." He acted hurt. "I tried to give you a hand — play fair, but you," a sweep of his hand indicated the war zone of the lobby before us, "you had to pull this stunt."

"You know why I did it."

"Maybe. Maybe it's even a good idea. But I don't care. If this guy kills again — if he keeps going and you're wrong and he just laughs, I'll help the media plant you so far you'll be lucky to pull factory assignments from Strouss Security."

I wanted to say something else, but Ray wasn't in the mood. He'd made a mistake, busting up the press conference, and pulling me down to the station. Unless—

I turned to Hu and Billy, telling them to take their triumphant smiles and wait with them in the lobby. Feeling just swell, I stepped back into Ray's office, shutting the door. I asked him, "Feeling clever?"

"No more than usual."

"That's nice."

"It sure is." He took a pull on his cigar. Putting his feet up on the desk, he smiled. Smoke curled through his teeth. "You complaining? I set you up with a juicy case, good money, lots of press — now I make you a hero, and help your stupid dog-ass plan along.

"Milk it for all it's worth, Jack. This is all you get from me."

Ray had sent Falcone to me; I'd known that since he'd slipped earlier, telling me that he known I'd take the case. He'd done that, and then helped my press maneuverings along in the background, keeping them interested in me, waiting for the moment to give them their big chance to uncover some dirt.

"We both know what's next. They're going to spread this all over the tube. Police rough up detective…Private Investigator reveals police secrets… Detective calls Chef 'coward'…film at eleven — same old song. If we're right about this lunatic, he'll be stewing real good about five minutes into the first newscast he sees. And he's going to start stropping his razor with your Windsor knot in mind. I'm thinkin', all in all, we now have a good chance of smoking this little fuck out."

Ray was enjoying himself. For a moment, he made us both forget how hot it was. "Just keep yourself alive, Jack."

"I'll do my best."

What a chump. Trenkel had sent Falcone to me, knowing there was a good chance I'd take the case. He'd kept the press informed, and when the time was right, purposely roughed me up knowing I'd be 'saved' by the 'heroic,' self-congratulatory media. I hoped now that he'd staked me out, he'd at least pick a good tree to watch from for the tiger. I grabbed up the sleeve of his jacket hanging near the door and mopped at the sweat on my face. As I turned the doorknob, he gave me another bit of news.

"Oh, and Jack — don't forget. If you were even a little wrong to do that — if he does start doing them up again like so much kobalsi — then, of course, I'll be forced to take action against any citizen who does such rash, damaging things."

The closest thing I had to a pal on the force. Shit — the closest thing anyone has to a pal on the force. I made to move, but he held me up one last time.

"By the way, Jack. There's an unofficial reward for this guy. A name you don't need to know is willing to go 50 thousand for the Chef's elimination. On any level. Of course, I'd need, ohhh — around 20% of that to keep things quiet if you were to bring him in in less than the best of health; still — 40 grand buys a lot of Gilbey's.

"Think about that, Jack; all of it. And stay real healthy."

He put his cigar back in his grin. I shut the door behind me and walked out into the sea of flashcubes and jabber to find Hubert and Billy. I couldn't wait to tell them how smart the three of us had been. Boobs of a feather. The cops had maneuvered me into being their excuse, and suddenly I found myself a working man of limited options.

Working men are real chumps.

He watched the lips move as anger inched through his system. His fisting fingers tore into the arm of his chair, tearing threads, gouging padding. One fingernail caught the edge of a tack. It shredded raggedly, blood gasping free, soaking the gray cotton, droplets splashing the rug. His eyes never left the set, staying fastened on the voice telling him what Jack had said. Clever. He knew it was clever.

"Fuck you, Jack," he told the air, hearing the echo, knowing his opponent couldn't. "What," he quizzed the room, "I was born yesterday? I know what you're after."

He reached for the evening edition again, staring at the front page, at the man in the picture.

HAGEE CALLS CHEF COWARD

He stared, back and forth, from the words to the man. Jack looked big. He measured the height, took in the thick shoulder muscles, the hardness, the qualities of the man he had challenged — who had challenged him back. "I'm not stupid, Jack — you fuck. You don't get me that easy."

And yet, had anyone else stood up to him — by themselves, one face alone, eyes open — to him? He'd brought the whole city low — terrified them all. But if Jack set out to bring him low — if he made a fool out of him, then no one would be afraid. He'd have to start over — he'd have to teach them all over again—

His smile leered. Why, they'd slip back in a minute, if they thought it was safe; if I were — gone. Jack only looked tough, sounded tough. "I can take care of him." Just like all the rest. That would teach them.

It would...

He relaxed as he smiled.

MONDAY

I knew it wasn't going to be as easy as it seemed. It had been almost two weeks since the Chef had done anything. The city had started ringing the chimes, declaring that the big bad wolf had gone back to the forest. I had the feeling he was still around, waiting to see if my bluff was made of straw or sticks or bricks or what. It was his move, and I'd just have to wait to see what happened.

I'd talked to Falcone, explaining what I'd done, and what I would be doing. I told him I was going to cut my fee in half and wait. He understood. To him, two weeks without terror was payment in full. He said Anna hadn't had a single nightmare since she'd seen me on T.V. calling out the Chef. He also confirmed my suspicion that Trenkel had sent him to me. Ray and I had kept in contact over the past two weeks as well. The police hadn't come across anything that looked like the Chef's handiwork. There'd been no more letters with his trademarks. Ray was a little more confident than I was, but not much. He told me he'd been impressed by Hubert's coming to the station to bail me out when he and Billy had thought I was in trouble. He didn't know anyone else Hubert would risk publicity for. I'd been surprised myself.

It hadn't hurt him, though. He'd slipped out without being cornered easily and met Billy and me later. The three of us had discussed Ray's maneuvers, and tried to pinpoint what the Chef might do. Actually, it was Billy that came up with it.

"It's their clothes, you know," he said. When we asked what he meant, he told us, "All the bodies that have been recovered, they've been nude — just dumped in lots and alleys in garbage bags and sacks. The one thing we've never known is how they were dressed."

"S-S-ure," stuttered Hubert. "That might be it. We've checked everything else."

Hu was right. Between us and the cops, everything had to have been gone over — hair color and styles, nail polish and makeup, measurements from the obvious to the inane — everything but their clothes, because no clothes had ever been found. That one we kept to ourselves. I was sure the same thought had crossed someone's mind on the force, and that they probably already had a file on what the victims had been wearing. I told Hu to sniff it out. He did.

A friend of a brother of a woman who worked in the D.A.'s office was able to get a xerox from someone she went to lunch with every Friday from the Records Building. All it told us was they were all neatly dressed. No jeans, or tank-tops, square-hole jackets, no, as my pal Tony would put it, 'slut clothes.' They all had been decently dressed, not so much expensively, as, well, tastefully. Most of them had been in suits when they'd disappeared. Everyone had been wearing hose and their best shoes and good, well-tailored outfits, all of which meant only nothing to any of us. They'd all been dressed as if on their way to job interviews at I.B.M. As desperate as we were for an answer, none of us thought that was the one we were looking for. As Billy said:

"It wouldn't actually be the clothes, but what they represented. It's the woman he really hates who dresses neatly. But who she is isn't going to be revealed to us by just the one clue. Did his mother dress that way? His ex-wife, his sister? The same questions again. I'm sure it's an important link, actually. The fact the police compiled this detailed of a list proves we're on the right track. But just like them, it isn't enough by itself to tell us anything."

Hu thought that maybe our boy might be keeping the clothing as trophies; the little doc's suspicions said 'maybe' to that idea, but ran more towards the idea of a sort of ritual stripping, a peeling of the armor, just another part of his degradation process toward his victims. It had given us possibilities, but nothing definite; just like everything else, no lines. We kept waiting.

So far, the Chef was acting just as we'd figured he might. That had me worried. We'd thought he might hold off for a while, trying to lull everyone into a false sense of security, just to be able to shock them all the more with a bloody return. I sat with my feet up on the sill. ignoring the noise and heat leaking in the window, trying to imagine that return's where and when. A glass was out, in case I suddenly got an overpowering urge. I hadn't for some time, but one never knows about urges. I like to be ready.

The sudden knocking at the door didn't surprise me. Neither did the knocker. The Press had been dropping in on me fairly regularly. Sally came in, creme skirt, powder pink blouse, creme jacket, all pressed and neat and feminine-but-business. I told her, mopping my brow uselessly with my soaking handkerchief, "I marvel you can keep creases in this weather." Dragging my feet down, I pointed her toward a chair. "What's up?"

"My," she cooed, "no hit-the-bricks-bitch today? What happened? You go and get civilized on me, Hagee?"

"No;" I pointed to the haze and humidity outside. "It's just too muggy to fight. Unless you insist, or something."

She laughed, running a hand through her hair, "I'll pass. I think we have enough on our hands." Something in her voice triggered me. I leaned forward.

"What's that mean?"

"It means things are going to get hot again."

"We talking speculation, or premonition here," I asked. "Or something worse?"

She opened her shoulder bag, pulling a small cassette player from it. Handing it across the desk to me, she confirmed, "Worse. Lot's worse."

I pressed play. I couldn't think of any questions that couldn't wait. The first thing I heard was Sally telling the world she couldn't come to the phone, and could everyone please leave a message. One was important.

"Hello, Sally. I thought we should talk." It was a cold, flat voice — something out of a slasher movie. I wondered if he'd practiced. "I have been considering giving myself up. I'm tired — I'm so tired." There was a pleading edge, almost as if he meant what he was saying.

"The police — I can't go to them. They wouldn't understand — they might... hurt me." The cold, flat child's whimper begged at us. I looked at Sally while it rambled. There was a chill around her. The voice had wrapped her in cold, cutting off the humidity and sticking clamminess which had dampened the city for the past weeks. She lit a cigarette, pulling deeply while the Chef talked.

He wanted her to come for him. He wanted her to get the story, because she'd been so fair — almost as if she'd known why he'd had to do everything he'd done. Yeah — right.

"You buy this?" I asked her. Smoke curled out of her nostrils, hurrying in jags as she breathed. Her finger halted the cold flat voice in mid-plea.

"I don't know." She bit her lip. "Maybe. Some of it. I don't think he believes it, though."

"Do you think he wants to give himself up?"

"Yes." She said it as surely as she'd ever said anything in her life. "He does. Somewhere inside."

I caught the hesitation. "But what?" I asked her.

"He wants you, too."

"I'd stick in his throat."

She stared at me levelly. I hate when women do that. She jammed her cigarette out in my ash tray, a paperweight kind of thing shaped like the cone and sphere from the '39 World's Fair. Drumming her fingers on the sphere, she said, "Doesn't it seem a bit hot for the chest-beating shtick right now?"

"Could be," I admitted. Reaching down to the big drawer in my desk, I pulled out my latest Gilbey's bottle. I'd bought it before I'd met Falcone, and yet I hadn't gotten the level down past the label yet. I offered Sally a chance to change that with me. She accepted. Passing her a glass, I reminded her, "No ice around here, you know." I passed her glass over.

"Is it wet?" She asked. As she sipped, I told her:

"Wet as gin gets."

"That's good enough."

We clicked glasses, then proceeded to knock back a few and drop the edges, getting sociable. There's nothing like your name being on the same bullet as the person's in the next seat over to start up a conversation. She clicked the tape back on. Our pal told us how my standing up to him had made him realize he'd been wrong. Now he wanted to repent. He wanted to begin repenting on a rooftop in Queens that night. No cops. He'd know, and if he saw anyone but us, he'd never surrender. Never. In fact, he knew just the kinds of things he'd do if things weren't done his way. He was kind enough to share a few of them with us. We played the tape out, drinking more, getting more sober with each glass.

"Please — no policemen. Just you two. I'll surrender to you — honest. Please Sally; get Mr. Hagee to come. I promise to be good. I promise. Please?"

It was good. Just the right amount of guilt, flattery, and innocence. Sally started to laugh. This time I stared at her levelly. She started to explain. Women must hate it when we do it, too.

"I was just thinking that this guy has sure gone to a lot of trouble to set two smart types like us up."

I smiled back. "So what?"

"Sure would be funny if we got up there and he just shot a lot of holes in us. Or blew up the roof."

"Yeah," I agreed. "But wouldn't it look good on tape?"

She started laughing in mid-swallow, suddenly choking, blowing gin and mucus through her nose long after a sober person would have. I smiled at her; she told me dryly, "You're very funny."

"Yeah; I'm always at my best before I walk into some lunatic's crossfire."

Knocking back the last of her drink, snot and all, she asked, "Think we've had enough?"

"I don't know — you want to go to bed with me?"

"Sure. A woman who's going to get pumped full of holes and blown up all for the greater glory of the 10:00 report deserves one good fuck in her life."

"Yeah. We've had enough."

"Goody." she clapped. "Let's go to my place." Before I could ask, she told me, "Yes. 4500 BTUs in each room."

Happy to close up my sweatshop in favor of an air conditioner palace, I threw the empty in the wastebasket and started to straighten my tie. She told me, "Don't bother. You won't be needing it."

Taking her at her word, I pulled the sweaty knot loose and stashed the tie in my middle desk drawer. Then, unlocking the bottom right-hand one, I pulled my shoulder holster out, along with a pair of handguns. I've kept a number of the unregistered weapons that have come into my hands over the years for special occasions. This seemed like one of those times. As I slipped into the holster, Sally cooed again, "Ooouuh; you going to take me home and pistol whip me?"

"Play your cards right — who knows?"

She giggled again. I joined her. As I started us for the door, however, I couldn't help but wonder if we were laughing at the same things. I gave her the benefit of the doubt. I wanted to enjoy myself.

Sally and I were right on time to walk into the Chef's set-up. He'd asked for 9:00 which was when we entered the building at the address he'd given. He'd said the door would open easily — that we wouldn't need the buzzer. He was right. Taking the elevator to the top floor, we got out cautiously, both noticing at the same time that the other was holding their breath. As we inched out of the car, Sally asked:

"Do you think we're being a little over cautious?"

"Not in the least."

The hallway was well lit; the doors looked well locked. I pulled the flashlight I'd brought from my car and pointed it toward the stairwell.

"Let's go," I told her. "You wouldn't want to go first? Equality and all?"

She did the level thing with her eyes again. I chuckled and started up the stairs. It had been hours since we'd left my office. The gin had worn off long ago. We'd sweated most of it out at her place, rolling and thrashing in desperation, tearing her sheets, leaving them caressed with perspiration and blood and cum. The air conditioning hadn't helped; nerve juice, that beady kind of sweat that forms in little droplets around small hairs had returned again and again until we tired of licking it off each other and had just settled down to live with it. Rounding the first landing, we started up toward the metal door that led to the roof.

I looked back; Sally's grin was in place, but her teeth were clamped a little too tightly, ruining the effect. I gave her credit, though. If all she wanted was a story, she could have gotten it staying safe downstairs in the car. But actually getting the Chef off the streets, that took her coming here with me — meeting his demands — maybe the most dangerous thing she'd ever done. I had to admit she had guts. As I fingered the handle, I hoped she wouldn't have to use them.

"Well," I told her, easing the way open, "here goes nothing."

"Right," she agreed as we stepped out onto the roof, "isn't that the truth."

We looked both ways; as expected, no one was in sight. What we did find was a bargain-brand walkie-talkie, illuminated by a small flashlight. I grabbed it up, using my own light to figure its controls. Handing Sally the second flash, I clicked on the talker and crossed my fingers.

"Okay," I said. "We're here."

No answer came for too many seconds. Then, meekly, "Where are the police?"

"Gimme a break. You said 'no cops,' and there are none. You've been watching the street. You're watching it now. No one's here but us, and you know it. So why don't we get this show on the road?"

"Why," he answered, the meekness disappearing, "it sounds like you don't want to play my game by the rules." It was going to be as bad as I'd thought. His voice was a pout—

"Come, come now, Jack. How many rocks could there be up here? I'm sure you won't have to turn over that many to find me."

Sally and I scanned the rooftops, but nothing showed. It was one of those long extender roofs, where fifty buildings all connected up together — the kind Queens is full of. The static crackled again.

"Just standing around? No adventure in your souls? Let's go you two."

The voice bubbled like a camp counselor's, trying to egg the last pair of kids onto the bus. I whispered to Sally. She shrugged. I thumbed to the left. We moved. The radio whined at us.

"Not that way — go the other way."

We kept walking. The speaker cried, "Come back. You won't like it that way. Honest."

Moving as quietly as we could, we continued forward, searching our way through the early gloom. With all the lights they turn on in this city, the rooftops never really get darker than a heavy gray. But there are black areas, shadows cast from the odd walls and exit rooms, and all of the other strange little structures that top New York's skyline. We played our flashes in the dark spots, searching for whatever it was our playmate didn't want us to find. We found it.

Guessing, I'd say her age had been leveled off for her in the mid-seventies. We fingered the brittle, once living sack gently — she'd been dead a good while. She was cold, stiff and broken and dried out. Sally turned from the sight of the old woman, and the half dozen jagged shafts ripping through her.

"I told you you wouldn't like it that way." Laughter sparked nastily through the speaker. Turning my light from the body, I pulled Sally away, forcing her legs to take step after step. She latched onto me, tight, dragging at my clothes in little fist grabs, until suddenly she let go, bunching her clenched hands atop her breasts. I looked over.

"I'll be all right," she whispered. "If I tangled you up, he could get us. Maybe that's even what he wants."

She might be right. I eased a .45 out of my shoulder holster, making another pass over the roofs around us with my light. Nothing. We walked forward, Sally dragging her feet, trying not to. As we clicked our lights off, I called into the machine.

"So, when's the 'giving-yourself-up' part start?"

"Now, Jack. You didn't really come here for that. That's why there really are no cops. You two are here in the hopes of catching me. Right? Some overpowering duty to the race...yes — I think we all know each other here." I moved in the darkness, Sally trailing behind me. Coming to an edge where one roof was higher than the next, we had to clamber up to the next level while the machine chuckled.

"Now you're getting warmer. Something up there for you. Is it me? *Is it?*"

Something was in front of us. It lay in a bizarre heap, moving in awkward, thrashing motions. My flash proved it to be a canvas bag, something like a small military duffle. I nudge it with my foot. It flopped. Moving Sally back, I reached down and pushed free the snap which fastened its top. The cover flap came open. I dropped it and jumped away as the first rats came skitting out. Several abandoned the bag, but some stayed inside.

Carefully grabbing the bottom, I snapped it, spilling its contents. A half dozen more eggplant-sized rats flopped across the roof, chattering with mad gnashes, their claws and teeth digging at their prize. Blood crusts flaked from the once living shape that thudded across the roof with its passengers. Several of the rats vanished into the darkness but two stayed with the head, angrily snapping at each other. I clicked my light off, not wanting Sally to see the remanents of little girl face peeking out through the tatters remaining. I was too late.

She started to cry as the machine spoke to us. "Oh. No. I guess it wasn't me after all."

I snapped back, "I didn't think this was your speed."

"You didn't see her before — all whored-up in mommy's idea of a good little woman. Just another trainee, Jack. Like mommy. Or Sally. No pots and pans and brooms for that one. Oh, no. Nothing so menial as a stay home life for that little business woman. No, by the time mommy got done with her, she'd have been polishing her name on the manager's door of some company, not a kitchen counter for a husband. Not that one."

And suddenly, everything clicked. "*It's the woman who dresses neatly that he really hates,*" is what Billy had said. It was only a hunch, but I knew deep inside I was right — knew the reason the never-ending horror had been unleashed. Playing my only card, I crossed my finger and answered:

"But she was just a kid. She couldn't have been your boss for years."

The machine went silent. Sally stared at me, questioning. I put my hand over the box, whispering, "Playing a hunch."

The speaker muttered in my grasp. I let it talk. "—you mean, Jack?"

"Like you said, pal — we know each other pretty well."

A harsh note clanged out — a piece of pipe striking another. It sounded through the machine and the air. It clanged twice more, ringing in the heat. I hefted my gun, looking at it in my hand, making sure it was still there. Sally was back against the wall, looking around us, watching the dark. Stepping back to her side, I asked if she'd spotted anything. She hadn't. Handing her my light, I told her, "Keep moving around. Go back towards the door. Play both lights around. Try to make him think we're still together. I'm going to see if I can smoke him out."

She nodded. Reaching into her purse, she pulled out the revolver I'd given her at her apartment. She doubled it in the same hand with the small flashlight, and then motioned me off. Lois Lane had nothing on her. Stepping off into the black, I moved in the direction from which the pipe noise has sounded. The box talked to me. "Come on — you two can't be that shocked. I am a maniac; remember?"

I ignored him. Trying to get a fix on his position, I kept the walkie talkie away from my head, hoping to hear him talking wherever he was. It didn't work. Listening in again, I waited for my turn and then tried to provoke him. "What's the matter — no more clues to give us?"

The pipes clanged again. I was headed in the right direction. He'd moved since the first time — right in to my path. I whispered to him, "Bang-Bang. Big deal. Even your boss could figure out you're not going to stay put, and I'm twice as smart as she is."

"Fuck you, Hagee!"

I heard him. Over the box, and through the air. He'd screamed; mistake number two. Inching forward a stairwell exit, I peeked around its corner, spotting the Chef. He was hunched over a roof edge, watching Sally with her two flashlights, chuckling to himself. There was a shotgun in his hand. Slowly, I started to reach around the corner, trying to edge out beside him. My hand hit something out of sight. It was a leg.

I stuck my head around. A female torso, maybe ten, maybe twelve years old, hung upside down from the stairwell wall strung up spread eagle. It was cold to the touch, except where the wet slime draped itself, dripping from her crotch over her torn and burnt belly. I'd found the part that wouldn't fit in the duffle.

The Chef looked my way. I froze in the darkness, my hand plastered motionless in the sticking smear wrapped between the body's legs. The shotgun came up. He was cautious, suspicious, but not certain. He took a few steps, and then suddenly turned back. Sally had started to move our way. He looked at the flashlight beams, catching our trick, and then back in my direction. I jumped.

The distance was too far; I couldn't close it. As he stepped back, the shotgun straightened, searching for me. I hit the roof, but kept scrambling forward. The night split open as shot tore past, gouging up the tar behind me. Coming up under the gun, I hit the Chef hard as the other barrel erupted. Our collision sent the metal spray scattering through the sky, raining down over the edge. I slammed my .45 into his side, jamming it hard into his ribs, listening to one crack. He shrieked and swung the shotgun at my head.

Grabbing it, I held it with one hand, stopping the swing; bringing my left up, I clubbed him across the face with my gun, smashing his nose. Jerking the shotgun down, he pulled back to swing. I stepped away saying, "Don't do it."

He swung. I fired. He took the bullet in the side. It didn't stop his swing. He connected with my arm, sending me flying. I could hear footsteps, running, but couldn't tell which way they were going. I'd dropped the .45 somewhere in the darkness. His weapon was still in his hands. Not bothering to look for mine, I charged him; he finished reloading calmly and sent another blast my way, clipping my calf with the edge of the scatter. I fell into him, both of us crashing against the wall behind. He lost his grip, the shotgun spinning away.

Grabbing a handful of his hair, I dashed his face against the bricks, slamming it repeatedly, hearing the broken nose become so much like jelly. He clutched for my throat, kicking, working his teeth toward me. His thrashing flamed the fire in my leg. I clamped my teeth and then grabbed his neck, jerking him forward into my fist. He popped away from the contact, his face making the sound a dropped milk carton does when it hits the floor.

Light hit us. It was Sally.

"Don't move."

She held her gun out where it could be seen.

"Jack — are you all right?"

"Sure."

I limped over to her. The Chef sat panting, his back against the wall. Taking one of the flashlights, I played it about, finding both the lost guns. Noise from the street came up at us. Someone must have heard our little party. I hoped they'd called the cops to complain about the ruckus. The Chef laughed.

"Well done." Blood puddled and fell from his face. I wasn't sure how he could talk. I didn't even think about it. I just listened.

"I guess it was only a matter of time." Struggling to his feet, he leaned against the wall. "Come, come. Check me. Make sure I don't have anything else." Coughing and spitting, he laughed as he hung against the bricks. "Let's get this over with."

I leaned on Sally for a moment, balancing the pain in my leg. She said, "You're sure in a hurry to get what's coming to you."

His laughter came in bubbles and coughs. "Hey, my lawyer and I can't wait."

"And what exactly does that mean?"

"You two are so stupid." He laughed again in a way that had me feeling he might be right. "You think I don't have this all planned? I contacted a good man in the field weeks ago." The blood on his face had started to clot. As my breathing became regular, Sally shouted:

"You went too far. You'll never get off — you're crazy if you think so."

"Well, you're convinced. Now for the rest of the suckers." His sputtering had stopped. The coughing had settled. He was stiff, walking with a pain, but that was all. We didn't move.

"Awww, what's the matter?" he asked. "This not working like you expected? Maybe I'll send you a copy of my book, and you can figure out what went wrong." As we started, he grinned, "It won't take long to finish. My publisher's just waiting for the last few chapters, and we wrote the hardest of those tonight." His hands gestured. "I can see it now — my joy over being captured — facing the truth — my shame. Oh, doctor — you have to help me.

"hahahahahahaaaaahahahahahaaaaahhha!"

My first bullet ripped through his chest, spinning him around, sending him reeling. The next tore through a hip. He screamed. As I crouched over him, Sally's hand caught my wrist. Looking at him, not me, she asked, "don't I get a chance?"

I swept my hand over his body.

"Take your pick."

She took a knee. It erupted against the roof, the back of his leg splattering my pants. She moved for the other, but I stopped her. It was my turn. We shot again and again — while he screamed, and after. We left the way we came. No one stopped us. No one bothered us. Eyes peeked out of doors as we went down in the elevator. By the time we reached the street, there were still no sirens, no police running in our direction, no one there at all. Just like always. We got into my car and drove away. The windows watched us but they didn't say anything. They never do.

Sally cleaned the shot of my leg, and then we spent the night together, mostly not sleeping, huddled together for warmth in the stifling dark air of my apartment. Before she left for work, I got a call from Ray, telling me he heard from a gun collector from upstate who wanted to offer me 50 grand for a couple of pieces I might be interested in selling. He told me there'd be a slight handling charge, but that he would like to see me get my due. I told him I'd limp over later.

The papers had split ranks, half of them urging the city to rejoice now that the beast had been slain, the others howling for the blood of the beast's slayers. I had a drink of sludge with Ray. We talked.

I explained about Billy's observation about the clothes, and how we had decided he must have something against some female in authority. A lot of guys have started hating women promoted over them in these days of 'equality.' I'd played the only decent hunch we'd had. Ray confirmed that the monster had worked for a small publishing house under a woman ten years his junior. Some guys can't take reality very well.

I took my 40 grand and left, not going anywhere in particular. I thought about Falcone, and how he and Anna could get on with there lives. What might be left to them I wasn't sure, but at least the shadows were lifted. I also thought about Sally, and when I'd see her again. I knew I would. Nothing pulls people together like sharing the job of emptying guns into someone who really deserves it.

I also thought about the fact that a guy like the Chef would probably inspire copy cats, less imaginative types, but just as dangerous, sitting around waiting for some new hobby to occupy their time. I didn't let it bother me. Things like that happen, or they don't, and nothing anyone does can stop them.

Shrugging off the need to dwell on it all, I started for the train station, and then stopped. I wanted to get something to eat, but I figured I'd take my time. I just kept walking, letting the sun wash over me. The heat had finally started to feel good. And, I figured, if I did get bored with walking, for once I had the money for a cab.

The Things We Do

I WATCHED THE cab pull away through a front window.

"Well…," As it rounded the corner past the first edging hedge at the driveway's end, I thought, "That's that."

The house was mine. Mine and the dog and the kid's. I guess especially the kid's. She lived there. I'd only been rented to live there over the weekend.

My name is Jack Hagee; I'm a detective. The dog was Balto. He's mine. Half-husky, half-German shepherd. One hundred and ten hard-muscled pounds of two year old playful energy — some times a pain in the ass but, pretty much my best friend in the whole world. There'd been times, I think, over the past hellish forever, that that hundred and ten pounds of lung and life and unquestioning love had made the never-ending nights bearable.

The kid was the daughter of my client; I was the babysitter. Double my daily fee, just to eat and live better than I usually do and make sure nobody bothers the house. Maybe Sally and Hubert were right. Maybe it was time to start living as if there were a tomorrow. I'd been doing a lot of thinking like that lately.

It hadn't taken much to get me started, either. Just the hideous murders of two dozen women, a panicking city of eight million losing its collective mind, and a killer so unredeemable that in the end I hadn't cared what the law said about the situation I was in, and neither had any of the seven million around me. When it was over, I had a first-in-my-lifetime five figure bank account and a beautiful blonde lady friend. We hadn't turned into Tracy and Hepburn yet, but it was getting close. It was a hell of a way to get ahead in life, but if someone had to do it, all in all I was glad it was me.

And that was what had started me thinking. Suddenly I had all the money in the world and an attractive, possibly loving, female companion, all with thirty-five still ahead of me. The morning I met Ms. Karen Stadler I was firmly convinced I was on a winning streak. I was also firmly convinced that a man on a winning streak does not goof up the big chance.

I'd walked through the doors of Morrison, Mason, and Cahil, the city's third biggest advertising firm, ten minutes before my meeting with Ms. Stadler. Her secretary had made the appointment the day before, his tone promising that promptness was still a virtue in some circles. He met me in reception with a handshake, passing me a menu while we walked to the elevator bank, apologizing for the fact that while I might be on time, Ms. Stadler was going to be a bit late.

"She's really stacked up against it today," he confided. "It is just brutal this time of year. Campaigns for the new fall season — everyone's first, everyone's best — oh, what a headache. Ms. Stadler was afraid she could be delayed up to fifteen minutes. She beggggs you to bear with us."

The chatter continued into the elevator, while we rode, exited, and worked our way back to the bosslady's office. I learned that it was time for lunch — thus making our meeting a tax write off, so I should get whatever I want — that the firm handled alll the big ones, just alllll the big ones — that the competition would give just anny, annnything to get their hands on what she was doing for the Radiant account so they could use it — that Karen Stadler was one very heightening woman — and that the coffee bar around the corner, there-there, had well you know anything I desired. Just anything.

I ordered a pair of medium bacon cheeseburgers with onion rings and a tall lemonade. He gave me a smile that told me there was fun in my future and asked me to take a seat. I gave him a nod that I'm not sure told him anything and sat down.

I thumbed the magazines around me for a moment but gave it up quick. The subject matter was mostly snooty or childish, the politics naive to the point of humor. The models used in them didn't do much for me, either. It wasn't their shapes or hair or outfits. It was their sneers — the condescension they wore as perfectly as their makeup. I'm not afraid of women, but I'm damn tired of the ones who think I'm supposed to be.

Waiting for lunch, I studied the architecture around me. It was the usual mid-town Manhattan throw-together of easily erected and equally destroyed corners, arches, and cardboard facades one finds everywhere nowadays. The walls held plastic block-protected blow ups of some of their campaigns and fine art posters, but nothing that told me anything essential about the corporation itself, about its character. Then again, I thought, I wasn't being hired by the corporation.

About ten minutes after I tired of trying to entertain myself, Stadler's flunky took two calls; one told him lunch had arrived — the other told him to get it and me in to see his boss. Seconds later, a small platter of vegetable slices, green pepper, carrot, mushroom, and some things I didn't recognize, a platter of bacon cheeseburgers and myself were all presented to Ms. Karen Stadler, vice president in charge of special network promotion. Handshakes she did not deem necessary. She told Flunky to hit the fan to pull the meat smells out of the office as he left. The look on her face had me wondering if she was referring to me or the burgers.

As we sat on opposite sides of her desk, I tried to drink in everything around me quickly. Stadler herself was a fairly non-descript woman. Her height and weight were average; hair a neutral shade of brunette, cut to a functional, easily maintained length. She was not an unattractive woman, just one who did absolutely nothing with what she had. Her suit and office decorations fell much into the same range.

"I've got a very tight schedule, Mr. Huggie..."

"That's Hay-gie."

"Excuse me...?"

"Hay-gie. Gie — rhymes with lee. Everyone gets it wrong. You were saying?"

"Ah, yes." She drew a pepper slice to pop in her mouth, encouraging me to eat. I did. "I'm sure my assistant explained everything to you."

"Yes, ma'am," I assured her. "You're going to Hawaii for the weekend to work on the set of one of the network's new shows. I'm to provide security for your home, grounds, and daughter. A registered nurse will be staying with us to act as chaperone, and obviously as nurse, if necessary. Everyone is their own cook. You have an alarm system, but after the two B&Es in the area last month you don't want to chance your home being hit. I've already studied what newspaper clippings I could find on the two incidents as well as the diagrams of your property which you had sent to my office, and talked with your local police.

"Your daughter has last weekend rehearsals for a school play, which is why she has to stay in New York. The nurse is already installed in the house. I have three different numbers for you in Hawaii — hotel, studio set, and the network's mobile remote wagon. I also have the numbers of your father in Westchester, your friends, the Crandells — next door down to the left — and your doctor's. I have two routes to the school memorized. I will take her to her rehearsal, wait for her to finish, and take her back home.

"I also have xeroxes for you of my insurance, my license, weapon's registration, and my carry permit."

I took another bite while she studied her copies. The burgers were perfectly medium, the thin line of soft pink in their centers the only bit of them not bursting with hot, tongue-pleasing juices. The bacon was perfect as well, four pieces to a burger, all of their folds clogged with sweet bubbling mozzarella. As I was finishing the first of the pair, Ms. Stadler said:

"You seem to have everything mapped out, but there's one more thing. No one comes near Leslie." She swallowed another bite and then added, "Especially her father."

"I wasn't told anything about this."

"Don't you dare think you're going to walk out on me at the last minute..."

"I didn't say anything—"

"Or run your charges higher..."

"Excuse, me," I blurted, loud enough to force a pause, "all I said was, nobody's given me any information about this. I'll need your husband's name...a photo...some idea of why I should be worried about keeping him from her. Would he harm her? Kidnap her? What are we talking about? Would he use a weapon? Would he use her as a hostage if he got desperate? Did you break up because of something between the two of you, or between him and Leslie?"

Ms. Stadler held up a finger and then apologized.

"All right. I'm sorry. I jumped the gun and I sprung this on you badly and at the last minute. No. I've worried that John might try to kidnap Leslie on occasion, I'll admit it — but I don't think he really would. Why don't we finish eating and I'll answer your questions as best I can."

From there on I got the last details I needed to know, including all the details to the inside story on her ex-marriage to her boring, investor/accountant husband, which made me a lot less calm about John than she was. Leslie'd been Daddy's little girl, but because of the nature of the breakup, Daddy, whose name was Fitzgerald and not Stadler, was being denied little girl visitation rights for the moment. Of course, maybe she was just delegating worrying over the situation to her newest employee. It *was* what she was paying me for.

And, after giving me a set of keys, that was that for Thursday afternoon. Twenty-six hours later I watched her taxi pull out, and then turned to find out what life with a twelve year old was all about. Pointing at Balto, she asked:

"Does he like cats?"

"He tolerates them. Why? Do you have a cat?"

"Yes. And I'd like it if he wasn't eaten by your wolfhound."

"I think that can be arranged."

Bending over, I grabbed Balto around the neck, and pulled him to me. Shaking him back and forth, I yelled at him, "No cats on the diet, you monster. Got that? No cats!"

Balto growled out his playtime roar, letting me know he would eat anything he pleased. I responded by flopping him over on his side. He snapped at me, catching my wrist in his mouth several times, but never breaking the skin. I raised my fist, threateningly, "No cats, your horselizard. Got it?"

Balto barked his version of 'yes, sir' and we straightened ourselves up. Leslie might have been amused, but if she was she did an admirable job of covering it up. Looking at us as if we were both in clown makeup, she said:

"You're pretty silly for a detective."

"My friend, Ray Trenkel, says that."

"Who's he?"

"He's a police captain." Before she could ask anything else, I pointed at Leslie and commanded, "Balto — take the measure."

Understanding that we had shifted into our business mode, Balto trotted forward, sniffing Leslie front and back, top and bottom. She reacted uncomfortably, asking, "What's he doing?"

"Recording your scent. We're both here to work. To do his part of the job, he has to record everyone and every place here. Once he knows all the smells in the house, he'll know everything he needs to in case there is any trouble."

"Our house doesn't smell." I was told.

"Everything smells. Some things smell bad and some good, and most have such a slight smell that you and I can't smell them at all — but he can."

"Prove it."

"Okay. Get me something Balto can carry in his mouth."

The girl thought for a moment, and then ran out of the room, returning seconds later with that week's T.V. Guide. After giving Balto a chance to get its odor, I told her to go and hide it. After she returned I gave Balto the fetch order. He was back with it in a tenth of the time it had taken her to hide it, looking quite pleased with himself. She was impressed.

Before we knew what happened, Balto was fetching the T.V. Guide from every corner of the house. Every time he brought it back, Leslie's face lit equally with delight and frustration. After the pair of them had gotten to the point where they could play by themselves, I took my bag to the room where I'd been told to store my things. While unpacking, Ms. Stadler's nurse stuck her head in the door.

"Hi; welcome to the staff."

"Thanks," I told her with a sour grin.

"The things we do for money, eh?"

She was an attractive woman — late twenties, black hair, dark eyes, nice figure — strong Spanish blood in there somewhere. Just my luck. Why is it, I wondered, that good looking women only wander into your life once you have a steady relationship. We bantered back and forth while I unpacked, taking each other's measure.

I discovered her name was Tori — that she'd been a nurse for seven years, that she'd stayed with Leslie many times in the past — that she wouldn't mind doing the cooking if I'd help with the dishes, and that she had a nice laugh and a coltish manner I was sure came unconsciously which is what made it so attractive.

She discovered I'm a sucker for women who call me 'blue eyes' — that I'd been in Military Intelligence and then with the Pittsburgh police department, before finally ending up with a private ticket in New York City — that I like Gilbey's gin if I'm going to drink — that I still smoke cigarettes, but that I've been thinking of at least moving up to filters — that I've never been to the ballet and rarely watch T.V., but that I hit the movies roughly once a week, mostly to see comedies. She also made a point of finding out if I was seeing anybody. I told the truth. That got a question.

"Can I ask you why you told me that?"

"What d'ya mean?"

"I mean, here we are, man and woman, locked up for the weekend together, and before you find out whether or not there could be a chance for a little whoopie between us, you just blurt out the truth. I'm curious what makes a man do that. I haven't met many who would." As we headed back downstairs, I told her.

"Not to try and go pompous on you but, my life's been one long look at what lying does for people. Whether it's country to country or person to person, lies kill. They kill everything. I've watched the Russians use them, the C.I.A. — your local police, politicians…I guess it's just that I make my living unscrambling other people's lies and bringing them down for telling them.

"I hate lies. I'm just sick to death of them."

She smiled at me as we stepped down into the hallway leading to the living room.

"You sure come on strong," she told me.

"I know," I agreed. "Sally, the woman I've been seeing, she says the same thing. It's, well…like anybody, I harp the most on the chords I need to hear the most. I, I saw some dirty games when I was in the service. I don't like to remember it. It's easier to forget lies you've told if you don't tell any new ones."

"Wait a minute." She snapped her fingers. "I know you — you're the guy who killed the Chef!"

I turned sharply, staring at her. The Chef was the serial killer I'd put away the month before. But no one knew that except Ray Trenkel who'd backed me into the corner where I'd done it, and Sally, who'd helped me do it. If Tori had looked into my eyes she'd have know she was right. I asked:

"What makes you say that?"

"I remember it — you challenged him on the T.V — on the news. You called him out. A few days later he was dead. Nice job. My girl friends and I, we wanted to—"

I cut her off with a shake of my hand so I could ask, "Yeah, yeah — but what makes you think I killed him?"

"Are you saying you didn't?" She smiled as she asked, but her tone told me it wasn't a question.

"Well, menza, menza," I stalled, "first I just want to ask what makes you think I did it."

"Oh, but everyone knows. I mean, everyone assumes it was you. Who else? I mean, if it wasn't you, it could've been anyone."

"Well, why don't we say it could have been anyone and just be glad he's dead. Okay?"

"Sure. I was going to...ohh, wait — you said your girl friend's name was Sally. It's Sally Brenner, isn't it? That anchorwoman from QQT you were on television with. Ohhh, she's so beautiful. Wow. Stadler really hired herself a hotshot, huh?"

My neck grew red. I pursed my lips to one side in a frowning grin. I was flattered and a part of me swelled with the artificial importance that comes from being recognized by a stranger, but part of it was damned uncomfortable. It sounds like a comic book, but if a nurse with no special interest in my life could put two and two together that fast about Sally and me, how long would it take someone who wanted to hurt me? It was something I was going to have to think about — long and hard. Answering Tori, though, I said:

"Well, it would be bad for business for me to deny any of that, so why don't I just plead the Fifth, okay? But thanks for the vote of confidence, anyway."

Tori smiled as if I'd just made her my special confidant. She asked if I was hungry. I told her 'yes.' She agreed and headed for the kitchen. As she walked away, I asked her, "Hey, since I'm a big celebrity, do I still have to help with the dishes?"

"You want to eat," she called out without turning around, "you work."

I headed into the living room, smiling. So much for celebrity.

The rest of Friday went smoothly. I took Leslie to her school for evening rehearsal right after dinner. Five hours later we were back home, cleaned up, and tucked in — Leslie in her room, Tori in one down the hall, me on the living room couch. The Stadler women had a guest room, I simply chose not to use it. Couches are less comfortable than beds. That makes them better for light sleeping. Also, break-and-enter specialists expect to find people in beds, not the living room. It's a small advantage, true, but sometimes small advantages are all you get.

I'm not sure where Balto slept. When I take him on a security job, he scouts the area we're watching and then picks his own spot. I think it has something to do with finding the core of a place's sounds, the area where he can hear the most noises a place has to make. I'm not sure, obviously because he's never told me one way or the other, but it's my best guess. Nothing happened Friday night, however, so it was all academic.

The next morning Leslie found me in the living room cleaning my .38 when she finally got up. The first thing she asked me was where Balto was. I told her I didn't know exactly. She told me, "He's pretty smart."

"Sure, he's Balto, the wonder dog."

"What're you doing?"

"Cleaning my gun."

"I know that. I mean, what're you doing it for? Why do you have to clean it?"

"Well," I answered, finishing up, "this isn't a full cleaning. This is just maintenance. I clean it every few days. You want to keep your guns free of dirt because they'll rust if you don't. Dirt, grease, dust — anything inside the barrel can cause your shot to pull to the left or right. Rust never sleeps." Then, looking at her watch me, I got a thought and said, "Guess you've probably never seen a real gun before. Would your mother mind if you looked at it?"

"Yeah," admitted Leslie with a dragging sigh. "Probably."

Suddenly feeling like a conspiratory uncle, I held the unloaded revolver, chambers open, out to Leslie, saying, "Then, I guess we better not tell her."

Leslie smiled, taking the gun in her hand. Surprised at the weight. The gun dragged her hand down a foot before she compensated and brought it back up.

"Wow," she whistled, "just like television," and then flicked her wrist to snap the cylinder into place. I flinched. Reaching out, I took the gun back for a moment and the said, "Let me show you something."

Releasing the cylinder again, I told her how cop-show dramatics can hurt a real gun, and then showed her how to lock it back into place correctly by just shoving it in with your other hand, or even against your chest. "Even a one-handed shooter doesn't have an excuse for treating his gun that way."

"Is everything on television wrong about policemen?"

"Well," I told her, "not everything, but most of it."

"Like what?" I showed her how to swab the barrel and told her.

"Where to begin? Well, no one gets hit over the head two or three times in one day and then goes off on a date. They die because their gray matter's been denied oxygen. Or maybe they're lucky and they just end up with brain damage. Cars can't fly through the air and slam against the street and keep driving. You get a bent axil or a cracked drive shaft — you at least lose your hubcaps. AAhhhh, there's so much..."

I told her about how boring and truly dangerous police work is. I told her about the long hours and the futility they induce in those struggling through them. Focusing our physical attention on the gun, we slid everything into place as I told her about different criminals I'd known.

"You have to understand," I said, "nobody thinks they're a bad guy. Everyone has the best reasons for the things they do. What you have to remember is that people who steal, or murder, or rape — do you know even what rape is?"

"Sure, my mom and I had a long talk about it after a TV movie where a guy tried to rape this woman and she caught him and tortured him for it."

"Uh-huh. Okay, well, anyway — the people who do these things, they don't think of themselves as bad people. It's always someone else's fault they did what they did."

"Why is that?"

"Because no one wants to be responsible for their actions anymore. People..." Suddenly I stopped. What did I think I was doing, I asked myself. Bad enough to risk offending a rich client by teaching her twelve year old about proper weapons ordinance — popping off about the criminal justice system to a grade schooler was no way to endear myself, either. When Leslie asked why I stopped talking, I told her:

"Oh, let's just say I was getting carried away. Believe me, you don't want to hear me go on about the civil irresponsibility of our politicians and legal system and the such."

"Why not," she asked. "My mother says I should learn about the world any chance I get."

"Maybe so, but I don't think 'The World According to Jack Hagee' is what she had in mind. Besides," I answered, pointing toward the clock over the living room's fireplace mantle, don't we have a school to get to?"

"Nutzoidal ruination," she shouted, seeing the time. "I'll go get my stuff — I'll meet you in the driveway." She headed upstairs, then stopped to yell back, "can Balto the wonder dog go with us?"

"To school?"

"Sure, all the kids would love him. He's tiger-ready."

I told her "Sure, why not?"

She ran upstairs. I found my "tiger-ready" — whatever that means — canine, and got us both headed toward the front door. Sticking my head into the kitchen, I told Tori we were off, and then left for the car. Leslie and Balto talked in the back seat. I chauffeured.

We returned in the dark, hours. Leslie was exhausted. I was pretty done in myself. Balto bounded out first, but was tired enough to wait for us. The play's director, extremely pleased with his cast's progress, had taken everyone out for pizza. I had to go where they did, and Balto goes with me. So, after more pizza and stupid pet tricks than are good for either one of us, we staggered into the driveway, making Leslie laugh through her yawns.

"Hey," I told her, "I'm an old man. He's an old dog. We're usually both in bed by now with some hot milk."

"Whatever you say, Jack."

Leslie continued to giggle, however, making me think she wasn't really convinced. Well, I thought, that was all right. I didn't really want people to believe Balto and I were the hot milk types, no matter what I said. Leslie begged me to let her take Balto to the back yard.

"All right," I told her. Then, looking down at Balto, I told him, "Listen, horselizard, Leslie's in charge. You listen to her, but keep an eye on things — okay?"

Balto barked out his interpretation of "okay." I decided that was good enough for me and headed upstairs.

I called out for Tori, but got no response. Checking my watch, I saw it was even later than I thought and figured she had already sacked out for the night. Fine by me. I decided to give Leslie ten minutes play time and then call her inside. Shrugging out of my shoulder holster, I left it on the coffee table near my couch and headed upstairs to the bathroom. As I hit the landing I fumbled for the lights, still not quite adjusted to someone else's living space. That's when he hit me.

The blow came from the side, low and crushing. I fell back down the stairs, tumbling and yelling the whole way. I tried to get back to my feet, but my attacker had followed me down. Two kicks kept me on the floor, my head spinning. The lights went out again. Hidden in the darkness, a voice told me:

"Be smart. Stay where you are. I don't know who you are or what you're doing here. I don't want to know."

My head started to clear as he talked. I stared at him in the darkness, but couldn't tell anything from the form I could see, especially with the stars still spinning in my head.

"To put you at ease," he told me, "the nurse is tied up in her bedroom. Cooperate, and that's where you'll go, too. I haven't found what I came for, but something tells me you've got the answers I need."

Holding my head, a thought hit me — John Fitzgerald. Somehow he had found out about his wife's weekend absence and had decided it was time to make his move. I didn't want to go hard on him, and yet my job was to keep him from what he wanted to do. Figuring I wouldn't hurt him too badly, I nodded when he motioned me toward the bedroom, acting more hurt than I was. He bought it. As I stumbled past him, I planted my right foot and then side-stepped hard to the left — elbow out — digging. My attacker went down like a fat lady on ice…but so did I.

While I'd made my move someone else hidden in the shadows'd made their's, clubbing me from behind. The pain shot over both ears and re-filled my eyes with a star field the size of the Milky Way. I hit on my knees and then toppled to my side. I was hurt and gasping, holding my head, forcing back the screams and tears raging at me to give in to the darkness and forget all about the two gentlemen with the saps. I couldn't imagine who they were, or what they wanted. The pain tore at me, making thinking about what was happening too hard to maintain.

Thoughts sped through my brain, relaying past each other in a jumble; not a random break-in, they weren't thieves — well trained, used to working together — not Fitzgerald, was it? He was — what, what'd she say — oh god, it hurts — just an accountant—

Pain hit again — a kick told me it was the first one, on his feet again. I had grown used to his kicks and knew how he placed them. The little whisper that tries to protect all of us told me I had to do something, fight back, but I couldn't focus past the ringing in my ears. Something finally got my attention, though. The sound of a .38 hammer being cocked, and the second's voice saying:

"Kill him."

There was more noise, then gunfire blasted away in the background behind the stabbing drumming in my ears.

"Wait a minute," Sally stared past the fettuccine on the end of her fork. We'd gone to Louie's, my favorite restaurant in the Village, to celebrate my still being alive. We didn't manage to get seats under Charlie, the sailfish that hangs from the ceiling in the main dining room, but at least we had a good view of him. She asked with a little impatience, "You're getting ahead of yourself. Who were those guys?"

I smiled. Never date a reporter if you want to be able to finish a story the way you want to tell it.

"Well, dear," I answered, "believe it or not, you almost lost me for the greater glory of Radiant Lady cosmetics."

Sally waved her fork. "Oh, I get it. Corporate spies. They were there trying to steal her notes." She slid the last of her forkful into her mouth in triumph.

"Yes," I told her. "They already knew she kept her most important account notes at home, so home is where they came. Not expecting yours truly, of course."

"Oh, and a big lot of help you turned out to be. How'd you even get out of that mess in one piece, anyway?"

"Well, that noise I mentioned…that was Balto taking down one of the guys. The gun shots, that was Leslie. She took my .38 from the coffee table and started blasting."

Sally smiled, the backs of her eyes lighting with mischief.

"Honestly, Jack, can't you be around a woman for more than a day before she starts shooting up bad guys?"

I frowned back, hiding behind a mouthful of fried sole.

"So, did she kill anybody?"

"No, no. She hit one guy — a nick, really. Balto was the hero of the day. He downed one while the other whined about the hit he took from Leslie. Mrs. Stadler didn't like the results much, lot of blood on the living room carpet, but she agreed the consequences could have been worse. And, all in all, that's pretty much that."

"I think I'm disappointed."

Knowing I was being teased, but no more immune to the effects of it than the next guy, I asked, "Okay, I'll bite. What's so disappointing?"

"Well, heavens, what kind of hardboiled detective are you turning into? I mean, you take a rich client you can hardly stand, you pass up a chance to sleep with a sexy woman, you don't even raid the liquor cabinet...then, you let two hoods beat you up, your dog and a little girl have to save you...I don't know, I don't know, what happened to all the beating and shooting you're so famous for? This doesn't sound like the tough guy that swept me off my feet."

"Wha — haven't you heard, all that tough guy stuff is tres passé these days. Why, I don't think I could ever do the wild kinds of things you're suggesting any more. I've grown far too refined in your company to even think of such things."

It was her turn to smile. She stared at me a moment, eyeing up her prey, then leaned forward.

"Oh, yeah?"

"Really. I've seen the error of my ways. I'm just looking forward to a genteel life from now on."

"No more fun or excitement now, eh?"

"No," I said, trying not to laugh, "that's all past now."

"Well, what if I suggest..." she leaned even further across the table, whispering her suggestion in my ear.

"Why, I'm shocked," I told her. "You mean, you and me..." she nodded.

"Now?" I asked. "Here and now?" She nodded again. I flicked my gaze toward the glass-eyed sailfish hanging a handful of yards away. "I mean, what would Charlie think?"

She laughed. I joined her. We raised our glasses in a silent toast, clinked them, and then drank. The rest of the night was ours.

MORE C.J. HENDERSON FROM MARIETTA PUBLISHING...

The Things That Are Not There

by C.J. Henderson

Teddy London was ready to close his detective agency after a demon-driven storm trashed his offices. Then fate led a beautiful woman to him — one being pursued by winged monsters determined to use her to unlock a doorway that will lead the entire world to madness.

$13.99 – Trade Paperback

ISBN 1-892669-08-0

The Occult Detectives of C.J. Henderson

by C.J. Henderson

Here are thirteen tales of the greatest otherworld investigators ever created tackling witches, werewolves, and every other terror that crawls, flies, or creeps through the night. It's the best stories ever from the reigning monarch of macabre mysteries!

$15.99 – Trade Paperback

ISBN 1-892669-10-2

Beluga Stein Mysteries From Marietta Publishing...

Last Resort

by Wendy Webb

Beluga Stein is a hit-or miss psychic who never travels without her familiar, a black cat named Planchette, a far more gifted psychic. An ill-conceived gift lands Beluga and Planchette at the opening of a new luxury spa. Opposed to healthy pursuits of any kind, Beluga is ready to leave – until a body is discovered.

$13.99 – Trade Paperback

ISBN 1-892669-21-8

Bee Movie

by Wendy Webb

Beluga Stein is back — with her loud muumuus, pastel cigarettes, and hit-or-miss psychic ability. This time she's called to investigate strange events on the set of a low-budget horror movie. But after a fire mysteriously erupts on the set, an actor in a bee costume is found dead. Is the set haunted, or are the supernatural stirrings the result of special effects?

$13.99 – Trade Paperback

ISBN 1-892669-24-2

New Mythos From Marietta Publishing...

Lin Carter's Anton Zarnak Supernatural Sleuth

Edited by Robert M. Price
Featuring stories by C.J. Henderson, James Chambers, Joseph S. Pulver, Sr., and more

Being stalked by terrors from beyond? What do you do? Where do you turn? To only one person: Anton Zarnak. Featuring not only *all* of Carter's Zarnak stories, but also thirteen tales written by others — at the request of the author and then later by his estate.

$19.99 – Trade Paperback
ISBN 1-892669-09-9

New Mythos Legends

Edited by Bruce Gehweiler
Featuring stories by Hugh B. Cave, Norman Partridge, Tom Piccirilli, Don D'Ammassa, Jeffrey Thomas, and more

H.P. Lovecraft has influenced many of today's top writers of science fiction, fantasy, and horror. This book contains cutting edge fiction from authors who have been inspired by his work, but have taken the Mythos to a new level....

$25.00 – Illustrated Hardcover
ISBN 1-892669-06-4
$15.99 – Trade Paperback
ISBN 1-892669-19-6

Also Available From Marietta Publishing…

Four and Twenty Blackbirds

by Cherie Priest

A southern gothic ghost story from Cherie Priest. Although orphaned at birth, Eden Moore is never alone. Three dead women keep watch from the shadows, bound to protect her from the violence that took their lives a century ago. But in the woods a gunman waits, convinced that God has spoken. Now Eden must pay for the sins of her great-grandfather or history may do far worse than repeat itself….

$13.99 – Trade Paperback
ISBN 1-892669-22-6

The Ghost Finds a Body

by Brad Strickland and Thomas E. Fuller

Leigh Bradford wants nothing more than to get on with his life as a struggling freelance writer, but before he knows it, Bradford — better known in the Panhandle of Florida as "the Ghost" — finds himself in a murder investigation involving a gaggle of romance writers, a stately old hotel, a red-headed lovely, and a killer who seems dead set on killing again.

$14.99 – Trade Paperback
ISBN 1-892669-23-4

Ordering Information

Marietta Publishing's books are available from Ingram Book Distributors and Baker & Taylor Book Group. A catalogue can be found at www.mariettapublishing.com. Or simply use the order form below.

Title	Qty	Price	Amount
Bee Movie	_____	@$13.99 =	_______
Four and Twenty Blackbirds	_____	@ $13.99 =	_______
Frontiers of Terror	_____	@ $17.99 =	_______
The Ghost Finds a Body	_____	@ $14.99 =	_______
Last Resort	_____	@ $13.99 =	_______
Lin Carter's Anton Zarnak Supernatural Sleuth	_____	@ $19.99 =	_______
New Mythos Legends (Ill. Hardcover)	_____	@ $25.00 =	_______
New Mythos Legends (Trade Paperback)	_____	@ $15.99 =	_______
The Occult Detectives of C.J. Henderson	_____	@ $15.99 =	_______
The Things That Are Not There	_____	@ $13.99 =	_______
Warfear, A Collection of Strange War Tales	_____	@ $14.99 =	_______
		S&H ($3.00 per book) =	_______
		Total =	_______

Name ______________________________

Address ______________________________

____

E-Mail ______________________________

Phone ______________________________

Send to:
Marietta Publishing
PO Box 3485
Marietta, GA 30061-3485

MP

Printed in the United States
201468BV00005B/160-189/A

9 781892 669186